From Other Shores

an omnibus

Chad Oliver

edited by Priscilla Olson

The NESFA Press
Post Office Box 809
Framingham, MA 01701
2007

FIRST EDITION
March, 2007

International Standard Book Number:
ISBN-10: 1-886778-66-3
ISBN-13: 978-1-886778-66-5

Dedicated to...
the ape that walks like a chicken

Contents

From Other Shores

Introduction

This book has been too long in preparation: real life has a way of inter-fering. So, I was delighted anew (when I got back to working on it) that I enjoyed the material so much.

Some of it made me smile. Some of it was pretty scary. Most of it made me feel pretty good about being human. And that's not a bad thing to say about something, is it?

While working on these Chad Oliver books (two previous collections of short material: *A Star Above It* and *Far From This Earth*, along with this omnibus) I feel like I've gotten to know the man. I've gleaned bits of what he was like through the memories of George Zebrowski and Howard Waldrop – but his works themselves were perhaps my greatest sources of information. Besides being a respected professor and anthropologist, Chad was a pipe-smoking fishing enthusiast with a remarkable zest for life. And he was a *good* guy, too! In these three "Alien Trilogy" novels, he presents us with his often understated thoughts on what actually makes us human…. and why this humanity is so special.

I never had the pleasure of meeting Chad Oliver: I wish I had.

- Priscilla Olson

Introduction - Shadows in the Sun

Shadows in the Sun (1954) was Chad Oliver's second published novel, and his confessed favorite throughout his life. The Ballantine Books edition appeared in simultaneous hardcover and paperback, and was followed by British, French, German, and Italian editions published between 1955 and 1967. The second American edition came out in 1968, in the Ballantine Bal-Hi books paperback series for students, featuring a special two-page introduction to parents and teachers about the novel's theme and a reading level indicator at the back of the book. Crown's edition of 1985, in my ten volume set of rediscovered books, with a general foreword by Isaac Asimov, was the novel's first American edition in nearly two decades.

"The theme is an alien masquerade on Earth," wrote Damon Knight in the May 1955 *Science Fiction Quarterly;* "the treatment is original and compelling." J. Francis McComas, the great co-founding editor of *The Magazine of Fantasy and Science Fiction* wrote in *The New York Times Book Review* for December 5, 1954: "With this, his first adult book, Chad Oliver, author of a number of excellent short stories and a first-rate juvenile, has written what is very likely the best science fiction novel of the year. In a quiet, realistic, entertaining story, he has brought one of the great science fictional themes down to earth. For, in this book, the almost insoluble problem of the Terran man versus the superman from outer space is worked out...within the confines of one small American town. To the men of other star systems, Terran man may be nothing more or less than a savage. And what happens to the savage when he meets civilization head-on? What happened to the savages of our own world when their lands were colonized by the culturally superior white man? In essence, then, the problem posed by this novel is the salvation of the savage. And while the whole equation is not worked out-—no earthly anthropologist is yet wise enough to do that-—enough of the solution is intimated to make this one of the most thought-provoking pieces of fiction, scientific or otherwise, this reviewer has read in years."

One of Oliver's wry solutions to the problem of the earthborn savage is to let us live in "reservations" known as cities, where we can be contained and managed by the aliens, who will control the liberated countryside. Another solution is to let us destroy ourselves. Alien control will simply follow our natures, since we exhibit both the tendency to crowd into cities and to threaten our survival through warfare. The aliens would go unnoticed.

Writing in *The Magazine of Fantasy and Science Fiction* for April 1955, Anthony Boucher, the other great editor and cofounder of that publication, announced that *Shadows in the Sun* "...clearly establishes Chad Oliver as one of the leading young talents in the field...Oliver is a trained professional anthropologist as well as a skilled writer; and he uses his knowledge of anthropological field techniques to revitalize completely the familiar theme of "There-Are-Alien-Observers-Among-Us." I can't think of anyone who has more sensibly and convincingly portrayed members of a highly advanced civilization who are not supermen, or who has treated more logically and humanly the problems of one of us in adjusting to such a culture."

P. Schuyler Miller, writing in *Astounding Science Fiction* (May 1955), stated that the novel showed "Chad Oliver's study of anthropology sinking into his thinking and writing, and I'm inclined to say that it's the best science fiction with an anthropological theme that I have seen." He also underscored one of the book's key ideas: that humanoid intelligence may be common in the galaxy, and that the greatest differences between its civilizations may be cultural, not physical. Oliver at one point in the novel does permit the existence of wholly alien Others, "...intellects vast and cool and unsympathetic," in H. G. Well's famous phrase, with which Oliver will deal in *The Shores of Another Sea,* the third novel in his Aliens Trilogy of escalating otherness. But in this opener the problem for Paul Ellery, anthropologist, is to decide whether he wants to be educated to take his place in the alien society. This opportunity holds a great attraction for a scientist; so much will be revealed to him. His other choice is to remain with his own kind and help its development as best he can.

Kingsley Amis's disappointing view of *Shadows in the Sun* (in *New Maps of Hell,* a study of science fiction published in 1960), shows him blind to the novel's anthropological materials. Paul Ellery is, for Amis, an unlikely anthropologist: six feet tall, two hundred pounds, and an American from Texas, of all places, but in fact a fair physical description of Chad Oliver himself. Certain features of genre fiction are, of course, completely overcome by the novel's scientific authenticity revealing the impotence of purely literary or formal critiques of genuinely scientific science fiction. The similarities in Oliver's novel to conventional genre narrative strategies are superficial, the differences profound.

Amis's lapses into literary and cultural parochialisms seemed strange in a critic who professed to understand science fiction, especially when discussing a novel of first contact with an alien civilization. But his confused reaction may also explain why too few readers appreciated Oliver's work in the 1950s; they failed to notice the subtle use of anthropological dilemmas in his stories and novels. This was not the case, happily, among the better critics and reviewers; Amis seemed to have been the most noteworthy exception.

An interesting professional notice for *Shadows in the Sun* appeared in a 1955 issue of the *American Anthropologist*. Evon Z. Vogt of Harvard University wrote: "...this delightful book calls the attention of social scientists to Chad Oliver (a graduate student of anthropology at UCLA) as a first-rate science fiction writer. The plot is similar to Huxley's *Brave New World* but with an interesting extension in scope. Instead of dealing merely with Earth, Oliver brings 'civilized' man in from other Earth-type planets. The 'savages' are not American Indians but ourselves. This startling discovery is made by Paul Ellery, Ph.D. in Anthropology, who is making an anthropological study of Jefferson Springs, Texas. Throughout the book, effective use is made of the concepts and data of contemporary anthropological writers. Anthropology definitely comes of age in science fiction in this unusual book..."

This description of Oliver's novel shows how far removed it is from routine commercial genre efforts involving aliens and flying saucers.

Today, *Shadows in the Sun* has lost nothing of its reputation. Readers who take anthropology for granted in the works of Ursula K. Le Guin, Michael Bishop, and others, responded with interest to the 1980s Crown editions of Chad Oliver's three alien novels. A major article on Chad Oliver by L. David Allen appeared in Everett F. Bleiler's *Science Fiction Writers: Critical Studies of the Major Authors from the Early Nineteenth Century to the Present Day* (Scribner, 1982), in which only seventy-five authors are covered. Oliver was ranked in the top ten percent of science fiction writers. Oliver's books are listed in Neil Barron's influential *Anatomy of Wonder* (1976, and in continuing editions). Harlan Ellison wrote: "I have been an enthusiastic admirer of *Shadows in the Sun* since it was originally published. Among other virtues, it was one of the first genuine New Wave novels, and that long before there was a New Wave. Chad Oliver was among the most underrated writers in science fiction."

The New Wave description called attention to Oliver's focus on character and place, its here-and-now reality and to the emotional undercurrents that show up in all of Oliver's fiction. The science is real, however, and so the novel might also be claimed for the "hard science fiction school" as well, except that this description is still incorrectly applied to science fiction based on physics, astronomy, chemistry, and even biology, often lacking in writerly virtues. But Oliver, the scientist, did bring his professional sensibility into his fiction and was compared to scientist-authors Arthur C. Clarke, Isaac Asimov, and others; and it was this combination of science and human character, expressed in a graceful, literate style, one of the professed ideals of the science fiction's New Wave of the 1960s, however often that movement rode off in other directions, that won Oliver that comparison. The challenge of combining the writerly virtues with those of genuine science fiction is still with us.

One example of how Oliver met this challenge, as both a writer and anthropologist, and as a science fiction writer, is made clear when Paul Ellery decides to stay on Earth rather than be educated by the aliens. He stays *because it would be bad anthropology for him to go;* he would be exchanging one set of cultural problems for another, for ones that he would have to learn from scratch. Character, plot, science all move dramatically forward at the same time, subtly, with feeling and poetry, streaming implications in all directions from the main action. Compare this with Richard Dreyfuss donning a red suit and rushing to board a flying saucer in *Close Encounters,* a movie with more than a few echoes of Oliver's work in it, but less of his sophistication.

The final, moving moments of Paul Ellery's decision to stay on Earth in order to delve more deeply into himself and his kind, reveals a profound anthropological commitment, one that I suspect is much like Oliver's dedication to his own work as a scientist and teacher.

Suddenly we see that cultures are angular views of the universe, and that their unique physical and cultural perspectives are to be treasured and defended; each is a response to the mystery of existence, but Oliver raises the problem beyond the level of nation-state, to a planetary awareness. Here is mine, hard won, with its own integrity, such as it is—a statement of natural identity, and a source of irrationally prideful conflict when attacked militarily.

Paul Ellery chooses his humanity, knowing that progress cannot be imported without a price and free of all harm; to be real, it must be won from within, in endless ways, just as understanding must be built up afresh in each individual.

—George Zebrowski
Delmar, NY 2007

Shadows in the Sun

1

At first it had had been plain stubbornness, disguised as scientific curiosity, that had kept Paul Ellery going. It was different now.

He *had* to know.

He sat at the corner table of the Jefferson Springs Cafe, alone as he had always been alone in Jefferson Springs. There wasn't much to look at in the small dining room—a grimy electric clock that had been exactly six minutes slow for the past two months; a somewhat battered jukebox, with tired technicolored bubbles, dying on its feet; the inevitable painting of Judge Roy Bean's *Law West of the Pecos;* a greenish-glass case filled with warm candy bars. Paul Ellery looked anyway, with restrained desperation. Then he pushed back his plate with its remnants of chicken-fried steak and French fries, and began to draw wet circles on the varnished table with the bottom of his beer bottle.

There was a boxlike air-conditioner stuck in one window, consisting of a fan that blew wet air into the room. Ellery could hear the water from the fan hose dripping down to the ground on the other side of the wall; and inside the cafe it was so humid that even the wood was sweating.

Except for the hum and drip of the air-conditioner, there wasn't a sound. It was like sitting in a cave, miles beneath the earth.

Waiting for an earthquake.

Ellery tried to ignore the unwanted little animal that kept shivering up and down his spine on multiple ice-sheathed feet. He tried to remind himself that the animal was imaginary. He tried to tell himself that he had nothing to fear. He tried to look calmer than he felt.

It was incredible.

The month was August, the day was Thursday. He was in Jefferson Springs, a town of six thousand inhabitants, in the state of Texas; a part, usually, of the United States of America. It was eight o'clock in the evening and it was hot. Some one hundred and twenty miles to the north was the city of San Antonio, where the Alamo had given way to the Air Force. Sixty miles to the south was Eagle Pass, and on across the river was Piedras Negras, in Mexico. Everything seemed perfectly ordinary. Indeed, Jefferson Springs could hardly have been a more average town if it had tried.

On the surface, there was no cause for alarm.

He finished his beer, and it was as hot and sticky as the rest of the cafe. He briefly considered ordering another one, but abandoned the idea. Instead, with great deliberation, he dug his pipe out of his back pocket, where he carried it like a .45, and filled it with tobacco from a cloudy plastic pouch. He lit it with a wood stick match, broke the match, and dropped it artistically into the beer bottle. Then he aimed a wobbly smoke ring in the general direction of Judge Roy Bean and watched it battle the current from the air-conditioner.

"The hell with all of you," he said, silently but inclusively.

He was the only customer in the Jefferson Springs Cafe. He had been the only customer, so far as he could tell, for the past sixty-one days. Cozy.

The first week he had been in Jefferson Springs he had played the jukebox religiously. It had seemed like sound field technique, and it had helped to fill up the emptiness with a semblance of life. As he was somewhat selective in his choice of popular music, however, this hadn't proved precisely a sedative to his nerves. The jukebox in the cafe was typical of those in small Texas towns. There were a number of nasal cowboy standards, including *When My Blue Moon Turns to Gold Again* and *San Antonio Rose*. There were several old Bing Crosby records: *White Christmas* and *Don't Fence Me In*. There were a number of year-old blues sides, featuring honking one-note saxes and leering pseudo-sexual lyrics leading up to inevitable anticlimaxes. There was a haphazard collection of middle-aged hit-parade agonies, notably *Doggie in the Window* and *Till I Waltz Again with You*. And finally, slipped in by mistake, there was an old Benny Goodman Sextet number, *Rose Room*. He played that ten times during the first week, and then gave up.

In a way he could not quite understand, the record had violated an unseen pattern. It was not a simple and obvious case of the records being out of place in Jefferson Springs; rather, it was the fact that music was being played at all, *any* music. The pattern was a subtle one, but he had been trained to be sensitive to just such cultural harmonies and configurations.

Paul Ellery had often remarked elsewhere that he would just as soon eat his food without the collective sobbings of the music industry in the background, to say nothing of an endless babble of human voices earnestly reciting the current cliches. Now that he found himself faced with total silence, however, he found the experience unexpectedly unpleasant. The silence cut him off, isolated him. It put him in the middle of a bright stage, without a script or an orchestra, alone, with the curtain going up.

He sat for what seemed to him to be a long time, smoking his pipe. Somehow, only fifteen slow minutes crawled by on the greasy electric clock above the doorway. The doorway led to a small alcove, which faced both the kitchen and the dark, deserted beer bar. He listened closely, but could hear nothing. The other door led outside, into the town.

He was afraid to go out.

He shoved back his chair and got to his feet, annoyed with himself. He told himself that there was nothing to fear. He remembered a time many years before, when he was just a kid. He had gone to a midnight show with another boy to see *Son of Frankenstein.* Then he had had to walk home, through the city of Austin. He and the other boy had walked all the way back to back, one walking frontward and the other backward, in order to keep an eye peeled in both directions at once. It wasn't that they *believed* in such things, of course, it wasn't that they were afraid—

You know.

It was that way now. What was he afraid of? No one had tried to harm him in Jefferson Springs. After all, it was just a little Texas town, just like a thousand others drowsing on the highway or tucked away on a back road, wasn't it? *Wasn't it?*

He left a dollar bill and two quarters on the damp table and walked out of the cafe. After the gloomy humidity of the dining room, the dry heat outside was a tonic. It wasn't cool yet by a long shot, and the sidewalk was still warm under his feet, but the burning sun had gone down. There was even the ghost of a breeze rustling in from the desert and trying to work its way down the street.

He stood in front of the whitewashed cafe and considered. He was a big man, standing a shade under six feet and pushing two hundred pounds. His brown eyes were shrewd and steady. He was dressed in the local uniform—khaki shirt and trousers, capped with a warped, wide-brimmed felt hat at one end and cowboy boots at the other. His Ph.D. didn't show, and he didn't look like the kind of a man who had often been frightened.

Jefferson Springs waited for him quietly. The cafe was at the northern end of the town, on Main Street. Main Street was split down the middle by the railroad, with its little station and loading platforms. Orange trees were planted on both sides of the tracks. To his right, two blocks away, he could see the lights of the Rialto, where a Mitzi Gaynor movie was now in progress. There were a few street lights, a few passing cars moving very slowly, but Jefferson Springs was dark and shadow-crossed.

Jefferson Springs. To the casual onlooker, it was nothing. A place to drive through on your way to the city. A place to get gas, if you were lucky enough to find a station open after dark.

Paul Ellery knocked the ashes out of his pipe against the curb. He had read many books written by men in search of the unknown, the mysterious. They had looked in the Arctic. They had looked in the jungles of South America. They had looked in Africa, in Egypt, in Polynesia. They had taken telescopes and spectroscopes and looked out into space, at the moon, at Mars, at Jupiter, at the stars beyond. They had invented the electroencephalograph and had looked in the human brain.

No one had ever looked in Jefferson Springs. Jefferson Springs was no place to look for the unknown. How known could you get?

Paul Ellery had spent the summer in Jefferson Springs. He hadn't merely lived there—he had studied the town. He had made schedules and charts and investigations, because that was his job. He had asked questions and checked up on the answers. He had read the paper, examined the records, interviewed the people. He had looked at Jefferson Springs the way he would at an Eskimo settlement or an African village.

And Jefferson Springs didn't add up. Jefferson Springs wasn't what it seemed to be. Jefferson Springs was—different. Unknown? You could call it that, all right, and more.

He looked up and down the street. There was not a single human in sight. He walked around the corner slowly, and got into his car, a Ford. He stuck the key in the ignition and just sat there, not knowing where to go. He was beaten, and had he been anyone else he would have admitted the fact and gone his way. Paul Ellery, however, was a stubborn man.

"The joint is jumping," he said aloud, staring at the empty town. "I wonder what's doing down at the morgue."

The stars were coming out above him now. He could smell the fragrance of the orange trees along the railroad tracks. It was a lonely smell, and a nostalgic one. It made him think of Anne, less than two hundred miles away in Austin. Two hundred miles—that was four hours' driving time. If he left now, he could be there a little after midnight. And why not? What was he accomplishing here?

But he knew he wouldn't go. He couldn't go, not yet. Not until he knew.

He had read a few lines, years ago, that had intrigued him enough to start him out on a career. He thought of them now, as he had thought of them many times the past two months in Jefferson Springs

The fact is, like it or not, that we know more about the Crow Indians than we do about the average citizen of the United States. We know more about Samoan villages than we do about American cities. We know a thousand times as much about the Eskimos as we do about the people who live in the small towns of the so-called civilized world. Who lives there, in those unexplored communities we drive through on our way to and from the great cities? What do they do, what do they think, where do they come from, where are they going?

A shocking *handful of small American villages have been scientifically studied by cultural anthropologists and rural sociologists. The sample is so small as to be meaningless. The data are hopelessly inadequate. We know as much about the planet Mars as we do about ninety-nine per cent of our own country.*

Look at the towns and villages and whistle-stops of America. Go into them with your eyes open, take nothing for granted, and study them as objectively as you would a primitive tribe. There is no man on this planet who can predict what you may find.

Well, he had found plenty, if he could only put it all together and make some kind of sense out of it. He had found more than the author of those lines had ever dreamed of.

He started the motor, cut in the lights, and began to drive aimlessly through the dark streets. He made the long square of Main Street first, not sure what he was looking for, not even sure he wanted to find it.

He drove down past the drugstore, which was open but deserted, past the bank and the dry-goods store and the jewelry shop and the Rialto. The Rialto was bright with lights, and he caught a fragment of tinny music and deep, mechanical voices as he drove by. There was a girl sitting in the glass ticket booth, doing her nails.

He turned left, bouncing across the railroad tracks, and then left again down the other side of Main Street. It was much the same, with minor variations: another drug store, this one closed, a Humble gas station, an "American Club" that was actually a combination pool hall and domino parlor, the Hot Chili Cafe, a grocery store, a few houses, and the Catholic Church. He turned left again at the big, square icehouse, jounced across the tracks, and looked over into the Mexican section of town. There was a little more life there—a few scattered lights, a woman laughing somewhere, the faint strumming of a guitar.

Paul Ellery pulled up along the curb, put the Ford in neutral, and left the motor running. He refilled his pipe and lit it. He didn't want to go back to his hotel room at the Rocking-T. He just couldn't face another long night of sitting alone and wrestling with the senseless data he had got in Jefferson Springs.

He constructed a newspaper headline for his own amusement: YOUNG SCIENTIST BAFFLES LEARNED SOCIETIES; MIXES FACTS IN LABORATORY AND GETS NOTHING.

He noticed that his hands were sweating, and it wasn't that hot now. He tried to analyze his fear. Partly, it was the result of two months of overt and covert hostility from Jefferson Springs. Partly, it was the result of working on a research grant and not coming up with the right dope. Partly, it was the pattern that always just eluded him—the pattern that would make sense of his charts and files and statistics.

Mostly, it was a feeling. He had lived in Texas all his life, except for a stretch in the army and two years at the University of Chicago. He knew his state pretty well. It was a diverse state, despite all the stereotypes. The coastal city of Galveston was utterly unlike the capital city of Austin, just as booming Houston was quite different from Abilene or Amarillo or Fort Worth or Laredo. Nevertheless, happily or otherwise, a man knew when he was in Texas.

Jefferson Springs didn't belong. It wasn't quite Texas. It wasn't even quite America. In fact, it wasn't quite—

What was he thinking of?

"Cut that out, boy," he said to himself. "You're headed for the funny factory."

He made up his mind. He wasn't going back to the hotel, not yet. Somewhere, there had to be the clue he needed. Somewhere, there had to be an answer. Somewhere—but where?

There was one possibility.

He put the car into gear and drove back along Main Street, and on out of town. He drove south, along the highway that led eventually to Eagle Pass and Mexico, toward the Nueces River. The land was flat but rolling, and his headlights picked out the dark twistings of mesquite trees and brush. The night was almost cool now, and the breeze slanting in from the window vents was fresh and crisp. The Ford hummed along the empty highway. Ahead of him, the lights stabbed a path through the early darkness. Behind him, the night shadows flowed in again and filled up the hole.

Paul Ellery knew, with complete certainty, that there was something terribly wrong with the town of Jefferson Springs. He meant to find out what it was.

2

Five miles outside of town, he turned off the highway to the left. The car purred along, still on a paved road, with plowed fields on either side. The stars were coming out above him.

Trying to calm himself, he switched on the car radio. The faded yellow light on the dial clicked on, together with a vast humming. Ellery hadn't been able to afford the standard radio when he had bought the car, so he had installed a special model he had found on sale. It had its drawbacks, but it worked. It warmed up and the first thing he got, naturally, was one of the huckster stations with mailing addresses in Texas and transmitters in Mexico, where they could pour on the power:

Yes sir, friends, I want to remind you again tonight of our big special offer. My daughter and I are offering you absolutely the biggest hymn book you've ever seen. This beautiful book, which will give you hours and days of pleasure and consolation, is two feet high and one foot wide. Yes sir, that's feet we're talking about—and remember that there are twelve inches in every single foot. And now, before my daughter sings one of these grand old hymns for you, just let me mention the price of this huge hymn book. The price is the best part of all, my friends, and remember that it's your contributions that keep this faith broadcast on the air—

Ellery tried again, and picked up a network show out of a San Antonio station:

(Burst of crashing music.) *Oh ho! And our next contestant, whose name is Ambrose Earnest, is from none other than Sulfur Creek, Colorado!* (Wild applause.) *Well now, Mr. Earnest, you're not nervous are you?* (Laughter) *Oh ho! Now then; Mr. Earnest, for two hundred and sixty-eight dollars in new quarters, can you tell me under what name William Frederick Cody became famous in the West?* (Long pause) *What's that? Speak right up, please. Oh ho, I'm sorry—Billy the Kid is not* the correct answer. (Moan) *But we don't want you to go away yet—*

Ellery turned the radio off. Nevertheless, his mood had brightened considerably. It was all so utterly prosaic—the peaceful country road, the night, the radio. How could there be subtle terror in a world of two-foot-high hymn *books?* How could there be horror in the land of Ambrose Earnest from Sulfur Creek, Colorado?

He rumbled across the old bridge that spanned the Nueces, and turned sharply to the right along the river. The road was gravel now, and his tires crunched through the ruts, although there was no need to slow down. A screen of trees blocked his view of the Nueces on his right, and a fenced pasture stretched away into the darkness on his left. He was getting close to the ranch road.

What was there, really, that alarmed him in Jefferson Springs? Paul Ellery told himself that he was neither wildly imaginative nor given to flights of occult speculation. He was an anthropologist working on a community study, and he had experience both as a teacher and as a research scientist.

Apart from his profession, he was skeptical by temperament. He liked facts and was apt to ask embarrassing questions to get them. He had a habit of being right, and a rather poor memory for the few times he had been wrong. This led him to a certain cynical bullheadedness, which wasn't as objectionable as it might have been, because he was saved by a lively sense of humor and a pleasant, unpretentious personality.

In any event, he wasn't given to seeing ghosts.

Okay. Rule out the supernatural. Chins up, and all that rot. How could he explain the facts?

ITEM: When he had first chosen Jefferson Springs as the subject for a community study, and had got a grant from the Norse Fund in New York to carry it out, he had met with nothing but hostility from the inhabitants of the town. When that happened, in ordinary circumstances, an anthropologist with only a few months for research usually picked out another town where he could get quicker returns for the time invested. Ellery, however, had been stubborn. He wasn't to be licked by Jefferson Springs.

ITEM: After a few weeks, the people had changed their tactics. Instead of clamming up, they had talked willingly and volubly. They had told him everything. Unfortunately, hardly a word of what they said rang true.

ITEM: There was not one single person in the town of Jefferson Springs who had lived there longer than fifteen years. The town had a population of six thousand. Now, Jefferson Springs, for all its woebegone appearance to a stranger, was no ghost town. It had been continuously occupied for one hundred and thirty-two years. There had been no disasters, no social upheavals, no plagues, no crop failure, no nothing.

ITEM: That meant, in a nutshell, that the entire population—six thousand men, women, and children—had been *replaced*. What other word was there to use? The original citizens, one by one, had moved out. The last had left only a few years ago. At the same time, different people had moved in. None of them had been there longer than fifteen years, and most of them had lived in Jefferson Springs a much shorter time than that. It was a totally new population.

ITEM: In view of the average Texan's devotion to his land and his town; in view of the old families who lived in all such small towns, resolutely facing the past; in view of a million things this unexplained shift in population was impossible.

ITEM: But there it was. What do your learned books have to say on the subject? Nothing? How sad.

ITEM: The culture of Jefferson Springs, as described to him by informants after everyone had decided to talk, was a lovely textbook example of a typical Texas small town. Everything was in precisely the right place and in the right amounts. It was exactly as though you had read that three out of four men wore chlorophyll bags in their ears, and then you went out into a busy street and there they were. One, two, three men with chlorophyll bags; one without, doubtless self-conscious. One, two, three men with chlorophyll bags; one without. As regular as clockwork. And as phony as hell.

ITEM: The people of Jefferson Springs just didn't *feel* right. Paul Ellery was ready to swear that they were not the genuine article. They said the right things at the right times, and more or less did the right things at the right times. But it wasn't spontaneous. They were play-acting. The stage setting was absolutely authentic, and they had all memorized their lines. But the play was a fraud. It was a soap opera with no soap.

ITEM: *Why?*

He came to the Thorne Ranch gate and stopped the car. He left his headlights on, got out, and slid the wooden bar back to release the gate. He pushed it back and drove the car through, then rode the gate back shut and fastened it again. The night was very still. Except for the frogs down along the Nueces, croaking their ancient song, and the gentle breeze sighing across the fields, there wasn't a sound. The stars were bright now, and diamond-hard. There was no moon.

He eased the Ford along the dirt ranch road, taking it slow. When he had gone almost a mile, he topped a small rise and looked down on the buildings of the Thorne Ranch ahead of him. They were completely dark, without a light on anywhere. Either everyone was asleep or away, or else they could see in the dark. It was an indication of Ellery's frame of mind that he rather favored the latter view. As a matter of fact, he had noticed that there were far too few lights burning in Jefferson Springs at night. The town was kept dark, and once you got off the main highway it was exceptional to see a lighted window after eight or nine o'clock. What did that mean, if anything? Was it significant?

He stopped the car, pulling into the rut by the side of the road. Trying to organize his thoughts, he cut the motor and turned off his lights. Whatever was going on at the Thorne Ranch, he had neither excuse nor authority for prowling around the grounds in the dark. His mission was hardly urgent enough to rout Thorne out of bed—or was it? How could he tell? He would have liked to examine the grounds further, just on the off-chance of picking up something useful, but that was a good way to stop a bullet on any ranch, mysterious or not.

He was reluctant to turn back. There was no place to go. He sat and listened to the frogs, welcoming their familiar music. He watched the stars, clean in the smoke-free air.

Melvin Thorne was a big, gruff, soft-spoken Texan. Correction: *appeared* to be. Ellery wasn't taking anything on faith anymore. Nobody, he decided, ever questioned the obvious. Therefore, if you were trying to put a fast one over, the obvious was a good place to start.

Thorne was something of a leader in Jefferson Springs—neither rich nor poor, but a man who commanded respect. He had been cordial enough to Ellery when Ellery had interviewed him, and had urged him to drop in again. He had even made the more or less inevitable suggestion that when Ellery got tired of fooling around with all them books he could always get an honest job on the Thorne Ranch.

The stuff that Thorne had told him about the ranch was average information, and absolutely identical with the information given him by Jim Walls, who had the place out near Comanche Lake. As usual, it was *too* identical. It was a carbon copy.

Ellery had decided to try an experiment. He would fake all the data given him by Walls, making it flatly contradict what Thorne had told him of ranching conditions, and then ask Thorne to explain the discrepancies. It wasn't much, but it might be a lead.

He sat in the darkness, feeling a little foolish. It was all so incongruous, really. That was one thing that made the whole problem so tough: it didn't *look* like a problem. You had to go back constantly to your notes to make certain it was really there, and not just a figment of imagination, or a rationalization for sloppy work. The setting was all wrong for a mystery—no dark castles, no murders, no thunder and lightning, no mad scientist, no beautiful girl.

Just a soft summer night on a country road. Just a sleepy ranch and frogs by the river. Just earth and air and stars.

It was then that he got the feeling.

He couldn't place it at first. He sat up straight, suddenly tense. He held the steering wheel tightly in his hands, ready to move. What was wrong?

He listened. There was only the breeze, and the frogs in the distance.

He looked. There was the ranch, dark and deserted. There was the land around him. There was the night, frosted with stars.

And something else.

He held his breath. His heart thudded in his throat. He looked up, above the outbuildings of the Thorne Ranch, into the night sky.

There was something there—something enormous.

Paul Ellery released his breath in a hissing whisper. He felt the cold sweat pop out on his forehead and his hands felt sticky on the plastic of the steering wheel. Very quietly, he opened the door of his Ford and stepped out on the dirt road. Free from the distortion effect of the windshield, he looked up again.

The thing was still there.

Actually, it wasn't what he *saw* that frightened him. It was what he *didn't* see. He couldn't really see the thing at all, but he could feel its presence in the skies.

His neck ached but he kept his head back, staring. It was a perfectly clear night—he must remember that. There wasn't a cloud in the sky. The moon was just rising, but it was still swelling on the horizon and did not interfere with his line of sight. There were millions of stars burning in the darkness.

Except, of course, where they were blotted out.

That was what he saw. There was a dark mass in the sky over his head that covered up the stars. He could trace its outlines without difficulty, but he could not actually *see* it, apart from an occasional dull glint of reflected light. Its outlines were long and slender, rather pointed at one end, rounded off at the other. It was difficult to judge, because he could not tell for certain what its altitude was, but he roughly estimated its length as at least five hundred yards. It hung in the sky, completely motionless. It neither threatened nor promised. It was just there.

Paul Ellery did not know how long he stood in the dirt road, but it was a long time. Finally, he was rewarded by a flash of muted flame under the cylindrical shadow. A small shadow detached itself from the larger one, and started to float down. Unmistakably, it was headed for the Thorne Ranch.

Ellery's first impulse was to run. He felt utterly helpless, utterly alone. Worst of all, he felt insignificant. But he stood his ground. This was his chance. If he let it go by, he would never sleep soundly again. If he took advantage of it—

He stood very still, watching.

He could see the descending shape fairly clearly now. It was spherical, featureless, about ten feet in diameter. It looked like nothing so much as a huge metal beach ball.

It landed without a sound in the yard of the ranch house, not a quarter of a mile from Ellery's Ford. Five figures got out of it. They didn't speak. In the light of the rising moon, he saw that one of them, unmistakably, was the rancher, Melvin Thorne. The other four, at least at that distance, were strangers to Ellery—a man and a woman and two children. They went into the ranch house and closed the door behind them. Surprisingly, they turned a light on.

The metal globe hummed very slightly and floated back into the air, where it rejoined the massive shadow above. There was a flicker of light, so brief that Ellery could hardly be sure that he had seen it, and that was all.

The shadow in the sky was gone. The stars looked down on him, twinkling.

Paul Ellery got back into his car and carefully closed the door. He was completely stunned, and it took a real effort to keep his hands from trembling. He looked at his watch. It was half-past ten.

He couldn't think. Nothing made sense to him, not now. The most important thing in the world to him at that moment was to get his mind back on the tracks. He had to make some sanity out of the world in which he found himself—a different world, surely, than the one he had thought he knew. Otherwise, he was just an animal—a rat in a maze.

It might be that he was not entirely rational that night. He had been through a lot, and subtle pressures can sometimes build up and explode with frightening violence. He had always thought of himself as an essentially practical man. Certainly he was not the hero type. And yet—

He had been treated like a fool. He didn't like it.

He clamped an iron grip on his mind, refusing to panic. He started the engine. He turned his headlights on bright. Making plenty of noise, he drove straight down the dirt road toward the ranch house. He would have to do it some time, or go crazy.

He had driven out here tonight to ask Melvin Thorne *some* questions, and that was what he was going to do.

3

Ellery knocked on the door. There was a long heartbeat while the world held its breath. Then heavy footsteps thudded along from inside the house, coming toward the door.

The door opened.

Melvin Thorne stood there in the yellow frame of light. He could not have looked less mysterious. He was a big man, bigger than Ellery. He stood a good six-feet-three, and he was solid. He might have weighed two hundred and twenty pounds, and it was all rock-hard. His hair was brown and thinned down against his skull as a result of years of wearing a hat to shade his pale eyes from the sun. He was dressed in style—khaki trousers, light shirt with the throat open, boots. He needed a shave.

A *perfect imitation,* thought Ellery.

"Howdy, Paul," said Melvin Thorne. His voice was slow and friendly, and the drawl was unmistakable. "What can I do for you this time of night?"

Easy now. Take it slow.

"I'd like to ask you a few more questions, Mr. Thorne, if you could spare me a few minutes."

"My name is Mel," said Melvin Thorne. He paused. "Kinda late," he suggested.

"I know this is a poor time to come calling, Mel, but I surely would appreciate your help. I'm running into some things that are like to tying me in knots."

"Well, now, Paul, that would be a shame."

Ellery said nothing. His hands were wet with sweat. "Well, come along in, son," Thorne said, smiling. "Reckon a few minutes won't hurt none."

Ellery followed Thorne inside the house, and Thorne locked the door behind him. Ellery pretended not to notice—why shouldn't a man lock the door in his own home? Why shouldn't a *man*—

The house seemed deserted; Ellery couldn't see a sign of the four people who had come in with Thorne from the sphere. He listened, but all he heard was the sound of his own footsteps and a big, noisy clock ticking in the living room. The house was typical of small Texas ranch houses, which meant that it resembled a standard frame farm house. There were no wagon wheels, buffalo rugs, or brands on the furniture. The rooms were comfortable, but hardly flamboyant. It was a clean, middle-class, town-on-Saturday, church-on-Sunday house. It had a no-nonsense air about it.

Thorne led him into the kitchen, of course. There was the big farm icebox in the corner, the big iron stove against the wall, the shelves of mugs and plain dishes, the battered wood table with a fresh red-and-white checked table cloth. They sat down at the table. There were salt and pepper shakers on the table, each of which was inscribed with a deathless bit of verse. The salt shaker said: "I'm full of SALT, all nice and white; some use me heavy, some use me light." The pepper shaker said: "I'm full of PEPPER, don't shake me a lot; use me sparingly, I'm pretty hot."

Mystery?

"Coffee?" asked Melvin Thorne.

Ellery nodded. "Please," he said.

Thorne poured from the big black pot on the stove.

Where did the coffee come from? Paul Ellery wondered. *There hadn't been time to make any fresh.*

Ellery drank it black. It was warm, but not really hot. He decided that Thorne must have just turned the fire on under the old coffee when he had heard the knock on the door.

Thorne made a face. "Coffee's right poor," he said. "The missus hasn't been feeling none too well lately. Anyhow, you know how women are—they all like weak coffee. Now I always say the more coffee the better. You're not drinkin' the stuff to taste the *water.*"

"That's sure right," Ellery agreed, searching for an opening. What could he say to this man? *By the way, Mel, I've just been wondering—are you a Martian?*

That would hardly do.

"Well, son," Thorne said, "start firin' in those questions of yours. I can't read your mind, you know."

Paul Ellery looked at him sharply, but the others face was smiling and unsuggestive.

It was very quiet in the house. The big clock ticked in the living room, and that was all. Four people had come inside with Thorne, had come down out of the sky. Where were they? Hiding behind the door? Under the bed? In a secret passage?

Absurd. It was all absurd. And the ship—

Ellery licked his lips slowly. He was good and tired of beating around the bush. He was afraid and uncertain and confused, for the first time in his life, but he knew he had two choices in Jefferson Springs: he could go on with the farce, write up the data he knew to be false, and go on his way; or, if he dared, he could go after the truth, no matter where it led him.

He smiled. He knew that he had no choice at all. "Mel," he said, "I need your help."

Thorne poured more coffee for himself and refilled Ellery's cup. This time, it was steaming hot, and a big improvement over the first batch.

"Happy to help out, son," Thorne said. "'Course, I don't claim to know nothing about all this stuff of yours, but I know Jefferson Springs as well as the next man and better than some."

Ellery nodded, feeling his way. "Look here, Mel, did you ever notice anything—well, strange—peculiar, about Jefferson Springs?"

"I'm not real sure I follow you there."

"Don't you?"

"Well now, you take that Pebbles woman, lives over there by the high school. I'd be the last man in the world to say that woman was *crazy,* but it's a fact that she's plumb peculiar. Now, I recollect one time, I was driving along in my pick-up, and I looked over thataway, and there she is, in broad daylight, pushing that old lawn-mower of hers, and she was plain naked, naked as the day she was born—"

"I don't mean that kind of peculiar, Mel."

"Well, you're dealing this hand. What kind of peculiar *do* you mean?"

Ellery retreated to his favorite defense mechanism—his pipe. He was smoking too much these days, but it gave him a chance to collect his thoughts and look occupied when he wasn't really doing anything. Anyhow, the most mundane statement took on a certain profundity when it was pushed around the stem of a briar. He lit it, broke the match, and dropped it into his wet saucer.

"Here's the kind of peculiar I mean, Mel," he said slowly.

"You ever been anywhere where things just didn't feel right, even when you couldn't quite put your finger on what was wrong? I remember one time—wasn't far from here, either, up around Sabinal—I was riding a one-eyed white mare down the road one afternoon, just as calm and peaceful as you please. Well, all of a sudden that mare shied away from her blind side so quick she almost jerked me out of the saddle, and the next thing I knew she took off like a bat out of hell. Took me a good ten minutes to stop that mare."

Thorne laughed. "Nothin' to it," he said. "She seen a snake or something on her blind side and it scared her. Happens all the time."

"Suppose," suggested Paul Ellery, "that there was no snake there? Suppose there was nothing there?"

Thorne shrugged. "So she was jumpy, son. What's peculiar about that? Don't *you* never get jumpy?"

"Sometimes," Ellery admitted. He looked evenly at the man who sat across the table from him. "I've had a funny feeling about Jefferson Springs almost ever since I got here," he said. "In fact, it's more than a feeling. I'm absolutely positive there's something wrong with this town."

"Wrong?" There was a long silence. "With Jefferson Springs?"

"You've never noticed it, I suppose."

"Can't say as I have. Course, there's Mayor Cartwright. I've heard tell the man's a little slippery, but he's a politician, after all. You take that mess in Washington now—I'm not too surprised at anything I might see here at home."

Ellery blew an uncertain smoke ring at the salt shaker.

Clearly, he wasn't going to trick Thorne into saying anything revealing. The man was refusing to talk, about anything important. And he was a good actor, no doubt about that. Already, despite what he had seen, Ellery began to feel unsure of himself.

Well, he'd just have to get blunter—hit him over the head with it and see what happened. No one had tried to harm him yet in Jefferson Springs, and until they did he meant to keep digging.

He leaned forward. "Cards on the table now, Mel," he said evenly. "I was parked down the road in my Ford when you came home tonight."

The silence deepened. Outside, the summer wind whispered across the land.

Melvin Thorne didn't bat an eye. "What's that got to do with it?"

Ellery took a deep breath. "You came down out of the sky," he said. The words bounced around the prosaic ranch kitchen, trying to find a place to fit.

"I don't follow you, son, not at all. What might you be trying to say?"

"Four other people were with you," Ellery went on doggedly, "a man, a woman, and two children. They came into this house."

Melvin Thorne grinned, big and confident and completely at his ease. "Is this a game, Paul, or have you been hitting the old bottle? Come down out of the *sky!*"

Ellery kept talking. He felt as though he were on a treadmill and couldn't get off. "You came down in a metal sphere. I saw you. What's it all about?"

Ellery felt like a fool, like a complete sap. *Yes, that's the way you're supposed to feel. That's the best defense in the world—the fear of ridicule.*

"You can't be serious. More coffee?"

"Thanks. I'm serious. Damn it, you *know* I'm serious!"

Thorne laughed. "Sphere? Ain't no sphere in *my* yard. Got a old oil drum out in the shed yonder, if that'll help any."

Laugh it up, buddy, Ellery thought, getting mad. *Make with the truisms and the phony accent.* "Stuff a cold and starve a fever," he said. "Still water runs deep. All that glitters is not gold."

Thorne looked at him with concern in his pale eyes. "You're not making very good sense, Paul."

"Neither are you."

"No call to get riled up. I tell you what—if you think there's one of these spheres in my yard, why don't we just go outside and have a look? If you find one, you can keep it and take it home with you."

"I didn't *say* it was in your yard now. I said you came down here in it. I said you came down with four other people out of the sky. Don't humor me, Mel. I know what I saw."

Thorne shrugged. "Anything you say, son. I might as well tell you the truth, since you already know part of it." He smiled. "Fact is, I been herdin' my cattle from a flying saucer. Traded in my jeep and my ridin' stock and bought one out of a mail-order catalogue. They're right nice, too, exceptin' that I always fall off when I try to do any ropin'."

"Cut it out, Mel," Ellery said.

"It was your idea, son. I was just trying to give you some more good ideas."

"I'm mighty grateful." Paul Ellery got to his feet, his fists clenched. He looked the big man in the eye. "I want you to know something, though."

Melvin Thorne got to his feet also. "Yes?"

"I want you to know that I don't believe one damned thing I've heard since I walked into this house. I don't believe one damned thing I've heard since I got to Jefferson Springs. I don't *believe* in Jefferson Springs. I saw you get out of some kind of metal sphere tonight, right out there in your yard, and I saw the ship up above it too. I don't know what the hell is going on around here, but I mean to find out. I don't take kindly to being treated like a two-year-old. I want you to know I'm not leaving this town until I know the score, if it takes me the rest of my life. And spare me the Texas drawl, what say? It stinks."

The big man looked at him. "I'd say you got powerful bad manners, son. I don't know what they're teachin' in the schools these days, but it sure ain't neighborliness."

"Can it," Ellery said. "You're not fooling anybody." The two men stared at each other across the kitchen table.

Somewhere, far out on the range, a coyote cried.

Melvin Thorne laughed, abruptly. It was a big laugh, a loud laugh. It rebounded around the room, sure and confident and unconcerned.

"I like you, Paul," Mel Thorne said. "You oughta give up them books before you go completely loco, and come and work for me."

Paul Ellery felt tears of helpless rage well up in his eyes. How could you fight an enemy who refused to act like an enemy? How could you deal with a man who refused to meet you on any terms except his own? He measured the man before him carefully.

"Steady," said Melvin Thorne calmly. "You better run along home before you do something foolish. You'll feel better in the morning."

Paul Ellery was not inexperienced, and had been a competent-enough athlete in his time. He wasn't in really poor condition, but Mel Thorne could probably tear him apart if he felt so inclined. He knew the type. Socking him on the jaw would be like kicking a tank in a moment of irritation.

"Okay, Mel," he said. "Thanks for the coffee."

"You're surely welcome," said Melvin Thorne. "Come back any old time."

He led him back through the living room to the front door, unlocked it, and saw him out. The door closed behind him and the lock clicked.

Paul Ellery looked at his watch. A quarter to twelve. Less than four hours ago, he had been finishing up his meal in the Jefferson Springs Cafe.

He walked over to his Ford and got in. He started up the motor and turned around in the dirt drive. His brain spinning, he started back toward town.

It was still a beautiful night, soft and dear and sprinkled with stars. The moon had climbed high above him now, like a great pale eye in the darkness. Everything was so normal it hurt. The frogs were still croaking down along the Nueces, in splendid unconcern. Maybe that was the answer: be a frog.

It was, Paul Ellery thought, like a movie in a nightmare. The people didn't go with the scenery, and the dialogue didn't go with the plot.

What *was* the plot?

He drove fast, and he did not look back.

4

The next day was exactly like the previous sixty-two: hot.

The blazing white sun hung in the sky, almost motionless, as though it too were too hot to move. No cloud braved that furnace, and the heat beat down like boiled, invisible rain. Heat waves shimmered like glass in the still air and the parched earth took on the consistency of forgotten pottery.

Jefferson Springs, from the coolest corner in the thick, square icehouse to the baked metal of the top of the water tower, held its breath and waited for evening.

In his room at the Rocking-T, Paul Ellery sweated. His room was an uninspired boxlike affair, and the resemblance to an oven was more than fleeting. He sat on the thin, plain bed and nursed a pitcher of ice water from the drug store three doors down. His notebooks were scattered over the floor in unscholarly confusion, liberally sprinkled with spilled tobacco. The morning paper, from San Antonio, was stuffed in the wastebasket, and the symbolism was intentional.

He was trying to think. The heat didn't help, and neither did the events of the preceding night. But he knew the trouble now, knew it clearly: the whole situation was completely outside human experience. The human mind is so constructed that it works on past experiences; these are the data which it tries to utilize. Human beings store up past experiences, both those of the individual and those of the group, and carry them as integral parts of cultures. When a man runs up against a situation, even a novel one for him, he doesn't really have to deal with it alone. He has at least *heard* of such situations, he at least has *some* facts he can bring to bear, he at least has *some* notion of how to proceed.

Most situations, that is.

Not this one.

This one was unique. In a nutshell, that meant he had to figure it out for himself. That sounds easy enough, being one of the familiar figures of speech of the English language, but Paul Ellery knew that it was not so simple. Most people live and die without ever having to solve a totally new problem. Do you wonder how to make the bicycle stay up? Daddy will show you. Do you wonder how to put the plumbing in your new house? The plumber will show you. Would it be all right to pay a call on Mrs. Layne, after all that scandal about the visiting football player? Well, call up the girls and talk it over. Should you serve grasshoppers at your next barbecue? Why, nobody does that. Shall you come home from the office, change to a light toga, and make a small sacrifice in the back yard? What would the neighbors think!

But—how do you deal with a Whumpf in the butter?

What do you do about Grlzeads on the stairs?

How much should you pay for a new Lttangnuffel?

Is it okay to abnakave with a prwaatz?

Why, how silly! I never heard of such things. I have enough problems of my own without bothering my head about such goings on. A Whumpf in the butter! I declare.

A situation completely outside human experience.

Paul Ellery could see just how lovely the situation would appear from the other side of the fence. If you wish to devise a problem that cannot be solved, the simplest way is to make it appear that there is no problem. So long as everyone is convinced that all the answers are on file, nobody bothers to devise new answers. And if the problem is so constructed that you cannot even accept it as real without doubting your own sanity—?

How *could* the Earth go around the Sun? Any fool could see that it was the other way around, just by watching. How *could* there be anything alien and inexplicable in a little Texas town right on the San Antonio highway? Any fool could drive through it and see that it was just like any other town.

But when you introduced astronomy and mathematics—

Or anthropology and community-study techniques—

Paul Ellery frowned at his scattered notebooks. It was all there, the whole pat, unbelievable story.

There was the expected class structure, ranging from "that no-good trash" through the various ethnic groups to "those big shots who think they're better than anyone else." The pattern was closer to what West reported from Plainville than to Warner's elaborate class divisions from Yankee City, but that was in line with the size of the communities involved.

There was the expected emphasis on the high school as an upward-mobility mechanism. Clyde Kluckhohn and others had long ago pointed out that education had tended to supplant the frontier as a pet way to get along in the world, and this seemed to be as true in Jefferson Springs as elsewhere. Americans expected their children to get a better deal than they had, and the high school was usually the ladder that led upstairs.

There were the expected racial stereotypes about Negroes and Mexicans, and it was depressing to see that so little had changed since Powdermaker had written her *After Freedom* in 1939. There was the expected rural-urban ecology, the expected small-town kin ties, the expected suspicion of "those crooks in Washington."

But, somehow, it didn't fit together into a coherent whole—or more precisely, it fitted together *too* well. The neighborhood maps, the statistics, the symbol systems, the values—they added up to a perfect, ideal "type" that simply could not exist in reality. Social science was one devil of a long way from being that precise in its predictions. No one had ever found an ideal "folk" society as conceptualized by Redfield, and no one could expect to find a community as typical in every way as Jefferson Springs.

Still, he had found one. There were no ragged edges, no individual peculiarities, no human unpredictability.

It was, in a word, faked data.

It was a false face.

The entire population of Jefferson Springs had been replaced within the last fifteen years. Even a superficial look at courthouse records, supplemented with names and dates from Austin, had told him that much. The town had been taken over. The old residents had moved out—under what kind of pressure?

Okay.

Say it. Are you afraid of *the words? This little town is in contact with— something—out in space. Thorne knows. They all know.*

The cowboy hats and the boots and the Texas drawls and the inane weekly paper meant nothing. They were clothes worn to a costume party. Whose party?

Toward evening, when the intolerable heat eased off to become merely acutely uncomfortable, he left the hotel and endured another meal at the Jefferson Springs Cafe. Whatever the things were he was up against, he reflected, they had certainly learned the secret of Texas cooking: fry it in too much grease, add day-old French-fries, allow to cool, serve on soiled plate. When he had finished, he went back to his hotel.

There were two men in his room.

They were pleasant enough in appearance, quite unsinister, young, and casually dressed in sport clothes. They might have wandered in from a yacht club. One of them smoked a pipe. Ellery had never seen either one of them before.

"Hello, Ellery," said the man with the pipe, as though Ellery had just dropped in for a visit. "I hope we haven't alarmed you by waiting for you here."

"You've scared me to death. So what?"

"The fact is, Ellery, that we'd like to talk to you, if you're not too busy investigating us." He gestured at the notebooks with his pipe. "Interesting reading."

"Thanks," said Ellery. He stuck his hands in his pockets. "Make yourselves at home, gentlemen. My time is your time."

The men hesitated. "We'd rather hoped you'd come with us," offered the one without the pipe finally. "We think we can save you some time, if you're interested."

"I'm interested," Ellery looked them over carefully. "Where are we going?"

The pipe-smoker smiled. "To the ship," he said. "I believe you caught a glimpse of it last night, isn't that correct? I'm sure you'll find it interesting."

Paul Ellery lit a cigarette; he smoked them whenever his pipe got too foul even for him. He felt as though he were caught up on a treadmill, pushed and pulled by forces over which he had no control. And yet, the choice was his. The two men had asked him if he wanted to come along, and seemingly that was what they meant. They had not told him that he *must* go with them.

Strangely, much of his fear had left him. He didn't know whether it was because he was getting used to the situation or because the situation was too implausible to be feared. You can't fear the totally unknown—what you fear is something within your experience that you cannot fully understand but have reason to believe is dangerous.

These people were X factors—unknowns.

Obviously, they were not melodrama villains, twisting their black mustaches while they fed the babies to the meat grinders. They seemed reasonable enough. If Jefferson Springs had wished to harm him, there had been many chances. And if these people had really come from a ship in space, they were probably more intelligent than he was, or at least had far superior knowledge. If they were out to get him, they could deliver the goods at their own convenience. If not—

The ship, up there under the stars.

"Would you object if I carried a gun?" asked Ellery. "You gentlemen are strangers to me, you know."

The man with the pipe shrugged cheerfully. "You'll be perfectly safe with us," he assured him, "but by all means take a gun along if it makes you feel better."

Humor the native, Paul Ellery thought wryly. *If he wants to take his spear, let him take it.*

Well, it would make him feel better. He walked over to the dresser and took his .38 from the middle drawer, where he kept it hidden under his shirts. As a man who had to do a lot of moving around, Ellery kept the revolver with him as a precaution. He checked the cartridges, smiled at the two men who were watching him, and dropped a spare box of ammunition in his pocket. Then he stuck the gun in his belt and changed his shirt to a short-sleeved seersucker, replete with designs of palm trees and improbable dancing girls. He left the shirttail out, which at least served to make the .38 a little less conspicuous.

"Lead on, MacDuff," said Paul Ellery.

The man with the pipe nudged his companion. "That's him," he said, in perfect seriousness. "That's Shakespeare, remember? Misquoted, I believe, from *Macbeth*."

Ellery stared at the man, but said nothing. He switched out the light and followed the two men out of the hotel. The air was pleasant now, dry and warm but invigorating after the blistering sunlight.

They got into a perfectly ordinary black Buick and drove out of town. The two strangers sat in the front seat, leaving Ellery alone in the back. He could have shot them both without any difficulty, but of course he had no reason to —yet. The Buick went the other way from Thorne Ranch, out the San Antonio highway for seven or eight miles, and then veered off to the right along a dirt road. They went two miles on that—Ellery checked the speedometer over the drivers shoulder—and then purred to a stop.

Ellery spotted it instantly.

The big ten-foot globe, looking like a giant metal beach ball, swayed lightly in the middle of a plowed field.

They left the Buick by the side of the road, wriggled under a barbed-wire fence, and walked across the field to the gray sphere. A sliding panel lifted at their approach, and white light spilled out. They stepped inside and the panel closed. There was a sensation of lifting, very much the same as riding in a smooth elevator.

The interior of the globe was unremarkable. It was simply a hollow sphere, with a flat floor section built in, furnished with a soft gray wall-to-wall carpet, and two comfortable green couches. There was a very faint smell of electricity—or something like electricity—in the air. The globe hummed slightly, and there was a barely discernible vibration.

The two men sat on one couch, clearly not thinking about the ride at all. Paul Ellery sat on the other one and tried not to look like a country boy on his first trip to the big city.

His heart was thumping much too fast for his peace of mind, and his blood sang in his ears. What he felt was not fear, nor even wonder. He accepted it, all of it, because there was nothing else he could do. Here he was, and that was that. It was quite beyond his comprehension, and he knew it.

There was no name for what he felt, floating through the night sky with two men who were not of Earth.

The sphere stopped, very gently. There was a muffled thump as something locked into place. The two men stood up, and Ellery followed their example. The sliding panel opened. Outside, there was a glow of subdued yellowish light.

"After you," said the man with the pipe, smiling.

Somehow, Paul Ellery walked through the door. He passed through a short corridor—out of the garage, he thought rather wildly—and then he was inside of it. Inside the great shadow that had blotted out the stars.

Say it. A spaceship.

A long hallway stretched before him, with soothing indirect lighting in the walls. The floor was spotlessly clean and polished. There were panels along the sides, evidently leading to rooms of some sort. What could be in those rooms? How many secrets did this ship hold, secrets as yet unguessed by the men of Earth? Where had this ship been built, and when, and what ports had it seen as it cruised the greatest sea of all?

The hallway ahead was deserted and silent.

They don't want to scare me, he thought. *Caution! Do not frighten the aborigine!*

"Just walk straight ahead," said one of the men behind him. "You have nothing to fear, I assure you."

Paul Ellery walked straight ahead. Superficially, it was not unlike walking along an air-conditioned corridor in some modern skyscraper. Almost, you could imagine that you could stroll over to a window and look out, and there would be the familiar towers and gray, honking streets of a large city.

Except that there weren't any windows.

Except that you were hanging in the air, far above the cities of Earth.

Except that the .38 in your belt suddenly seemed an amusing toy, nothing more.

He walked for what seemed to be a long time, with the footsteps of the two men clicking behind him in the hallway. Actually, by his watch, it took him a little over one minute.

But it was a long minute.

At the end of the corridor, there was a heavy door, set flush with the wall. There was no knob on it.

"Just go right on in," said the man with the pipe. "The door will open and let you through. We'll be back for you a little later."

The two men turned and walked down the corridor, and disappeared into a branching passage. Paul Ellery was alone.

"Here goes nothing," he said, not giving himself time to hesitate.

He stepped forward and the big door swung open without a sound.

He walked inside.

5

A little red-faced fat man was waiting for him.

"Ellery!" he exclaimed, extending a stubby hand and getting up from behind a large and untidy desk. "Damn glad to see you—been really looking forward to making your acquaintance. Say, haven't you been the stubborn devil though! I like that, I admire that. Have a drink?"

Paul Ellery got his own hand out in time to have it pumped up and down with enough enthusiasm to make him worry about his shoulder socket. He could not have been more surprised if he had encountered an alligator in a spacesuit. This jovial little fat man simply didn't fit the bill as a mysterious alien. He was about as mysterious as Lassie.

"What the hell," said the fat man, hands on his hips. "Don't stare at me like that, Ellery. This isn't a zoo, old man, and I have always flattered myself on a roughly humanoid appearance."

"Sorry," Paul Ellery managed to say. "I didn't mean to stare. It's just—well, you sort of caught me off base, that's all."

The fat man frowned with what seemed to be genuine petulance. "What do you want me to do, confound it—act inscrutable or something?"

"Or something," Ellery admitted.

The fat man laughed. "Well, anyhow," he said, "my name here is John. Frightfully original, hey? And now that we've been formally introduced, how about that drink? Permit me to assure you that it is not mere hospitality that speaks—I, the amazing monster from beyond the stars, am thirsty."

Paul Ellery hesitated. This was all coming at him so fast that he hardly knew how to react to it. The behavior pattern just didn't exist. It was just last night that he had stood on the dirt road on the Thorne Ranch, looking up—

But he felt himself relaxing. John seemed an amiable enough old buzzard. At least he wasn't a second-hand Texan, and that was a relief.

Careful. He may be a trick.

"What kind of a drink?" he asked cautiously.

The man called John laughed again. "What kind of a drink? Why, there's only one possibility, of course! I'll let you in on it, because I'm really not John at all—my name is Buster, and I'm an undercover man from the F.B.I."

Incredibly, the little fat man began to pace the floor, making wild theatrical passes at the air and frowning hideously. "The drink—ah, yes, the drink. You want to know about the drink?"

Ellery caught himself gaping again. Was the man a lunatic? A—what was the phrase—a mad scientist? Oh no, that would be the last straw! *Call the attendant, Doctor. I'm ready.*

"The drink," announced John, rubbing his small hands together with great relish, "is none other than a magic potion which will make you our willing slave in our diabolical scheme to turn the Earth into roast beef!"

Ellery laughed out loud, unable to control himself. It sounded a little hysterical.

John abandoned his pose and pretended disgust, but it was evident that he had enjoyed playing his brief role. "Damn it all, Paul," he said, "you're a rational man. You've got to get hold of yourself and calm down. We're banking on your intelligence, old man. Pray don't disappoint us. There's nothing up my sleeve, and I'm not going to turn into a spider and feed you to my young. You chaps, if you don't mind my saying so, have the most monstrous stories about us. There's a whole literature down here that's positively stuffed with invading monsters, ghouls, and a frightfully dull army of dim-witted supermen who dash about through the air thinking at each other and throwing things about with mental force, whatever that is—you read science fiction, of course?"

"Well, no," Ellery admitted. "I haven't had much time for that sort of thing."

John clucked sadly. "Deplorable. The worser sort, that is. Well, no matter. When I say a drink, I mean a *drink*—in your terms, of course. I rather like your Scotch—do you?"

"Yes," said Ellery. "Yes, I do, and I could use some." He sat down in a chair in front of the large messy desk. He couldn't pretend to himself that he knew what the score was, but at least he could try not to make a fool of himself.

The little fat man sat down in a plush, padded chair on the other side of the desk and produced a bottle and two glasses from a drawer. The bottle was a familiar one—White Horse. John filled two glasses and handed one to Ellery.

"To sin," he said, and swallowed a good two jiggers in one gulp.

Ellery matched John's drink with one of his own, and the Scotch felt good. He needed it. He looked around the room, trying to get a line on the man who occupied it. The place was jammed with books—all kinds of books. Many of them were totally unfamiliar to him, alien in language and design, but there were others that he had seen before: Thomas Wolfe's *Of Time and the River*, Mark Twain's *Huckleberry Finn*, Ernest Hemingway's *The Sun Also Rises*, A. E. Housman's *A Shropshire Lad*, Thomas Mann's *The Magic Mountain*. Books by Chekhov and Dostoevski, de Maupassant and Sartre, Eliot and Shakespeare. Detective stories by Conan Doyle, Chesterton,

Cornell Woolrich. Science fiction by Arthur Clarke, Ray Bradbury, Edgar Pangborn, Clifford Simak. And magazines and newspapers and tapes and cans of film. Ellery even spotted Kroeber's *Anthropology* and Howell's *Mankind So Far*—two books by anthropologists who knew how to write.

"You read a lot," he commented without brilliance.

John grinned and refilled both glasses. "I know you're wondering about many things, Paul."

"Wouldn't you be?"

"Of course." The little man produced a cigarette which glowed into a light when he puffed on it. He frowned. "I'm not playing with you, Paul. I hope you'll excuse my ham acting when you came in—you have no idea how it feels to shake hands with someone and all the time have him look at you as if you were about to sprout wings and squirt fire in his eyes." He drummed his fingers on the untidy desk. Almost, he looked nervous and ill at ease. "You see, Paul, this is rather a ticklish situation. Hard to explain, hard to get across. This isn't easy for me, either. Doing the best I can, do you see?"

Paul Ellery thought he saw. *No use kidding myself. He's the anthropologist and I'm the aborigine.*

"Maybe I can help," he said.

"Maybe you can," John agreed. "I hope you'll try."

"Question one," Ellery said, "what am I doing here?"

John frowned again and puffed on his cigarette. "Look at it this way—and please understand that there is nothing personal in what I say. The fact is that we regard you as an intelligent man. Further, you are a patient man, a persistent man. You even have a basic grounding in the scientific approach to phenomena. All right. You have blundered into a situation, quite by accident, and you've been smart enough to see through the window dressing and formulate a problem. That in itself is remarkable, and we are properly impressed. You are not, frankly, dangerous to us. You *are* a nuisance, if you will excuse my bluntness. Therefore, we have decided to do the only logical thing from our point of view."

"Which is?"

"Remove the nuisance, of course."

Paul Ellery raised his eyebrows. "What do I do—walk the plank?"

John frowned, changed his mind, and laughed. He laughed rather too much for comfort, Ellery thought. But then, he seemed concerned about Ellery's feelings, not his own. Sincerity, or part of the job? Or both?

"Nonsense," the little fat man said. He tossed his cigarette into a small depression in his desk and the cigarette disappeared. "Utter rot. Our methods are hardly so crude as all that. As a matter of fact, Paul, I can set your mind at ease a bit by telling you one simple fact. It is this: we are forbidden by the laws under which we live to harm physically any native of your planet. Ah, I see this surprises you! You find it hard to imagine that the monsters from space live under laws of their own?"

"To tell you the truth," said Ellery, "I never thought about it."

"Ummm. Well, be that as it may, the fact is that you probably have less to fear from us than from your own people. So do try to relax. You're making me nervous."

Paul Ellery savored the Scotch in his mouth. He tried to picture the scene he was enacting: a young man sitting across the table from some sort of an alien, an alien with what almost amounted to an inferiority complex about being an alien, in a spaceship hanging over the Earth, discussing the nuisance value of the aborigines. It wasn't easy to visualize. It was still less easy to accept as reality—it had all happened too fast. But only an idiot could bury his head in the sand and convince himself that what was happening *couldn't* happen.

"Question two," said Paul Ellery. "Are the people in Jefferson Springs—well, human?

John poured more Scotch. He must, Ellery thought, have a capacity like a storage tank. What did they drink where *he* came from?

"You'll have to define 'human,' I'm afraid, before your question will make much sense," John said, inserting another cigarette in his mouth. "Do you mean, to employ your own terminology, a creature that may be classified as kingdom Animal, phylum Chordata, class Mammal, subclass Eutheria, order Primate, sub-order Anthropoidea, family Hominidae, genus Homo, species sapiens? Do you mean a divine creature with a soul, and do you care to specify any particular religious faith? Do you mean the highest product of evolution? Do you mean people born on Earth, or in America, or perchance in Texas? Do you mean a highly complex animal which, by means of glandular interaction, possesses rare spiritual qualities? Do you mean an essence, a vapor, an ultimate this-or-that? Do you mean something, say, with a cranial capacity of over a thousand cubic centimeters? Do you mean someone with whom you are not at war at the present time?"

Paul Ellery digested that slowly. To cover his own confusion, he resorted again to his pipe, filling it and lighting it with slow deliberation. Whatever else he might be, the little fat man was no fool. All right, then—what did *he* mean by "human?"

"Suppose we rephrase my somewhat childish question," he said. "First of all, as to your physical type, if I can use the term, I should judge that these people are indeed Homo sapiens, at least externally. Right?"

"You have answered your own question," John said. "Isn't it surprising how much you know if you will just stop half a second and think?"

"Okay," Ellery went on. "Next, were you born on Earth? I presume not. Next, if you weren't born on Earth, where *were* you born? More important, are you the product of a completely different evolutionary chain, unconnected in any way with Earth? As an anthropologist, I find it hard to understand how man could be repeated so precisely somewhere else in the universe. The line of development that produced man is so improbable and twisted—"

"If I may say so," John interrupted him, "there are a good many things anthropologists do not understand."

"I would be the last to deny that," Ellery admitted. He felt relaxed now, almost at his ease. It was like a bull session in college—except that college was a spaceship, high above the sleeping Earth.

"No offense, Paul," the fat man assured him. "Anthropologists are no worse than other natives of your planet. In fact, they are less certain than others, which means they are almost on the road to average intelligence. But we digress, my friend. The Scotch has loosened your tongue, and it has made me arrogant."

"It hasn't made you answer my question, however."

"Ummm. Well, it's no secret. The galaxy has spawned man many times, although its motive for doing so, if I may anthropomorphize a bit, seems obscure. In fact, man is a rather common animal. All it seems to require is a planet that closely resembles your own—and planets are a dime a dozen, you know—and a sun of the proper type; and man, by one road or another, becomes disgustingly inevitable. One of man's attributes, by the way, is that until a certain rather low level of development, he always is quite certain that his own planet is the only fortunate one in the universe, being blessed with his presence."

Ellery downed his Scotch and puffed on his pipe. "Let's try another question, then," he said. "The gentlemen you sent for me mentioned saving me some time. I was given to understand you had some concrete proposal you were going to make to me. What were they talking about?"

John refilled both glasses and then got to his feet. He began pacing up and down behind his desk. Ellery got the distinct impression that the little fat man really had been enjoying their talk, just as he had enjoyed acting out the role of one of Frankenstein's afterthoughts when Ellery had first come in. Now, he was working again, and none too happy about it. Why?

"It's quite simple, Paul," he said, jamming his hands into the pockets of his loose-fitting gray tunic. "You are, to put it candidly, an investigator who has been annoying our people. Now, suppose our positions were reversed. Suppose that you found an investigator who went around bothering *your* people—one without official immunity, let us say. What would you do with him?"

"Try to get rid of him, I suppose," Ellery said.

"Precisely. And how would you get rid of the investigator?"

"Well, you could lock him up if he had performed any criminal act. Or you could make things so hot for him he would have to go away and leave you alone. Or, failing all else, you might try to buy him off."

"Logical enough," John admitted, still pacing up and down. "Logical, but rather crude. I might almost say primitive—nothing personal, you understand."

"Naturally," said Ellery.

"Yes," said John. "We think we have a much more efficient method for getting unwanted investigators out of our hair."

"Which is?"

"Simplicity itself, old man. We simply take the problem that the investigator is trying to solve, and solve it for him! After that, we present him with the solution, with our compliments. Then, you see, the investigator finds himself in the untenable position of having nothing left to investigate. He has got the answers he was looking for and—presuming that he is an honest investigator—he can leave us in peace."

Ellery stared at the little man. "You mean you brought me up here to tell me what I've been trying to find out?"

"That's the general idea." John walked back to his desk and sat down. "There are things in the town of Jefferson Springs which you do not understand and which bother you. You've seen ranchers come down out of the sky in a metal sphere, and you have seen this ship. You might think, incidentally, that Thorne was a bit careless in letting himself be spotted that way, but sometimes it *is* necessary to transport people back and forth. After all, it was done at night on Thorne's own ranch, and Thorne's land does not lie along a main road, you know. Even if it did, most people wouldn't spot that shadow in the sky. The few that might would be dismissed as flying-saucer addicts, and in any event we'd be gone before any lasting harm was done. Well! I'm going to tell you the works, Paul, the true story. After that, I'm going to make you an offer. Clear enough?"

"Clear so far."

"Okay," said John. "Here we go."

6

The story the fat man told was a strange mixture of the familiar and the unique. It was man—another race of man, perhaps, but man for all of that—writing the old, old stories on new paper with new machines.

There were many earthlike planets in the galaxy—rather small, unspectacular planets, orbited about quite ordinary suns. On everyone, the alchemy of life had produced miracles in the seas, and the chain had begun. From the sea to the land, from reptile to amphibian to mammal; from simple to complex; from tiny, scuttling animal, sneaking a living from the domain of monsters, to man, proud and powerful and almost intelligent enough to be a long-term success instead of a flash in the pan.

The details were often different, but the generalized outline was the same. If you started with an Earthlike planet, you got an Earthlike man. Man was not quite an accident, and neither was he planned. He was the result of a set of conditions. Each group of men, when they arrived at a stage when they began to wonder about such things, naturally assumed that they were altogether too remarkable ever to be duplicated elsewhere in the known universe. Therefore, man's first inevitable contact with other men—for all men looked out at the stars, and all men wondered—always came as something of a shock.

People who had been living in villages found themselves also in a universe.

People who worried about nations discovered galaxies.

People who had learned to live in one world were dismayed to learn of a hundred thousand more.

Eventually, of course, great organizations and federations developed— man was an organizing animal. Planets which had reached a relatively high level of culture joined forces with other advanced planets. This was not easy, and took many centuries, for of course each planet felt that it had unique qualities; and it was difficult to trust foreigners. Each planet knew that it was superior and, what was more, each could prove it to its own satisfaction.

But civilization, which was another name for complexity and larger social aggregates, spread. At first, it was a few planets that had banded together, each for selfish purposes and each speaking loudly of brotherhood. Then it was many planets—for how could one lone planet survive against the power of many?

Man was an animal with big ideas.

The federation, loose and suspicious at first, thrived. Ideas were exchanged, and fresh viewpoints. Cultures flowered. A vast galactic government evolved, weak in the beginning, and then strong. Man could not live without organization.

When man on Earth was a clumsy thing climbing down from the trees, the first civilized planets were making overtures to each other.

When man on Earth found himself with a brain of sorts, and learned to make fire and pick up rocks with which to bash in other brains, a tenuous galactic federation was struggling to be born.

When man on Earth was yet a Neanderthal, slowly evolving the ideas of religion and an afterlife, other men he could not see had a civilization that spanned the known universe.

When man on Earth was a Cro-Magnon painting the walls of caves, he might look up at night, perhaps walking homeward from a mammoth hunt, and see the stars. Out there, a hundred thousand planets were jockeying for position on a galactic scale.

When man on Earth was an Indian, coming into an empty America across the Bering Strait from Asia, the star civilization was running into difficulties.

When man on Earth was developing agriculture and cities and mushrooming technologies, the galactic troubles grew.

They had to be solved.

The interstellar civilization had thrived. When man thrives, he multiplies. The birth rate had gone up with the cultural vitality. Man filled up his planets, and the civilized planets of the galaxy became overcrowded.

The expanding population had to find some place to go. At first, non-human planets had been tried. Unfortunately, this had not worked out. The existing life-forms which occupied these other planets had been part of the trouble, but only a small part. For the most part, they were so utterly different that they had no interest in human beings one way or the other, and competition with them was out of the question—different life-forms lived different lives, and required different things.

The basic problem, however, was the planets themselves. If a planet was naturally suitable for human life, human life evolved there. If it wasn't naturally suitable, the mere question of survival for men posed tremendously difficult problems. It had been said many times that man was an extremely adaptable animal, and so he was—on his own planet, or on one closely resembling it. He didn't adapt very well to a planet with twenty gravities; he didn't exactly thrive on a methane atmosphere; he didn't find temperatures that melted rock very pleasant.

To be sure, there were some relatively unoccupied planets that man could exist on. He could build atmosphere domes and enclosed villages;

he could substitute his technologies for nature. But only up to a point. Human populations didn't do well in plastic bowls. In some cases, they managed to stay alive, but they—changed.

Obviously, the "different" planets were no solution. Man needed Earthlike planets for his homes, because it had been Earthlike planets that had spawned him. On the right kind of a planet, on *his* kind of a planet, man worked. On other kinds, he didn't work, because he was a man. It was that simple.

The population continued to expand. The galactic civiization had to have Earthlike planets, had to have colonies that could drain off the overflow of men. Where could it find them?

There was only one place. If you want an Earthlike planet, a Marslike planet won't do. You can irrigate a desert and make it green, but you can't turn Jupiter into England with a slide rule. If you want an Earthlike planet, you must pick an Earthlike planet in the first place and go there.

It was unfortunate that *all* of the Earthlike planets were occupied.

It was more fortunate that all the Earthlike planets were not at the same level of cultural advancement. Many of them were quite primitive, others were just experiencing the growth pangs of civilizations.

Now, cultural simplicity has consequences over and beyond any moral condemnation or exaltation of the noble savage. It has consequences in terms of populations. A culture that exists by hunting and gathering, on the average, must be a small one. If the population of New York City alone had to live in New York State by hunting wild animals, it is a safe bet that the population would be drastically reduced. A culture that has farming can support more people on the available land surface. With the beginnings of machine technology, still more people can live on the same amount of land.

But it takes a galactic civilization *really* to fill up a planet. As a result, most of the Earthlike planets which had not yet become a part of the larger civilization still had some room left for expansion.

Earth was one of those planets.

The galactic civilization found itself in an odd position. On the one hand, it had developed to a point which made the ruthless conquering and exploiting of other worlds unthinkable. Its own citizens would never stand for such an action.

On the other hand, it had to drain off population, and there were only the occupied Earthlike planets which offered any possibilities in that direction.

They did the best they could. Man, when forced into it, is a compromising animal. They decided to colonize the undeveloped Earthlike planets left in the galaxy, but their colonization was no crude and slapdash affair. In order to appease public opinion within the federation, they had to work within a framework of principles, restrictions, and laws.

First of all, the primitive planet must not be aware that it had been colonized, for that would destroy initiative and rob whole worlds of their futures. Secondly, the natives could not be harmed in any way, and could not be interfered with except in the initial setting up of the colony, when various psychological techniques were permitted. Finally, there was a limit to the percentage of a planet that could be colonized. This percentage varied with the planet, but in no case could it exceed fifteen per cent.

Earth was one of the primitive planets selected. There was nothing intentionally cruel about this idea, although it had its imperfections and unforeseen consequences. It was just an emergency solution to a pressing problem, and it postponed, at least, the necessity for long-term, sweeping reorganization and restriction. It was a practical program for thousands of years, in most cases, and as for the future—well, perhaps they would have other solutions then.

They were not *proud* of their solution, but they were stuck with it.

Ironically enough, there was a precise parallel on Earth itself, if on a more limited scale. On many parts of the planet, expanding Western civilization had reached out and enfolded more primitive cultures. In some cases, it had simply exterminated the natives. In others, it had just taken away their land and deposited the aborigines on reservations. It had happened quite strikingly in North America, among other places. The Europeans came in, and the Indians were presented with the short end of the stick.

We weren't a vicious people, the Europeans said afterward. *We weren't bloodthirsty fiends. But it was inevitable—all that land, supporting only a fraction of the people it could support. And we needed land, needed it badly. Perhaps we were wrong, in an abstract sense, but what happened couldn't be helped. No practical man could imagine leaving a whole continent to the Indians. We didn't always like it, but what else could we do?*

What, indeed?

And, argued the civilized peoples of the galaxy a few hundred years later, *what else could we do?*

When civilization came furtively to Earth, sneaking in by the back door as it were, it was all done with great finesse and subtlety. Advanced peoples employ advanced methods. There was no drum-thumping invasion, no excitement, no death rays, no battling space fleets. No one got hurt. The Earth never even knew it had company.

Planets had been colonized before. Methods were smooth and routine. No fuss, no muss, no bother.

Defense? How could there be a defense? Defense against what? Where was the offense?

Naturally, the colonists confined themselves to the small towns and villages. They had other uses for the cities.

Picture a small town, any small town. A Main Street and a drugstore and a movie. Houses with unpainted, honest fronts and hamburgers cooking in the kitchen. Snow in the winter, sun in the summer. Rain on the night of the big dance. Rotary Clubs and gas stations. Gray ladies worried about the new preacher—he smokes, you know. A boy and a girl on a night in spring, the family car kissed by magic, a soft moon forgotten among the stars.

The town, though caught in the web of nation and state, is isolated. The people there see the same people every day. The next town is twenty miles away, and of course the people in the next town are hardly the *proper* sort. Strangers aren't wanted, because strangers always want to change things. We like our town the way it is.

The small town has a reputation in the city. The people who live and die there are ignorant, so the legend goes. They are fifty years behind the times. You can't ever tell about small towns—they're funny. They're full of local color and strange rural customs and the damnedest characters you ever saw.

An isolated society, then. A clannish society that doesn't want strangers poking around. A backward society where odd things and unusual-looking people are a part of life. Buildings all up, crops all planted, stores all stocked. A rustic colony. Ideal conditions. Ready for immediate occupancy.

The scientific experts from an unsuspected civilization go to work. Buy here, sell there. Tamper with a crop here, dust a few cattle there. Alter the rainfall, just a little. Spread a few pointed stories around—why, they're cleaning up down the road in Oakville, or out in Indiana, or right over there in the city. Opportunity!

And new people move into your little town. Funny people. They don't mix. Why, they're taking over the town, I declare! It's all poor Mrs. Smith can do to keep body and soul together. And so many of your friends moving on, after all these years, selling out, going to the city.

It's just not the same in your town any more. And you've heard of such wonderful chances somewhere else—the Wilsons went there, remember, and the Wades and the Flahertys—

Will, I've been wondering—

It was a snap. Duck soup for the experts from the stars.

One population moved out, another population moved in. A colony.

Of course, it was unfortunately true that if you moved the natives off their land you had to be sure they had somewhere to go. Fifteen per cent of a planet was a lot of real estate. There had to be, in a sense, reservations for the natives.

Earth was ideal. Earth already had its reservations, ready and waiting. They were called cities.

Where did the unabsorbed small-town people go when they left home? Where had they always gone? Into the cities, of course.

The cities of Earth became preserves for the aborigines.

It was beautiful, really. What sane man would prefer to live in the shrieking chaos of a city, stacked in like sardines with his neighbors in the smoke and the dirt and the sweat? What sane man would voluntarily leave the sunshine and the green fields and the quiet companionship of home for a factory and a tenement and the grinding of machinery?

Answer: almost all of them. Wasn't it the thing to do? Wasn't the city the place to go to get ahead? Wasn't the city where all the smart people were? Weren't you an ignorant hick if you stayed at home?

There was nothing new in this. Man had always gone to the city. But he could be helped along if necessary, and he was. Psychological conditioning techniques, when administered by a really advanced culture, were remarkable things.

If you want to build an escape-proof prison, there is a way. Just don't tell the prisoners that they're in jail. Make them compete with each other for life-sentences.

Call it home.

There was one colossal irony in what was happening on the Earth, and it afforded the colonists with no end of amusement. The technicians of Earth were busily engaged in trying to build a spaceship of their own—one of the first primitive types, of course, with chemical fuels. With this spaceship of theirs, if it ever got off the drawing boards, they hoped to transport colonies of *natives* to other planets! They were bravely hoping one day to go out and "conquer" and populate the galaxy—a galaxy that was already so overcrowded that it had overflowed to Earth!

Naturally, they would find that the other planets of their solar system were quite unsuited for colonies of any sort, and they were still many centuries away from a workable interstellar drive. Still, it was amusing.

Since Earth was now entering a primitive phase of what might be termed pre-civilization, with savage war patterns coupled with semi-advanced destructive techniques, it might well be that an atomic war could occur. Earth was at a crisis period in her history, and could easily go either forward or backward. Many of the Earthlike planets had reached this stage many times, only to be blown back to the beginning for another start. Some planets never did get any further.

Now, an atomic war, under present conditions, would primarily affect only the large cities. This was not a pleasant prospect, of course, but for the colonists it was far from being a tragedy. The longer it took Earth to evolve a true civilization, the more time the colonies had to live their lives undisturbed.

Mind you, they would not start the war. They were not immoral beasts. Starting a war would be very unethical. On the other hand, they were forbidden to interfere. They just wouldn't *prevent* the war. Savages were so warlike.

The town of Jefferson Springs, obviously, was one of the alien colonies. It went through the typical well-trained motions of an American village, but this was no village of Earth.

This was different.

And that was the story the fat man told.

7

There was a brief silence while John paused for breath.

He occupied himself by refilling the neglected glasses with Scotch and indulging in another cigarette. He looked just faintly bored—the look of a college professor explaining evolution to a freshman.

"Well, that's that," he said. "I hope I haven't bored you?"

"Not at all," said Paul Ellery. *When all else is gone,* he told himself, *put up a good front.*

"No monsters, no fiends, no wicked prime ministers," the fat little man observed, rather sadly. "Not even much drama, I'm afraid, to say nothing of melodrama. Just expediency. Just politics. Just human littleness in the face of something big." He sipped his drink. "I sometimes think that men are too small for their universe, Paul. We have such a magnificent backdrop, and our plays are so confoundedly uninspired and monotonous."

"Yeah," said Paul Ellery. "Monotonous."

"I'm quite serious," John said. "You will find that life on a galactic scale can be every bit as humdrum as life confined to a planetary anthill. Sam still loves Mary, and Mary still wants Sam to be a bigger wheel than Philip. It's all damnably dull if you ask me, which you didn't."

Paul Ellery, Ph. D., born in Austin, Texas, and raised on the planet Earth, puffed on his pipe in a spaceship room, hanging in the night. It was his fourth pipe, and his mouth felt like sandpaper. The rest of him felt worse.

He felt numb with what he had heard. It was not so much that it had come as a complete surprise, for much of his information had pointed the same way. Rather, it was the fact that his wildest conjectures, his most fantastic guesses, had been reduced to the level of a commonplace, everyday existence.

Little green men living in your furnace? Why, of course! Didn't you know?

John's matter-of-fact attitude toward the whole thing had made him feel oddly distant from the whole problem. It was like an intellectual exercise, a bedtime story in bedlam, a motion picture about another world.

It wasn't easy to remember that *he* was an aborigine. Ph. D.? He had never been unduly proud of it, but it *was* disconcerting to have it calmly reduced to the level of Witch Doctor, Third Class. *Some of his herbs really work, you know; but all that mumbo-jumbo is just too much for me.*

He couldn't doubt the story he had heard. It fitted the evidence too well, and the quiet ship that surrounded him squelched any qualms he might have had with complete authority. There was no reason for John to lie to him. He had heard the truth and he knew it.

He had one question, however.

"Look, John," he said slowly. "You kept talking about the inevitability of these colonies. You kept speaking of the necessity for what you did, and you used some examples from our own history to justify your viewpoint. But isn't there a basic difference? After all, this outfit of yours is a galactic civilization. It's big business. Wouldn't birth control have solved your whole population problem very neatly?"

John smiled. "No, it wouldn't," he said.

"Why? Surely your people are sophisticated enough—"

"That's not the point, Paul. Look here—you have birth control available and widely practiced right in the United States, isn't that right? And has the population gone up or down since the introduction of birth control techniques?"

"Up," Ellery had to admit. "But I still think—"

"No, my friend. It isn't that simple. Many other factors are involved. For one thing, the galactic federation is not a dictatorial set-up—and it takes a dictatorship to impose that sort of a rigid restriction on people. You will find that as people advance they insist on a certain amount of individual freedom; they will submit voluntarily to some things, but not to others. Birth control is practiced to some extent, just as it is in the United States, and you will observe that the birth rate in Jefferson Springs is actually lower than in most American towns. That isn't enough, however—it's a phony solution."

"Why?"

"You know the answer to that one, Paul. Permit me to refer you to one of your own scientists, V. Gordon Childe. What has *always* happened when there is a technological advance? What happened in the Neolithic? What happened during the Industrial Revolution?"

Ellery saw the point. "The population expands," he admitted.

"Check. And you are *sitting* right smack in the middle of a technological advance—a spaceship. Spaceflight *always* means more population, not less. That's just the way it is. If there's a method of cutting down population without killing the culture, we haven't found it yet. It's a problem for the future. We don't know all the answers, Paul, and we never will."

Ellery let that sink in a minute. There was just one thing he could say. He said it. "You spoke of an offer, John."

John put the tips of his fingers together and twiddled his thumbs. "Paul, you're an intelligent man. The fact that I am from what we have modestly described as a high civilization and you are a citizen of, shall we say, a less developed culture, has no bearing on your *intelligence*. We respect your brains. We know our own self-interest when we see it, and we think we could find a place for you in Jefferson Springs. Not much of a place at first, to be candid, but with hope for the future. We want you to work for us. That way, we gain and you gain. The other way, nobody gains. You have a saying on your planet, I believe, one of the few that makes a modicum of sense: If you can't beat 'em, join 'em. Crude, but I'm sure you see the point."

Ellery looked at the fat little man—the friendly blue eyes, the lines in the pink forehead, the earnestness that filtered through the easy mannerisms. Whatever else he was, John was an intelligent man. More to the point, he seemed to be an honest man. "Suppose I don't accept your offer?"

"You are indeed a suspicious man:" John sighed. "I'm afraid you still think of me as a monster of some sort."

"Not a monster, John," Ellery said truthfully. "I'm trying to deal with you as a human being."

"What is there to say, my friend? If you don't accept our offer, you don't accept our offer. That's all. Nothing will happen to you—although the psychological effects are apt to be rather overpowering. You are free to leave here, go anywhere you want to go, say anything you want to say. We think you have a brain, and we hope you use it. It's up to you."

Ellery hesitated. "You mean I am actually free to leave, after what you've told me?"

John nodded at the door. "There's the exit. You will be escorted back to your room, unconditioned and uninfluenced. You're a free agent—or as much of one as a human being ever is. You know Mel Thorne. If you want to take us up on our offer, go out and see him. If not, I wish you well."

Paul Ellery got to his feet, slowly.

"So long, Paul," John said, shaking his hand firmly.

"So long—and thanks. I appreciate—well, everything."

"It was a pleasure, my friend." John looked as though he meant it.

The big door opened silently for him. He left the fat man alone at his desk. He seemed a little lonely, a little sad. The two escorts were waiting in the long, cool corridor.

Ellery followed them down the timeless, deserted tunnel, past the side panels that lined the walls. There was the door, the short passage, another door—and he was back in the sphere. He sat down on the green couch on the gray carpet, and the humming vibration came again.

When the sliding panel opened again, he emerged into the moist coolness of false dawn. He heard crickets chirping in the damp grass. He looked at his watch. It was five o'clock in the morning. There was the ride in the Buick, hardly remembered, and then he was back in his hotel room. His two guides left, and he was alone.

He sat down on the edge of the bed, in the darkness. He felt terrible. Too much Scotch, too much tobacco, too much everything. At long last, a hollow reaction caught up with him. He had left one world a short two months ago, his life secure and his future comfortable. He had come back to a new world this morning. His future might be—anything.

He got up, pulled the .38 from his belt, and stuck it back in the dresser drawer. Then he fell down on the bed, clothes and all, and stared at the gray light of morning until he fell into a light and fitful sleep.

He twisted and turned as the hours passed and the blistering heat came again. Twice, he cried out.

He woke up shortly after noon; it was too hot to sleep any more, and his pillow was wet with sweat. He managed to shave and take a cold shower in the bathroom at the end of the hall, and when he had put on fresh clothes he felt a little better.

He didn't even try to think until after he had downed four cups of black coffee at the cafe, and managed to choke down two overdone eggs and some passable sausage. Then he got into his car, opened all the windows, and just drove. He wasn't going anywhere, he just wanted the air to circulate a little. The sun was like a big brass shield in an absolutely empty sky.

He thought, briefly, of going to Austin, but he couldn't quite face it. He had dimly hoped that when he woke up, despite John's assurances, he wouldn't remember a thing that had happened the night before. But he remembered it.

All of it.

He simply couldn't go into the city yet.

He recognized, with painful clarity, the utter hopelessness of his position. Things weren't the same any more, and they would never be the same again, not for him.

Sure, he had the whole story now—or most of it. There was no more problem. He had the answer he had sought.

Great.

Fabulous.

What could he do with it? *Nothing.* Absolutely nothing. He thought of every conceivable angle. He analyzed every possible course of action. He planned at least fifty different moves, and promptly discarded everyone of them.

It was impossible for him, being what he was, just to put Jefferson Springs and all that it meant out of his mind, leave the place for good, and try to find any meaning in the life he would have to lead. It was a shock, to put it mildly, to find out that he was a primitive, a savage, sitting in his little village and calmly assuming that he was king of all he surveyed. A man—or at least Ellery's kind of man—couldn't go on with his work, knowing that all he was working for was thousands of years old-hat to a civilization of which he could never be a part. He couldn't face his friends every day, working, laughing, dreaming their dreams—when all the time he knew.

He would look up at the stars at night, and one night he would pull the trigger.

He could not write up what he had discovered in a technical paper. The idea was laughable. *Some Evidence Pertaining* to *an Alien Colony in Texas, with Suggestions about a Galactic Civilization.* No reputable journal would touch such an article for a million dollars. And if it were published, what difference would it make? Who would believe it? Even if the world's most famous scientist seriously advanced such a theory, he would be quietly carted off to an insane asylum.

And Paul Ellery was not the world's most famous scientist. There were several hundred thousand or so ahead of him.

He could not go to the newspapers or to the police; What could he say? He could hear himself: "Look, do you know the town of Jefferson Springs? It's been taken over by aliens, people from out of space. That's right, *space.* You know. You see, they took me into their spaceship one night and told me the whole story. It's like this…"

He couldn't even tell his best friend. "Look, Joe, a funny thing happened to me while I was working in Jefferson Springs. I know this sounds nuts, but…"

It was hopeless.

It was hopeless precisely because the colonists really *were* far more advanced than the cultures of Earth. The whole problem that the colony posed, a problem in philosophy and psychology and ethics as well as in survival, was virtually inconceivable as a serious situation to a planet at Earth's development stage. It was precisely analogous to a Neanderthal shouting into his cave that he had just split the atom.

Hopeless, too, because there *was* no Earth. There were only the hostile nations, glaring at each other in armed truce. There was only the U. N., fighting to be born in a world that needed it desperately but wasn't ready for it yet.

Could you address the United States Senate and suggest that aliens from outer space made up many of the senators' constituents? Ellery didn't even want to think about that possibility.

A revolution as an answer was sophomoric. Who would revolt? Against what? The plain fact was that Earth had evolved no technique even faintly suitable to handling the situation. It was outside Earth's experience, outside her expectations. It was even worse than trying to stop a tank with a bow and arrow. Earth could not even recognize that the tank *existed.*

There was only one thing he could do, obviously. There was no answer to the new problem that had been created by the solution to the old problem. All right, accept that. Therefore, his job was easily stated: *find one.*

He actually knew little or nothing about what really went on in the town of Jefferson Springs. He knew the familiar patterns designed for public consumption, and he knew at least something of the true story behind the colony. Beyond that, he was ignorant. The inner life of the colony, the genuine, functioning community culture—all that was unknown.

What was the actual relationship of the colony to Earth? Was it at worst a harmless parasite, as John had suggested? Or were these people human enough to want their colony to continue for always? Would the colonists *really* leave Earth alone to work out its own affairs? How could they be controlled that closely?

And how did the damned thing *work?* How could people, real people, live out their lives in a masquerade, pretending to be virtual savages from their point of view? Roughing it was fine for a vacation, even for a year or two. But for a lifetime?

Paul Ellery thought about Jefferson Springs—the real Jefferson Springs that he had never penetrated. Possibly—just possibly—there was a clue there. If he could find it.

He didn't really think he could. It was a needle in a haystack, at best. He wasn't even sure what it was he would have to look for. It was a million-to-one shot. But Paul Ellery was a stubborn man. He was also a practical man. He repeated the words to himself: *If you can't beat 'em, join 'em.*

He told himself that he was motivated by pure self-interest. He told himself that he was too sensible to try to save the world. Saving the world was a large order, with or without colonists from the stars. The hydrogen bomb was a tough opponent in a debate.

If he could come up with no solution, he would just have to make the best of things. He would have to adjust. He had been given a chance. Many a native before him had had to leave his tribe and try to learn the strange ways of civilization. He remembered his friend Two Bears, his interpreter among the Hawks. Two Bears was one of many Indians he had known, caught between two opposing lifeways. What were they called in the literature?

Marginal men.

He would try to find a flaw in the colony's armor. He would do the best he could. That was all he could do.

It was evening when he turned his Ford around and drove back to Jefferson Springs. The long shadows lay like soft fingers across the fields and the brush and the cactus. The faint breeze was only another shadow, whispering over the clean, sweet land. Jefferson Springs baked in the late sun, one hundred and twenty miles from San Antonio, sixty miles from the Rio Grande and Mexico.

Paul Ellery had made up his mind.

He had become a hired man. Not a *hired* man, he reminded himself, but a hired *man*. There was a difference.

Tomorrow, he would drive out again to see Melvin Thorne.

8

The next day was like all the rest. The burning sun was up early, sucking the night moisture out of the air, and again turning Paul Ellery's hotel room in the Rocking-T into a boxlike oven. It was wrong, somehow, that the day should still be the same. So much had happened, so much had changed, that the most incredible thing of all, the most difficult fact to accept, was that the world went on, inevitable and unimpressed.

Ellery ate a perfectly ordinary breakfast—no worse than usual—and was faintly surprised to find that he had a good appetite. In fact, he felt fine. The pressure was off, and if that was left was mainly resignation—well, that was still an improvement.

He went back to his hotel room, took off his shirt, and propped himself up on the bed, using a bulky copy of *Anthropology Today* as a writing desk. His handwriting was none too beautiful, but his typing was worse.

He had three letters to write.

The first was to Winans University. Winans was a small, privately endowed school, a few miles north of Austin, near Round Rock. It had been established thirty years ago by old Edgar V. Winans, an eccentric Texas millionaire who had, surprisingly, graduated from Harvard. Winans had failed to see why his native state could not support a really *good* small college, and to prove his point he had built Winans University. Winans was a man who knew what he was doing, and when he was through he had a first-class school on his hands, and one that attracted high-caliber students. Ellery, who had been teaching at the University of Texas, had resigned before coming to Jefferson Springs on the Norse grant. He had an offer from Winans University, which he had tentatively accepted because he liked small schools and the pay was good.

That, of course, had been in the other world.

Now, he dropped a note to Bud Winans, the old gentleman's capable son, and told him that he couldn't make it by September. He said that his plans were indefinite for a while, but that he would give him a definite answer as soon as he could. Hardly standard operating procedure, but Bud was a good guy, and would pull the necessary strings.

The second letter was to his parents. This was a more conventional item, hinting broadly at hard work and unexpected complications, and said in effect that he would be very busy for a while, but would try to see them soon.

The third letter was to Anne. This one required more skill. He had to prevent her from getting lonesome and coming to see him; and on the

63

other hand he had to keep in her good graces in case he should decide to see *her*. This wasn't too difficult, being a type of letter that all young men learn to write to their girls, although Ellery had a sneaking suspicion that Anne was never fooled a bit.

He thought of Anne, only a short distance away in Austin, and felt a strong desire to go to her, be with her. But he rejected the idea almost before it was born. Nice, yes—but the answer to *his* problem wasn't in Austin.

He took his camera off the dresser and loaded it. It was a most unspectacular box Brownie. Ellery wasn't certain what he intended to do with it, but he figured that a few pictures here and there wouldn't hurt anything.

He dropped the letters in the slot at the ramshackle post office, across the street near the Rialto. Now showing at the Rialto: *Rocketship X-M*. Ellery guessed that *that* one would be well attended. Coincidence—or did all the colonists have an odd sense of humor?

He got into his Ford, stopped and bought gas at the Humble station, and tried to tell himself that the station attendant was an alien colonist. It didn't work. The overalls, the clumsy shoes, the red bandanna hanging out of a back pocket—the man was just too damned *ordinary*.

He had to keep telling himself: *This is not real, this is an alien colony, this is not real*—

The words were not real, either.

He drove off, back out of town and out across the Nueces bridge to the Thorne Ranch. He did his best to choke off both his mood and his train of thought. The treadmill thinking that kept rolling off *this-can't-be-real-but-it-is-real-but-it-doesn't-LOOK-real* wasn't helping a bit. He had to keep his mind clear.

For himself, of course. He came first.

He drove along through the familiar country, along the familiar gravel road, and turned off at the dirt road that led to the ranch house. He looked up, half expecting to see a great ship swimming in the air, but the pale blue sky was empty.

There was only the sun, relentlessly pressing the attack.

He pulled into the ranch driveway and parked. No pictures yet, he decided. He got out and knocked on the door.

He heard footsteps, but they were not those of Thorne's clumping boots. His wife, maybe?

The door opened. It wasn't his wife.

"Hello," said the girl, smiling. "Are you Paul Ellery?"

"I used to be," Ellery said.

"Please come in, Paul. I'm Cynthia. I'll call Mel."

Ellery followed her into the house, caught off base again. The girl was a surprise. She was a blonde, with her hair piled up on top of her head, careless of her looks because she had them to spare; She wore a man's white shirt with the sleeves rolled up, and gray shorts. Her feet were bare.

"Sit down; Paul,' she said.

Ellery sat down. He was in the living room this time, on a brown couch. The big clock ticked monotonously in the heat.

"Mel's out in the barn," Cynthia said. Her voice was soft, but it had a definite Texas slur in it. "Don't go 'way."

She left, and Ellery heard her call. She had a good pair of lungs, among other things. Ellery tried to add her into the equation. Mistress? New colonist from the ship? Bait? Friend of the family? Vampire?

Cynthia came back. "My God, it's hot here." she said.

That, Ellery reflected, was a statement with at least two hidden jokes in it. Who or what her God might be, he had not the foggiest notion. And the way she said "here" suggested strongly that she had just arrived from elsewhere. However, if nothing else, the sentence neatly destroyed the picture of her as a *femme fatale* he had been building up in his mind.

"It is hot," he said wittily. Then, ashamed of himself, he tried to do better. "Do you live here?" Not much of an improvement.

"Yes," she said, sitting down next to him on the couch. "In town," she added. "I teach home economics in the high school."

Ellery let that digest a minute, and discovered that her eyes were the standard blue. Age? Early twenties, probably.

"That's nice," he said. "For the students, I mean."

She smiled. "Thank you, Paul," she said demurely.

The back door slammed and there were more footsteps. Clumping ones, this time. Melvin Thorne walked into the room, big and solid and sweating. He held his hat in his hand, and he was wearing tight, faded blue jeans and a dirty khaki shirt. The cowboy boots were scuffed.

"Howdy, Paul," he drawled. "Mighty glad to see you again."

Oh no, thought Ellery a little wildly. *Not the dialect again.*

"Hello, Mel. How are you?"

"Fine, mighty fine." The big man paused. "Cynthia, you get the hell out of here." He said it in exactly the tone of voice he would have used to say, "Cynthia, please pour me another cup of coffee."

Cynthia raised her neat eyebrows but made no objection. She stood up, looking very cool and slim next to Thorne. "See you later, Paul," she said, and left the room.

"You want to watch out for that one, son," Melvin Thorne said. "She's trouble. Come on into the kitchen where we can talk."

They went back into the kitchen and sat down at the battered wood table with the red-and-white checked tablecloth. The salt and pepper shakers still carried their inane legends, unashamed. Before Thorne had a chance to say anything, his wife padded into the kitchen. She was dumpy, white-haired, scrubbed. She had nice brown eyes.

"Pour us some coffee, Martha," Melvin Thorne said.

Martha obliged, pouring from the big black pot on the stove into two mugs that had seen better days. She didn't bother about sugar or cream. She eyed Ellery for a moment, and then put a strong hand on his shoulder.

"You'll be Mr. Ellery," she said. "You look like a nice young man, and I hope you like it here with us."

"Thank you, Mrs. Thorne," Ellery said. "Thanks a lot."

Again, he looked at Mr. and Mrs. Melvin Thorne. Could these people really be "alien," and what did that mean? If they had evolved on a planet that circled another sun, was that so horrible? What was the difference?

Why is there a threat to *Earth at all? A threat to me? Why shouldn't they live here, the same as anybody else?*

But he remembered, even there in that cozy kitchen. He remembered all those primitive peoples who had come face to face with the white man. The white man had evolved on the same planet they had, and was indistinguishable from them except for a few minor traits. Where were those primitive peoples now? These aliens, or whatever they were, said that they had no desire to "conquer" the Earth. As far as Ellery could tell, that was true. But more of them were coming all the time, looking for living space. They were not machines. They had their weaknesses the same as other people.

Some day, that meant trouble.

Paul Ellery wondered: *Had any colonized planet ever climbed out of savagery? Or were they—helped—to stay where they were?*

He thought, too, of the hydrogen bombs and all that they represented. The civilized aliens could prevent those bombs from ever going off, could wipe war from the Earth forever. But they wouldn't. Here, if anywhere, they would not interfere. What chance did Earth have, on its own?

Paul Ellery clenched his fists. Well, here was one way out—for him.

"I guess John told you the story," he said.

"I heard from old John, that's right," Melvin Thorne said, drinking his coffee. "Reckon you've decided to tie up with us, that right?"

"That's right," Ellery said. He swallowed his coffee more out of politeness than desire. Gulping hot coffee in the middle of the day in summer was one Texas custom he had never made his own. "He told me you'd tell me what I needed to know."

"Mighty glad to help, Paul," Thorne said slowly. "Though there ain't an all-fired lot to tell."

Melvin Thorne was still employing his Texas drawl, and Ellery suddenly realized that it wasn't faked at all. *This was the only English the man knew.* He had been trained for this particular culture—for how long? Ellery began to appreciate something of the stake that Thorne and the rest had in staying in Jefferson Springs. Where else could they go?

"It will have to be sort of odd jobs at first, Paul, until we're sure and you're sure that you want to stay on with us," Mel said, pouring more coffee. "You understand, I reckon, that it will take you a spell to fit into the *real* life of our town. You've got a lot to learn, just like I had a lot to learn before I came down here and set me up a ranch. I think the paper would be a good place for you to start, since you like readin' and all that stuff anyhow. We'll keep you at that a spell, and then give you a shot at something else. It won't be very exciting at first, Paul, but we think we've got a nice little town here and we're proud of it."

Ellery listened in growing wonderment. Thorne was just the same as he had been before-evidently he really *was* more or less what he appeared to be on the surface. Personality type screening? Right man for the right job? Somehow, he hadn't expected an alien from an advanced civilization to be of no better than average intelligence. But why not? It was the civilization that was advanced, not the citizen. The fact that Joe Blow lives in the same culture as Albert Einstein does not mean that Joe Blow can't be a Grade-Q moron. And Mel Thorne seemed to be—what? A Texas Babbitt from another planet? It was a vaguely frightening thought.

"I'll do my best, Mel," he said.

"I'm sure you will, son. And later on, if you get along okay, they may send you—back—for the full treatment."

"Back?"

"That's right—back. You know. But for right now it'll have to be the newspaper."

"Well," Ellery said, "it could be worse. They used to have a standard joke in college that all the guys with a Ph.D. wound up digging ditches."

Melvin Thorne laughed—a big, booming, noisy laugh. "That's a good one, son," he said. "I always said that there book learnin' was a waste of time."

Ellery sighed. The man *meant* it. It was no act. "Well, I'll try to rise above it," he said.

Mrs. Thorne came back into the kitchen, smiled vacantly, and padded out again.

"One thing we *can* do for you right at the start," Mel told him, "and that's get you out of that Rocking-T hotel. That place is just to scare the tourists off."

He laughed. Ellery laughed with him, unamused.

"You just go on into that little white house across from the high school," Thorne said. "Ain't nobody living there, so that's your house now. You'll find the key in the mailbox."

"Thanks again," Ellery said. His mind set up a pleasant equation: house plus high school equals Cynthia.

"And keep an eye out for Cynthia, son," Thorne said. "She's trouble, like I said. She teaches high school, you know."

"I know," Ellery said. "I'll wear my armor."

"Uh huh," Thorne said doubtfully. "Well, that's about it, Paul. I want you to feel free to come out here and see me any old time. And remember this, son: you're not a prisoner here. This is your *home,* if you want it. You're free to leave whenever you want to. We're right proud of what we've done in Jefferson Springs; we've worked hard for what we've got. Just remember, it ain't half as funny to you as it was to us when we first came here.'

Ellery caught just a glimpse then of Jefferson Springs the way the colonists saw it. An alien town on a strange and distant world, a tiny spot torn out of a hostile wilderness, a fragile container into which they poured their lives and their loves and their hopes. An adventure on another world, as surely as though it had been men from Earth journeying to the stars....

"Thanks, Mel," he said.

"Don't mention it, son."

Paul Ellery went back through the living room and out the door. He didn't see Cynthia. He gunned his Ford down the dirt road. The brilliant sunshine touched the blue sky with gold, and the heat was heavy with the rich smell of the river and the cypress trees.

He breathed deeply of summer and tried not to think.

9

His first day on the weekly newspaper was singular enough for any man.

The *Watchguard* office, located across from the Community Hall, was a long, narrow, and magnificently drab shed. It was so palpably ancient that Ellery half expected to find that all the writing was done by hooded scribes with goose-quill pens.

Instead, it was done by Abner Jeremiah Stubbs.

Mr. Stubbs was tall, stooped, and thin. He was pleasantly grotesque. His hair was a precise nothing-color, and it was kept out of his eyes by a faded green eye shade. He dressed in a black suit. His shapeless coat was hung on a hook on the door, and he worked in a shiny vest. He had a big gold watch, and Ellery knew without checking that it was scrupulously accurate.

Abner spoke in funereal tones, when he spoke at all. Everything he said came out sounding like, "Ah, the pity of it all, the *vast* pity of it all."

To Ellery, he said: "Typewriter's in the next room. Telephone's there, too. List of stories on the pad. You know make-up?"

"Only the kind that goes on girls' faces," Ellery confided.

Mr. Stubbs nodded wearily. Another day, another burden. "You'll learn. Get ink in your blood."

Ellery nodded. Mr. Stubbs leaned back in his swivel chair and gazed blankly at the wall, so Ellery decided that the interview was over. He went into his office, if it could be dignified by that name, and risked the wrath of ageless gods by wrestling up a window that acted as if it had been shut since the Flood. The Flood hadn't washed it any too clean, either.

The heat was stifling. Outside the window, a single forlorn oak tree drooped in the sun and tried to remember what rain looked like. Ellery sat at a small, unpainted table and contemplated a typewriter that must have been older than he was.

He had, of course, studied the paper intensively in his work in Jefferson Springs. Every item in it for months before he had arrived in the town had been classified and filed. The news items had given him information on kinship connections, meetings, parties. They had furnished valuable interview leads. The editorials of Mr. Stubbs had yielded insights into the value system of Jefferson Springs.

Ellery knew the paper. He had never been much of a writer, but he felt supremely confident that he could attain the required stylistic excellence. The paper was called *The Jefferson Springs Watchguard*. Its slogan: OUR FIGHT FOR THE RIGHT IS ETERNAL AS THE PLAINS.

Not much of a slogan, he reflected, but better than some he had seen. There was one town in East Texas with a paper called the *Jimplecute: Join Industry, Manufacturing, Planting, Labor, Energy, Capital (in) Unity Together Everlasting.*

He studied the scrawled pad for thirty minutes and then stuck a yellow sheet in the typewriter. In three hours he wrote four stories, and between the battered typewriter and his own unskilled fingers he managed to produce a mess worthy of any seasoned reporter. Casting inexperience to the winds, he composed four headlines to go with the stories. He was happily ignorant of word-counts and allied trivia, but he caught the tone of the *Watchguard* to perfection:

MILDEW IS COMMON PROBLEM OF SUMMER.
LITTLE JODY DAVIS IMPROVED AFTER BEING KICKED IN FACE BY HORSE.
A 4-H CAMPER WRITES HOME TO MOM.
LIONS CLUB BANQUET IS VERY ENJOYABLE EVENT.

His day's work done, Ellery examined the last issue of the paper, trying to find something in it that would prove useful to him. Here again was the basic anomaly of Jefferson Springs. The town was an alien colony but there was nothing advanced about it that he could see. It was as average as dirt. Now, acting or no acting, false-face or not, the colonists actually *were* living in Jefferson Springs. No matter how insincere—and it did not strike Ellery that they were insincere at all in the lives they led—the mere business of going through the motions of life in Jefferson Springs took time, a lot of time. These people spent, without any doubt, the majority of their lives acting out the parts of small-town Texas citizens.

And that didn't make sense.

These colonists were human enough, as far as Ellery could tell. No group of people would willingly spend at least seventy per cent of every single day pretending to live in a culture without meaning for them.

Ellery reversed a few positions in order to see the problem more clearly. Suppose that the cultures concerned were those of the present-day United States and a Southeastern Indian group, say the Natchez who had once lived on the lower Mississippi. The gulf between the two cultures was roughly comparable to the gulf between a galactic civilization and the United States, though possibly not as profound. Okay, that was the setup. On one hand, modern industrialized America. On the other, seven villages of thatched huts, agricultural, with temple mounds and undying-fire ceremonies, together with a well-defined class system ranging from a supreme Sun down through Nobles, Honored Men, and commoners, the last known as Stinkards. Now, suppose that for some reason the present-day Americans wish to set up a colony among the Natchez, and do it in such a way that the Natchez are unaware of the colony's presence. First, of course, there would have to be an intensive period of detailed training, to say nothing of time travel. But, assuming that the United States citizens could turn themselves into a reasonable facsimile of Natchez Indians, how long would they be willing to *live* like the Indians, cut off from all the comforts and conveniences and values of the life they had known? Not for a week or so, not for a summer's outing, but for *keeps?*

Ellery could see only one possibility there: if the United States citizens were taken as children and brought up as Indians, then they would, of course, be perfectly content with the Indian culture, since they would, in effect, *be* Indians. They would not, however, be typical United States citizens any longer.

That was the possibility. It was unfortunate that the aliens weren't working it that way.

Quite clearly, it wouldn't work in their case. Their problem was considerably more complex. They must both fit their citizens for life in a primitive colony and at the same time retain them as participants in a galactic civilization. Simply dumping them down in Jefferson Springs as children wouldn't do the trick, and in any event he had already seen enough to indicate that the procedure was quite different. Some of the colonists came to Jefferson Springs as young adults; that called for one technique. Some of them came as children; that meant another technique. And some, apparently, were born in Jefferson Springs and then trained as full galactic citizens elsewhere.

Sent "back for the full treatment," as Thorne had intimated that Ellery would be eventually?

The question remained: how could they be both? How could they live in and *enjoy*—for they must enjoy it—Jefferson Springs, and at the same time maintain their unity with a vast and complex interstellar civilization?

Ellery had no answer for that one.

He read the paper carefully, digesting every last "personal" ("Mr. and Mrs. Joe Walker spent two happy days last week visiting in Garner State Park") and advertisement ("Mr. Merchant: Don't Preach Home Patronage then Send Your Printing Elsewhere"). In the entire paper, he found only one small item that was at all suggestive. It was suggestive only because it was cryptic; there was nothing blatantly mysterious about it. It was a small squarc on the back page:

THORNE RANCH
COMPULSORY
AUGUST 25   9 P.M.

That was all. And the date was the day after tomorrow. Paul Ellery didn't know what it was, or even what it might be.

He did know that he was going to be there.

He walked out of his office and handed his completed stories to Mr. Stubbs, who was still seated in his swivel chair gazing with complete absorption at the wall. Stubbs fished out his gold watch, shook his head sadly, and said nothing.

Ellery chose to interpret this as both approval and dismissal, and left for the day. He drove home to his new white house across from the high school, which was deserted for the summer. The house was just beginning to cool off from the afternoon roasting, but it was still plenty warm. There was a slight breeze out of the north, but Ellery had no instruments delicate enough to detect it.

The house was plain but comfortable: living room, bathroom, bedroom, kitchen, a few closets, all put together without a single trace of either ingenuity or imagination. There was one painting in the place, a waxen floral study, and when it had been carefully turned to face the wall it was passable.

Ellery fried himself a hamburger, preferring even his own cooking to that of the Jefferson Springs Cafe, and opened a bottle of beer. He armed himself with a notebook and a pencil and sat down at the kitchen table.

He asked himself what he, as an anthropologist, knew about the problems of culture contact that would be useful to him. He was not given to getting in over his head and asking questions afterward; he had found that it was to his advantage to figure things out ahead of time. If he could.

When the knock on the door came, he was halfway through the hamburger. On the problems of culture contact, his progress was less remarkable. He stuck the notebook in a drawer in the kitchen table and opened the front door.

It was Cynthia. The equation ran through his mind again: house plus high school equals Cynthia. Well, better late than never. And better early than late.

"Are you busy?" asked Cynthia, smiling.

"Not that busy," Ellery assured her. "Won't you come in? I'm just finishing up my caviar."

She came in, and Ellery closed the door. She was wearing a dark green skirt and a white silk blouse, and her blond hair was down. She was slim and tanned and she looked good.

Very good.

"Now that you're a reporter," she said, "I thought I'd bring you a story."

"Fine," said Ellery. "Bring it on into the kitchen and I'll give you a beer for a reward."

She followed him into the kitchen and sat down at the table, wrinkling her nose slightly at the hamburger. She accepted the beer without complaint, but she didn't look like the beer-drinking type.

"Sorry I don't have anything better," Ellery said. "I just moved in here, and I haven't stocked the cellar yet. In fact, I haven't got a cellar."

She laughed gently. It was a pleasant laugh. It said: "That wasn't a bit funny, but it was a reasonable try."

"Do you eat hamburgers every night?" Cynthia asked.

"Not at all," Ellery assured her. "I fry a mean egg too, so there's no monotony in my diet."

"Poor man," Cynthia said. "You need a cook. Will I do?"

There it was. No stalling, no fumbling for invitations, no beating around the bush. Cynthia wasn't being coy, and she wasn't kidding. Ellery decided that he and Cynthia were going to get along fine.

"Lady," he said, "you will do splendidly. I won't even ask for references."

"That's good," she said, "because I haven't got any."

Ellery finished his beer and opened another. "When do we start this charming arrangement?" he asked.

Cynthia smiled her man-killer smile. "Let's make it tomorrow night," she suggested. "I'll bring the groceries and see if I can impress you."

"With or without groceries," Ellery assured her, "you will impress me."

"Good," said Cynthia. She crossed her legs pleasantly. "Let's not forget about the story, Paul."

Ellery, who had done just that, nodded. He went into the living room and got an empty notebook. "Let's have it," he said, sitting down again. "I'll phone Stubbs and have him stop the presses."

"No hurry," Cynthia said. "It's about the high school. It opens on the third of September, and all new students will have to have a birth certificate, small-pox vaccination, and diphtheria immunization."

Ellery stared at her. She wasn't fooling, so he wrote it down. He remembered that Cynthia taught home economics in the high school. My God, maybe she *was* going to cook him a dinner!

Period.

"That all?" he asked.

"That's all." She smiled. "I just thought I'd save you a little work."

"Well, thanks. Thanks a lot."

Ellery took a long pull on his beer. Just when you thought you had these people all figured out they always pulled another rabbit out of the hat.

No matter. Cynthia could be useful. Anyway, he liked rabbits.

"Cynthia," he said, "I wonder if you'd tell me something."

"I'm sure you do," Cynthia said.

Ellery ignored that one. "Look," he said earnestly, "I'm in a tough spot here-you know that. You're about the only person I've met who's acted—well, who's acted—"

"Human?" Cynthia suggested.

"Friendly," Ellery corrected. "I don't feel so much like a freak when you're around."

Cynthia laughed. "What do you want to know, Paul?"

Ellery put it on the line: he had a nagging suspicion that it would be a stupid man indeed who thought he could put over a fast one on Cynthia. "I saw a notice in the paper, last week's paper," he said, "about a compulsory something at the Thorne Ranch the day after tomorrow. I saw you out there, and I wonder—"

"What it's all about," finished Cynthia. She patted her hair.

"Check," said Ellery. "If I'm going to play on your team, I've got to know the signals."

Cynthia pursed her lips. "I don't know, Paul," she said. "I'd like to tell you, but I'm not sure that it's permitted. Tell you what I'll do, though—I'll find out just where you stand on this, and if I can get an okay I'll do better than explain it. I'll take you out there with me, and you can watch."

"Fair enough, Cynthia. Thanks."

She finished her beer and stood up. "We'll see what we see," she said. "Thanks for the beer. Have to run now."

"So soon?"

"So soon." She walked toward the door, the green skirt rustling around her legs.

Ellery caught her at the door, touched her cool arm with his hand. He could smell the perfume in her hair.

"Cynthia—"

"Good night, Paul," she said, softly but firmly. "See you tomorrow."

And she was gone, into the gathering shadows of night.

10

Next morning, Paul Ellery was up early. It was still cool from the night before, but the sun was already climbing into the sky for the day's bombardment.

However, he did notice, on his way to the newspaper office, that there were just the bare suggestions of gray clouds hanging on the horizon. They might mean nothing, but there was a chance they spelled a break in the heat. August was a hot month in Texas, but usually the rains came in by September. They were long overdue.

The cadaverous Mr. Stubbs had not yet arrived, so Ellery went into his office and hacked out a story on the high school's opening He finished just as Stubbs came in, and he took it in and placed it on his desk.

A. Jeremiah Stubbs looked at him as he might have looked at a stray goldfish in his drinking water and said nothing. Very carefully, he took off his shapeless black coat and hung it on the hook on his door. He then rolled up his sleeves, freeing his white, skinny arms for action, and donned his green eye shade. His work for the day presumably finished, he lowered himself wearily into his swivel chair behind the editor's desk and resumed his fascinated contemplation of the empty wall.

"If you don't have anything urgent that needs doing," Ellery said, "I'm going out to look for some news."

Mr. Stubbs gazed at him in mild astonishment. He blinked his eyes as though he had difficulty keeping him in focus. "Look for news?" he repeated.

Ellery nodded.

Mr. Stubbs concentrated mightily and one corner of his upper lip twitched. The unaccustomed smile almost fractured his jaw. "Only one real story in this town, sonny," he said, "and that's the one we can't print."

Ellery waited respectfully, but that was all there was. Mr. Stubbs spoke mainly in silences, and it was up to his listener to figure out the drift of his inaudible conversations. Having no real evidence either way, Ellery again chose to interpret the silence as approval, and so he left. In truth, there was very little that needed to be done on *The Jefferson Springs Watchguard,* and Paul Ellery found it hard to take the job too seriously.

There must be something more than this.

And yet, weren't there still the tiresome little jobs filled by colorless people, even in interstellar civilizations? Surely not *everybody* spent his time cruising around in spaceships. If Earth joined the galactic league, wouldn't someone still have to work in the gas station, clerk in the grocery store, take tickets at the movie?

Ellery drove home, without the vaguest intention of looking for any news. He had his own work to do. He noticed hopefully that the gray clouds were massed more thickly on the horizon. It might—just might—rain.

At home, he sat down at the kitchen table and sipped his coffee. Everything was happening so fast that it was getting away from him. He didn't like the prospect of getting swept along by the current. He wanted to steer a little.

What did he, as an anthropologist, know that might help him in the life he found himself living?

The cards were all stacked against him in Jefferson Springs, no matter how much the dealer smiled. If he wanted a wild card in his hand, he would have to pull it out of his own sleeve. If he wanted to win, or only to break even—

The first step was finding the right question to ask. After that, he had to be able to recognize the answer when he saw it.

Well, this was clearly a problem in culture contact, and that had a name: acculturation. Unhappily, however, the problem wasn't really an acculturation problem. Of the two cultures—correction, more than two; this thing wasn't limited to the United States—one was unaware of the contact! And, in a very real sense, they weren't in contact.

Still, *he* was in an acculturation situation. He was a savage, rubbing his nose in civilization. The principles of acculturation must apply to him as well as to all the other primitive peoples who had found themselves in the same boat. Could he make the jump, blowgun to atom bomb? Cave to skyscraper?

What were the choices open to him?

He sweated it out. There had been a great deal of work done on problems of acculturation, but very little of it seemed applicable to the fix he was in. Facts were more insistent than theories: his thoughts constantly returned to Two Bears, his old interpreter. He had done his first field work among the Hawk Indians of Montana, and he had made many friends there. The Hawks were a former Plains tribe, with the customary bison-hunting economy, and they had never taken too kindly to agriculture. The old people still had a security of a sort, living in the past. But the younger men and women were trapped between the old and the new. Two Bears was inclined to be a little contemptuous of the ways of his ancestors, and in any event their culture was practically extinct. At the same time, he was enough of an Indian, culturally speaking, so that he didn't fit into the pattern of American life around him.

Two Bears was a very mixed-up man, trying to fit fragments of opposing lifeways together into a meaningful whole.

He spent a lot of time getting drunk. He spent a lot of time, too, off in the hills by himself—alone with the gods that he could not quite accept.

Paul Ellery understood him a little better now.

He took a fast, cold shower, and shaved too quickly, nicking himself twice. He got dressed, abandoning his work clothes for a pair of brown slacks, white shirt, and tie, and loafers with noisy yellow argyle socks.

At a quarter after six, Cynthia drove up outside.

He lifted two large sacks out of the front seat and carried them into the house, setting them down on the kitchen table. One clinked and one didn't.

"I didn't expect you to have an apron," Cynthia said, "so I brought one of my own." She took a plastic apron out of her purse and tied it around her hips. "Now you get out of here, and I'll start supper."

"Yes, master," Paul Ellery said. He walked into the living room and sat down, reflecting that of all the mysteries in Jefferson Springs, Cynthia certainly wasn't the least. He fired up his pipe and listened to Cynthia's heels clicking around in the kitchen. He timed her. In fifteen minutes flat she was out, a glass in each hand.

"I hope you like Martinis," she said, handing him one.

"I'm enchanted," Ellery said. He examined his glass. "And two olives! You've read my mind."

"No," Cynthia said seriously. "Just guessed."

She sat down next to him on the couch. Ellery could feel his pulse thudding like a schoolboy's, but he let it thud. He couldn't figure Cynthia out, and for now he was content to let it go at that. Of course, it was flattering to think that he was just plain irresistible, but if that were the case then he could think of a large number of females in the past who must have been blind.

Cynthia had on a smooth but simple black dress, nothing fancy, and she had a green ribbon in her soft blond hair. Her dress caught the light and rustled when she moved, and she seemed quite conscious of the effect.

Ellery sipped his Martini, which was extremely dry and extremely potent. "What did you find out about tomorrow night?" he asked. "Am I included out?"

Cynthia patted his knee. "Not at all, Paul," she said. "I talked to John and he fixed it up. You can come."

"You know John?"

"Of course. Have another?"

"Sold."

She went back into the kitchen, bustled around a bit, and came back with two fresh Martinis. This time, his had three olives in it.

"This," Paul Ellery said sincerely, "is the life. I'm converted. Where do I go to enlist?"

"I'm not trying to sell you anything, Paul," Cynthia said, with a directness he found disconcerting. "I'm here on my own. Wait until tomorrow night, then see what you think of us."

"What *happens* out there tomorrow? Black Mass?"

She laughed, the Martini putting a flush in her cheeks. "Not exactly," she said. She had nice white teeth. "It's sort of a—well, sort of a ceremony. Only not exactly that. Not a ritual either, really. And not quite a political meeting. It—draws us together, all of us, on all the worlds. Do you understand that, Paul?"

"Not exactly," Ellery admitted. "But I'll say Rite of Intensification; that sounds good."

"To tell the truth," Cynthia said, downing her Martini, "I think the whole thing is kind of corny."

There it was again. The offbeat note. The wrong chord. If these people would just be human or alien, one or the other, it wouldn't be so bad. But when they were both—

"You won't find it corny, though," Cynthia added. "I promise you that. The first time is apt to be—uncomfortable."

"You hold my hand," Ellery suggested. "I won't be scared."

"We'll see," Cynthia said. "And now we'll eat."

She vanished into the kitchen again. Five minutes later she called him, and there it was. Thick steaks covered with mushrooms. Mashed potatoes with natural gravy. A crisp green salad. A glass of cold water and another Martini.

Ellery pitched in. "By God," he said, "you *can* cook."

"I have my talents," Cynthia said, and met his eyes without wavering.

After supper, with the dishes stacked in the sink and another Martini under his belt, Ellery was feeling amorous.

"And now," Cynthia said, "we cool off a little. Let's take a walk."

"Walk?"

"Walk."

They walked.

They walked under a darkening sky, through a hushed and breathless night. They walked along the street toward town, arm in arm, like any two lovers since time began.

He thought: *just like two average people in an average sort of town. How could you doubt it?*

Cynthia was warm and soft in his arm. They walked down past the icehouse and across the tracks. Ellery could smell the orange trees, their fragrance suspended in the electric air. They turned to the right and walked on into Mexican Town. The pavement ended, and they walked on a dirt road, like a path, but there were more lights now, and laughter floated out of the night.

Someone, somewhere, was strumming a guitar. The sound was happy, and a little lonely too.

They passed several Mexican couples, strolling along, talking in Spanish. The Mexicans nodded, friendly but reserved. They were better dressed than the native Texans of the town; the men with ties and sport clothes, the women with bright, flowing dresses that were designed to please. Ellery liked them, as he had always liked Mexico.

A distant rumble ruffled the still air. The night tensed itself, waiting.

"These people," Ellery said quietly. "Are they—part of it?"

Cynthia laughed, her voice faintly husky. "Yes, Paul. They're part of it too, all of them."

"But—well, are they happy here? I mean, the lot of most Mexicans in Texas leaves something to be desired. I'd think that people of your civilization—"

She squeezed his arm. "You can't understand us yet, can you? Paul, there are all sorts of physical types in the universe. On one planet, one type is running the show, and somewhere else it's a different group. It's purely a matter of historical accident, and if you *know* that, it doesn't matter. These people know that they're just as good as we are, and we know it too, so the tension isn't there. It isn't where you live that counts, it's how other people think of you. We go where we can, and live as we must."

"Thanks for the anthropology lesson."

"You're welcome, love."

There was a deeper hush, sudden and complete. Then the thunder crashed, and there was no doubt about it this time. A small, cool breeze began to whimper along the street.

"We'd better get back," Ellery said.

"Yes. Come on."

They walked back down the dirt road, and back to the paved highway again. They crossed the tracks and hurried past the big square icehouse, squatting like a cement monster in the darkness. They could see the lightning now, flashing down in livid forks out of the massed black clouds that blotted out the stars. The thunder was a continuous rumble in the north.

They walked faster, and the wet breeze became a wind, sighing down the street. The smell of rain clogged the air, rich and sweet and heavy.

Ellery rolled up the windows in Cynthia's Nash, and they half ran up to the little porch of his house.

They just made it.

There was a flash of lightning that charged the air, quick and close and turning the night into pale silver. Then the thunder that crashed down, splitting the skies. A gathering, a hush, a pause—

And then the rain.

Sheets of it, smashing down in big fat drops. Buckets and tubs and rivers of it, gushing into the dry gray street. The street glistened and little brooks gurgled down the gutters.

Ellery caught his breath, his arm holding Cynthia close. The lightning flashed and flickered and the thunder rolled. The storm roared in from the desert wastes, and the wind and the rain washed through the streets of Jefferson Springs.

They went inside and closed the door behind them. The storm pattered and surged on the roof, and the air was released and fresh. Ellery flicked on the light.

Cynthia smiled at him and Ellery could feel the tightness in his stomach, the blood in his veins.

She reached up, slowly, and untied the green ribbon in her hair. She shook her hair gently and it caressed her shoulders. He could smell its subtle perfume.

She came to him and loosened his necktie, her hands cool and sure.

"Well," she whispered softly, "what are you waiting for, Paul?"

11

Next morning, it was still raining—a gentle rain now, that pattered against the window panes and splashed into little puddles off the roof. Thunder muttered furtively, far away and lonely, rumbling around on the horizon, looking for a way back to town.

Cynthia was already up and dressed when Ellery opened his eyes, and he could smell breakfast cooking in the kitchen. He lay quietly for a long minute, sniffing the rich aroma of percolating coffee and the fresh tang of frying bacon, and then he eased himself out of bed and into his bathrobe.

He felt good. He felt better than he had felt in a long time. He told himself that he was certainly satisfied, and probably happy.

Still, he wasn't positive he liked everything he remembered about the night just past.

What do you want, boy, he thought, *egg in your beer?*

When he walked into the kitchen, after more or less combing his hair, Cynthia had her back to him, frying eggs. Her blond hair was tied back again with the green ribbon and she looked cool, beautiful, and collected. He kissed her on the ear and she smiled.

"I think I'll call you Cyn for short," Ellery said. "Spelled with an 's' and an 'i' and an 'n.'"

"I'm flattered, Paul. Two eggs or three?"

"Make it three," Ellery said. He found himself feeling playful, but he sensed that Cynthia wasn't having any.

Breakfast it was, then.

"Will the rain hurt things tonight?" he asked, working on his second cup of coffee.

"Not too much, Paul, unless it rains harder than it's raining this morning. It's too important to call off, you know. They'll be electing delegates."

"Delegates?"

"You'll see. You mustn't be impatient, love."

"Okay. All things come to him who waits, so I'm told."

"Well," said Cynthia, "you wait for me this evening and we'll test your proverb."

"You can't stay?"

"Sorry. You know I'd like to. But I've got—things—to do before to-night. Can you wash the dishes and make the bed? I'll be back for you about eight."

"Fair enough," said Ellery.

Cynthia got to her feet and smoothed her dress down over her hips. She picked up her purse and glanced at her watch.

"Cyn?"

"Yes?"

"Is anything wrong? You seem so—well, different."

Cynthia put her purse down. She came to him and put her arms around his neck. She kissed him, hard and expertly. Her body was cool as silk, and Ellery began to tremble. She let him go and smiled, her white teeth very sharp.

"See you at eight, love. Don't forget about me."

Ellery laughed, a little hoarsely, and she was gone. Ellery stood at the door and watched her drive away. The blue Nash turned left at the high school and vanished into the gray mist.

The gray day darkened and became night, and still the drizzle came. There was more rain in the sky, more real rain, but it was holding off.

Waiting.

Ellery found himself afraid again, and stuck the .38 in his pants pocket. He hoped it wouldn't show under the raincoat.

Exactly at eight o'clock, Cynthia came back. He had hoped that she would come in, but she honked the horn for him and he went out. The street was glistening under the car's headlights.

"All set?" she asked.

"All set," he said. He wished that it were true.

The Nash purred off through the drizzle, its windshield wipers ticking and shushing against the tiny, hesitant rain spray. Cynthia looked inviting as ever, in brown slacks and a gray sweater, with a raincoat tossed over her shoulders; but she seemed distant and preoccupied, so Ellery didn't try to talk.

It was hard to believe that just sixteen hours ago——

Well, the hell with it. Ellery watched the yellow headlights cut wetly through the town, licking at the empty glass windows and the pale gasoline pumps, and then they were on the highway, the tires hissing through the dampness.

Before he was really ready, they were at the Thorne Ranch.

They got out. There were already at least one hundred cars parked around the ranch yard, glistening dully in the drizzle, but otherwise the ranch looked normal enough. There weren't even any lights on inside. The cars in the yard might have been sitting in a parking lot outside a fair or a stock show or a football game.

Cynthia set off with a quick, determined stride, out across a wet field, away from the ranch buildings. Ellery, feeling rather like a faithful dog curious about a missing bone, turned up his coat collar and followed her dark shadow. The soaking rain of the previous night hadn't been a drop in the bucket to the thirsty fields, and the ground was not muddy, although it was a trifle slick.

The thunder rumbled distantly, promising to do better.

They worked their way along toward a bend in the river, and Ellery could sense other figures moving along with them through the night. They topped a slight rise, too small to qualify as a hill, and at first there was nothing.

And then there it was.

It was a large square of pale blue lights, invisible until you were almost on top of them. Pale blue lights, like glowing, bloated bugs hanging in the mist. Beyond them, the poplars and cypress that fringed the river made a black wall. Inside them was the population of Jefferson Springs, Texas.

They were all there, or soon would be. All six thousand of them. Ellery's first reaction was one of surprise—surprise that a whole town could fit in that pale blue square. But then he recalled that it was nothing for fifty or sixty thousand to watch a football game.

There seemed to be a screen of some sort around the square, a wall of invisible force. Cynthia had to take his hand and lead him through. The citizens of Jefferson Springs stood quietly, waiting. A few had brought along canvas chairs. The people were all different in their attitudes. Ellery saw old women, dressed in black funeral dresses, who were rapt and consecrated. He saw wide-eyed children, and children who clearly had their minds on other things. He saw thoughtful men, impatient men, bored men. One portly gentleman with a cigar was loudly issuing orders that nobody listened to.

And there was Mr. Stubbs, looking gloomy. Clearly, Stubbs expected a hurricane at any moment. He was prepared to be blown away.

Ellery started to relax a little. Nothing alarming here.

Just like a big meeting, or even a picnic.

The music started.

It was soft, subtle, insidious. Ellery couldn't see where it was coming from. It throbbed and beat softly, almost inaudibly. You had to strain to hear it, and yet you couldn't get away from it. It was inside your head—searching.

Ellery thought of stars.

He heard the voices now. People were talking. They weren't talking English; they were speaking their own language. It had tones and buzzes and clicks.

Ellery shivered. He wished that it hadn't been quite so dark. The pale blue lights tricked the eyes. He wished that it would start to rain. Really rain. He would like to hear rain now.

"I'll have to leave you," Cynthia's voice said. Hers was the only voice speaking in English. "Enjoy yourself, love."

She was gone. He was alone. He had never been so alone. The music began to beat at him. The pale blue lights began to blur. Sweat trickled down under his arms, icily. He was afraid to move.

A hand touched him on the elbow.

Ellery crouched without thinking, his hand clutching for the butt of his .38. He almost drew it out, and then he saw who it was.

A jovial little fat man with shrewd, laughing eyes. John.

"Still hunting monsters, Paul?" he whispered.

"No. Sorry! Yes. Dammit, am I glad to see *you!*"

"Not so loud, old man. You just try to keep your eyes open, and I'll cue you in when I can on what is going on. Deal?"

"Deal," agreed Ellery gratefully.

A pickup truck came jouncing across the field toward the square of blue lights, feeling its way with only its parking lights on. It came inside and two men unloaded a large metallic box. They placed it carefully on the ground in the middle of the square. It had no connections, dials, knobs, or levers of any kind, as far as Ellery could make out. It was just a box.

All the lights winked out but one blue eye, staring at him. The beat of the music throbbed through his veins. "News report," John whispered.

The box talked.

It talked for perhaps fifteen minutes. The voice was not unduly loud, but it had a compelling quality to it. Ellery could not understand a word of it, but it did not *sound* terribly different from an ordinary news summary coming over an ordinary radio.

John whispered: "More attention promised for colonials...that old bunk...some economic difficulties in Capella Sector...a scrunch play won the Sequences; you wouldn't get that...a new treaty with the Transformists ...a suspected sighting of the Others...a Two Representative says there is corruption in Arcturus Sector... some guff about the traditional planetwide conference coming up in Sol Sector; that's a special tossed on the line to inflate our egos—they'll never hear it outside the system...the Evolutionaries agree to a compromise on Spicus Six, just opened up...the usual stuff."

Oh sure. The usual stuff.

The box stopped.

A smooth-shaven, portly man moved to the center of the square. Ellery recognized him as Samuel Cartwright, mayor of Jefferson Springs. He began to talk persuasively in the alien tongue—persuasively, but with just a hint of a lisp that Ellery had noticed before, as though Cartwright were having trouble with his false teeth. He talked for ten minutes, pausing now and then to wipe the mist from his face.

When he stopped, there was scattered finger-snapping, which Ellery took to be applause, and several quite Earthly catcalls. A lively wrangle ensued, and some of the citizens appeared to be getting hot under the collar.

Clearly, they were electing some representatives.

"Delegates to the big conference," John whispered, confirming Ellery's guess. "They're going to discuss our colonial policy toward Earth. Want to come?"

"You're kidding," Ellery said.

"Not at all, Paul. I can fix it up. I carry some weight around here, you know. Anyway, it's high time you got an education. I'll notify you."

The election was over, with two men and a woman picked to represent Jefferson Springs. Ellery waited, wondering what was coming next. For a long minute, there was nothing.

The people, however, were very quiet. Ellery could hear the tiny ticks of the rain on his coat. Suddenly, the one blue light winked out. There was total darkness. The beat of the music, almost forgotten, picked up. It grew stronger, much stronger.

And stronger still.

Ellery felt himself swaying on his feet and tried to steady himself.

"Don't fight it, Paul," came John's voice from far away.

He was floating on a gray cloud, a warm gray cloud. He could feel the cloud in his hands. He could pick it up and shred it like cotton.

He drifted, lost and entranced.

He saw colors, smelled smells, tasted tastes. He spun lazily, a moth in the summer night, swallowed in euphoria.

He saw his home with a strange, distorted clarity. He smelled fried chicken in the kitchen. He saw his old books on the shelf in the room he had grown up in: *The Wind in the Willows, Just-So Stories, The Wizard of Oz*. He saw his old model airplanes suspended from the ceiling, their tissuepaper wings shredding where the glue was wearing off. He saw his mother, young again, and his father, snorting at the evening paper.

The scene shifted, noiselessly and completely. He was playing football for the Austin Maroons, racing down the green field under the lights. He heard the crowd, on its feet and yelling. He shook off one tackler, throwing a hip into him, and angled off to his right. The broken strap on his rib pads twisted sweatily. He saw that he wasn't going to make it past the safety man, who wasn't going to be faked out of the way. He set himself to run over him, fighting for the extra yard, and then there was a *smack* as the safety man went down in a heap, blocked out by his end. He cut for the goal stripe. He was going all the way—

Again the scene shifted. He caught his breath. There was a planet, a blue and green and brown planet, hanging like a jewel in black velvet. It was his planet. His vision flickered, and the scene expanded fantastically. His field of sight was enormous, vast beyond imagination, and yet the whole thing was crystal-clear. There were many suns, and many planets. Together, they formed a Titanic design that he could barely grasp. Between the worlds, almost invisible, were spun gossamer silver threads, tying them together. Atoms, atoms of worlds—

Something else. Something down in the corner, down dark in the corner. Something vague, amorphous—

He wanted to scream. Perhaps he did. He whirled, twisted, spun. Dizziness and mist....

It was over. He blinked his eyes and saw that John was holding him up. The blue light snapped back on. The spray of rain cooled his forehead.

"All right?"

"I—think so."

"It's a little strange at first. You didn't get it all, old man. Designed to reinforce, do you see, rather than to dramatize. You've got to supply most of the images, and you won't see what the others see until you go to a Center and get the full treatment. You should have picked up the drift, though: nostalgia for home, the relation of the one to the many, the unity of civilized life—that sort of thing. Quite unimaginative, really."

Ellery listened to John's clipped, matter-of-fact voice and was more than ever grateful to him for being on hand. The rotund little man with the fringe of hair around his pink skull looked like a worldly friar out of Chaucer. He was something solid and real to hang onto. He was a man you could deal with as a man, without worrying about culture or status or formalities. In a word, Ellery thought, John was one hell of a good guy.

An old woman, gray-haired and earnest, stood up in the glow of the blue lights and intoned some syllables, letting them collapse from her thin lips in monotonous cadences. There was considerable shuffling of feet among the audience.

"Poem," said John. "Very bad."

The old woman sat down. The blue lights brightened, almost imperceptibly. The music switched its key. It sounded proud, and a little sad. It swelled up in stirring sweeps, suggesting ancient kings and magnificent temples and acts of bravery long forgotten.

"You'll get more of this," John whispered. "It's the first landing here, the first colonists."

The music pounded, then faded to a low murmur.

The blue lights dimmed, and then began to brighten again, very slowly and steadily.

The people chanted, their voices filling the great night silences.

Ellery saw Earth through alien eyes—wonderful, mysterious, frightening, compelling.

He saw a hidden ship in the night, a globe that floated down in a deserted field, a handful of colonists turned loose near a waiting car. The men and women alone in a strange world, ready to carve a life for themselves out of a primitive planet.

The colonists walked to the car, got inside. They were well trained and they knew what to do, how to move in. They were part of a superlatively well-organized immigration. They knew every step they had to make.

Still, they were afraid.

This was a new world for them, a new home, a chance for their children. They were pioneers in an occupied land.

The car started. They drove toward town, a square of lights far away but clear in the clean, cool air. They were dressed like the natives, they looked like the natives, they talked like the natives. They were ready, and their eyes shone with a hard determination.

They must not fail.

They *would* not fail.

The car purred on down the highway, through a strange and marvelous land....

The music stopped. The chant died. Ellery opened his eyes.

He saw them all around him, the people of Jefferson Springs, ghostly in the pale blue light and the drizzle of the rain. The people of Jefferson Springs, the colonists—proud, confident, superior.

And, somehow, a million million miles away.

Ellery felt sick and tired. He was not a part of them. He was not *one* of them. He was just—

Nothing.

Nobody.

He looked at Cynthia, on the other side of the square.

Blond hair, blue eyes, brown slacks, gray sweater, a raincoat tossed over her shoulders. She was lost in pride. She was smiling, as a queen might smile. She was *somebody*. She didn't even look at him. She wouldn't have seen him if she had.

He felt John's firm hand on his arm. There were words. He felt the field, moist and earthy under his feet. A car, and the highway again. His house, dark and empty and alone. "You'll be all right, Paul."

"I know."

"It takes a little time."

"Sure."

"I'll be back in a few days."

"Thanks, John."

John was gone. He went inside and turned on the lights. He threw himself down on the couch in the living room. He lay very still and listened to the cold sound of thunder rumbling in from the other side of the world.

12

Sleep did not come.

At three in the morning he got up, changed his clothes, packed a bag and left. It was cool in the morning mist, and very dark. He started his car and drove out of Jefferson Springs. By five, he was through San Antonio, circling by way of Loop 13. He stopped to get gas, drank a coke, and drove on down the Austin highway.

He was not quitting. He knew he would go back. But right now he needed a break.

He needed Anne.

He smiled a little. He always ran to Anne when he was in trouble, and Anne was always there. Someday, she wouldn't be. He knew that. No girl would wait forever.

But that was in the other world.

By half-past six, he was in Austin. It was sultry already, and he opened all the windows. He drove past Hill's—how many steaks had he eaten at Hill's?—and past Irving's, and crossed the bridge over the Colorado River. He drove down the broad sweep of Congress Avenue, almost deserted in the early-morning gloom. He stopped at the P-K Grill, which was open all night, and drank three cups of coffee. Then he drove down and parked on the corner, across from the Capitol Dome, and just sat. Anne wouldn't be up yet, and he didn't want to go home.

He watched the city wake up. Austin was his city. He tried to remember that. It wasn't easy.

The sky lightened to a gray glare. He looked back down Congress. Humphrey Bogart at the State, James Stewart at the Paramount, Roy Rogers at the Queen. The bulk of the Austin Hotel dominating the street. Shoe stores, department stores, ten-cent stores, banks, cafes, offices. The Capitol Building, with its big Lone Star Flag. Newspapers stacked on the corners. And—yes, there was Norman, the thinnest and most energetic newspaper seller in the United States, already hawking the morning headlines. How many papers had he bought from Norman, over on the Drag in front of the University?

The cars came first, and then the people. The cars dribbled down the street in the beginning, fed into Congress Avenue by a network of side streets. As the sun climbed higher into the leaden sky, the cars came faster. They squirted into the street, and then flowed like rivers, compressed and controlled by the dams of traffic lights. The horns honked, the brakes screeched, the gears ground. Hot-rods and motorcycles charged up and down the street with a clatter and a bang, and vacant-eyed female drivers consistently managed to turn right from the left lanes. By eight o'clock, the first ambulance had moaned through the street, scattering the cars like toys. Somewhere, energetically, a cop blew a whistle.

The people seeped out of the walls. At first, there had been only a scattered few: a neatly dressed man with a cane, who was undoubtedly never late to his office; a pale woman gazing into store windows; a tired young man in need of a shave who had come hurriedly out of a hotel via the side entrance. Then, as though the few had divided like cells to become many, the sidewalks were jammed. Big ones, little ones, fat ones, thin ones. A blind man sitting hopefully with his box of pencils. A girl and her mother getting new clothes for school. The lights clicked through their memorized routine, and human beings and cars took turns testing the pavement.

The heat hit like a bombardment. It was an unseasonal, humid heat. The hot air was caught between the cement and the gray clouds. Whatever god was responsible for such matters fumbled around for the rain trigger and couldn't find it.

Ellery felt choked, and his hands were shaking. His hair felt sticky. His eyes burned. He felt like hell.

It wasn't all the heat.

He looked at his city and didn't recognize it. The city had changed. It had been comfortable and soft and familiar. It was now distressing, hard, and alien.

It was a reservation for savages.

It *had* changed—if only in his mind. And he had changed, too. He wasn't the same Paul Ellery who had left Austin to spend the summer justifying a research grant. He didn't quite know what to make of Paul Ellery Number Two. He did know one thing: he wasn't very comfortable to live with.

He started the car and drove slowly out past the University of Texas, a collection of vaguely Spanish structures dominated and presided over by a white skyscraper with a Greek temple perched in perpetual surprise on top of it, and on to the greenish apartment house on King Street where Anne lived.

He went up the outside stairs and rang the bell. There was a short pause and the door opened. It wasn't Anne.

"Paulsy!" exclaimed Peg, Anne's eternal roommate. "My dear, you look like the *wrahth of Gawd,* I mean you *really* do."

"Thank you, Dale Carnegie," Ellery said. "Is Anne around?"

"But of *coawse!* Come in for heaven's sakes, I'll *call* her."

"Fine," said Ellery. He walked inside and slumped in the chair by the phonograph.

"Now you be careful of my etchings," Peg said. "They smear *dread-fully.*"

"No more rug-weaving?"

"Oh, heavens no! I gave that up months ago. Paulsy, it's so good to see you."

"It's good to see you too, Peg," Ellery said, and he meant it.

Peg disappeared to attempt the Herculean feat of waking Anne up, and Ellery reflected that he had always liked Peg, and didn't quite know why. She was a dizzy blonde, not devastating but well informed, and she had an arty personality that in anyone else he would have detested cordially. But Peg never took herself any more seriously than she deserved, and she was one of those curious and wonderful people who were always just "around" when you particularly needed a friend. You had to take Peg on her own terms, but she wore well.

Ellery took in the well-remembered apartment with real affection, and felt himself beginning to relax a little. There were books all over the place, and they were stacked in untidy piles that indicated they were being read instead of exhibited.

But the place was clean, comfortable, and quiet. It was subtly feminine, with unexpected frills and flowers popping out here and there, but its sex wasn't flaunted. It was an apartment resigned to being a girl, and enjoying it, but still given to playing tomboy now and then.

There was a swish and Anne was in his arms. "Ell," she whispered. "I've been so lonesome."

"Me too," said Ellery.

He looked at her, holding her at arm's length. Her dark hair was mussed and she didn't have any make-up on. Only her clear gray-green eyes hinted that she could be beautiful when she wanted to. She had on a shapeless blue bathrobe, and from underneath it peeked a sleazy pink silk nightgown. Anne's pet vice was an addiction to secret-agent nightgowns and harem pajamas, and Ellery had never objected yet.

"You look good," he said. "You look wonderful."

"You don't, Ell. I love you, but you look shot. Want some breakfast?"

"I could use some."

Anne went into the kitchen, taking Ellery with her. She brewed up sausages and poached eggs and toast and coffee. Suspecting a hangover, she made a quart of orange juice and made him drink most of it. He did feel better when he finished, and his nervousness turned into weariness.

"Now, you lazy man," she said, kissing him lightly, "You're going to bed. I've got to work this afternoon, and tonight we're going out. I refuse to go out with somnambulists. I'll wake you up when I get home."

She put him to bed, firmly. She kissed him again, picked up clothes from various places, and disappeared into the bathroom to get dressed. Ellery stretched, feeling tired and delighted.

He heard Anne come out of the bathroom after a while, and he heard her phone somebody named Ralph and break her date for that night. He heard the door open and she sneaked in and kissed his nose.

"Good night, or good day or something," she whispered. "Nice to have you back in the house of ill-repute."

"Night, hon," he said. "I think I love you."

"What, again? It must have been something you ate."

And she was gone. Peg had kept discreetly out of the way, and he didn't know whether or not she was still in the apartment. He yawned, hugely.

Jefferson Springs seemed far, far away.

He slept.

Hours later, he awoke when Anne shook his shoulder. "Rise and shine, handsome," she said. "You're taking me out to supper tonight, or didn't you know?"

"I didn't know," Ellery mumbled. "I thought perhaps your magic touch in the kitchen—"

"No thanks, pal. I get tired, you know—it's one of my little idiosyncracies. If I'm supposed to be charming, gay, and lovable tonight, then you're supposed to dig down in the vault and buy me some eats."

"I'll pay," Ellery said. "Don't beat me any more." They changed clothes and went out to Irving's, where they disposed of two charcoal-broiled filets. Then they drove out to Lake Austin and stopped at the Flamingo. It was still hot and overcast, with no stars in sight. They bought a fifth of Scotch from the adjoining liquor store before going inside—the quaint Texas liquor laws ruling mixed drinks evil and corrupting unless you bring your own fifth and pour it in yourself.

They got a quiet booth at the Flamingo, held hands, and Ellery settled down to some serious drinking. The Flamingo was pleasant and modern, and its most distinctive attribute was a painting of a sensational nude, which hung over the piano. Confirmed barflies had a legend that after twenty-five beers, no more and no less, you could watch closely and see the nude roll over. Ellery had tried it one time, in his younger days, but had been rewarded with only a slight twitch of the right shoulder.

It seemed that everyone in the Flamingo knew Anne, and stopped to say hello. Anne was a girl with a lovely split personality. About half the time she was the gayest of the party-party crowd, and the other half she holed

up in her apartment and read. Ellery was about the only man who had
seen both sides of her character, which gave him a certain distinction.

"Anything wrong, Ell?"

"Wrong? Of course not."

"You're the worst liar I know. I must remember that. What is it—work
going badly, bored with me again, just ornery?"

"Ornery, I guess. Let's pretend it isn't there, okay?"

"Okay. Laugh and be merry, for tomorrow we will have hangovers."

She was merry, too, at least on the outside. She took Ellery in hand,
made him dance, and poured Scotch into him. It was a therapy that had
worked before, and tonight it was *almost* successful. Except that Ellery
got too high.

He took to monopolizing the jukebox, feeding it with handfuls of
quarters. He started out with good swing, showing marked favoritism to
records cut prior to the bop mania, and then, with more Scotch, proceeded
to sloppy ballads that would have sickened him if he had been sober.

"I love you, Annie," he said along about midnight. "I really love you.
You're the finest, sweetest—"

"There, there," Anne said, patting his hand. "You always love me when
you're drunk. You love everybody when you're drunk."

Ellery downed another drink, hurrying to get it in before the midnight
curfew. "I don't know about that," he said slowly. "I just don't *know* about
that." He was feeling very wise and lucid. "It's my theory that drink reveals
a man's character. You see, Annie, when I get drunk I *do* love everybody.
I love *everybody*. You see?"

"That's wonderful," Anne said.

"You *do* see. You see, if *everybody* loved everybody when everybody was
drunk, you see, why then, everybody...everybody..."

"I see," Anne said, as Ellery trailed off into uncharted vistas of the
mind.

Finally, Ellery surged to his feet. "We go!" he announced.

"Goody," said Anne. She carefully picked up her purse and tipped the
waitress.

Ellery set himself in motion toward the door. He was confident that he
had never walked with more dignity. Anne artfully removed a forgotten
paper napkin from his belt to add to the illusion. He paused once before
the jukebox and listened with great concentration.

"Terrific," he announced, after due deliberation. And then, at the top
of his lungs, he added: "Oh, play that THING!"

Anne steered him to the car and shortly they were home.

Ellery mounted the stairs, singing lustily, and carried Anne over the
threshold into her own apartment. He dropped her on the floor, missing

the chair with great precision, and then carefully dived at the couch, and made it.

He didn't move. His eyes were open, but decidedly glassy.

Peg came out of the bedroom, rubbing her eyes. "Oh, bro-*ther!* Do I have to put *both* of you to bed?"

Anne picked herself up off the floor, laughing. "Nope. Just lend a hand with Junior here."

"Well," said Peg, "at least I don't get tossed out of my bed tonight."

"Hush," said Anne.

They went to work, trying to arrange two hundred pounds of inert mass. The inert two hundred pounds said, quite distinctly: "I am thoroughly capable of putting my own self in the sack." It said it twelve more times before they got him arranged on the couch and tossed a sheet over him.

"Night, baby," Anne said, and kissed him.

She undressed and went to sleep in the other room. She slept soundly as always. Once, very early in the morning, she thought she woke up and heard someone crying in the living room.

13

The next morning was on the miserable side, and by the time Ellery really began to sit up and take an interest in things, the girls had to go to work

Ellery sat in the apartment and wondered what to do.

Jefferson Springs sat there with him, smiling.

Last night, he had managed to shut out Jefferson Springs. He had stuffed it down in to a back corner in his mind and poured alcohol on top of it. It had worked, too—

Except for the dreams.

"Damn it," he said. "Damn *me.*"

He wished, fervently, that he could forget all about Jefferson Springs, and forget everything that had happened there. He wished that he could simply unpack his bag where he was and never go back. He could go on and live a life, some kind of a life, and tell himself that it was none of his business. He didn't have to go on being a scientist; science was not a religion to him. He could just relax and persuade himself that a few facts didn't really matter. He would just say to himself, "I once knew a town less than two hundred miles from my home, a town where people lived who thought of me as a savage. I once knew such a town, but the hell with it."

He liked the idea.

Too bad that it was impossible.

Impossible for *him.* Paul Ellery had been cursed with a mind that asked questions, looked for answers. His mind worked whether he wanted it to or not, and he had never been able to find the button that would turn it off. He had been cursed with a stubborn streak a yard wide, and he had never been broken. He had been cursed with a cynical soul that he wasn't proud of; he had always thought that he should have been better than he was, or at least dumber.

He could no more walk out of Jefferson Springs, licked, than Cortez could have walked out of Mexico, or Columbus could have quit before sighting land. It wasn't heroism, and it wasn't noble. It was selfish pride, and he knew it.

Either he was going to beat Jefferson Springs or Jefferson Springs was going to beat him. If he won, which he knew was impossible, then he had done something for his people and for himself. If *they* won, which was certain, then he would be one of them, and he would have done something for himself.

Neat.

He wished he believed it in his guts instead of in his head.

Okay, bright boy, he told himself. *You came up here to think things out. Start thinking.*

The flash of illumination, the insight that would have made the impossible easy, didn't come. Ellery paced the floor, swearing diligently under his breath. He looked out the window at the hot gray sky and cursed that explicitly. Why didn't it rain?

He picked up the morning paper and stared at it glumly. The same old crud. He read the story over, and a thought waded around below the surface and tried to be born.

He sat down, his head in his hands. He had three hours left before Anne came home. Three hours. Had he made any more progress, really, toward understanding what went on in Jefferson Springs? He told himself that he had not, and then he wasn't so sure.

For one thing, now that he thought about it, that ritual in the blue lights at the Thorne Ranch had told him plenty. It had given him a needed clue into the workings of the colony culture. If that was a prime source after the "full treatment," and if the citizens of the colony spent all or most of the rest of their time in living the lives of small-town Texans, then there was only one possible technique they could be following.

If all human beings in all their variety had to start with an almost identical skeleton—

Well, leave that for the moment.

Take that story in the paper about China. That was interesting, definitely. What *was* the attitude of the United States toward China? That depended. Which China did he mean—the one on the island or the one in China? Did he mean the official policy of the United States Government? Which administration—past, present, or future? Did he mean the individual states? Which ones? Did he mean the "man in the street?" Which man? What street?

That was interesting. That was another clue.

So—how about the alien culture? What was he up against there, and how could he come to terms with it? What was the attitude of the whole alien civilization toward its colonial policy? John had hinted of friction there, hadn't he? Wasn't that what the big conference was going to be about?

What did they think of savages who climbed up the ladder?

Had John told him the *whole* truth about Jefferson Springs?

Questions. Always questions. Find the right question and you get the right answer. Questions—

How about the aliens, the people? Were *they* all identical robots, thinking alike, speaking alike, looking alike? The little fat man, high above the Earth, reading bad science fiction with a persecution complex? Mel Thorne,

running his ranch in the sun? A. Jeremiah Stubbs, sitting on the one story
he could never send out to the A. P. wire?

Cynthia?

And how about the *billions* of others, out there beyond his imagination? No conflicts, no disagreements, no factions? Nothing that he could
use, nothing that he could turn to his own advantage?

Well, leave *that* for the moment. But don't forget it.

Of course, the whole problem posed by Jefferson Springs was a problem
in acculturation, a problem created by the contact of cultures. One culture
was extremely advanced, so advanced that he could hardly do better than
to catch tantalizing, unsatisfying hints as to its true nature. The other
culture was his own.

Or had been.

There was the catch he had thought of before: there was no acculturation
problem for the two *cultures* involved, since one of them wasn't even aware
that the other existed. But there was acculturation for *him.* He knew.

He thought, again, of Two Bears.

What happened to men caught between two cultures? What happened
to a savage when civilization reared its metallic head? Well, he could be
killed, of course, either literally or spiritually. He might try his luck with
a spear against a tank, or he might watch his people die and smile. He
might make himself useful to the civilized men, might even go to school
and become one of them. He might run away, if there was any place to
go. What else might he do? Was there *anything?*

Maybe. Just maybe.

In spite of himself, Paul Ellery felt a growing excitement. He was a man
again. He would go back. This time, he knew what he was looking for.

By the time Anne and Peg came home, Ellery had shaved and taken
a shower and put on clean clothes. He even managed to stick a smile on
his face that was almost as good as the genuine article.

"Whee!" said Peg, kicking off her shoes and rubbing her ankles. "He's
alive again! I like you so much better that way, Paulsy. I mean I really
do."

Ellery kissed each girl impartially. "I'll make some coffee," he said. "You
all sit down and radiate."

"My," said Anne, obeying orders. "What are we supposed to radiate—gamma rays?"

She looked trim and provocative in a white blouse and dark skirt with
a red silk handkerchief around her throat. Ellery kissed her again for good
measure. "You radiate beauty, of course," he told her. "Maybe a bath would
help, but right now you do the best you can."

"Wait until you see that different, mysterious me," she said. "I come on after five, or at least that's what it said in the glamour magazine. Right now I *do* stink a little. You feeling better, hon?"

"Wait and see," he said cryptically and went out to make the coffee.

He proved it to her, taking the rest of the night for a demonstration. They didn't do anything spectacular, but when they were right they didn't have to do anything at all. They had something to eat at Dirty Bill's Drive-In, and then they just drove, outside of Austin, out in the hills.

There was beauty around Austin, an unsuspected beauty that waited patiently for someone to come out and look at it. It was not a sensational, color-postcard kind of beauty. It was a beauty that asked for a pair of seeing eyes.

There was a long, comfortable lake, made by a dam across the Colorado. There were low hills, blanketed in sweet-smelling cedar. There was empty farmland, rolling away into the shadows. They drank it in, and neither talked of it. Then he drove Anne home.

"Paul," said Anne, "will you ever come back for me?"

"I don't know," Ellery said, hating himself. "I hope so. I want to, Anne. Remember that."

"I wish I knew what had happened to you down there. You're different, Ell. It's not just another woman this time."

"No. Maybe I'm growing up."

"Don't grow away from me, Paul. We're not so young anymore, and it's lonely sometimes. You need me, too."

"Yes. No one else would put up with me."

"Could I come and see you?"

"No, baby. I don't want you down there. Don't make me explain."

"I'm only human, Paul."

"That's enough. Don't say any more. Don't talk."

It was three o'clock when he took her home.

"Come back to me, Ell. I can help, whatever it is. I've always helped you, haven't I, Paul?"

"Always," he said. "You're my girl."

"You'll come back, Paul? Please say you'll come back."

"I'll try, Annie. That's all I can say."

"Okay, hon. Sorry I love you so much. 'Night."

"Good night, Annie."

He drove away, trying to ignore the knot in his stomach.

He stopped at the University and walked across the gray campus, deserted in the early morning hours. He walked to steady himself, to clear his head.

And he walked to remember.

The cold gray buildings that he knew so well were like a living past. He knew them all, from Waggoner Hall, where he had taken his first course in anthropology, to the Tower that housed the library. He even knew buildings that were no longer there, like old B Hall, now just a plot of grass.

And the old faces came back, laughing and crying and unconcerned.

An icy melancholy crept over him as he walked and his blood was cold in his veins. With an almost numbing shock, Paul Ellery began to understand that his problem was far more than it had appeared to be. All his life he had rejected, questioned, rebelled. Not altogether, of course, and perhaps mainly in his mind. Maybe, even, it went with his kind of mind. Maybe it was necessary, if he was ever to understand. But the fact remained that even this was not wholly his.

He was an outsider not to one culture, but to two.

He shook the feeling off and went back to his car. He got in and drove through the sleeping city, back out the San Antonio highway and on toward Jefferson Springs.

And all through the night he thought. He thought of the Osage, who had discovered oil on their reservation....

14

September hurried by, trailing rain and a crispness in the morning air. The land turned green, hurriedly, and the cactus flowers bloomed. The hot afternoon sun blazed down recklessly, not knowing what month it was, and tried to suck the moisture from the ground. But the rains had come and the rivers flowed, and then, quite suddenly, it was October.

John sent the same two men to escort Ellery to the ship. One of them was still smoking a pipe, and Ellery got the distinct impression that it had not gone out since he had last seen him. They came for him while he was at work.

"We must be quick," the man with the pipe said. "The delegates are already aboard, and we have a lot of territory to cover before the conference."

"On my way," Ellery said, yanking a sheet from his typewriter and handing it to Mr. Stubbs. "Here's the story on the garden club."

A. Jeremiah Stubbs did not look up. He slowly extracted his big gold watch from its nest and examined it with marked distaste. He adjusted his green eye shade and hooked his fingers in his black vest. "Young cub," he said gloomily. "When I was your age—"

Ellery slapped him on the back, startling him to such an extent that he actually tilted his swivel chair a full inch from its usual position. "I'll bet you were a demon!" Ellery assured him. And then to the two men: "Let's go."

Time twisted back on itself and played a remembered scene again. There was the black Buick and the country road, and then there was the ten-foot globe. He sat on the same green couch on the same gray carpet, and there was the same faint smell of electricity in the air. The globe lifted through the golden sunlight, carrying him very high this time, and then the panel slid open and there was a glare of gentle yellow light.

He was back in the giant spaceship, floating over the Earth.

Back down the long polished corridor, and even as he walked he felt a new vibration in the ship. It was subdued, but it carried a hint of power that was beyond his comprehension. For the first time, he was on the ship while it was in flight. He knew a fleeting moment of terror. He pictured the massive silver tube of the ship standing on her tail and pointing her nose up and out, flashing into the abyss of space, leaving the Earth far behind her, a dot in the infinite, and then nothing, nothing at all—

He pulled himself together. The ship would only be circling the Earth, picking up representatives from the star colonies.

He laughed shortly. That was all. Just alien delegates. How strange it was, he thought, this endless adaptability of the human mind....

Back to the heavy door set flush in the end of the corridor, the door that swung open without a sound as he approached it. Back to the familiar room, the padded chairs, the cluttered desk.

And John.

The fat little man beamed. He chuckled, hugely, like Santa Claus. He got out his bottle of Scotch and poured out two glassfuls. *He's glad to see me,* Ellery thought, and he was grateful. *He's really glad to see ME.*

"Ellery, old man!" John exclaimed. "Welcome back to the den of the fat monsters!"

"Howdy, John," Paul Ellery said, taking his drink and sitting down. "Thanks for not forgetting me."

"Nothing, nothing at all," John said, tossing down half a glass of straight Scotch at a swallow. "Ah! The delicate glow of hot machine oil. I've missed you, Paul. You have no idea how deadly dull it is to have to sneak around and be mysterious all the time. Damn it, I hate mysteries! I'm a straightforward man. How do you like being an alien, son?"

Ellery hesitated. "I don't know," he said finally.

"Fine!" said John. "How was Austin?"

"Strange," Ellery said truthfully. "Strange, and rather wonderful. How the devil did you know I was in Austin?"

John shrugged, his bald dome gleaming above its fringe of hair. "Elementary, my dear Paul. Nothing omniscient about it at all. I left you in a state of shock, and the next day it was noticed that your car was missing. I know you pretty well, old man; and it wasn't hard to guess that you'd go home. As a matter of fact, it's easier to keep track of you out of the colony than in it."

"Meaning?"

John pulled out a big black cigar and stuck it in his mouth. "Follow your instincts, Paul. At its somewhat primitive level, your science doesn't much believe in instincts any more, but you follow 'em anyhow."

"You're hinting at something, John-boy. What?"

John ignored the question. "I want you to see the ship before the yak-yak starts. And I want you to meet Withrow. He's been in the same situation you're in, and you two should have a lot in common."

They started to walk, with John leading the way. Ellery could feel the ship sliding to stops and then easing into motion again.

Picking up passengers, around the Earth.

They walked until Ellery's legs ached. John plunged on like a plump, eager puppy, and he never seemed to tire. Ellery once had estimated the length of the ship at five hundred yards, but he decided now that he would have to revise his estimate upward.

Way upward.

What he saw was astonishing enough—astonishing in its vastness and in its cool, comfortable efficiency. But what he could only sense was more astonishing still: a million engineering problems solved and hidden under his feet, problems as yet unformulated in the world he had known. A million answers to questions that might never be asked....

There were computers and planetwide survey graphs. There were acres of files on unbelievable subjects. There were libraries and compact weapons that could wipe out a world at a touch of a button. There were hospitals and galactic communications equipment, bewildering in its complexity.

But he saw only the simple stuff, the toys.

And there were men and women, more alert and intense than those he had known in Jefferson Springs, technicians and engineers, and men who had long ago made a science out of anthropology and psychology and sociology, and then had gone on to something else.

When he saw the navigation room, he caught his breath. Three-dimensional mock-ups of galactic sectors, with stars and planets and moons and asteroids moving frigidly in magnetic fields, a universe stuck in a glass cage. And when two of the technicians computed a driveline, a triangular segment of star systems blurred eerily, so that the eye could not follow it, and the three dimensions that Paul Ellery had lived with turned into—something else.

He not only knew, now, that this ship could go a long, long way; he *felt* it.

"Don't forget, Paul," John said, watching his eyes when they were alone together for a brief moment "they're just people. Take a jackass and give him an automobile, and he's still a jackass."

Just people. What was he trying to say? "This conference," Ellery said. "It's about colonial policy, right?"

"Check. Maybe that's too much of an inflated term, though. This is just one planet, son. Peanuts. Strictly peanuts."

"I've been wondering," Ellery said slowly. "I'm not sure I understand your part in all this. What are *your* views about Earth?"

John looked him right in the eye and didn't smile. "Me? Why, I'm absolutely non-political. I have no views. I leave thinking to the smart men."

"Oh," said Paul Ellery. *Damn liar,* he thought.

"And now," John said, "you get to meet Withrow. Come along."

Ellery moved his legs again and wondered when the numbness would go away. "Who's Withrow?"

"Well, he used to be a writer—quite a popular one, as a matter of fact. He got to poking around in a little town in Maine about six years ago, and we made him the same offer that was made to you. He took us up on it, and he's been to the Center, so now he's one of us. You can probably learn a lot from Withrow."

Ellery was intrigued. Maybe here at last was someone who could be closer to him than either of the two cultures, a man who had been in the same boat that he was in. Maybe—

I need a friend, he thought. *I need one in the worst way.*

They found Withrow in a scanning cube, studying. Ellery sized him up. He was a thin, confident man with iron-gray hair, perhaps forty years old. He had cold, flinty eyes. He nodded at John and introduced himself to Ellery.

"Paul," he said, extending a businesslike hand, "I've heard a lot about you. I'm Hamilton Withrow. I hope very much that I can be of some help to you; I know how confusing things can seem at first." He smiled.

"I'm sure we'll get along," Paul Ellery said.

"Mr. Withrow has consented to do us a favor," John said. "Since you can't understand our language as yet, Hamilton has kindly offered to stay with you during the conference and let you know what is going on. I'll be busy elsewhere, being a non-political person."

"That's mighty nice of you," Ellery said.

"Not at all," said Hamilton Withrow.

John left them, presumably to go back to his office.

"Strange man," observed Withrow.

"John? He seems like a pretty good guy."

Withrow shrugged and didn't pursue the subject. "You know, Paul," he said, "I was in exactly your position once. I know the difficulties you're going through. If I may say so, all your doubts will vanish utterly after a short time at the Center. Your old life—and I mean no offense by this—will seem an amusing childhood, and your old friends just fondly remembered children. We must learn to take the long view, Paul, the *long* view."

"I appreciate your advice, Mr. Withrow."

"Please! My name is Hamilton—or even Ham, if you prefer." He laughed.

Ellery laughed, dutifully.

The hours passed, and the great ship swam around the Earth, scooping up her passengers like fish from a shallow sea. In what was really a remarkably short time, Hamilton Withrow led Ellery to the conference room, where things were starting.

It was a long, low room, staggering in its immensity. It was filled to overflowing with the strangest people Ellery had ever seen.

There were Chinese, English, American, French. There were Africans, Danes, Brazilians, Poles, Swedes, Japanese. There were Filipinos, Swiss, Australians, Russians. There were Negroids, Whites, Mongoloids. There were rich men, poor men. Men in business suits and men who were half naked. Women with rings through their noses, women with rings in their lips, women with rings on their fingers.

But the strangeness was more than their diversity. The strangeness was in their *similarity*. They were all self-assured, sophisticated, well-behaved. Even a bit smug, perhaps. They had a tangible sense of belonging, an unconscious air of superiority, an aura of power.

The people were human, all right. If a man could apply strictly objective criteria, they were undoubtedly the most human people on Earth. But they were not human beings as Paul Ellery had known them. They were somehow different, somehow alien. Almost, they were the Cro-Magnons as seen by the Neanderthals.

"Look at them!" Withrow exclaimed, his cold eyes shining. "Aren't they splendid?"

Ellery hesitated. "Splendid" wasn't quite the word that he would have used, but he decided against saying so. "Remarkable, no doubt of that," he said.

There was a great deal of soft conversation, filled with buzzes and clicks, and Ellery couldn't understand a word of it.

"We can't speak to each other in our adopted Earth tongues, you know," Withrow told him. "Each group knows only its own local language. So, when we get together, we have to use the mother tongue."

"Oh," said Ellery, glancing at Withrow. "The mother tongue."

Hamilton Withrow, however, failed to notice the speculative look. He was thoroughly wrapped up in the conference, his thin body proud and alert. Occasionally, he exchanged words with someone he knew, speaking quite fluently in the clicks and buzzes of the alien language. Ellery began to feel uncomfortable.

The conference started.

Ellery was unable to fathom the rules of procedure. Small groups appeared to work together, examining documents and talking softly, and then the various different groups would compare notes. Periodically, and seemingly apart from the group arrangements, someone would address the convention. While he spoke, perhaps five or six of the delegates would pause and listen to him. This, too, seemed to be somehow prearranged.

On one wall, there was a large white square, bordered in some black metallic substance. As the conference wore on, colored lights flickered into life on the square. They arranged themselves into flowing patterns, and altered after each speech. From time to time, a small group would send someone over to check the pattern against a small black gadget that fitted into the hand, and when the checker went back to his group there would be a renewed flurry of activity.

To Ellery, the whole thing took on a hypnotic, lulling quality. Very important and all that, but a little removed. Withrow could not translate a fiftieth of what was said, and Ellery could not understand a fourth of what was translated.

He listened and did his best.

"All automatic, you know," Withrow said. "All the variables are integrated, and then the free-choice element is factored out and manipulated."

"Ummmm," said Ellery. *And don't put the bananas in the refrigerator!*

"He's saying, essentially, that we must be practical about this thing. He says that our colonial policy was not a choice, but a necessity. He says we should give the colonials a greater voice in galactic administration. He suggests that Earth will soon blow itself back a thousand years, and then we can safely bring in more colonists. He says we must think of our children, and of our children's children."

"I see," said Ellery.

"This one's a bit wild. He says that our whole solution to the problem of overpopulation is nothing more than sticking our head in the sand. He says he isn't any aborigine-lover, but just the same he thinks we're headed for trouble. He says we should resurvey the whole galactic colonial system. I wonder where he thinks *he* would go if we left all the planets for the savages! You can see how muddy his thinking is, Paul."

"Sure," said Ellery.

"The next speaker—see him, the one with the abominable haircut—is saying—well, he is saying—you see, it's about the relation of the Prime Force to the Quadrant—I mean—well, I'm afraid it's a bit over your head."

"Don't worry about it," Ellery said.

He listened, and the meeting seemed to go on endlessly. There was a great deal of bickering about local problems: the position of the colony in the galactic economy, the possible importation of luxury items into backward areas, the problem of fraternization with the local savages. Ellery just couldn't take it all in. He had to keep telling himself, over and over: *This is Earth they are talking about, this is—was—my home they are discussing, my people—*

The voice droned on in his ear: "This one is advocating more interference to maintain the status quo...this one wishes to send missionaries among the savages; that's a good one...this one thinks we should send all colony-born children back to the Center *before* the high-school ages...this one...this one...this one..."

After an eternity, it was over.

The pattern of lights on the board flowed, steadied, and stopped. The result was announced.

"Same old thing." Withrow yawned. "The galactic colonial policy is approved, and more attention is requested for local problems. Doesn't mean a thing, but it keeps the colonists happy."

Ellery looked at Withrow. Unbidden, an image came into his mind. An image from many years ago, from high school. A boy who had come out for football during the last month of the season, when it was too late for him even to get in shape, and had thenceforth referred to himself as "one of the team."

"You can probably learn a lot from Withrow," John had said.

John was subtler than he looked.

"I appreciate your help, Hamilton," Ellery said.

He was exhausted, mentally and physically. He let Withrow lead him out of the conference room, and back to John's office. He was glad when Withrow left him alone; he simply didn't feel up to talking to the man.

John wasn't in. Ellery thought dimly that this might be a good time to pick up some secret information from John's desk, but he rejected the idea. He already had more information than he could possibly handle; he was flooded with a deluge of information. His problem, he knew, was never going to be solved by any remarkable item filched from a desk.

There were no magic formulae.

Ellery compromised by walking over to a wall couch, stretching out, and going to sleep in seconds. It was the only retreat he had left, and it was good to get away for a while.

John woke him up, hours later, and brought him a cup of hot coffee, which he drank thankfully. He was stiff and sore, and he felt thoroughly insignificant.

"Jefferson Springs," John said quietly. "Time to go home."

"Thanks, John. What do I owe you for the room?"

"Not much, my boy. Shall we settle for your grandmother's arm and the mortgage on the family homestead?"

"It's a deal."

John himself escorted him down the long corridor, walking with deceptive speed. "You know, Paul," the little fat man said, "you're just beginning to get an insight into the size of this mess. That whole conference you witnessed was classed as a strictly rural affair. Maybe it'll get one line in the Galactic Administration Report, and nobody'll even read it. It's a bit shocking at times—did you know that more than ninety-nine per cent of the civilized people of this galaxy do not know that the planet Earth exists? It's strictly specialized information."

Ellery started. *Ninety-nine percent did not know—*

Well, how could they?

"Quite stupid," John said, shaking his head. "The conference didn't even have the guts to *mention* the real problem."

Ellery raised his eyebrows.

"There are the Others, you know. I believe you caught a glimpse of them at the little gathering on the Thorne Ranch?"

Ellery remembered. *The galaxy, with gossamer silver threads. Atoms of worlds. And something else. Something down in the corner, down dark in the corner.*

Had he screamed?

They came to the panel that led to the metallic sphere which Ellery was beginning to think of as an elevator.

"You'll be sent to a Center soon, Paul," John said. "Don't sleep too long."

Ellery stared at the fat man, waiting, but John said nothing more. The panel slid open and Ellery walked into the globe. He sat down on the same green couch, but this time it was more crowded. The two ship escorts were there, one of them still with his pipe in his mouth, and in addition there were the three conference delegates from Jefferson Springs, two men and a woman. The men wore boots and big hats, and the woman wore a black dress and a shawl. They sat next to him and made small talk, but the atmosphere was strained.

The great floating globe touched down, and they stepped out into a plowed field. It was night, and the blackness was frosted with stars. There was a cold moon, coating the Earth with silver. Ellery wasn't sure what night it was.

They got into the black Buick, and the car jolted over the dirt road, and then purred down the highway toward Jefferson Springs. Ellery sat in the back seat, crowded in with the three colonists. He didn't look at them and he avoided their eyes.

Too big, too big, he thought. *Too big to fight.*

He felt himself growing tense as the little town came closer. He sensed the vast bulk of the spaceship, lost in the stars over his head. He felt very small.

He couldn't beat them. Being what he was, he couldn't ignore them. After seeing Withrow, he wasn't even sure he could join them, and stay sane.

He thought about Anne, and wondered what she was doing.

He tried to think about Indians who had found oil on reservations.

He was very tired, and the big black Buick rushed on, into the shadows and the night and the pale splashes from an empty moon.

15

Autumn flowed softly by, easing its way toward winter. The land lost its brief flush of green and stood nakedly before the wind, but there would be no real freeze until January.

Paul Ellery kept digging, looking for the chink in the armor of Jefferson Springs. He knew that he was not learning fast enough, and he knew that it would not be long until they shipped him off to the Center for the "full treatment."

After that, he wouldn't care.

He saw Cynthia, occasionally, using her to fight the empty loneliness he felt in the town that was not his own.

Once, out walking on a country road, he spotted a piece of worked flint half buried in the dry, hard-packed earth. He picked it up and looked at it. It was a crudely made, pointed artifact about five inches long, bearing the characteristic flake scars of human workmanship. It was too long for an arrow point; it might have been a spear point, a dart point, or a stone knife. Probably not Comanche or Apache. Ellery wasn't certain, not being an archaeologist, but the flint had probably been used by one of the nameless hunting-and-gathering Indian groups that had been common throughout Texas before the beginnings of the written historical records.

Another way of life—vanished in the dust.

He stood in the chill wind and shivered.

The humble, long-overlooked bit of flint called forth a host of memories. He remembered the kick he had got out of his first anthropology courses. He remembered the long, all-night discussions, and the books that had seemed to open up wonderful, uncharted vistas of the mind-the excitement of Malinowski, the sweep and daring of White, the vision of Linton dedicating a work of social science to the next generation. He remembered his young confidence, his certainty that he had a key that would unlock doors that others could not see. And he remembered the subsequent plodding of graduate school, the hot digs, the quizzes on bone fragments, the wrestling with German. Fun, all of it; but what had happened to the excitement and the hope and the promise for the future?

When had it turned into uncertainty and caution and even fear? When had the kick in his work gone out the window?

Was it the apathy of his students? Was it the preoccupation with trivia of many of the scientists? Was it the discovery that social science had many questions but few answers?

Was it the flowering hell of the hydrogen bomb that reduced what he was trying to do to hopeless insignificance?

Was it a climate of cultural hysteria in which a scientist could not work?

Or had he failed himself, somewhere along the line?

He stood for a long time, the old artifact in his hand, and then walked back to town under the thin, pale sun.

He kept trying. And one day he found something.

It was late in the afternoon of a warm day. He stepped into the American Club for a beer. There was a little bell on the screen door, and it jingled as he walked through. The front room was furnished with four faded green pool tables and a few crooked wire stools. There were calendars on the walls, showing bathing beauties in love with Coca-Cola, cowboys in love with horses, and business executives in love with trout. There was a stained bar along one wall, made of plywood. There was no one in the room.

There were voices coming from the back room, behind a thin wood partition. Voices, and the click of dominoes.

He moved quietly over to the wall and stood with his ear pressed against it. He kept his eyes open. He could hear the voices clearly:

"I don't care what you say, dammit, the Administration is gonna throw us to the wolves."

Administration? That would be the galactic government.

"What're we supposed to do—just sit on our tails and let 'em take our homes away from us? You listen here to what I'm tellin' you boys—"

"Me, I say we oughta do more—a hell of a lot more! So maybe the Preventers are illegal—so what? They're workin' for *us,* and they're the only ones who give a good goddam about us."

Preventers? He had come across references to them before—an organization that believed in preventing a colonized planet from ever reaching civilized status, as opposed to the Evolutionaries who felt that colonized planets must be left alone to progress as best they could, without interference.

"Ahh, you take yourself too blamed serious. They'll blow their ratholes sky high without any help from us. Let the Preventers stick their necks out if they're a mind to. Me, I ain't forgettin' that ship up yonder, and don't *you* forget it neither. You remember what happened to that colony down south, don't yuh? Polio, they said—"

"They're a pack of damn Evolutionists in One Sector, if you want my opinion. I ask you, what do them jokers know about *practical* problems?"

"Take it easy, there, you're not yellin' into a tornado."

"Ahh, what're yuh scared of—the F.B.I.?"

Laughter.

"Yeah, the hell with it. Bill, what say to a couple more beers?"

The sound of a chair scraping the floor. Footsteps.

Ellery hurried across the room and out through the screen door. He had forgotten the little bell, and it tinkled as the door swung. He walked down the sidewalk, then crossed the street and entered a narrow alley. He stopped by a garbage can and listened.

Nothing.

He kept moving, back on Main Street, down the block to his car. He got in, backed into the street, and drove past the club. There was no excitement there. No one was in the front room. Either he hadn't been seen or else they didn't care. He went home to get dressed for a date with Cynthia.

While he dressed, he thought over what he had heard.

The pieces were beginning to fall into place a little.

If only he had more time....

Evidently, the aliens had not been able to eliminate an old, old problem in the field of government. There was a marked conflict between basic administrative policy, set by the Galactic Administration, and the colonies actually living in the field. The basic policy was fair and even altruistic. The great spaceship was there to see that the hands-off policy was followed to the letter. Unfortunately, the ship couldn't be everywhere at once, and some colonists didn't think too highly of basic policy. They were human enough to think of themselves first and ethical questions later, if at all. If the Preventers could only prod the native planets into atomic wars that would blast the city reservations, then the colonies were safe from eventual interference.

Probably, the Administration could handle the Preventers. Ellery was sure that John and the rest knew all about them, and were quite competent to deal with the problem. For Ellery, the important fact was simply that the colonists were divided in their sentiments.

That could be helpful.

Cynthia picked him up at eight. He climbed into her blue Nash and gave her a kiss.

"Hi love," she said. "In a dancing mood?"

"More or less. But I'm getting old for that sort of thing."

"You're not old, Paul."

"I feel old," he said, and meant it.

"We'll see if we can't rejuvenate you."

"You're the doctor."

They pulled up in front of the Community Hall, which was a drab, barn like structure rearing up out of a lot of bare ground and a few earnestly struggling blades of grass. Her arm in Ellery's, Cynthia swished up the cement walk, cool and aloof in an off-the-shoulder dress of green taffeta. Ellery didn't mind dancing, and the Community Hall struck him as genuinely quaint, but walking into a building full of colonists still made him nervous. It was not fear so much as it was awkwardness and a sense of uncertainty, much as he had felt as a child when he had been cajoled into performing in a grammar-school play before an audience of adults. He had, he recalled all too vividly, dropped his spear and tripped on his toga.

He hoped that the inevitable punch was spiked, but he knew that it wouldn't be.

They made their entrance. Cynthia took the frankly admiring glances of the men in stride, accepting them as her due, and she returned the critical looks from the older females with icy disdain. She held Ellery's arm tightly, possessively.

It seemed to take forever, but eventually the buzz of conversation picked up again and filled up the sudden hush.

The inside of the Community Hall easily fulfilled the promise of its unglittering exterior. Primarily, it was empty space. Along the sides were folding chairs, and upon the chairs were seated the old women of Jefferson Springs. There were two doors at the back of the Community Hall which led to a kitchen. Music was provided by a portable phonograph plugged into a light socket. The phonograph was manned mainly by the high-school crowd, who watched Cynthia with frank speculation. Ellery wondered what she taught the kiddies in home economics.

The records in the Community Hall were somewhat dated, which suited Ellery fine. There was a lot of Glenn Miller, a sprinkling of Harry James, and a minimum of trick novelty records produced for the moron market.

The music played: *On a Little Street in Singapore. At Last. Serenade in Blue.*

Ellery danced, or at least shuffled his feet around. Cynthia politely turned down men who tried to cut in on them, and she felt light and pleasant in his arms. Ellery tried to forget where he was and just enjoy himself. All things considered, he did rather well.

The Community Hall simply wasn't very alien. And the girl in his arms was a beautiful young woman.

Along about eleven o'clock, after too much sweet and fruity punch, one of the boys decided to liven things up a bit. He seemed to be a standard Jefferson Springs product, with huge, rawboned hands dangling out of a too-tight and unfamiliar blue suit, but he had a taste for an upbeat tempo in his music. He diligently plowed through the Community Hall record stacks and turned up a dozen instrumentals. He risked the wrath of the football coach—who wasn't visible at the moment—by lighting a cigarette with airy unconcern. Then he proceeded to play the records, one by one.

He started off with *In the Mood,* and the dance floor cleared as if by magic, Paul started to join the exodus, but Cynthia pulled him back.

"Come on, love," she urged, her face flushed. "Show your stuff."

Ellery did his best, reluctantly at first, but warming to his task as he danced. He had never been the best fast dancer in the world, jitterbugging being an art that he had mastered solely to save himself embarrassment, and it had been a long time since he had really had to work up a sweat on the dance floor.

Watching the few remaining dancers out of the corner of his eye, however, he began to feel better about the whole thing. Unsensational though he was, he was better than *they* were. They were going through the motions easily enough, but they weren't letting themselves go. They seemed slightly uneasy, like a group of wrestlers dancing the minuet.

So, he thought, *there's* one *thing I know more about than they do!*

The music went from *No-Name Jive,* with its hackneyed but effective tenor sax solo, to Harry James's old *Two O'Clock Jump.*

Paul Ellery and Cynthia were alone on the dance floor.

Ellery began to show off. He twirled Cynthia around like a top, and she loved the chance to show off her legs. Ellery really got with it, closing his eyes in pseudo-ecstasy, and contorting himself. Cynthia kept up with him, but by God he was the star of *this* show!

He strutted half the length of the floor, and then the record stopped.

He laughed, his heart thumping merrily.

Then he heard the applause. It came at him from all sides, waves of it. Jefferson Springs was impressed.

Even Cynthia was clapping.

Paul Ellery stopped laughing.

The applause ended, and there was a sudden silence. Conversations started up, a little too quickly, and someone went over to the phonograph and put on a slow record.

Ellery stood very still.

"Oh, Paul!" exclaimed Cynthia, breathing hard. "You were positively *unique!*"

"Shut up." said Ellery.

"Why what's wrong, Paul?" She was smiling.

"Shut up." His voice was louder than he had intended.

Some of the old ladies were looking at him.

He heard a whisper: "Savage!"

Blindly, Paul Ellery pushed his way outside, out of the building, into the cool night air. He stood alone, leaning against the wall. His sweat chilled and he clenched his fists.

Fool! I did it, right there in the middle of *them. I did it, and I was proud of myself!*

An exhibition. An exhibition of primitive dancing.

She made me do it. Damn her soul, she knew what she was doing. She tricked me, showed me off like a smart animal.

Paul Ellery saw red.

He looked around him in the starlight and found two rocks, one for each hand. He gripped them tightly.

He started for the door, where Cynthia stood framed in the yellow light.

He moved through a red haze, step by step.

And then he stopped. The whisper stuck, stinging his ears: *"Savage!"*

He dropped the rocks, listening to them thud when they hit the ground. He stood still, trying to control himself. He stood there for a long time, until he was sure that he was calm.

He was going to show them something about savages.

He didn't have his pipe, so he settled for a cigarette. He lit it with a steady hand; and blew a smoke ring up into the still air. He breathed deeply.

Then, quite casually, he strolled back into the Community Hall. There were three men watching him closely, but he didn't even look at them. He went straight to Cynthia and took her hand. She tensed, first in fear and then in surprise.

Paul Ellery smiled pleasantly. "Come on, dear," he said softly. "Let's go home."

Her blue eyes widened. "So—soon?"

His smile widened. "Not afraid of *me,* are you, Cyn?"

She hesitated. "Of course not."

"Then let's go."

"All right," she said. "All right, Paul."

They went home, to the little house across from the high school. It was a long night, and Ellery never touched her.

By morning, there was a certain respect in Cynthia's eyes.

16

Paul Ellery kept digging.

His job on *The Jefferson Springs Watchguard* didn't take up much of his time. He checked in almost every morning, typed up a story or two, and left. Mr. Stubbs handled the advertising, which was the biggest job on the paper, and how he did it was a mystery to Ellery. He never saw Stubbs move from his precisely-tilted chair, and the old gentleman's eyes remained fixed on the blank wall, as though searching for impudent termites.

As a matter of fact, he supposed that Stubbs had his paper down to such a routine that it was virtually automatic. All of the accounts were handled by mail, and whenever anyone had a bit of news he always brought it in to Stubbs, like a faithful dog with a dead duck.

For a long time, Ellery had been puzzled by the absence of lights at night in Jefferson Springs. The town was never completely dark, except after midnight when everyone was asleep, but on the other hand it was never illuminated properly, either. The houses, particularly, were darker than they should have been. By eight or nine o'clock, there were seldom more than a dozen lights to be seen away from Main Street, and frequently there were none at all. In a town of six thousand, that didn't make sense.

The problem did not turn out to be unduly difficult to solve, once Ellery decided to investigate it. It was surprising, really, he thought, how many questions could be answered if only someone would go out and look. His method was simple, if unheroic. He became a Peeping Tom. He felt like an idiot, but he got his answer.

He spent two nights prowling through the dark streets of Jefferson Springs. He walked by houses first, to find out whether or not there was a dog around, and if he didn't draw any canine howls of fury he went back. The streets were poorly lighted, and except for passing cars, there wasn't enough light to pick him out. He just walked through the yard to the side of the house and looked through the windows. Or tried to.

All the windows had blinds over them, covering what was inside. The blinds were old-fashioned roller types, however, and he could usually find enough of a gap at the sides to look through. He saw very little at first, because the houses were dark, but he stuck with it, and eventually began to spot things.

A glimpse here, a hurried look there. The back of a head, a table, a shadowy figure.

And the blue lights.

Many of the houses were empty, but whenever he found one with people in it he found the blue lights with them. They were simple blue bulbs, as far as he could see, which were screwed into ordinary sockets. They gave off a pale blue light, identical with the blue light he had seen before, that night at the Thorne Ranch.

Around the blue lights were seated the people of Jefferson Springs, ten or more to each occupied house. They sat very still, in chairs or on the floor, and they never spoke. Their eyes were open—he could see them glinting dully in the eerie light—but they were fixed and unseeing.

Ellery listened closely, but he could not hear a sound. If there were any transmitters in operation, they were very quiet.

He never saw one of the meetings start, because they began early and he was afraid to risk sneaking around while it was still light. He did see two of them break up. At an invisible signal—evidently a time lapse of some sort, since it hit them all at the same moment—the people came out of their trances. The host turned off the blue lights and replaced them with plain white light bulbs. There was coffee and casual talk, and then the visitors went back to their own homes.

Ellery stayed hidden. As long as he was careful (and didn't leave town) no one would spot him. The colonists were not omnipotent.

He had enough data now to make some sense out of what he saw. Clearly, the colonists took turns acting as hosts for small groups of people; one night at one house, the next night at another. The blue lights had been used at the community ritual at the Thorne Ranch, and evidently these smaller gatherings served much the same purpose. They were ceremonies, ceremonies with a distinct religious flavor.

How did they work? There was no talk, and no apparatus that Ellery could see. The people just sat down, the blue lights went on, and the people entered into a state of trance. What happened then? Well, the colonists must have been conditioned in such a manner that they could go into a kind of direct voluntary hypnosis by looking into the pale blue lights. Something more than hypnosis, probably, but certainly related to it. What did it accomplish? Ellery was certain that it served to open their minds to some form of suggestion that had been previously implanted in them. Sitting there in the blue lights, they looked at nothing. And they saw—

Who could say? Scenes and events and commands that tied them to the larger whole of which they were a part, experiences that Paul Ellery could only guess at. Experiences he could never know, until he went to the Center.

That was what Centers were for.

The citizens of Jefferson Springs. Watching scenes undreamed of on Earth.

Back in *his* house, Ellery sat alone at the kitchen table and wondered about Cynthia. She, for one, passed up a lot of rituals. Perhaps she wasn't a good citizen. But she had gone to one ceremony, and she had done her bit.

Ellery was making progress. He knew that, and felt a certain satisfaction in it. But he knew, too, that he wasn't making progress fast enough. Still—

He had the key to the alien culture now. His notebook was paying off. His notebook and the long, lonely hours. He had the key.

What made it possible for members of a galactic civilization to live in a primitive culture? How could they possibly spend their lives going through the motions of what was, to them, an alien life? How did the galactic colonial system *work*?

It wasn't a masquerade. That was the first thing to remember. These people, up to a certain point, believed in the lives they were living. These were their lives, and this was their culture. It had to be.

But it wasn't their *only* culture. That was the catch.

What the galactic administration had done was to indoctrinate its colonists with a hard core of civilized premises and beliefs. That was the skeleton, the same for every citizen, no matter where he might live. On top of that core of culture, the administration had grafted the customs and habits of the area to which the colonist was to be sent. That was the face and flesh and fingerprints, different for every citizen as it was for every human being.

It took some doing, of course. There was plenty of opposition. The whole scheme would have been utterly impossible in an uncivilized society. That, however, was just the point: these people were civilized.

They had learned, long ago, that it was the cultural core that counted—the deep and underlying spirit and belief and knowledge, the tone and essence of living. Once you had that, the rest was window dressing. Not only that, but the rest, the cultural superstructure, *was relatively equal in all societies.*

Human beings, by virtue of being human beings, had certain structural "musts" that had to find outlets. They had to eat and sleep and mate. All societies provided for such needs. And if you were conditioned to live in one specific society, you did it in the way the society specified, and you liked it—because that was your way, too. Beyond those basic needs, all cultures provided systems of handling the products of group living. Families? They could be monogamous or polygamous, matrilineal or patrilineal. You liked the one you were brought up in. Economy? It might be hunting or fishing or raising crops or buying food in a can. You liked what you were used to. The arts? They might include beating on a log drum, dancing in masks, or reading books. You were pleased by what you had been trained to like.

The colonists had the core. Beyond that, they could be taught to live with any cultural trapping—*and they could be happy in any society in which human beings could be happy.*

The core of civilized culture was reinforced and kept alive by community rituals that maintained contact with the mother culture. The techniques varied from society to society, but the purpose was always the same, and it worked, within human limits. It worked because the galactic administration knew what it was doing. It worked because the civilization involved had learned enough to pull it off.

It worked, too, because the really intelligent and successful citizens attained responsible positions in their native cultures. In a word, they stayed home, or worked in the Galactic Fleet. The ones who were farmed out to the colonies as population overflow were the weak and the dull and the uncaring—and the misfits. That wasn't the way it was planned, but that was the way it worked.

Adults were conditioned in the Centers before they were permitted to move into colonies. Children who were born in the colonies were indoctrinated by the colonies at the same time that they received instruction in the culture in which they found themselves and then before maturity they were sent "home" for intensive training and conditioning for a period of three Earth-years.

Paul Ellery had the key to the alien culture. He understood it as well as any outsider could ever hope to understand it.

But what could he do with his key?

How could he *use* it?

He didn't know.

And so he went on, doing the best he could, while time ran out on him. He was convinced now that he wasn't going to *find* any secret weapon that would turn defeat into victory. He didn't give up, but he did reaffirm his earlier decision.

He did it, oddly enough, at a football game. It was the last one of the season, and it was played on Thanksgiving. Jefferson Springs was playing Eagle Pass. The game was played at night, as always, under the lights. This was because the merchants were all busy on Saturday or holiday afternoons, when the ranchers came to town; and the games drew bigger crowds at night.

Ellery went with Cynthia, who looked fresh and young and almost innocent in skirt and sweater and loafers. He had a good seat and he enjoyed the game. Texas high-school football was rough, tough, and fast. It was played for blood. The fields were apt to be pitted and rock-strewn, the bands were customarily out of tune, and the pep squads were more strident than effective. But the games were good and hard and well played.

Cynthia watched with complete detachment, although she uttered the correct noises at the proper times. Ellery, who had been under the lights himself a long time ago, was quieter than he should have been, because he was rooting for the wrong team. He was pulling, desperately, for Eagle Pass.

They had two brothers, Dave and Tom Toney, at quarterback and halfback. They were good, giving all they had and then some, and Ellery cheered them silently.

Come on, Dave, he thought, *come on, Tom. Sock it to 'em!*

Dave and Tom socked it.

Ellery felt a thrill of pride. The Jefferson Springs boys played earnestly, but they lacked the sparkle. They felt a bit superior, and that was deadly. Eagle Pass surprised them, with a bruising line and a tricky backfield.

Come on, Dave; come on, Tom!

The lights on the towers soaked the field and hid the stars. The creaky wooden grandstands swayed whenever the fans stood up and hollered. The referee blew his whistle, and the yardage chain moved up and down the sidelines, following the ball.

Ellery kept his fingers crossed. He was still an outsider. He didn't belong to Jefferson Springs. He didn't even belong to Eagle Pass, but he felt closer to them. They, at least, had been his kind.

Ellery watched the field and wrestled with his thoughts. He decided, again, what he had to do.

Sock it to 'em!

He could not go on living a life without meaning. He could not go back to Anne and live a life in a zoo. He could not bring children into a world in which they would live on a reservation, devoting their lives to finding out things already a million years forgotten by others, facing a frightful future in which cities disappeared in a searing flash.

There was no secret weapon that he could find. The galactic set-up was simply too prodigious to be overthrown by one man, and particularly not by an ignorant savage.

He would keep trying, yes, because he had to. But if he could not come up with a real solution to his problem by the time the aliens decided to send him to the Center, there was just one thing to do. He would go to the Center and make no fuss about it.

After that, he wouldn't be Paul Ellery any more.

Come on, Dave; come on, Tom!

Now that it was lost to him, his world looked pretty good. He thought of it, with all its laughter and sadness and beauty and squalor, and he wanted it. He wanted it very much.

But not a world without purpose or meaning. Life was too tough if it was all for nothing.

Maybe he wouldn't have to be another Hamilton Withrow—Withrow, probably, hadn't been any prize specimen even before the "full treatment." Maybe he could even be another John. He liked John. It would be better than the life he was living now—tolerated, but not a part of things. Any culture was better than none, if you believed in it. And he *would* believe in it, after the Center. No doubt about that.

Attaboy, Dave! Attaway, Tom!

Eagle Pass won, and whooped jubilantly off the field. It was Thanksgiving, and in his own way Ellery give thanks. He was proud of his boys.

Dammit, there must be *some* way! If only he had more time...

Someone tapped him on the shoulder as he stood up. He turned around. It was Samuel Cartwright, portly and with his pink face gleaming with shaving lotion. The mayor of Jefferson Springs.

"'Lo, Cynthia," he said, with just the trace of a lisp in his speech. "Good to see you, Paul. How are you getting along?"

"Fine," lied Paul Ellery. "I'm getting along fine."

"Mighty good," said Mayor Cartwright. "I'm happy to hear that. By the way, Paul—"

"Yes?"

"I wonder if you'd drop around to my office tomorrow—you know where it is, over in the Court House. I'd like to talk to you a bit."

"What about?"

"Oh, a few plans for your future, and things like that. It's important that you be there, Paul. You know."

"I know," said Paul Ellery, his heart sinking. "I'll be there."

"Fine," said Mayor Cartwright. "I'm sure our talk will be satisfactory."

Cynthia smiled.

17

The Jefferson Springs Court House stood alone, its brick arms outstretched to try to cover a city block. It was a relatively modern-looking structure, and it had an air of distinct surprise about it, as though it still had not recovered from the shock of finding itself in Jefferson Springs. It stood on a side street, just across from the water tower. It was surrounded by elderly gentlemen engaged in an endless contest to determine the best and most consistent expectorator in Jefferson Springs.

Mayor Cartwright perched in haughty aloofness in an office on the second floor. To prove with crushing conclusiveness that he was a politician not to be ignored, he had both a water cooler and an open box of cigars in his office.

Paul Ellery waited until almost ten to give the great man plenty of time to settle himself in his sanctum, and then knocked on his door.

"Come in, come in!" urged the Mayor, in his best never-too-busy-for-my-constituents voice.

Ellery went in.

Samuel Cartwright shook his hand and offered him a cigar. Ellery took it, out of politeness, although he was not overly fond of cigars.

"Close the door, Paul. That's the spirit. Now sit down, take a load off your feet. There. Nice day, mighty nice."

Powerful nice," Ellery said.

"Yes, sir. Go on Paul—light up that old cigar! I like to see a man comfortable. No airs in *my* office, son. I'm a plain man."

Everybody calls me "son," thought Ellery. *What kind of biology do they have where they come from?*

Mayor Cartwright flicked on a lighter that actually worked, no doubt a product of alien super-science, and set Ellery's cigar on fire.

"Thank you," said Ellery, and blew out a big cloud of smoke to prove that he was enjoying the cigar.

"You're mighty welcome, Paul. Now we can get down to business. I reckon you know why you're here, Paul."

"More or less. I hope I haven't done anything wrong?"

"Not at all, son, not at all. Your conduct, if I may say so, has been exemplary."

True blue, that's me. "Nice of you to say so, Mayor."

"I know it hasn't been easy for you, Paul," the Mayor said slowly, speaking carefully to avoid his lisp. "You've been with us now for almost six months, and you've been in a difficult position. It isn't easy for a man to throw away his old life and start in on a new one. All of us know that, Paul. We've been through it ourselves."

"I guess you have, at that."

"We surely have. We've been watching you, and you've handled yourself very well. However, we have found it advisable not to prolong the adjustment any longer than necessary. A man can't do it all by himself. There comes a time when he needs help. There comes a time when he has to get off the beach and swim in deep water."

"You're right, of course," said Ellery.

Cartwright puffed on his cigar. "That's what the Center is for, Paul. It's to help *you*. We want you to understand that. We ourselves have had to go through Centers, and we send our own children to them. It will take a few years, and there is a certain discipline that you will have to put up with, but in the long view it's all for the best."

"When do I start?"

"As it happens, there will be a convoy ship in this area very early on the first of January—about one o'clock in the morning, I believe. You'll be picked up in a sphere just outside of town, on Jim Walls's ranch. After that, you'll be under Center jurisdiction until they judge that you're ready to come back and take your place in society. I'm fairly sure that you'll be assigned to Earth, since you are already familiar with the customs and the language here, but of course that will be up to them. You'll be leaving on New Year's Day, actually." He smiled proudly. "Rather a nice touch of symbolism, I think."

"Very nice."

"You'll see things and experience things and learn things that are beyond your imagination, Paul. It will be more than a whole new world—it will be a whole new *universe*. And when you come back, you'll be one of us—really one of us. You will have to take my word for the fact that when you come back, Jefferson Springs will seem very different to you. You have barely seen the surface here, Paul. When you return your real life will begin."

"I understand that."

"I'm sure you do. And Paul—"

"Yes?"

"When you come back, you will of course be under our laws—or the laws of some other colony. You may have observed that they can be rather strict under some circumstances. I'm not threatening you, understand; the necessity for our laws will be impressed upon you at the Center. I'm sure that you can see that our position requires diligent law enforcement. This is, you realize, as much for the protection of the natives as for our own safeguarding. Until you leave here, you are legally classed as a native, if you'll excuse my frankness, and you are protected under our laws. We have taken pains to explain your legal position to you previously. If you have any intention of changing your mind about taking advantage of our offer, Paul, now's the time to do it. You can leave now, and still be under Administration protection as a native of Earth. But it will be too late once you board the Center ship, and when you come back you will not, of course, be quite the—same."

"I've made up my mind," said Ellery.

"Fine. Mighty fine. I'm sure everything will go smoothly for you. Until the ship picks you up, just keep right on at your job, and I hope that things will not be unpleasant for you."

"You've all been very kind."

"Well, we *try* to do the decent thing, Paul. We really do. Our position here has its own difficulties, and we take considerable pains, if I may say so, to conduct ourselves like civilized men and women."

"I appreciate it."

"All right, Paul. I'll probably see you again before you leave. The best of luck to you."

He shook Ellery's hand again, and Ellery left the Court House. When Ellery was safely away from both the building and the spitters, he carefully took the cigar from his mouth and ground it under his heel.

Well, now he knew.

He had a little over a month left. Thirty-odd days to be Paul Ellery.

It would be very easy to give up and take what was coming. He could almost do it now. A man could butt his head against a stone wall for only so long, and then he discovered that the wall wasn't going to come down.

He endured some chili and crackers at the Jefferson Springs Cafe, risking a volcanic eruption in his stomach, and then he went to work.

It was one in the afternoon when he checked into his office. Abner Jeremiah Stubbs placed both feet firmly on the plank floor and hauled out his big gold watch. He examined it distastefully, replaced it, and adjusted his green eye shade.

"Official business," Ellery explained. "I had to see the Mayor."

"You had to see the Mayor," Mr. Stubbs repeated, placing each word under a mental microscope. "You—had—to—see—the—Mayor."

"You've got the essence of it, Abner."

"My name, young man, is *Mister* Stubbs."

"But your friends call you Abner, isn't that right? Well, am I or am I not your friend? Now I'll get to work and write your front page for you. We can go to press early tomorrow."

"Well," said Mr. Stubbs, pleased. "Getting ink in your veins, eh son? I knew you had the makings of a newspaper man."

"Thank you, Abner," said Ellery.

He proceeded back to his office and heard the creak of the chair which indicated that Mr. Stubbs had resumed his customary tilt and had engaged his attention with the opposite wall. Ellery forced open the window, which seemed to close itself by magic every night. It was getting a little chilly, but the room was too stuffy to work in with all the windows shut.

He sat down before his venerable typewriter, stuck in a yellow sheet, and went to work.

One month to go.

HOME TALENT RODEO PLANNED.

Would Cynthia be waiting for him, if he came back? Did he *want* her to be?

NELLIE FAYE MOSELY WEDS BILLY JOE ADAMS IN CHURCH SERVICE.

Who were the Others? Where were they, what were they like, what did they have to do with all this? Why had he screamed when he had sensed them that night?

LOVELY PARTY IS COMPLIMENT TO CARRIE SUE ROBERTS.

What was John's role in all this? He had more than one, Ellery was certain, but *what were they?*

The phone rang. His phone. It was an ancient instrument in the corner, and he could not reach it from where he sat. It *never* rang. Ellery hadn't even been positive the thing was connected.

He got up and answered it.

"Yes?"

"Mr. Paul Ellery?"

"Speaking."

"We have a long-distance call for you from Austin, Texas. Hold the line please."

Ellery fumbled for a chair and sat down. Austin—

"Hello. Paul? Paul, is that you?"

Anne. His hand began to sweat.

"Yes, Annie. This is me."

"Paul, what on earth are you doing in a newspaper office? I called information and they said that's where you'd be. Paul, what are you doing?"

Mr. Stubbs's chair squeaked in the other room.

"I can't explain just now, Annie. But I'm okay. Don't worry."

"Paul, you sound so far away! Ell, this is Annie."

"I know, hon. It's hard to talk right now."

"Ell, I want to see you. I've got to see you."

"I want to see you, too, Annie. You know I do."

"I don't mean to be nosey, baby, but you haven't written or phoned or anything. Have you gotten my letters?"

"Yes. Yes, I've gotten them."

"Paul, I know it's none of my business. But it's been so long! You know I've tried never to bother you—but—but we've been so close—and I thought—"

"Yes, Annie."

"Ell, could I come down? Just for a little while? I know you must be busy and everything, but I could catch the bus here—I could come Friday and maybe we could drive back together—that isn't asking very much, is it Paul?"

"No, hon. It isn't asking anything at all."

"Can I come? Shall I come? I hate to be so silly—"

"Annie."

"What?"

"Annie, you can't come here."

"Paul, what's *wrong?*"

"I can't explain, I just can't."

"My gosh, you don't have to be so *mysterious* about everything! You talk like you were phoning from Dracula's castle or something. Why *can't* I come down?"

"You just can't, baby. If I could tell you why, I would."

"You—you mean you don't *want* me to come. Is that it, Paul?"

Ellery felt the floor spinning under him. *Go ahead, damn you,* he told himself. *Go ahead and act as if you don't care. Make her hate you. It's the only thing you can do for her now. Be decent for once in your life. Think of somebody else, just once.*

"Is that it, Paul?"

"Yes, Annie;' he said. "I'm afraid that's it."

Silence. A silence that rocked the room.

"Paul?"

"Yes, Annie."

"I loved you, Paul. I really loved you."

She hung up. The *click* in his ear sounded like an explosion.

Ellery slowly put the receiver back on the hook. He went over and took the yellow paper out of his typewriter. He gathered up his stories, and handed them to Mr. Stubbs, who was standing in the doorway.

"Easy does it, Paul," Mr. Stubbs said softly.

"Thanks, Abner."

He hurried outside to a pale afternoon sun. He walked fast, away from the office, not going anywhere special.

Just walking.

His eyes were stinging in the chilly air, and it was hard for him to see.

18

For Paul Ellery, time ticked itself out.

The days between Thanksgiving and Christmas had always gone fast for him. He could remember, in school, that the two holidays seemed to come so close together that they almost merged into one. He had never thought much about Christmas coming at the end of the year. It was just a needed break in the routine of classwork, a pleasant time of friendship and relaxation, and then before you knew it New Year's Eve had come again.

New Year's Eve was a party night. It was a night he had spent with Annie for—how long now?

A night of champagne, a night of laughs.

A night of auld lang syne.

A night of fun.

He had never really thought of it as the end of a year. To be sure, he had to remind himself to change a numeral when he was dating letters, but that was about all. He had always religiously skipped the tired editorials and the unfunny radio comedies about New Year's resolutions.

But now it was ending. An ending of his life, and of the Paul Ellery he had known.

It had been a chill, rainy December, and now it was Christmas Eve. Seven days left.

He had worked at his notebooks, half-heartedly, but he wasn't getting anywhere. The secret weapon stayed a secret. More likely, it wasn't even there.

It was seven o'clock in the evening—a nothing hour that was like the phrase someone had coined about the countryside between the cities, an hour that seemed to be designed as a gap between something and something else. It was already dark in Jefferson Springs, and there was little to indicate that it was an evening different from other evenings. Jefferson Springs hadn't even bothered to string up the colored lights and paper bells with which other small Texas towns tried to hide the fact that it almost never snowed in their part of the country.

Ellery had hoped that Cynthia would call, but she was busy somewhere else. He was pretty damned lonesome, and he didn't know what he could do about it.

He didn't have any presents, because they had all been sent to his home. He didn't even think about going home. Somehow, childishly, he missed his presents. He felt forgotten. He knew that it was strictly his own choice, but that didn't help much.

He did have a radio, and he let it play, just for the hell of it. He heard Santa Claus. Santa, it seemed, was spending Christmas Eve in front of the Alamo in San Antonio, and was sponsored this year by a big department store.

Ellery tried another station.

This time he got Christmas carols. They had a sort of melancholy beauty, but they depressed him terribly. He tried again, and suffered through a drama about a mean old man who was just pure gold way down deep, especially when he heard bells and smelled turkey, and whose crusty manner concealed a deep-rooted and decidedly senile sentimentality toward all small children, all homeless dogs, and certain selected cats.

At eight-thirty, there was a knock on his door.

He got up, hoping that it was Cynthia, and swung the door open. It wasn't Cynthia. Instead, like a scene from an old play, it was the two men who had twice escorted him to the great spaceship that hovered over the Earth. The only difference was that this time the perpetual pipesmoker was not smoking.

"Well, gentlemen," Ellery said, glad to see anybody, "won't you come in?"

They hesitated. "We brought you a note," said the one who didn't smoke a pipe.

"Come in anyhow," Ellery insisted. "You know, I must be an awful lot of trouble for you two."

They smiled, almost bashfully. "Not at all," said the pipesmoker. They came in, a bit reluctantly, and sat down on the couch. Ellery took his message, an ordinary white envelope, and tore it open. There was a single sheet of paper inside, with a typed note on it:

"Christmas Eve is no time to be alone. The Scotch is ready. Come on up and we can cuss out Withrow. John."

Ellery felt better. Much better.

"You know," he said to the two men, "I don't even know your names."

The pipesmoker said: "I'm Bob. He's Clark."

Maybe their specialty isn't conversation. "How about some wine, before we go back? Bob? Clark?"

"No thanks," said Clark. "We're on duty, you know."

"Thanks anyway," said Bob. "We're still working our way up, and that sort of thing can lead to trouble."

"Okay," said Ellery. "You know best."

He turned off the radio without regret, and switched on the porch light. After that, the journey was like the others. They got in the big black Buick—did the car stay out in the fields between trips, or what?—and drove out of town. This time the metallic sphere was resting on the Walls Ranch just outside of town. The thing was almost invisible, actually; even when you knew it was there, you could hardly see it until you were almost on top of it. They entered through the panel, and the elevator lifted, buoyantly, up into the night.

Ellery did get one piece of information out of the two men. Bob had fired up his pipe again, with an almost audible sigh of relief. Feeling expansive, he said: "You know, you're quite exceptional, Mr. Ellery."

"How do you mean?"

"I've never seen the old man take such an interest in one of the—in one of the—"

"Natives," supplied Ellery, smiling.

"Yes. Pardon me, I meant no offense."

"Forget it. Facts are facts."

Bob nodded, admiringly. "The old man is—hard to get to know," he said. "He must like you."

Clark nudged his companion, and Bob said nothing more. Ellery gathered that dealing with the natives was apt to be a tricky sort of business. As a general rule, no doubt, it was left to trained contact men like John. Ellery hoped that he wasn't just part of a day's work for John, but it was hard to tell.

Still, there *did* seem to be something more at stake, even though he was unsure as to what it was. John did his job, of course, but that wasn't *all* he did.

Well, if John had something up his sleeve he would have to shake it out this time. Paul Ellery wasn't going to be around much longer.

The globe hummed into the invisible ship and stopped. There was a muffled thump as it locked into place. The sliding panel opened, and the yellowish ship light flowed in.

The two men stood aside and let Ellery find his own way. He walked through the interlocking passage and into the long hallway with the closed panels. He walked down its spotless length, the vast ship throbbing ever so slightly around him, and stepped toward the heavy door set flush with the wall. The door opened without a sound, and Paul Ellery walked into John's sanctum.

The little fat man was seated behind his desk, his feet propped on a spare chair, reading a magazine. He looked up eagerly, and slammed the magazine down with a gesture of supreme irritation.

"Propaganda, that's what it is," he snorted. "Propaganda! Paul, I'm glad you could come. Damn glad!"

"Thanks," said Ellery, warming to the man's bursting personality. He shook his hand, firmly. "It was very kind of you to ask me to come."

"*Nonsense,* Paul. Nonsense and garbage! Don't you think I ever get lonesome up here?"

"Well," said Ellery, sitting down in the chair in front of the desk, "you have your job, your friends, all that."

"My friends are mutton heads," announced John. "I seem to recall that you like Scotch, so I've requisitioned a new supply. It's quite good, really, for a primitive drink. Got a kick to it, a little of the old sock. We're getting soft, sophisticated. Ought to get back to fundamentals."

He poured out two drinks, downed his own at once, and poured himself another one.

Ellery felt himself relaxing, forgetting his troubles. *Therapy,* he thought. *John's a pretty fair country doctor.*

"I see you're reading science fiction again," Ellery said, indicating the crushed magazine on John's desk.

John leaped at the bait, eagerly.

"Incredible," muttered the fat man indignantly. "Absolutely fascinating at its best, but so fantastically far off the beam so much of the time."

John polished off his second Scotch. Ellery, knowing John of old, fished out his pipe, lit it, and settled back for the deluge. But even as he settled back, he thought: *He brought me here for a reason. This is his last chance. If he's ever going to do anything, it will have to be now.*

John, however, seemed splendidly unaware of the role he was supposed to play. He was off on his pet peeve. He surged to his feet, bristling, and picked up the science-fiction magazine.

"Look at that," he ordered, holding up the cover. *"Look at that."*

Ellery looked, without much interest, humoring his host. The cover portrayed a bald gentleman with a swollen head. The bald gentleman was staring intently at a wrench, which was hanging in the air, fastening a bolt.

"You *see?*" demanded John.

"Well," said Ellery, "what is it?"

"It's a superman, dammit!" John exclaimed. "I *hate* supermen!"

The fat little man with the red face took another hefty pull at the Scotch and began to pace up and down his office. There was something compelling about the man, something dynamic, something that held your attention riveted to him. He held you, even when he was off on one of his crazy tangents, even when your mind was watching in amazed wonder, asking—

Why?

"You hate supermen," Ellery said. When at a loss for words of your own, he had long ago decided, you could always repeat the other fellow's. He tried to keep his voice matter-of-fact, but as far as he was concerned he might just as well have said, "You hate manhole covers." "Go on from there."

"Yes. Where was I? Ah, yes. Now, I'm a fair-minded man. I would be the last to condemn a craftsman for failing to incorporate in his work data that were unknown at the time he wrote. You wouldn't yell at Shakespeare because he didn't write a story about the hydrogen bomb, would you?"

"No, I wouldn't."

Ellery watched the little man—earnest, red-faced, pot-bellied, a fringe of hair girdling his balding head. John was a bundle of paradoxes. He was a man out of the future, but he resembled nothing so much as a jovial monk or friar from the Earth of long ago. He was frantic and incredible, but he was genuine. He kept out of reach, tossing around ideas that were irrelevant beyond belief, and yet he was communicating something, something that had to be said.

"You look here," John said, waving the magazine. "I don't mind when writers get to yakking about ridiculous mutations that take place without benefit of genetics, that just happen in the 'germ plasm' every time an atom bomb cuts loose. I don't mind when they blithely blow up whole planets filled with intelligent life just to keep the story going. I don't mind racial memories and Atlantis and *psi* factors. I don't mind when they portray everything in outer space as a ghastly monster. I don't object at all when I am depicted as a fiend, damn them. I *do* mind their confounded mutant supermen who take the normal, mixed-up kiddies by the hand and lead them forward to the promised land. Supermen *stink.*"

"Oh?"

"A profound observation. Look here, Paul. You're supposed to be a scientist, right?"

"I was, yes."

"You are, yes. Now, if that brain of yours has not atrophied from lack of use, what do you think about a theory that postulates that man progresses because his brain gets bigger and better? Do you think that the next great advance of mankind will come about because of some mutant superman who points the way ahead, like Og, Son of Fire?"

Ellery considered, puffing on his pipe. "I think the theory's wrong," he said.

John sat down in sheer exasperation. "Listen, Paul," he said, "you *know* that theory is wrong. You want some proof?"

"Sure."

John stood up again. *"I'm* proof. Confound it, man, do I have to hit you over the head with it? I represent a civilization as far superior to yours as yours is to the Cro-Magnons'. Here I am, Paul! Am I a superman? Hardly. Am I in any physical way superior to you? Absurd—you could demolish me with one swat. And I *assure* you I cannot read your mind, and have not the slightest desire to do so."

"Okay, John, but what's—"

"Don't rush me." John sat down again, and helped himself to the Scotch. "I'm going to tell you a story. You already know it, but I'll tell it anyhow. On this planet called Earth, a very old but never tiresome story is in progress. Its hero is an animal called man. We'll just dispense with all man's forerunners here—I'm talking about H. Sapiens, Esquire. Call him Cro-Magnon when we first look in on him; it's as good a name as any. There he is, living in caves, existing as a big-game hunter. *His brain is as good as yours, or mine.* Now, let's take a snapshot here and there, at long intervals. Our hero discovers agriculture. He becomes a food producer. His small village expands. A more complex technology develops, and specialists appear, and new kinds of social organization. Man has an Industrial Revolution. He lives in cities, a fact which we have utilized to our own advantage. He splits the atom, a fact which may also be utilized to our advantage. That is the first chapter of the story, Paul. The rest of the book has yet to unfold here on Earth, but elsewhere in the galaxy man has gone on to become a relatively civilized animal. *His brain is still the same.* It doesn't change much, because, as I have attempted to point out to you, *man doesn't change that way.* What *did* change, Paul?"

"His culture, of course," Ellery said, feeling a little foolish. "His way of life."

"*Very* good, Paul. Applause. His brain stayed the same—but it had more to work with as man learned more and more. Now, does man inherit his culture?"

"No. It's historically produced. He learns it." Ellery felt like a singularly dull freshman.

"Fine. Very good. You people are bugs on supermen. It's a very common primitive trait. Have another drink."

Ellery had another.

John put his feet back up on the chair and peered at Ellery intently. "You should think more about man, Paul. Plain old everyday man. He's a remarkable animal."

Ellery waited for John to go on, but John just looked at him, smiling.

"You didn't bring me here tonight just for the hell of it," Ellery said. "I don't know just what your part in all this is, John, but I know there's something that you want me to do. There isn't much time left. You've been talking—"

"That's right," the little fat man said. "I've been doing all the talking, haven't I? And I have accomplished two purposes. The first was to take your mind off yourself. The second was to give you the solution to your problem."

Paul Ellery stared at him, his pipe forgotten in his hand.

19

Christmas Eve had long since turned into Christmas.

The vast bulk of the spaceship floated high in the darkness above the sleeping Earth. It was a shadow, undetected and unseen, slipping through the shifting air currents as a mighty fish might balance itself in a shadowed sea. It moved without sound, wrapped in an envelope of force, proud and aloof over the dark villages it had seeded from the stars.

Alone in one tiny crevice within the leviathan that could swim to the shores of the galaxy, the two men talked.

The talk went on—seemingly trivial in a universe vast beyond understanding, just as the Earth was a trivial thing in a galaxy that had passed her by.

But trivia was slippery stuff to define.

Trivia had an unpleasant habit of turning into something else. Trivia was all art and literature and music and love and science, while all sensible people knew that it was battles and wars and headlines that were really important.

All trivia did was to build civilizations.

Sometimes, though, it seemed a little slow. To Ellery, it didn't seem to be moving at all. "Look here, John," he said, "this is one devil of a time to be playing games."

The fat man shrugged. "Depends on what game you're playing," he said.

Ellery helped himself to more Scotch. He was keyed up and tired at the same time, and he had reached that early-morning stage in which a few drinks one way or the other didn't make much difference.

"Let's just pretend that I am a small and rather dull child," he said. "You bring me up here when I have only a few days left before going though a mental meat-grinder, and you tell me why supermen strike you as illogical. You're a good talker, John, and I like to listen to you. But then you tell me that you've just solved my problem for me. Now, unless I'm greatly mistaken, my problem is a simple one. I've got to decide in six days whether or not I'm going to the Center. If I do, I start a new life, with new values. If I don't, I go back to live a life that has become meaningless for me. I can't live like that. You yourself told me, not so very long ago, what I should do. You said: 'If you can't beat 'em, join 'em.' If you've solved that problem, you're going to have to spell it out for me. I haven't got time for riddles."

John frowned, as though disappointed. "I had hopes for you, Paul, or I wouldn't have bothered with all this. I *still* have hopes for you. Let me draw you a small parallel, to help you understand my position. You have been a teacher yourself—I don't know whether you were good, bad, or indifferent, but I suspect that you were indifferent. But let's talk about a *good* teacher. If he's got a student who he thinks has some brains, he can give that student some facts to chew on. He can point out lines of inquiry that may bear fruit. But he can't do *all* the work. The student has got to relate the facts for himself, or else they will never mean anything to him. Most students never do forge a coherent whole out of the information that gets stuffed into them. Sometimes that's the teacher's fault, Paul. And sometimes it's the student's."

"Okay, okay," Ellery said impatiently. "So where are the facts?"

John sighed.

The aborigines are slow, Ellery thought. *You have to lead them step by step.*

"Let's do a little spelling-out then," John said. "We'll start with fundamentals. I am a man." He waved his hand. "No, I'm not making fun of you. You go ahead and get irritated if you wish, but don't let it keep you from thinking a little."

"Sorry," said Ellery. He refilled his pipe and lit it.

John said, "Very well. I am a man. As a man, I was by chance born into the culture in which you find me, and into a society with its customs and laws and policies. As a man, I have a job to do—I am employed, if you wish. Since I have a certain knack for getting along with natives, I am used by my government in contact work when such is needed. In my official capacity, I first met you. I gave you the business, and I flatter myself that I did it rather well. Now, however, I am not in my official capacity. Now I am trying to talk to you as a man."

"I see," said Ellery. "But can't you be more explicit? If you overestimate my abilities, we won't get very far."

John smiled. "If I have overestimated your abilities," he said, "then you are of no use one way or the other."

Ellery absorbed that. He was getting a bit tired of being patronized, but he knew that John was not doing it without a purpose. There were some people you had to sting into giving the best that was in them.

"I'll tell you why I can't be more explicit," John said. "To put it in a convenient nutshell, I am a law-abiding citizen. I *have* to be. I have not the slightest intention of trying to overthrow my government, and couldn't do it if I wanted to."

Ellery waited, almost hopelessly. If he was going to get anything useful, it would have to be soon. *Very* soon.

John drummed his fingers on his desk. "I'm not much of an idealist, son," he said. "My life has not left me starry-eyed and panting about the fate of the downtrodden. I'm not a reformer. I like to think that I'm a practical man, just as you are."

"What do you mean by practical?"

John brightened visibly. "Ah, semantics! A brain cell has stirred into reluctant life!"

"Dammit, John, climb off your high horse." Ellery smiled. "How would you like a swat on the kisser?"

John laughed, delighted. "Wouldn't bother me in the slightest," he assured him. "And it certainly wouldn't help *you*. But I like your attitude. It's a great improvement. Dish it out a little, Paul. You don't progress by just taking it."

"I'll send your sentiments to Edgar Guest."

John suddenly slammed his fist down with a bang on his desk. He stood up, and Ellery changed his mind in a hurry about what a pushover John might be in a fight.

"Practical!" he snorted. "I'll tell you what's practical. It's just one damned thing: being smart enough to survive. Not just you and me—we're nothing. But all of us, everybody! If man survives he's been practical. If he doesn't, he goes down the drain. What do you think of that?"

"Sounds good. What does it mean, specifically?"

"It means, my friend, that the civilization which I have the honor to represent is typical of man in every way. It's a pack of howling jackasses galloping over a cliff! We've made a lot of so-called progress. We've got spaceships and planets and gadgets a million years ahead of anything on that speck of dirt under our feet. And so what, Paul? I repeat: *so what?*"

Ellery smoked his pipe. Invisibly, he crossed his fingers.

John sat down again and folded his hands patiently. "You already have all the facts you need," he said. "You're supposed to be a scientist. Let me ask you a question. What is the one sure thing about colonial policies, in the long run? The one thing you can always count on?"

Paul Ellery said slowly: "They don't work."

"Fine!" John banged his fist down again and helped himself to most of what was left of the Scotch. "You see before you a civilization that covers the galaxy. You see technological triumphs that you can barely understand. And what are you caught up in the big fat middle of, son? A colony! A backward planet taken over as a colony! You see nothing fantastic about that, Paul? Eh? You see nothing fantastic?"

"I guess I've been a little stupid," Ellery said. His brain was churning, trying to digest what it had swallowed.

"Of course you've been stupid! You're a man, aren't you? What other animal could make the same mistake a billion times and still be around to talk about it?"

"You said," Ellery reminded him carefully, "that you were a law-abiding citizen."

"You bet I am. Most human beings are. That doesn't mean that I have to *agree* with all the laws I live under. If everybody had always agreed that current ideas were the ultimate in human wisdom, we would all still be huddled in caves. Indeed, son, we never would have *reached* the caves! Still, as I have pointed out before, I am a non-political person." He smiled. "Practically."

"And now—what?"

"Now," John told him, "I'm going to show you something. I have, in my small way, tried to set you to thinking about the Others. I hope that the problem has interested you?"

"Of course. What are they?"

"That," said John, "is what I'm going to show you."

The tireless little man surged up from behind his messy desk and led the way across the room, like a halfback leading the interference. Paul Ellery followed in his wake, and hoped he could find out where the ball was.

They passed through the sliding door into the corridor, and John set a fast pace through the ship. They passed a number of men and women, none of whom paid much attention to them. The ship was lighted normally; there seemed to be no difference between night and day on it. Or perhaps they hadn't bothered to adjust themselves to the daily cycle of Earth.

They hustled down long, antiseptic passageways, past a confusing multiplicity of doors, panels, and branching tunnels. They rode on elevators and walked up ramps. Finally, when Ellery judged that they were very high in the floating ship—he almost expected the air to be thinner—they came to a stop before a large, closed door.

There was a guard here—the first one that Ellery had noticed anywhere on the ship. The guard nodded to John, but looked a question at Ellery.

"He's with me," John said. "Everything's all right."

The guard said something, not in English, and activated the door. It slid open noiselessly and John led Ellery inside. Behind them, the door closed again.

The room was not large, and looked almost like a standard projection room. There were some twenty rows of comfortable seats, all of which faced one end of the room. At that end, replacing the standard white screen that would have been found on Earth, was a square of cloudy gray. The square was not just a surface, but was rather an area of well-defined substance, like thick, tinted air, gently in motion.

The two men sat down in the front row. John pressed a combination of buttons in the arm of his chair.

"Meet the Others," he said.

All the lights went out.

The gray square turned a milky white and seemed to fill the room.

Involuntarily, Ellery narrowed his eyes to slits against the smokelike stuff, but there was no sensation.

The milky white shifted into a sharp gray-black. Quite suddenly, Ellery caught his breath and felt a distinct sensation of falling. He held on tightly to the arms of his chair, but the chair was falling too. He tried to breathe and there was no air. There was only a vast black tunnel, bigger than the world, and he was falling down it, head first, toward a billion flashlights that picked him out and blinded him as he fell—

Faster and faster—

He saw three sleek spaceships swimming ahead of him. His eyes fastened on them, desperately. Perspective returned. He could breathe.

The spaceships looked like gray minnows, lost in immensity. They edged along the jet black tunnel, toward the staring flashlights that were a huge spray of stars.

The tunnel widened and became deep space itself. The lights flowed together and made an eye-searing splash of frozen flame. Around the edges, there was a scattering of lesser stars.

This was not the galaxy that had given birth to man.

The three ships slipped on through the clinging ink, with tiny white spots of atomic fire bubbling from their tails. Their movement was lost against the Gargantuan scale, but the splash and drops of light came closer.

There was something else.

Ellery could not quite see it. But he hunched back against his chair, and he wished that he could close his eyes.

He almost saw it. He wanted to scream. He remembered that night, a million years ago, that night in the pale blue lights....

It was naked in space. Unprotected. Alone.

It oozed and undulated in an oily slime.

It came toward the ships and it had eyes.

It did nothing that Ellery could follow, but one of the ships broke in two. Flame licked out into space and dripped away in every direction. Ellery tried not to see.

The two remaining ships started to turn, curving around in a long, agonizing arc. They were tragically slow. It took them forever—

A pale force started to surround the ships. It grew, shimmering. The ships turned—

And then there was one ship. The other disappeared.

The thing with the eyes *flapped*—that was the only word for it. It hung in empty space, coated with slime. It waited.

The last ship got away. It started back up the long black tunnel, away from the splash of light and the thing that rested in nothing. It blurred, and dimensions changed—

There was milky whiteness again, and then just a square of cloudy gray.

Paul Ellery was back in the projection room.

"Cute, hey?" said John.

Ellery didn't say anything.

The little fat man led the way out of the room and back down the tunnels and ramps and elevators to his office. He poured two glasses of Scotch from a fresh bottle, and this time both men downed them with one long, shuddering drink. John poured two more and sat down.

"That area is known to your astronomers as the Large Magellanic Cloud," John said slowly. "It is an irregular extra-galactic star system. It's where the Others live."

"They live in space? Empty space?"

John shrugged. "They're versatile," he said.

"How much do you know about them?"

"Not too much, but enough. There are other galaxies than this one, Paul, and other life-forms than man. The *Others* are hostile, if that is the right word. Who could possibly understand their motives, if they have any? They have been sighted within our own galaxy, and they mean trouble. Not now, as far as we can tell, but eventually. One day man will have to face them, Paul. If it came today, man would lose. He wouldn't even be in the fight."

Ellery sat very still. His mind seemed suddenly a tiny, hopelessly inadequate thing. His horizons had been blasted open to include a galaxy, and he had tried to face that problem. And now there were other galaxies—

An ant, lost in the jungle.

"It's getting late now," John said, "and the ship will be moving on. Our time is running out on us, Paul, and I may never see you again. I've almost finished what I had to say to you, and maybe it's been something of a disappointment." He waved at the crumpled magazine on his desk. "I flatter myself that I understand you pretty well. You were looking for a secret weapon of some sort, weren't you? A nice miracle, all wrapped up with a blue ribbon?"

Ellery considered. "I tried to tell myself that there wasn't any secret weapon," he said. "But I guess I was looking for one anyway."

John nodded. "There's only one secret weapon that's worth a damn in the long run, Paul. It's the only one you can't beat by dreaming up a better secret weapon. It's called man."

There it is. Your secret weapon.

"You see," said John, talking slowly and clearly now, with none of the exaggerations that Ellery had come to expect, "you've got to get to know us. You must not think of us as a culture—we're human too, Paul. Culture is an abstraction made up from the lifeways of many different people, all averaged together to get the human element out. A galaxy is a large place, and there are many opinions in it. Sentiment among our people, as among all peoples, is divided. We do the best we can. It's the *situation* that breeds the trouble. Hell, my friend, all of us have a long way to go. No system lasts forever. Someday, all men must stand together, or there will be no men left. You've seen the Others now, and I don't think you'll forget them. Just the same, your problem right now is not wandering around out in space somewhere. Your problem is a gent named Paul Ellery. You should get to know him. I think he's a pretty good Joe."

The silence flowed in and filled the air.

Ellery saw the room around him with a curious, sudden clarity. He saw the books, each one distinct in a brightly etched jacket of color. He saw the tapes, gleaming dully. He saw the desk, the chairs, the comforting walls. He saw the bottle, and the stale, filmy glasses. He saw John, and the words that he wanted to say wouldn't come.

"I guess we're not used to friendship these days," he said slowly. "It embarrasses us. It makes us uncomfortable. We don't know what to do with it."

"I know," John said. "The hell with it, though. If it's there, that's enough."

"Maybe I'll see you again."

"Maybe." John glanced at a clock on his desk. "It's time for you to go."

Ellery stood up, a little shakily. John began to fidget with papers on his desk. Without his solid wall of personality he seemed almost at a loss.

The two men shook hands.

"Hell, boy," John said. "I'll see you around."

"Yeah. Maybe we'll buzz up to heaven and play the same harp."

"Good deal. You'd better roll, Paul, before this crate winds up over Australia somewhere."

"Okay. I know the way. Thanks for everything."

"So long."

Paul Ellery walked toward the door. The door opened. Behind him, he heard John's voice: "Merry Christmas, son."

The door closed.

He walked down the long passageway, to the globe that would carry him back to Earth. Back to Earth, and back to Jefferson Springs He looked at his watch.

It was almost noon of Christmas Day.

20

The days that were left to Paul Ellery ticked quickly by.

One, two, three—

Four, five, six—

It seemed only a heartbeat, and then it was late morning on the last day of December. At midnight it would be a new year on Earth. At one in the morning, the Center ship would leave for deep space.

There was a place for him on that ship.

All he had to do was climb on board. All he had to do was kiss the Earth good-by.

He looked outside from his kitchen window. It was a gray, miserable day. The sun was pale and far away. A cold, biting wind scratched at the old glass in the window.

Kiss the Earth good-by.

Would that be so tough, really? Sure, it was always hard to overcome your own inertia, pull up stakes and leave. It was always hard, but it wouldn't be impossible.

Not now.

There was the diseased, hideous bloom of the hydrogen flower, waiting to flash into sudden growth on every hillside.

There were other charming new flora too—the gray-leafed cobalt tree, and the peaceful nerve-gas weed.

Ellery had seen war, and seen it close. He had been born in a century of war. He had lived with war always on the horizon. The stink of war was in his nostrils.

Hiroshima and Nagasaki had ushered in a whole new technology. They had made warfare obsolete, and the hydrogen-torn holes in the poorly named Pacific had underlined the lesson. The culture of Earth *had* to change, and would change, but would it change in time?

He had heard the voices so often: *"I say bomb the bastards now while we've got a chance. Hit them before they hit us. Maybe we'll get wiped off the map, but let's take them with us."*

War was not practical. War was suicide. But people did not know. They reacted as they had always reacted. No one had told them that times had changed. No one had told them that the solutions of twenty years ago were not the solutions of today.

No one had told them.

"Okay, pal, you tell me a better way. "

What was there to tell them?

They didn't trust the United Nations.

They could not believe in faith.

They had learned to be cynical in a tough school.

They did not know what science was. They did not know that science was a method. They thought that science was gadgets and bombs and automobiles and television. Why not? The scientists hadn't bothered.

And the scientists were human, too. They weren't just scientists. They were Frank and Sam and Bob and Heinrich and Luigi. They never agreed on anything. It was a point of honor. They would be debating value judgments when the world went *bang*.

There were the men and the women and the children. Each had his problems, his dreams, his fears. Each was right as he saw it. Each was hurrying, trying, working—

Ants in an anthill.

And then the bucket of scalding water.

Ellery wasn't scared of the Preventers. The Galactic Administration could handle them. He wasn't too worried about the Others, not yet. They were a long way from Earth.

Even Jefferson Springs didn't scare him, not by itself. He wasn't scared of the Americans or the Russians or the Chinese or the English or the Eskimos.

He was afraid of *all* the people.

He was afraid of Earth.

He ground his cigarette out in a dish on the kitchen table and lit another one. He listened to the icebox humming. He heard water dripping from a faucet over the sink. He got up and punched open a can of beer. Outside the window, the world looked very cold.

So much for Earth.

Suppose he left on the alien ship?

First of all, he would live. That was important to him; he could not pretend he wanted to be a martyr. The civilized people of the galaxy had learned to control their bombs. There was no danger of that kind.

If he went to the Center, he would be different. He would not be the same Paul Ellery. Was that any great loss? Was he so crazy about himself that he could not bear any change in great, big, wonderful Paul?

Different, but not completely so. Maybe he would be changed for the better. Certainly, he would be happy. The Center would see to that. They would give him new values and new goals, and they would equip him to get where he wanted to get.

Wherever that might be.

He would have most of his questions answered—at least the scientific ones. Possibly he could even continue to be an anthropologist, or whatever passed in their culture for an anthropologist. Take the problem of acculturation, for example. Culture change that took place when different cultures came into contact was fascinating stuff. On Earth, scientists were just beginning to get an inkling into the actual nature of the process. At the Center, he could check out a book and get the answers.

The answers to the questions he asked as a man might be more difficult.

He could carve out a life for himself there. A new life, a better life. He could not even imagine the things he might see, the things he might do. He could walk through the future with a notebook. The aliens were people too. He could start over, and face his new life with confidence. He could live in peace, and in safety. He could enjoy himself.

Perhaps, too, he would have an opportunity to help Earth—help her from *inside* the galactic organization. Surely he could do more good there.

Of course, he wouldn't be quite the same, and he might not want to help, and he would be fenced in with laws. But he could still do a lot for Earth. He could be like John.

He tried to believe it.

He looked at his watch. Six o'clock of New Year's Eve. At eight he would be going to Cynthia's to usher in the new year. In seven hours the ship would leave for the Center. He could be on it.

Outside, night had come. He wondered where John was now. He could almost see him here in the kitchen, leaning against the icebox, a glass in his hand. Eyes twinkling, bald pink dome gleaming under the bulb in the ceiling, waving his arms, talking, talking, talking.

John had given him a solution. It was not all tied up in a neat package, but it was there.

The Osage Indians had found oil on their reservation. The oil had been important because it had given them what they needed to amount to something in a commercial culture: money.

John had given him a different kind of oil to deal with a different kind of culture. John had given him information.

Information to bridge the gap.

"It's the *situation* that breeds the trouble," John had said.

The problem posed by the alien colony of Jefferson Springs had no solution because Earth was not far enough advanced to deal with the problem. A problem could not be solved until its existence could be recognized.

"No system lasts forever," John had said.

That was the key. The problem had no solution *at the present time.* That didn't mean that it would *never* have an answer.

The aliens could not legally interfere with Earth, and they enforced their laws. If man could pull himself up the ladder, then the aliens couldn't kick him back down again.

If the Earth could get that far—if there really *was* an Earth and not a patchwork of hostile nations—then the situation would be different. Earth would have found its voice. The alien problem would be understandable, and techniques would have evolved to handle it.

There was more than that. The galactic civilization would *need* a united Earth by then, and need her desperately. The shoe would be on the other foot. Ellery remembered:

"Meet the Others."

"If it came today, man would lose."

The human galactic civilization was not alone in the universe. Already, it had contacted hostile life-forms from another galaxy, the Others who had no name. Men had discovered that the Others were deadly, and one day they would have to be faced. Perhaps by then they would not have to be met with naked force, but man would still have to be united and strong to survive. There were wheels within wheels, always.

Even the Galactic Administration was young. Beyond the Others, who knew what lay in wait for man? He would need his strength.

Ellery could not deal with the colony now. He could not negotiate because Earth had nothing to offer. Applying the right force at the wrong time was worse than applying no force at all. But the right force at the *right* time—that would work. That would always work. The galactic civilization, too, would be interested in survival.

The solution was there. It was centuries away, but it was there.

In the last analysis, Earth's future was up to Earth. It couldn't wish the responsibility off on anyone else. It could pull itself up by its bootstraps until it was a world to reckon with, or it could blast itself to oblivion. At best, the answer was hundreds of years in the future.

Earth might never get there.

Meanwhile, Paul Ellery had a life to live. He looked at his watch. Eight o'clock. He was late. He still had a decision to make, and there was no use kidding himself. There would be no second chance.

There wasn't much time. The old year was almost gone.

He heard the click of a woman's heels come up the wooden steps to his porch. Cynthia would be doing a slow burn. He walked quickly across the living room and opened the door.

A woman stood there. Not Cynthia.

Anne.

21

He looked around for some words and couldn't find any.

"Hello, Ell. May I come in, or are the vampires feeding tonight?"

Anne just looked at him, waiting. Her soft gray-green eyes were shadowed and her dark hair was combed a little too hastily. She had on a blue suit with a white blouse, and the skirt was wrinkled from sitting too long.

"Come on in, Annie," Ellery said. "It's cold out there."

She came in, looked around, smiled faintly at the picture that still hung turned toward the wall. She took off her blue suit jacket, fluffed out her hair, and eyed him uncertainly.

"How did you get here?" Ellery asked inanely.

"I took the bus. The public transportation system is still in operation, I'm happy to report. There weren't many passengers tonight."

"Did you have a good trip?"

"Utterly delightful. I knitted you a ski-suit."

"Sorry, Annie. I'm all fouled up tonight. Want some coffee?"

"Not now. Thanks."

She stood there in his living room, looking for some answers of her own. He wanted to go to her but he did not move.

"Annie, why did you come here?"

"I had to come, Paul. I had to see for myself. We've always spent our New Year's Eves together—I didn't think you could forget them. I wanted to see her, whoever she is. I guess I just couldn't stand it." Her voice was less steady now. "I'm *not* going to cry."

"You shouldn't have come."

"I know that. I'm here, though." She managed a smile. "What are you going to do with me?"

"I'm going to ask you a favor, hon," he said slowly. "Will you do me one more favor?"

"I'll try, Ell. What shall I do—go out to the crossroads and drive a stake through her heart?"

"It's tougher than that. I've got to go out. I want you to wait here and not follow me. I'll leave you my car, just in case."

She looked at him, desperately. "What *is* all this, Paul? Are you in some kind of trouble?"

"You might put it that way," Ellery said. "Look, I can't answer your questions. I just can't. You'll have to trust me. I want you to wait here. Will you do that, hon?"

She nodded, not understanding. "How long do I wait, Paul?"

"Wait until one," he said. "I know I'm asking a lot—I would have saved you from this if I could. I tried. If I'm not back by one, take my car and go home and forget me."

"I guess I asked for it, Ell."

"I've got to go."

She was in his arms. He held her tightly, afraid to let her go. He tore himself away.

He grabbed a coat and left.

The night was raw and cold. A chill wind out of the north sighed through the flat streets and whistled nakedly through the bare branches of the trees.

He had less than four hours left.

He walked through the dark streets of the town. The rows of little boxlike houses squatted along the sidewalks, staring at him. Once he saw a glimmer of pale blue light leaking through a crack in a window. His footsteps clicked on the sidewalk. They made a lonely, hollow sound.

Jefferson Springs seemed utterly deserted around him. He climbed the steps of Cynthia's house and knocked on the door. He walked inside without waiting to be asked.

"Well," said Cynthia, getting to her feet from the couch, "fancy meeting you here."

"Sorry I'm late."

"Sober?"

"Yes."

"This is your big night, lover. Want a drink?"

"Sure."

Cynthia poured him one of her inspired dry Martinis, which he insulted by drinking it at a gulp. She made him another, and kissed him.

"Relax, baby," she said. "Don't you want to get civilized?"

He sat down on the couch. She looked terrific. She always did. Her blond hair was smooth as silk, her blue eyes cool as ice. Her dress was wicked. Cynthia knew how to use clothes.

"I've been lonesome. I'll miss you, Paul."

"Sure you will."

"What's eating you, lover?"

"Cannibals." He laughed, unreasonably.

"You're nervous. I'll fix you another one."

The Martinis warmed him. He could not think. He postponed his thinking and tried to relish what he had come here to do.

Quite suddenly it was eleven o'clock. Time was running out.

"Cyn."

"Yes?"

"I came here to tell you something."

"Say it, then."

The room pressed in around them. A warm room, secure against the outside cold.

He stood up. "I came here to say a lot of things, Cyn. I wanted to call you a bitch and tell you all about yourself. 1 wanted to tell you I knew what you were after—you wanted to sleep with a caveman, try out one of the natives for kicks. I've known it ever since the dance, maybe before. That's all I was to you, just a savage to play with. I wanted to tell you that I knew all about that. I wanted to say I stayed with you because you were the best I could get. I had it all planned. I was going to walk in here and toss it in your teeth and see how you liked it. It's funny as hell, Cyn. I've been nursing this for a long time—and now it doesn't seem worth doing. So where do we go from here?"

Cynthia sipped her martini calmly. "I knew you knew, Paul."

He sat down, feeling hollow.

She lit a cigarette. "Baby, we are what we are. Maybe you're just beginning to find that out. I'm a misfit here and so are you. I was lonely, too, if you like. I was *bored.* That was my crime. These people of mine are the supreme bores of all creation, if you want my honest opinion. They're here because they didn't have enough on the ball to stay home. I'm here because I didn't fit in any place. I'm just not a solid citizen, lover. I was alone, and you were something new. You were alone, so I gave myself to you. We had fun, didn't we, Paul? Does that make me evil? Does that make me a bitch?"

"Score one for your team." Ellery said.

She shrugged. "I'll go my way, Paul. I always have. When it's all over I'll have no regrets. When you get back from the Center, if they send you here, come on around and say hello."

"I won't be very interesting then. No more caveman."

She smiled, "We'll see."

"I've got to go, Cyn. Thanks for everything."

"Good luck, lover."

She kissed him, and then he was outside. He put on his coat, shivering in the cold, and looked at his watch.

Midnight. The time was now.

A metallic globe from the Center ship was waiting for him on the Walls Ranch. He would have to get outside the city limits and then pass the Garvin Berry place. Jim Walls lived in the next house. It was not too far to walk. It might take him half an hour—no more than that.

He stood in the cold wind, fists clenched, eyes closed. He had waited. Waited until the last possible minute. He was caught now. He was forced into it. He had to move one way or the other.

He watched to see what he would do.

The ship was waiting, half an hour away. Peace was waiting, a short walk down the road. A new life was waiting, waiting in a metal sphere.

He had his chance.

He smiled. He started to walk.

His steps clicked on the cold cement. Jefferson Springs was dark and cold around him. He walked through a village of the dead.

He did not walk alone. Memories of Earth walked with him.

Austin. A hot summer day. The lake around the aluminum canoe, still and glassy calm. The sun on his bare shoulders. Hank and Chuck drinking warm beer and munching stale bread. The fish that wouldn't bite. The wonderful, sharp coolness of the water when they had tossed aside the bamboo poles and lowered themselves into the green, green lake....

Home. A living room filled with the very special lamps and pictures and chairs that had been his world. Mom humming over the dishes in the kitchen. Dad laughing at some book he was reading. "Pop, can I have a dime for a soda? All the guys are going. Can I, Pop?" His street outside, and the dark sunset trees....

Los Angeles. A party late at night after a convention. Stale smoke in the air. George and Lois Sage sitting across from him. Everyone talking about what to do if an air-raid alert sounded. Everyone scared of the hydrogen bomb. Lois smiling. "Personally, I'm going to catch a bus for downtown L.A. That way you get vaporized all at once and miss the painful flash-burns....

Colorado. A tiny village nestled at the foot of a pass through the snow-capped mountains. Blue sky, clean air, tall pines. A swift river filled with trout. An unshaven old man with his shirttail out. "Sonny, I remember this town when the mines was here and they brung in a hundred whores from Denver...."

New York. Bright lights. A little club, a hole in the wall. A Dixieland band. A trumpeter almost completely paralyzed, playing in a wheelchair. Pale face sweating under the white lights. *Aunt Hagar's Blues.* A flushed, excited grin. "You had it then, Johnny, you had it then...."

God, it was funny—the things you remembered.

You never knew how much they meant to you.

He walked faster. Down one street, across another. The cold forgotten now.

Hurry, hurry, don't be late—

Don't be late for your new world. Don't be late for your new life!

He had found his place. He had found his people. The odds against him in the only life he could ever know were tremendous. He was a fool—

He didn't give a damn.

Hurry, hurry, don't be late—

Earth had a chance. He had only to believe in it. He had to have only a little faith, a little hope.

Earth was his.

He had a job to do. A little job, a job that paved the way. It was not the business of science to dictate to others. It was not the business of science to force people to its ways. All it could do was make the facts available to all, honestly and without fear.

Science, too, had to have faith in man.

Hurry, hurry, don't be late—

No man could say what might make the difference between chaos and civilization.

It might be a word in a classroom.

It might be one more man who would stand up and be counted.

It might be a faked community study to make men think a little.

There was the high school, frozen under the stars.

He began to run.

Across the street, past his parked car, up the steps of his house. He jerked open the door, ran inside.

And stopped.

Anne wasn't there. But—

He saw her then. In the kitchen, drinking coffee. She looked up, startled.

"Paul!"

He kissed her. He kissed her neck and her eyes and her hair. He knocked over the coffee pot. The hell with it!

"Happy New Year, Annie," he whispered. "Happy New Year!"

"Paul!"

"Quick now, Annie! Grab everything of mine you can get your hands on. Throw it in the car. Hurry!"

"But—"

"Are you too proud to marry me, Annie?"

Her mouth made a big round O. She looked at him speechlessly and then pitched in with the energy of a demon. They cleaned the house out in nothing flat. They turned out all the lights and piled into the Ford.

They laughed at nothing, at everything.

He gunned the engine and the tires screeched as he pulled away from the curb. He drove down the street as fast as he dared to drive. Right on Main Street. Past the shadowed square of the ice-house.

Out onto the open road.

Hurry, hurry, don't be late—

Past the Berry place. Past Jim Wall's ranch. The gray sphere was out there in the field, waiting for him. He could feel the prodigious might that hung high above his head, blotting out the stars.

He did not look up. He looked straight ahead.

"If you can't beat 'em, join 'em!"

That had more than one meaning. If you can't beat 'em the way they are now, then catch up with them!

"Hang on, Annie," he grinned. "Here we go!"

They went the back way, across the beautiful and lonely land. Up to Uvalde, over to Kerrville, on through the Hill Country.

There were stars all around them.

Far ahead in the east, where the low, dark hills touched the sky, Ellery could see the first faint rays from the morning sun. Beneath the rising sun, his city waited.

He prayed that this warm, golden sun might be the only one his home would ever know. He prayed that another manmade sun might never sear its shadows across his Earth.

He laughed, exultantly, into the night.

It was good to fight for life.

John was very near and smiling.

Anne was close at his side.

"Paul, it's so good to have you back!"

"It's good to be back," he said. "Annie, Annie, you'll never know how wonderful it is to be back."

Introduction - Unearthly Neighbors

Unearthly Neighbors (1960) was Chad Oliver's fourth novel and his fifth book of fiction (counting 1955's distinguished story collection, *Another Kind*). With it he closed a decade of impressive growth as a writer, by carrying forward his favorite theme of contact between intelligent species to a level of complexity and drama rarely seen in works of science fiction. "Chad Oliver continues to put his anthropology degree to good use," wrote Frederik Pohl. "Other science fiction writers have invented more 'alien' aliens than these for us to make contact with. Few, though, have been as able as Oliver to convince us that this is the way first contact is going to be."

As humankind reaches out across the light years to confront another humanity, we see how both forms of intelligence are compelled to face their own inner natures before they can even begin to understand each other. Being alien, in Oliver's sensitive analysis, is not just a matter of physiological differences, but also a dimension of culture and history overlaid on the biology.

Sirius Nine is a vividly imagined world; its alternate humanity is complex and deeply felt. The anthropological puzzle presented by the planet's humanoid civilization is fascinatingly detailed, as are the lives of the investigators from our own future Earth. It's a wise novel, probing our deepest feelings as it strives to answer the question: what is a human being? Seeking the answer, Oliver' story faces us squarely with one of the central points of all literature—that mostly we do not know well enough what we are under the overlay of civilization. There is nothing naively escapist about Oliver's fiction. He jolts feelings and provokes thought.

But even though he was not a writer of simple-minded adventures, Oliver's work is adventurous, exciting, suspenseful, and even harrowing;

no seeker of absorbing narrative will be disappointed. His portraits of our culture-bound humanity at odds with itself gain intensity when alien humanities come on the scene. Oliver had no illusions about the worst in us even as he presented what might become better. His all-too-human protagonists struggle with their own inner failings as well as with external problems. Oliver knew that we have not yet replaced given nature with a wholly successful creation of our own; in fact we may fail at this project of remaking ourselves and our environments and die off in waste and warring.

An outdoorsman and lover of nature, Oliver was also a romantic poet singing the subtleties of ecological-cultural adaptations. In this aspect his work has been compared to that of Clifford D. Simak, and to later writers Michael Bishop, Ursula K. Le Guin, and Eleanor Arnason. Anthropologist Oliver shows us humanity trying to transcend the natural system in which it evolved. Can this creature continue to adapt to its own changes or is it an exile incapable of either accepting itself for what it is or changing itself into something better?

Humankind, for Oliver, was an ongoing project of vast proportions, run by an intermittently enlightened artisan, humanity itself. Either we will learn enough to help ourselves mature as a culture—we do this better individually at every point—or we will remain on a historical treadmill, if we don't destroy ourselves. Combine this critical approach with an anthropologist's varied insights and a writer's careful attention to his own individual experience and you have an author who stands directly in the best tradition of a searching, probing science fiction—one in which, in the words of Anthony Boucher, "the science is as accurately absorbing as the fiction is richly human" and deserves the science fiction term because it delivers on its full, genuine meaning.

Unearthly Neighbors was first published as a paperback original in 1960. The distinguished-looking Ballantine edition was well received, even though H. W. *Hall's Science Fiction Book Review Index* lists only notices by P. S. Miller, Leslie Flood, S. E. Cotts, and Frederik Pohl. It was not a great year for science fiction publishing. There was no British edition and only one translation. For this new edition, the author made substantial revisions in the early chapters and various corrections throughout the text, thus making the Crown 1985 publication the first definitive hardcover edition. Unfortunately, the Crown editions of these three alien novels, despite good bindings, typography, and cover art, showed a marked reluctance on the part of production personnel to make galley corrections. More than a hundred were inexplicably ignored in all three novels, but these have now been made.

—George Zebrowski
Delmar, NY 2007

Unearthly Neighbors

Before the End

High above the tossing trees that were the roof of the world, the fierce white sun burned in a wind-swept sky.

Alone in the cool, mottled shade of the forest floor, the naked man sat with his back resting against his tree and listening to the sigh of the woods around him. He was an old man now, old with the weight of too many years, and his thoughts were troubled.

He lifted his long right arm and held it before him. There was strength in Volmay yet; the muscles in his arm were firm and supple. He could still climb high if he chose, still dive for the strong branches far below, still feel the intoxicating rush of the air in his face....

He let the arm drop.

It was not only Volmay's body that was old; the body mattered little. No. it was Volmay's *thoughts* that worried him. There was a bitter irony about it, really. A man worked and studied all his life so that one day he would be at peace with himself, all duties done, all questions answered, all dreams explained. And then....

He shook his head.

It was true that he was alone, but all of the People were much alone. It was true that his children were gone, but they were good children and he could see them if he wished. It was true that his mate no longer called out to him when the blood pulsed with the fevers of the spring, but that was as it should be. It was true that he had only a few years of life remaining to him, but life no longer seemed as precious to Volmay as it had in the lost, sunlit years.

He looked up at a fugitive patch of blue sky that showed through the red leaves of the trees. He had walked life's long pathway as it was meant to be walked, and he knew what there was to know. He had not been surprised—except once—and he had not been afraid.

And yet, strangely, he was not content.

Perhaps, he thought, it was only the weight of the years that whispered to him; it was said that the old ones had one eye in the Dream. Or perhaps it had been that one surprise, that one glimpse of the thing that glinted silver in the sky....

But there was *something* within him that was unsatisfied and unfulfilled. He felt that his life had somehow tricked him, cheated him. There was something within him that was like an ache in his heart.

How could that be?

Volmay closed his dark eyes, seeking the dream-state. The dream wisdom would come, of course, and that was good. But he already knew what he would dream; he was not a child....

Volmay stirred restlessly.

The great white Sun drifted down the arc of afternoon. The wind died away and the trees grew still.

The naked man dreamed. And—perhaps—he waited.

1

"Free will?"

Monte Stewart chuckled and tugged at his untidy beard. "What the devil do you mean by that?"

The student who had imprudently expressed a desire to major in anthropology had a tough time in choking off his flood of impassioned rhetoric, but he managed it. "Free will?" he echoed. He waved his hand aimlessly. "Well—uh—like, you know."

"Yes, I know," Monte Stewart leaned back precariously in his ancient swivel chair and stabbed a finger at the eager young man. "But do *you* know?"

The student, whose name was Holloway, was obviously unaccustomed to having his glib generalities questioned. He fumbled around for a moment and then essayed a reply. "I mean that the—um—bottom line is that we have the ability to choose, to shape our own Destiny." (Holloway was the type that always capitalized words like *Fate* and *Destiny* and *Purpose*.)

Monte Stewart snorted. He picked up a dry human skull from his desk and flapped the spring-articulated mandible up and down. "Words, my friend, just words." He cocked a moderately bushy eyebrow. "I will pass over a cheap shot at the derivation of the name *Holloway*. What type blood do you have, Mr. Holloway?"

"Blood, sir? Why—type O, I think."

"Let's be positive, Holloway." Monte Stewart was enjoying himself. "When did you make the choice? Prior to your conception or later?"

Holloway looked shocked. "I didn't mean—"

"I see that your hair is brown. Did you dye it or merely select the proper genotype?"

"That's not fair, Dr. Stewart. I didn't mean—"

"What didn't you mean?"

"I didn't mean free will is *everything*, not in biology. I meant free will in the choices we make in everyday life. Like, you know..."

Monte Stewart sighed and made a mental note to have Holloway do some nosing around in the history of sociobiology. He fished out a pipe from a cluttered desk drawer and clamped it between his teeth. One of his most cherished illusions was that students should learn how to think; Holloway might as well start now. "I notice, Holloway, that you are wearing a shirt emblazoned with an admirable slogan, slacks neatly trimmed off below the knees, and fashionably scruffy shoes. Why didn't you put on a G-string and moccasins this morning?"

"You just don't—"

"Your presence in my class indicates that you are technically a student at the University of Colorado. If you had been born an Australian aborigine, you would instead be learning the mysteries of the *churinga.* Isn't that so?"

"Maybe. I've heard about the revitalization movement in Australia. But just the same..."

"Ah, you have been paying some attention. We'll score that one a draw. Have you had supper yet, Holloway?"

"No, sir."

"Do you think that you are likely to choose fermented mare's milk mixed with blood for your evening meal?"

"I guess not. But I could, couldn't I?"

"Where would you get it this side of the Kazaks? Look, have you ever considered the idea that a belief in free will is a primary prop of the culture you happened to grow up in? Has it ever occurred to you that if the concept were not present in your culture you wouldn't believe in it—and that your present acceptance of it is *not* a matter of free choice on your part? Have you ever toyed with the notion that *any* choice you may make is inevitably the product of the brain you inherited and what has happened to that brain during the time you have been living in a culture you did not create?"

Holloway blinked.

Monte Stewart stood up. He was not a tall man, but he was tough and wiry. Holloway got up too. "Mr. Holloway, do you realize that even the spacing between us now is culturally determined—that if we were participants in a different cultural system we would be standing either closer together or farther apart? Come back and see me again next week and we'll talk some more. You might also reflect on the point that the timing of appointments is another cultural variable."

Holloway backed toward the door. "Thank you, sir."

"You're entirely welcome."

When the door closed behind Holloway, Monte grinned. Even with his rather formidable beard, the grin was oddly boyish. He had been having a good time. Of course, any moderately sophisticated bonehead could have given him an argument on the old free will problem, but Holloway still had some distance to cover in that regard. Nevertheless, the young man had possibilities. He just needed to unplug the computer now and then, stop coasting, and start thinking. Monte had seen it happen before—that startling transition from befuddled undergraduate to dogmatically certain graduate and, sometimes, on to the searching questions that were the beginnings of wisdom.

Monte enjoyed his teaching and got a kick out of his reputation as an old-fashioned fearsome ogre. Sometimes, he knew, he overplayed the role. He hoped that he had not been too forbidding with Holloway.

He moved over to the console, intending to punch up some data on the conversion factor in potassium argon dating for his class tomorrow. His short black hair was trimly cut, complementing the slight shagginess of his jutting spade beard. His clear gray eyes were bright and alert, and although he looked his age—which was a year shy of forty—he conveyed the impression that it was a pretty good age to be.

"Monte," he said aloud, "you're a damn fool."

He didn't need the data. Louise knew all there was to know about potassium argon dating; he could get it from her. Besides, his stomach was telling him that it was time to go home.

He locked his smoke-hazed office and rode the tube to the roof of the Anthropology Building. (It was not one of the larger buildings on the campus, having been built in the compact style that had come into favor early in the twenty-first century, but the status of anthropology had improved sufficiently so that it was no longer possible to dump the department into an improvised shack.) The cool Colorado air was bracing and he felt fine as he climbed into his copter and took off.

He did not know, of course, that Holloway would never be his student.

He did not even know much about tough choices—yet.

He lazed along in the traffic of the middle layer, enjoying the glint of snow on the mountains and the clean golden light of the westering sun. It had been a pleasant day, considering that it was a Wednesday.

He eased the copter down toward his rock-and-log home in the foothills of the mountains. He was surprised to see an unfamiliar copter parked on the roof right next to his garage. He landed, climbed out, and took a good look at it. The copter was a powerful machine. It had a discreet blue and-white U.N. logo on its nose and official tags.

Monte did not exactly feel a chill of apprehension. However, like the man in the tall building who glanced up and saw King Kong peering in through his office window, he felt something more than mild curiosity.

The top door of his home opened before him, and Monte Stewart ran down the stairs to see what was going on.

The man was seated in Monte's favorite chair in the living room, enjoying what appeared to be a Scotch and soda. Both of these choices, in Monte's view, indicated a man of intelligence. He stood up when Monte entered the room, and Monte recognized him at once. He had never actually met the man, but his craggy face and silver-gray hair were immediately familiar to any tri-di watcher. Besides, Monte had seen him at close range several times when they were both involved with the NASA project.

"You're Mark Heidelman," he said, extending his hand. "This is an unexpected pleasure. I'm Monte Stewart. Was there some communication I didn't get?"

Mark Heidelman shook hands with a solid I-really-mean-it grip. "The pleasure is mine, Dr. Stewart. I always intended to introduce myself on that NASA business—you did one hell of a job. But I have to plead political sensitivities and all that. Sorry." He took a deep breath. "No, there was no contact with you. I just sort of barged in. It's rather shoddy procedure for a diplomat, but I *have* cleared things with your dean—rusty old bird, he is—and I've met with President Kovar of your distinguished university. She was quite complimentary about you, by the way."

"Ummm," Monte said. He hardly knew Kovar. "I take it then that this is an official visit?"

"It is, Dr. Stewart. Very hush-hush but very official. We don't want to start tongues wagging and this concerns your wife as well as yourself. Have I intrigued you?"

"You might put it that way." Monte waved him back to his chair and pulled up another one. "What's going on?"

"We're going to try to put you on a very sticky spot, Dr. Stewart."

Monte reached for his pipe, filled it, and puffed on it until it lit. Where the devil was Louise? He knew, naturally, that Mark Heidelman was the confidential troubleshooter for the secretary-general of the United Nations, which meant that he was a very big wheel indeed. The U.N. had gone through its ups and downs since the long-ago days of the near-legendary Dag Hammarskjöld, but now with its overt and covert operations it was as much an integral part of life as spaceships and taxes. The obvious question filled the room. What did the U.N. want with Monte Stewart?

"Please call me Monte. I take it that you need an anthropologist."

Heidelman smiled. "We need you, if that's what you mean. And we need Louise."

The servomec wheeled itself in, carrying a tray with two fresh glasses of Scotch and soda. It wasn't much of a robot—just a wheeled cart with assorted detachable appendages—but Monte and Louise had not had it long, and they were inordinately proud of it.

Monte took his drink, raised it toward Heidelman, and proceeded to indulge in one of the great benefits of civilization. "Now then, Mark. What's this all about?"

Heidelman shook his head. "Your wife told me that you hated to discuss anything before supper, and I'm taking her at her word. Anyhow, she was good enough to invite me to share a steak with the two of you, and she's doing the cooking herself. I'd hate to get booted out before I could do justice to the meal."

Monte chuckled, understanding more clearly why Heidelman was one of the world's most successful diplomats. The man radiated charm, and there was nothing at all unctuous or phony about it.

"Give me a hint, can't you? Mysteries make me nervous."

"You may develop some dandy ulcers before this one is over with. Monte, one of our ships has finally hit the jackpot."

Monte felt a cold thrill of excitement. He raised his bushy eyebrows. "My God, do you mean—"

With exquisite timing, Louise Stewart picked that moment to enter the room. Monte noted that she had activated her I'm-still-female-when-I-want-to-be role, which was a sure sign that she approved of Mark Heidelman. She had put on one of her discreetly sexy dresses, her dark hair was coiled in the latest fashion, and her brown eyes sparkled. She looked devastating.

"Steaks are on," Louise said. "I didn't cook them with radiocarbon, either. Let's eat." She gave Monte a light kiss on the forehead. "Monte, I'm about to pass out with curiosity."

"How do you think I feel? Let's get this show on the road."

They escorted Heidelman into the dining room, which was in a separate wing of the house. It was too cold for the roof to be rolled back, but the stars were clearly visible through the ceiling panels.

The stars. It had to be the stars.

Stuck with their own conventions, they managed to give respectful attention to one of life's most underrated pleasures: genuine sirloin steak, cooked to perfection. Heidelman did not insult the meal by talking shop. He waited until they were back in the living room and the servomec had done its thing by supplying them all with coffee.

"Okay," Monte said. "We've got a quorum and wonderfully stuffed bellies. No more messing around, Mark. About this jackpot you mentioned..."

Heidelman nodded. "I hope this doesn't sound unduly melodramatic, but I have to say that what I am going to tell you is absolutely confidential. No matter what your decision, I know that I can rely on your complete discretion."

"Give it to us, man," Monte said. "Let's just pretend that we've run through all the preliminaries. What exactly have you got?"

Heidelman could not resist a pause for effect, but he kept it short. "One of our survey ships has found a planet with human beings on it," he said.

Monte tugged at his beard. "Human beings? What kind of human beings? Where?"

"Give me a chance, Monte. I'll spill it as fast as I can."

"Fine, fine. But don't skip the details."

Heidelman smiled. "We don't *have* many details. As you know, the development of the interstellar drive has made it possible for us—"

Monte got to his feet impatiently. "Not *those* details, dammit. We know about the stardrive. We know about the Centaurus and Procyon expeditions. What about these human beings? Where are they, and what are they like?"

Heidelman drained his coffee. "They were discovered on the ninth planet of the Sirius system—that's about eight-and-a-half light-years away, as I understand it. Maybe I was a little premature in calling them human beings—that's your department—but they look pretty damned close."

"Did you make contact with them?" Louise asked.

"No. We didn't expect to find any people out there, of course, but all the survey ships carry strict orders to keep their distance in a situation like this. We did get some pictures, and sensors were planted to pick up recordings of one of their languages—"

Monte pounced on the word like a cat going after a sparrow. "Language, you say? Careful, now. Remember that chimpanzees are very close to us biologically and they make a lot of vocal racket, but they don't have a true language. Even after a century of teaching them manual signs, there's a line they can't seem to cross. Language? How are you using the term?"

"Well, they seem to talk in about the same circumstances we do. And they are definitely not limited to a few set calls or cries—they yak in a very human manner. We have some films synchronized with the sounds, and several of them show what appear to be parents telling things to their children, for instance. How's that?"

Monte dropped back into his chair and pulled out his pipe. "I'll have to study the tapes. But if they *do* have a language, what about the rest of their culture? Things you could see from a remote position, I mean?"

Heidelman frowned. "That's the odd thing about it, Monte. The survey team was careful, but they were good observers. They couldn't see any of the things I would have expected. No cities or anything of that sort. Not even any houses, unless you call a hollow tree a house. No visible farming or industry. The people don't wear clothing. In fact—unless the survey was cockeyed—they don't appear to have any artifacts at all."

"No tools? No weapons? Not even stone axes or wooden clubs?"

"Nothing. They go naked and they don't carry anything with them. When they swing through the trees—"

Monte almost dropped his pipe. "You're kidding. Are you trying to tell me that these people brachiate—swing hand over hand through the trees?"

"That's what they do. They walk on the ground too—they're fully erect in their posture and all that. But with those immensely long arms of theirs..."

Louise laughed with delight. "This is too much! Show us the pictures, Mark. We can't take much more of this."

"Maybe that would be best." Heidelman grinned, knowing that he had his victims thoroughly hooked. He stood up. "I have some photographs right here in my briefcase."

Monte Stewart stared at the brown briefcase on his living room table with an excitement he had never known before. He felt like Darwin must have felt when he first stepped ashore on that most important of all islands....

"For God's sake," he said, "let's see those pictures!"

2

There were five photographs in full color. Heidelman handed them over without comment. Monte shuffled through them rapidly, his quick gray eyes searching for general impressions, and then studied them one by one.

"Yes and no," he muttered to himself.

The pictures—which were obviously stills blown up from several film sequences—were not of stupendous quality. They were a bit fuzzy and the subject matter was irritatingly noncommittal. The pictures looked like what they were: random shots of whatever had wandered into range. Still, they were the most fascinating photographs that Monte had ever seen.

"Look at those arms," Louise breathed.

Monte nodded, trying to get his thoughts in some kind of order. Only five pictures, but there was so much to see. So much that was new and strange-and hauntingly familiar.

The landscape was disturbing, which made it difficult to get the manlike figures into perspective. There was nothing about it that was downright grotesque, but the *shapes* of the trees and plants were subtly wrong. The colors, too, were unexpected. The trees had a blue cast to their bark, and their leaves were as much red as green. (Autumn on Sirius Nine?) There were too many bright browns and blues, as though a painter's brush had unaccountably slipped on a nightmare canvas.

The Sun, which was visible in two of the pictures, was a brilliant white that filled too much of the sky.

The whole effect, Monte thought, was curiously similar to the painted forests one sometimes saw in old books for children. The trees were not quite the trees you knew, and the pastel flowers grew only in dreams....

Of course, after the bleakness of the solar system, *any* trees and flowers provided a certain welcome reassurance.

"They are people," Louise said. "They *are*, Monte."

Yes, yes, he thought. *They are people. How easy it is to say! Only—what is a man? How will we know him when we meet him? How will* we *know her? Will we ever be sure?*

Superficially, yes—they were people. (And they were mammals too, unless females were radically different on Sirius Nine.) But Old Lady Neanderthal had also been part of the family, different only at the subspecies level. And even *Pithecanthropus erectus* belonged in the crowded genus *Homo.*

What is a man?

Monte's hands itched; he wished fervently that he had some solid bones to look at instead of these blurry pictures. For instance, how did you go about estimating the cranial capacity from a poor photograph? The skulls might be almost completely bone for all he knew; the gorilla has a massive head, but its brain is nearly a thousand cubic centimeters smaller than a man's.

Well, what did they *look* like?

The general impression, for what that was worth, was unmistakably hominid. The people—if that was indeed the word for them—were erect bipeds, and their basic bodily outlines were not dramatically different from earthly hominids—or at least hominoids. The legs, in fact, were very human, although the feet seemed to have a big toe sticking out at a right angle to the other toes. (Monte couldn't be sure of that, however. Unless the camera catches it just right, it's hard to see even on a chimpanzee.) The arms were something else again. They were extremely long, almost touching the ground when the people stood up straight. But the people were fully erect; there was nothing of the stooped posture of the ape about them. The bodies were hairless and rather slender, and the skin color was a pale copper.

Faces? Call them unusual, but within the human range. They were long and narrow, with relatively heavy jaws and deeply recessed eyes. Monte could not see the teeth, but it was clear that the canines, at any rate, did not protrude. The head hair was uniformly light in color and was very short—hardly more than a fuzz.

Heidelman's description had been accurate as far as it went. The people wore no clothing, but two of the men had vertical stripes painted on their bodies. The painting seemed to be confined to the chests and was quite simple—a streak of red and one of blue on each side of the chest.

None of the people carried any weapons.

Monte saw no tools of any sort and no houses. One of the men was standing in front of a large tree that appeared to have a hollow chamber in it, but it was difficult to tell.

There was a child in one of the pictures. He seemed to be five or six years old, if earthly analogies could be trusted, and he was hanging by one hand from a branch and grinning from ear to ear. A female was shaking her finger at him from the ground below, and the impression of mother and son was very strong—and remarkably human.

But then, of course, the mother-and-son relationship often seemed quite human, even in monkeys....

Monte carefully put the photographs down on the table.

"Brother," he sighed. And then: "Brothers?"

Monte abandoned his pipe for a cigarette, which was a sure sign that he was worried. He began to pace the floor.

"I don't get it," he said. "You say that they do no farmng, and yet they can't hunt because they have no weapons. So where the hell do they get their food?"

"Couldn't they live off wild fruits and roots and stuff like that?" Heidelman asked.

"It's possible, I suppose."

"Come on, Monte," Louise said. "Apes do it, don't they? And some of them hunt, too."

"Sure, but these people aren't apes—unless you want to call human beings modified apes, which *is* one way of looking at it."

"You're lecturing, Monte," Louise said.

"Sorry. But Mark says that they have languages, and that's a human characteristic no matter how you slice it. Forget about the ape hoots and whale whistles. If they have languages, you'd expect them to have cultures too; cultures and languages go together like Scotch and soda. I've never heard of any group of human beings without any tools at all. Even the simplest food-gathering peoples had digging sticks and spears and baskets and things of that sort. Either these people are the most primitive ever discovered, or else—"

Louise laughed fondly. "Monte! I never thought I'd hear you say what you were about to say. After all your caustic remarks about yarns involving primitive supermen..."

"The catch is," Monte said seriously, "that *primitive* is a pretty slippery word. We think we know what it means on Earth—it refers to a nonliterate culture without urban centers. The notion works fairly well here, but what can it possibly mean when it is applied to people on another planet? We don't really know a damned thing about them or their cultural histories, and fitting them into a ready-made category derived from a total sample of one world may be a gross mistake. As for supermen, I doubt whether the concept is a valid one at all—are we superapes or are we something else altogether? These people could be *different* without being super, if you get what I mean."

Heidelman smiled a quiet, satisfied smile. "Of course," he said, "the only way to find out the truth is to go and see."

There were the words, the words that had to be spoken. They were followed by a long silence.

Monte finally ground out his cigarette and lit another. "Yes, yes. Is that what you want us to do—or am I supposed to wait until I'm asked?"

"You *are* being asked. Do I have to wave flags and ring bells? We want you to lead a scientific expedition to Sirius Nine, and the sooner the better. We want you to start your planning now. We are determined to have a trained anthropologist make the first contact with these people—I'd like to think that we've made at least enough progress to avoid some of the more glaring errors of the past. How about it?"

"Just like that, huh?" Monte perched on the edge of a chair, feeling as though he had just been handed the gift of immortality. "Hell, of course I'll go. No need to waffle about it. But look, Mark, there are a couple of things we should get straight—"

Heidelman nodded. "I know what you're thinking, and you can relax. We know how important this is, and we're prepared to give you all the authority you need. You'll be pretty much your own boss. You'll be free to pursue any scientific work you want to undertake. All we ask is that you do your level best to establish a friendly contact with the people on Sirius Nine and make a full report to us when you get back. We'll expect you to make any recommendations you see fit, and you'll have a voice in seeing to it that they're carried out. You can select anybody you want to work with you. We'll supply a ship under Admiral York—he's a good man—and he'll get you there and be responsible for your safety. But in all relations with the natives you will be in charge. Your only superior will be the secretary-general. The U.N. will pay your salary and will arrange for you to take a leave from the university. Louise will also be on salary; we know that you'll need her to work out dating sequences. We can hash out the details later, but how does that sound?"

Monte was stunned. He had not, in fact, been thinking on such an exalted plane. He was close to being in shock, and his mind had seized on smaller questions: *Who will take over my classes? What about my graduate students? How about all the wretched committees, the curse of university life? Who will move into my house?*

He finally said: "Why me? I'm not the world's greatest anthropologist. There ain't no such animal anymore, not since the days of Boas and Kroeber. Shouldn't there be an election or something?"

Heidelman shook his head. "Impossible. I'll get to that, if it worries you. But I'll tell you flat out: this has not been a hasty decision. We want you because you're good and because you've got some sense. That's crucial. We know you and we know what you can do. That's crucial. As for who might be the world's greatest anthropologist—well, that's *not* crucial and we really don't give a damn. If you know such a mythological being, fine. Take him or her with you."

Monte tried to collect his flying thoughts. "It sounds too good to be true. There must be a catch in it somewhere."

"There is. You put your finger smack on it awhile back. We don't really know anything much about those people. It won't be an easy job, and it may very well be dangerous. I'm not going to try to minimize the danger. You'll be risking your life out there—and the life of Louise as well."

Monte shrugged. It wasn't that he did not have a high regard for his own skin, but staying at home now was completely unthinkable. He did not insult Louise by asking for her opinion; he knew his wife well enough so that words were superfluous.

"How long do we have?" Monte said.

"That's partly up to you. With the new stardrive propulsion, it will take the ship a little better than eleven months to reach the Sirius system. If you spend a year on Sirius Nine, that will put you back on Earth in about three years if all goes well. We can stall things that long, I think. We'll want to get going as soon as we can—I don't have to tell you that if word of this leaks out there'll be the devil to pay.

"Pardon our ignorance," Louise said, "but why? What's the need for all the secrecy?"

Mark Heidelman smiled. He was in his element now. "You are intelligent people, but you don't know one hell of a lot about politics. This would be the news sensation of all time. Once the people got wind of it, every government that could throw a starship together would start a race for that planet. Any chance of a genuine scientific expedition would go out the window. Those people out there would be tried and convicted a million times over by the media—either as subhuman savages or as dangerous monsters. There's another possibility—they might be exploited as the saviors of humanity, and half of the U.N. would insist that we genuflect out of respect for the Space Gods. There would be power plays you wouldn't believe. There's a real chance for a blowup here; you never know what's going to happen when people get excited and start to calculate political advantage. We can't afford that. We've got to have accurate information *before* this thing breaks."

Monte went back to his pipe. "What happens after you get your accurate information, if you get it?"

"That depends on what you find out, doesn't it? After all, those people may *be* dangerous. They could even be gods, for all we know. We picked you for the job because we think you're hard-headed enough to stick to the facts."

"It's a fantastic responsibility."

"Would you rather someone else had it? Who?"

Monte had no answer.

"I told you that you were headed for some ulcers. They go with the territory. This job isn't all cocktails and suave diplomacy, you know." Quite suddenly, Heidelman looked very tired.

Watching him, Monte had a flash of insight into the problems that faced the man. This Sirius thing, dramatic as it was, was only one of a vast series of interlocking and never-ending crises. It must have taken a mind-numbing pile of conferences before this job could even be offered to Monte. And at the same time there was the eternal task of keeping the U.N. afloat in a sea of distrust. There was the cute question of what to do about Brazil's insistence on testing atomic weapons. There was the border squabble in the Middle East. There were the renewed population explosions in China and India....

"I think it's time for a nightcap," Louise said and called in the robot. With expert skill, she turned the conversation into quieter channels. Without ever actually saying so, she implied that the heavy discussions could wait until tomorrow. The world could survive that long.

Monte discovered that Mark shared his passion for trout fishing, and the two men got into an amiable argument concerning the relative merits of the Royal Wulff and the smaller match-the-hatch flies. They solemnly swore that they would try Beaver Creek together when Monte got back from Sirius Nine.

By the time Heidelman reluctantly went off to bed at two o'clock in the morning, they all had a slight buzz on and they were all good friends. That helps a lot in any enterprise.

While the robot clicked and wheedled around cleaning up the room, Monte began to prowl aimlessly, too keyed-up to sleep. Go fishing when he got back from Sirius Nine! It had been a crazy day. He felt like a stranger in his own living room. He looked at the familiar books and cassettes that lined the walls, frowned at the early-period Tom Lea painting that had always had a calming effect on him, tramped down the corners of the still-bright Navaho rugs scattered over the muted red tiles of the floor. This was his home. As an anthropologist, he was no stranger to departures. But only a few short hours ago his life had been comfortable, his future pleasant and moderately predictable. And now, with the suddenness that was one of life's most characteristic calling cards, it was all new and strange....

Louise took his arm. "Let's go look at it," she said.

At first, he didn't understand her. Then he snapped his fingers.

Side by side, they walked over to the picture window and pulled back the drapes.

They looked out into a wintry blaze of stars beyond the black silhouettes of the Colorado mountains. Monte felt a brief shiver run through his wife's body.

"There it is," he said, pointing. "Funny, I even remember the name of the constellation: Canis Majoris."

"I wonder what constellation we're in," Louise said.

"I confess I never thought it would happen, really. After those completely alien things uncovered by the Centaurus and Procyon expeditions, the human critter seemed like a very unlikely accident. I was reading an article just the other day—remember, I told you about it—that estimated that there was less than one chance in a million for the independent evolution of manlike beings somewhere else. According to this joker's theory—"

"Theories! You know what you always say about theories."

"Yes. But it's a strange feeling just the same."

Strange, and more than strange. The light that took the picture I held in my hand a few hours ago won't reach the Earth for more than seven years. It is far, so far....

He held Louise tightly in the circle of his arm. He was not afraid, but she seemed even more precious to him than before. She was all that was warm and thinking and alive in a universe vast and uncaring beyond belief.

"Well, old girl," he said quietly, "I'm glad you're going with me."

She gave him a playful kiss. "We're going together, dear. You don't think you were selected on your own merits, do you?"

They stood for a long time before the window that opened on the night, watching and wondering and trying to believe.

They could see Sirius plainly.

It was the most brilliant star in the sky.

3

How do you go about setting up an expedition that is designed to make the first contact with an alien, extraterrestrial culture? Monte didn't know, for the excellent reason that it had never been done before.

Obviously, it was too big for the two of them. He couldn't just put on his boots and pith helmet and sally forth with notebook in hand. "Come, Louise. I will make penetrating observations and you calibrate the chemistry for the dating. Nothing to it."

Nevertheless, the other extreme was equally absurd: he couldn't take everybody who might have an interest in the problem. For one thing, that would have required a fleet of spaceships. (Lord, there would even have to be committees!) For another, unleashing a horde of investigators upon what seemed to be a relatively simple culture would have been a sure way of guaranteeing that no one would get any real work done.

Quite early, he decided on a minimal expedition. He would take the people he needed for the basic spadework and leave the more specialized problems for later. He told himself that he was motivated by practical considerations, which he was to some extent, but the fact was that Monte had a deep-seated suspicion of all massive and grandiose research schemes. Multiplying the number of brains working on a given job, he knew from long experience, was far from a surefire way of improving the quality of the final product.

Well, who did he need?

Monte himself was something of a maverick in modern anthropology. He was primarily a social anthropologist, and his major research had been involved with a search for regularities in the culture process. Characteristically, however, Monte hadn't stopped there. Impelled partly by a taste for the unconventional and partly by a conviction that biological and social anthropology belonged together, he had also made himself reasonably expert in the most technical field of physical anthropology, population genetics. (The thought of getting blood samples from the people on Sirius Nine made him as eager as any Transylvanian vampire would have been under the same circumstances.)

He needed a linguist. The whole shebang cried out for the best damned linguist available, and so Monte swallowed his personal feelings and chose Charlie Jenike. Charlie was a sour and faintly uncouth individual with a distinct resemblance to a dyspeptic penguin, and he had the quaint habit of wearing shirts for days on end until they virtually anesthetized unwary co-workers. Just the same, Charlie Jenike was a brilliant linguist. If anyone could crack one of the native languages in a hurry, Charlie could do it. Oddly enough, human animals being the strange creatures that they are, Charlie's wife, Helen, was a doll—tiny and dainty and singularly charming. She was also no mean linguist herself; the joke in the profession was that when Helen didn't work, Charlie didn't publish. Helen and Louise got on well together, which partially compensated for the sparks that flew when Monte and Charlie glared at one another over a supposedly friendly brew.

Harvard's Ralph Gottschalk was probably the best of the younger physical anthropologists, and he knew as much as any living person about the primates generally. In view of the rather gibbonoid appearance of the people on Sirius Nine, Ralph had to go along—and anyhow Monte liked to have him around for company. (Field rule number one: if possible, have somebody with you that you *like*. It helps when the going gets sticky, and it always *does* get sticky.) Ralph—a giant of a man with the build of a gorilla and the most gentle disposition Monte had ever encountered—was an unfathomable poker player and an eminently sane individual. Ralph was married to an enigmatic lady named Tina, and he invariably left Tina at home when he traveled. It was hard to say whether this was Ralph's idea or Tina's, but at any rate Ralph always seemed tickled to death to get away. In the field, Ralph tended to wear the secretive smile of a kid playing hooky from school.

If everything worked out according to plan—not that Monte thought for a moment that it would—a certain amount of psychological testing would seem to be imperative. Tom Stein's work in Micronesia had impressed Monte, and when he had met him for the first time at a meeting of the A.A.A. in San Francisco the impression had been strengthened. Tom was a tall, skinny guy, prematurely balding, with pale blue eyes that were almost hidden behind thick glasses. His shyness failed to conceal the fact that he had a razor-keen analytical mind; furthermore, although he was best known for his work in the culture and personality field, he had a genuine feel for social structure. He and his wife were inseparable. Janice Stein was a plain, rather dumpy woman with a radiantly pleasant attitude toward life. Many people underestimated her, but Monte was aware that she had designed some of Tom's most effective projective tests.

Finally, Monte picked Don King. It was a tough decision; Monte's first choice was Cal's Elizabeth Plascencia, but Louise insisted on Don King. She had worked with him before. Don was an archeologist, something of a lone-wolf in his ideas, and a decidedly sharp cookie. Monte didn't actually *like* Don——few people did—but the man was stimulating. He was a valuable irritant because he never accepted anybody's ideas at face value, and he loved an argument above all other things. Don, who was currently in his chronic state of moving from one sexual partner to another, was almost offensively handsome—a tall, well-built, sandy-haired man who habitually dressed as though he was about to pose for a fashion advertisement. Mark Heidelman had questioned the inclusion of Don, since the people of Sirius Nine did not appear to make tools, but Monte was certain that Don would pull his share of the load. A good reconnaissance ought to establish whether or not stone tools had been made in the past. In any event, the scanty pictures available were not a reliable guide, and if those people in fact lacked tools there was the key question of how they got by without them.

Eight anthropologists, then, to breach a world.

Presumptuous?

Sure—but (as Monte was fond of remarking) when there were no precedents you had to make up a few of your own.

The ship was a great metal fish of the deeps; it lived in space. Like the strange fish that live in the long silences and eternal shadows, the ship had never known the shallows that border the shores. It had been assembled in an orbit around the Earth, and its only home had been the vast seas of space and stars.

The exploration crew had been ferried up to the U.N. satellite and had boarded the ship there. The ship had flashed out past the Moon on conventional atomic thrusters and had then gone into the overdrive field that permitted it, in one sense, to exceed the speed of light.

By international agreement, all interstellar ships were named after human beings who had become symbols of peace. This one, officially, was the *Gandhi*. However, you just *can't* think of a tremendous sphere of hurtling metal as the *Gandhi*. Since it was the second ship to make the long run to the Sirius system, the crew, with the strained logic that sometimes filters up out of bull sessions, had promptly dubbed it the *Son of Sirius*. After some three months in space, the happy thought had occurred to one bright lady that Sirius was the Dog Star. From that point on, the evolutionary semantics were inevitable.

From Admiral York on down, everyone referred to the ship as the *S.O.B.*, although the polite fiction was maintained between officers and crew that the initials stood for "Sirius Or Bust."

Monte and Louise had found that packing for a trip to Sirius was annoyingly like packing for a trip anywhere. There were the same nagging problems about what to take and what to leave behind, the same soggy decisions about how to lease the house, the same frayed nerves and perpetual irritations. The force of habit was so strong that they even worked it out so that their departure took place between semesters.

When they finally got away, it was a relief; and the jump up to the U.N. satellite had been a wonder. The stars seemed so close that you could almost reach out and touch them, and the velvet abyss of space was a real and tangible thing. It was much the same feeling that a man had when he went to sea for the first time, and he stood on the deck with the wind in his face and looked out across the living green waves and the bowl of the sky and knew that the world was new and mysterious and anything could happen....

Once they were inside the swollen metal bubble of the starship, however, it was all very different. It rapidly became evident that the voyage to Sirius was going to be something less than a volcano of excitement. Admiral York ran a tight ship, and he smothered the possibility of emergencies with a calm efficiency that took everything into account and corrected errors before they could happen. There was nothing to see and very little for a passenger to do.

When you got right down to it, Monte supposed, an interstellar spaceship was the least interesting way to travel that there was. He made the discovery that millions had made before him: that riding in a big jet, for instance, isn't half as much fun as flying in a small plane, and that for sheer joy no plane can compete with a horseback ride through beautiful country or a canoe trip down a clear stream leaping with rapids. The more exotic the mode of travel—spaceship, submarine, what-have-you—the more people had to carry their own specialized environment with them. Further, the more specialized the artificial environment, the less direct contact with the natural world outside.

The hyperspace field surrounding the starship might have been a mathematical marvel, but you couldn't see it, feel it, hear it, or touch it. Your world was *inside* the ship, and that was a rather barren world of gray metallic walls and fragile catwalks and cool, dead air that whispered and hissed through damp gleaming vents and endlessly circulated and recirculated in the vault that had become the universe.

Eleven months in a vault can be a long, long time. Still, there was work to be done....

Voices.

Monte leaned against the cold wall of the small boxlike chamber that Charlie Jenike had rigged up for his equipment and absently stroked his beard. He listened to the sounds that came out of the speakers and perversely tried to make some sense out of them.

It was impossible, of course. The voices sounded human enough; he could recognize what seemed to be words spoken by both men and women, together with utterances that sounded like the speech of children. But the sounds picked up by the hidden sensors of the first Sirius expedition conveyed no meaning to him at all. They were voices that spoke from across the immense gulf that separated one species from another, voices of people who were more remote from him than a Neanderthal from the last age of ice....

"Doing any good, Charlie?"

Charlie Jenike twisted his aromatic form around on his stool and shrugged. Monte had the distinct feeling that he was about to spit on the floor, but he was spared that indelicacy.

"Good? I'll tell you something, Stewart. I'm right where I was a week ago, and that is precisely nowhere. Let me show you something."

"I'm all eyes. Or ears."

Jenike, moving with surprising grace and skill, set up a projector and fiddled with the computer that controlled the sounds from the speakers. "Got an action sequence here with a few sentences to go with it," he muttered. "Give you some idea what I'm up against."

A good clear picture formed in the air, sharp and three-dimensional. A male native of Sirius Nine dropped down out of the trees—there was a distinct thump when he landed—and walked up to another naked man who was standing in a clearing. The pickup was amazingly sensitive, and Monte could even hear the rapid breathing of the new arrival. The man who had descended from the trees said something to the other man. It was hard to catch exactly what he said, because the *sounds* of the language were utterly different from any language Monte knew. The man who had been there first hesitated a moment, then gave a peculiar whistle. The two men went off together and disappeared into the forest

Jenike cut the equipment off. "Neat, huh? That's about the best we've got, too. I've worked out the phonemic system pretty well; I can repeat what that guy said without much trouble now. But what the hell does it mean?"

"What you need is a dictionary."

"Yeah. You get me one first thing, will you?"

Monte shifted his position carefully; the low artificial gravity field that Admiral York was so proud of was apt to send you smashing into a wall if you forgot what you were doing. He appreciated Charlie's problem. It would have been a tough nut to crack even if he had been working with a known culture.

Suppose, for example, that two Americans meet each other in a hallway. Imagine that for some reason they speak in a private language that is quite unknown to a hidden observer. One of them looks at the other and says—something.

What?

It might be: "Joe! How are you?" (Health is a major concern of American culture, but you don't have that clue on Sirius Nine.)

It might be: "Joe! How're the wife and kids?" (Same clue, plus knowledge of the typical family structure. Elsewhere, it might be *wives* and kids or some other permutation.)

It might be: "Hey! You old bastard, molested any kids today?" (Joking relationships are common in America.)

It might also be: "Ah! I've been looking for you. We're late for the conference." (Americans are slaves to clock time.)

It might be nearly anything.

Without even the hints that might be provided by a familiar cultural system, the voices from Sirius Nine were just that—voices. They were sound patterns without meaning. It would definitely not be possible to land on the planet in a blaze of glory, stroll up to the nearest inhabitant, and say, "Greetings, O Man-Who-Is-My-Brother! I come from beyond the sky, wallowing in good will, to bring you all the jazzy benefits of civilization. Come, let us go arm in arm to the jolly old Council of the Wise Ones...."

"I'm going nuts," Charlie said. "Got any suggestions?"

"Just keep digging, that's all. We'll probably have to work out a non-verbal approach, but if you're set up to learn the language in a hurry once you get the chance, that's all we can expect. Anything I can do for you?"

Jenike smiled, showing singularly yellow teeth. "Yeah, you can get out of here and let me work."

Monte stifled a ready reply; he was going to keep things running smoothly if it killed him. "See you around, then."

He started to duck out through the door.

"Monte?"

"Yep?"

"Don't mind me. Thanks for coming by."

"Don't mention it."

Feeling a little better, he closed the door behind him. The door was not soundproofed. Almost instantly, the voices started up again. He could hear them faintly in the cold silence of the ship: laughing, solemn, playful, querulous.

He started gingerly along the catwalk, and the strange whispers followed him, filling his mind.

Sounds from another world...

Voices.

The large, somewhat egg-shaped off-duty room was supplied with tolerably comfortable chairs and grip-top tables. It had a bar of sorts, and the cool air was warmed a bit by the fog of smoke and voices that tended to characterize such watering holes.

There were two distinct groups in the room. Members of the crew formed a close, noisy circle around the bar. The anthropologists had marked out their own territory: they were in conference at one of the corner tables. Monte had no doubt that the crew thought they were just as alien as anything likely to be found on Sirius Nine, and there were times when he agreed with them.

"Garbage, old man," Don King said, crossing his long legs without disturbing the crease in his trousers. "Absolute garbage."

Tom Stein blinked his pale blue eyes behind his thick glasses and pointed a skinny finger at the archeologist. "It's all just too simple for you. You've poked around with projectile points and potsherds so long that you think that's all mankind is. I say it's a mistake to regard those people as simple until you know for sure what you are talking about."

Don finished off his drink with one long, meticulous swallow. "You're making problems where there aren't any, just like old Monte here. Dammit, man, there *are* constants in culture. We're long past the stage where you can seriously suggest that a culture is just a crazy collection of unrelated traits—a thing of shreds and patches, to use Lowie's unhappy phrase. Cultures, as you guys are always insisting, are hooked together internally. A simple technology, and we don't even know whether or not they've *got* any technology on Sirius Nine; I ain't seen any evidence of it yet—*means* a low level of culture. You don't invent algebra while you're out digging up roots, my friend. We're dealing with a rudimentary band of hunters and gatherers. Why make them more complicated than they are?"

Monte puffed on his pipe, enjoying himself. "That's what I'm worried about. How complicated *are* they?"

"For that matter," Janice Stein said, "what *is* a low level of culture? How do you measure it? Who does the evaluating?"

Don ignored the bait and shifted his ground, which was a favorite stunt of his. "It's complicated enough in one sense, I'll tell you that. It may have sounded nice and easy to Heidelman back at the U.N., but what does he know about it? Did you read that official directive we're supposed to be working under? It says we're to make contact with the natives of Sirius Nine. That's a laugh. How in the devil do you 'contact' a world like Sirius Nine? A world is a helluva big place. You'd think they would have found that out back at the U.N."

Ralph Gottschalk moved his big body on his chair. He had a surprisingly soft voice, but everyone listened to him. "I think Don's got a point there. So far as we know, there is no hypothetical uniform culture on Sirius Nine; there are thousands of isolated local groups of food gatherers. If a starship had landed among the San Bushmen of Africa ten thousand years ago, could it then make contact with *Earth?* It seems improbable."

"Why go back ten thousand years?" Louise asked. "If a ship landed on Earth right now, what would happen? Who speaks for all of us?"

Monte shrugged. "We all know that we'll be doing well to make contact with just one group; Heidelman knows that too. But we still have to be careful. A lot depends on what we do on Sirius Nine."

Don King raised his eyebrows. "Why?"

Monte, who would have asked precisely the same question if he hadn't been in charge of the expedition, took a stab at it. "Apart from the admitted possibility that we may be biting off more than we can chew, it might be argued that we have made at least *some* progress in ethics and law since the time of Cortes and the rest of his merry crew. We can't just sail into a new harbor, run up a flag, and line up at the hog trough."

"I wonder," Don said. "Maybe I'm just cynical because I'm between mates at the moment, but I doubt that line of reasoning very much. We say we're civilized and we carry weapons only to protect ourselves. Sure. We've got enough surplus to afford luxuries like high-minded philosophies. But if things get tough I'll bet we'll be right back where we started from quicker than you can say Cuthbert Pomeroy Gundelfinger; it'll be an eye for an eye, a tooth for a tooth, and a pancreas for a pancreas. If we can't hack it, the military will take over."

"We'd better hack it then," Monte said quietly.

Ralph Gottschalk stood up, looking more than ever like a gorilla. "I'm going back to work, folks."

Monte joined him, leaving the others to their interminable arguments.

Together, the two men walked through the cold metal ship to study the reports of the first expedition again.

When Monte came into their rather drab quarters after his umpteenth conference with Admiral York concerning procedures to be followed on Sirius Nine, he found Louise curled up in bed reading a novel. The book was entitled *Lunar Flame,* and Monte recognized it as a more or less current best-seller that—to quote the cover blurb—"ripped the plastalloy lid off the seething passions that boiled inside the Moon Colony."

"Doing a little research?"

Louise slithered around in her provocative silk nightgown, which she wore from time to time for their mutual enjoyment, and grinned at him. "Let's go to the Moon, dear. That's where the real action is."

He sat down on the bed. "I thought you'd be down at the hydroponics tanks."

"I spent an hour there," she said, brushing back her long, uncoiled black hair. "But it's too *chemical,* even for me. Dammit, Monte, I miss our roses. Stupid, isn't it?"

"I don't think so, Lise." He took her in his arms and nudged her cheek with his beard. Her perfume was sensational, which was a not-so-subtle signal. "Three years is a big chunk out of anyone's life. It's funny, the things you miss out here."

"I know. I catch myself thinking about those picnics of ours up in the mountains. Remember that time on Beaver Creek, when you caught all those rainbows and the storm came up? I think the worst thing about a spaceship is that there's no *weather.*"

"It's not all fun and games," Monte admitted.

Louise changed the subject. "What did Master York have to say?"

Monte hesitated. "Nothing much. He's a very levelheaded guy, I think. We were working out the details of rescue operations—just in case."

Quite suddenly, they became sharply aware of the cold metal of the ship around them, the thin icy sweat, and the great emptiness Outside....

Monte thought of the children they had never had—Louise had lost two babies in childbirth—and he knew that Louise was thinking of them too. It was a shared sadness between them. They had been planning to adopt a child, but somehow it had never happened.

Louise held him tightly. "You're all I have, Monte. All that counts."

"It works both ways, Lise."

He kissed her, and. she kissed him back, and the ritual between them began again.

It always comes back to this, he thought. *After all the small triumphs and major sorrows that make up a life, it comes back to the two of us alone in a room. Without her, my universe has no meaning.*

And then: *Monte, you're a sentimental slob.*

And then: *What the hell! I like it this way!*

"And so do I," Louise whispered, reading his mind with the ease of long practice.

In the darkness of the artificial night, with Louise asleep by his side, Monte Stewart woke up. He had been dreaming, and the dream had not been pleasant. He felt a chill in his bones.

He lay quite still, his eyes open, staring into blackness.

Maybe it's the ship that gives me the jitters. Maybe it's the cold dead air that sighs from the vents, or *the vibration of the stardrive,* or *the gravity that's never quite right. Maybe it's the gray metal coffin that seals me in....*

No.

Come off of it, Monte.

You know what it is.

Sure, he knew. The alien forms of life that had been found in the Centaurus and Procyon systems hadn't worried him. They were *really* alien, so utterly different from human beings that there was no possible point of conflict, any more than there was between a trout and a pine tree. When lifeforms are totally different, they can usually manage to ignore one another. But when they are close—well, there was unexpected truth in the old phrase about being too close for comfort.

In a way, Monte felt, they had all been talking around the central problem, pretending that it didn't exist. In the long run, it might not matter much whether or not the people of Sirius Nine had a culture that was more complex than it seemed to be.

The crucial point was simply that they *were* people.

The one animal mankind had to fear was man; so it had always been and might always be.

In one sense, Monte Stewart was going to meet a native of another world.

In another sense, and an equally real one, man was at last going to meet man—his sometime friend and his most ancient enemy.

4

There are a number of much-advertised facts, Monte discovered, that a man doesn't give a hoot in Hades about when he's actually *living* on an alien planet. Prominent among them are the following:

The star Sirius is twenty-six times as bright as the Sun of Earth, and two and one-half times as massive. It has a temperature of 19,700 degrees Fahrenheit. It has a white dwarf star for a companion, which revolves around it every fifty years. The dwarf is a long way off—twenty times the distance from the Earth to the Sun—and it is only a little more than three times the width of the Earth. Sirius has twelve planets, and the ninth one, very far out in an elliptical orbit, is similar enough to pass for a cousin, if not a twin, of Earth. The planet has five percent more nitrogen in its atmosphere than does the Earth, and slightly less oxygen.

On the other hand, there were certain facts that a man could not ignore. These were the ones that kicked him in the teeth:

The sun is a blinding white; a raging giant furnace in the sky. If you are not careful, it blisters your skin with disconcerting speed. The daylight hours—there are ten of them—are oppressively hot, and the air is humid; your shirt is plastered to your back ten minutes after you put it on. The gravity, particularly after the months on the ship, is a shade too strong and your feet feel as though they have picked up heavy gobs of mud with each step you take. Something in the air doesn't agree with you; your nose itches constantly and your throat is always sore. Strange animals sniff you on the heavy wind and panic at the smell. The rolling grasslands look very pleasant, but they are *never* level—you are always either climbing or descending a deceptive grade, and there is a liberal supply of burrs and thorns to rip at your skin and your clothing. The great forests that grow in bands along the bases of the jagged mountains are gloomy and still, and the reddish leaves of the trees remind you of a nightmare autumn. There are dirty-gray clouds on the horizon, and muted thunder mutters down the wind....

Monte wiped the sweat out of his eyes with his damp sleeve and tried to find a less slippery grip on his rifle. He had been on Sirius Nine for two weeks now, and in his considered opinion had accomplished precisely nothing. He had seen the natives with his own eyes, and knew no more about them than he had known on Earth. Journeying across the light-years, he thought, was sometimes easy when compared to crossing from one man's mind to another's.

For the first time in his life, he genuinely understood that a culture, a way of life, could be a totally alien thing—something for which there was no counterpart on Earth at all. Nothing in his previous experience had prepared him for the reality of the people on Sirius Nine. Now, struggling through the thick grass of the field with Charlie Jenike at his side, he could not forget what he had written the night before in his notebook. (He kept two sets of notebooks, an official one and one for himself. So far, the official one was virtually blank.)

It's frightening to realize how ignorant we are, and how thoroughly conditioned by our own limited experiences. Stories and learned speculations about life on other planets always seem to emphasize the strange and exotic qualities of the alien worlds themselves, but the life-forms that exist against these dramatic backdrops all live like earthmen, no matter how odd their appearance may be. (Or else they live like social insects, which amounts to the same thing.) All the caterpillars and octopi and reptiles and frogs have social systems just like the Vikings or the Kwakiutls or the Zulus. Nobody seems to have realized that a culture too may be alien, more alien than any planet of bubbling lead. You can walk right up to something that looks like a man—and is a man—and not know him at all, or anything about him....

Charlie sneezed. "Kleenex will make a fortune here."

Monte squinted, trying to see over the curtain of grass that surrounded him. "Dammit, I think we've lost him again." He glanced up at the large gray reconnaissance sphere that hovered in the sky above them, then spoke into his wrist radio: "How are we doing, Ace? I can't see a thing down here."

The soft, Texas voice of Ace Reid, who was piloting the sphere, was reassuring. "He's right where he was, sir. Just at the edge of the trees. You're right on target if he doesn't panic."

"Thanks. Stand by." He cut off the radio and concentrated on trying to avoid the hidden thorns in the grass. His throat was sore and his eyes were inflamed. The day was cloudy, fortunately, but the heat was almost unbearably sticky. He felt like the wrath of God, and he was none too optimistic about what he was doing. They had tried twice before to make contact—how he was coming to hate that phrase!—with the natives, and had gotten exactly nowhere.

However, there was a possibility that the two of them approaching on foot might not be overly alarming. And the old man they had scouted had *seemed* to be more curious than the others....

"This," Charlie Jenike said, "is murder."

"Earthman's Burden," Monte muttered. He would have preferred to have Ralph Gottschalk with him today, but he desperately needed the linguist just in case the native actually said something. Anyhow, Charlie was trying to be cordial; it wouldn't hurt him to reciprocate.

He pushed on through the sticky blue grass, talking to fill up the silence. "You know, Charlie, it's been a mighty long time since any anthropologist went in absolutely cold. I mean, even the early boys had some sort of a go-between—administrators, someone who knew someone, *somebody*. I feel like one of those Spaniards who washed ashore and looked up to find a bunch of Indians nobody had ever seen before."

"Give me the Indians every time. They're at least from the same planet we are—one of those Spaniards wound up being a chief, you know." Charlie began to sneeze again.

With startling abruptness, they climbed out of the grass and saw the dark shapes of the trees ahead of them. Monte stopped and surveyed the terrain. He didn't see the man. Of course, they still had a good hundred yards to go....

He cut in the radio. "Ace?"

"A little to your left, and dead ahead."

"Right. Thanks." He switched off the radio. "You ready, Charlie?"

"I haven't been taking this stroll to help my digestion." Monte took a deep breath of the irritating air and wished irrationally that he could light his pipe. It was out of the question, of course. If there were no tobacco-like plants on Sirius Nine, the native might not take too kindly to the spectacle of a strange man with smoke coming out of his mouth.

The two men walked steadily forward; their rifles at the ready.

"Hold it," Charlie whispered suddenly. "I see him."

The man stood right at the edge of the trees, half hidden by the faint shadows. He did not move at all, but he was looking directly at them.

Monte did not hesitate. "Keep moving. Stay behind me and on my right. Don't use that rifle unless I'm actually attacked, and for God's sake, Charlie, try to look friendly."

Monte walked straight toward the man, keeping his pace steady. His heart hammered in his chest. He was within twenty yards of the man, fifteen....

It was the closest he had ever gotten.

The man stood as though rooted to the spot, his dark eyes wide and staring. His pale copper skin gleamed wetly in the light, and the fuzz of golden hair on his head seemed almost electrically alive. His long arms almost touched the ground. The man was completely naked, with a series of vertical stripes painted on his chest. The stripes were all vermilion.

He carried no weapons of any kind.

Ten yards....

Monte stopped. *Dammit,* he thought, *he is a man.*

When you get up this close, there is no doubt at all. Monte put his rifle down on the ground and held up his hands to show that they were empty.

The man took one quick step backward. His dark eyes blinked. He was quite old, Monte noticed, although his muscles still seemed firm and supple. He looked frightened, confused, uncertain. But there was something else in his face, as though a struggle were raging within him. The dark sunken eyes were sad, and yet strangely eager....

Don't run away. Just don't run away.

Monte slowly fumbled in his pack. He took out a small piece of raw meat and a cluster of red berries. He held the meat in his right hand and the berries in his left. He extended them toward the man.

The old man looked at the food silently. He wiped the palms of his hands against the bare skin of his legs.

Monte took a step forward.

The man retreated a single step, standing now almost behind a tall blue-barked tree.

Monte froze, still holding out the food. He didn't know what to do. If only he could *talk* to the man....

He bent over and put the berries and the meat on the ground. Then he waved Charlie back and retreated ten paces.

They waited. For a long minute that seemed to stretch into eternity, the old man did nothing at all.

Then, surprisingly, he whistled—one long whistle, and one short. It sounded exactly like a whistle used to call a dog.

Nothing happened.

The man repeated the whistle, urgently.

This time he got results. An animal whined back in the trees. There was a sound of padded feet slowly moving over a carpet of dead leaves. The sound came closer....

The animal stepped out into the open and stood beside the man. It was a big beast, and the stink of him filled the air. He stood some four feet high and his coat was a dirty gray. His long muscles rippled under his taut skin. His ears flattened along his sleek head and he growled deep in his throat. He looked at the two strangers and bared his sharp, white teeth.

Monte held his ground. The animal looked more like a wolf than anything else, but he was built for speed. His head was very long, with massive jaws. He was a killer; Monte knew it instinctively. He felt exactly the same way he felt when he looked at a rattlesnake.

The wolf-thing sniffed the air and growled again. The old man whistled, once.

The animal went down low, his belly almost touching the ground, and inched his way forward. It snarled constantly, its long white teeth bared. It looked at Monte, saliva dripping from its jaws. Its eyes were yellow, yellow....

The wolf-thing paused at the meat, then kept coming.

Monte could feel the sweat dripping down his ribs.

The old man took a step forward, and whistled again, angrily. The beast paused reluctantly, still snarling. Then it turned, snatched up the meat, and trotted back to the man by the tree. The man patted its sleek head and nodded, and the wolf-thing disappeared into the forest, taking the meat with him. He held it gingerly in his mouth, not eating it.

Very slowly, the man stepped out and scooped up the berries with his right hand. He stared at Monte, his dark eyes fearful.

Monte took a deep breath. It was now or never. He pointed to himself. "Monte," he said distinctly. He pointed to Charlie. "Charlie," he said.

The man stood there with the berries in his hand. He made no response. His eyes began to shift from point to point, not looking at either of them directly. He seemed very tense and nervous. Once, he glanced up at the gray sphere hovering in the sky.

Monte tried again. He pointed to himself and repeated his name.

The man understood; Monte was certain of that. The dark eyes were quick and intelligent. But he said nothing. He looked like he was trying to make up his mind about something, something terribly important....

Quite suddenly, with no warning at all, the man turned on his heel and walked into the forest. In seconds, he had disappeared from view.

"Wait!" Monte called uselessly. "We won't hurt you, dammit!"

"Try a whistle," Charlie said sarcastically, lowering his rifle.

Monte clenched his fists. Somehow, he felt very much alone now that the man was gone, alone on a world that was a long, long way from home. His skin itched horribly.

He looked up. Great dark clouds filled the sky, and the rumble of thunder sounded closer. He saw a jagged fork of white lightning flicker down into the forest. There was a heavy smell of rain in the air.

Monte made up his mind rapidly. He was *not* going to let that man get away. He called the sphere and dictated a fast report of what had happened. "What's the extent of that forest, Ace?"

"It isn't very wide, sir—not over half a mile. But it stretches out lengthwise a far piece in both—maybe two or three miles before it thins out any."

"We're going in after him. I want you to come down low, just above the trees. Let me know at once if he comes out the other side. Keep a fix on us, and if we holler you know what to do."

"You're the boss. But there's a bad storm coming up—"

"I know that. Stand by."

Monte cut off the radio and wiped at his beard with his hand. "He was walking, Charlie. That means there must be a path."

Charlie Jenike eyed the gathering rain clouds without enthusiasm. "What if he takes to the trees?"

"What if he does?" Monte asked impatiently. "Didn't you ever play Tarzan when you were a kid?"

Charlie put his hands on his ample hips and tried to figure out whether or not Monte was seriously considering taking to the trees after the man. He couldn't decide, possibly because Monte himself wasn't sure at this point of what he would or would not do.

Monte picked up his rifle and pushed his way into the forest where the man had vanished. He thought for a moment that he heard the whine of an animal, but that was probably his imagination working. It was hot and breathless among the trees, and the subtly *wrong* shapes of the ferns and bushes gave the whole thing the improbable air of a make-believe world. The woods were dark with shadows. He felt cut off, as though he had stepped behind an invisible wall.

Thunder boomed high above them and the blue-black limbs of the tall trees stirred fitfully.

"Look there," he said. "There *is* a path."

It was just a narrow, twisting trail through the forest. In one place, where the leaves had been scraped away, there was a fresh print—the mark of a naked man-like foot, with the big toe sticking out at an angle like a human thumb. The path looked like a trail through the woods back home; there was nothing sinister about it.

But it was too still. Even the birds were silent at their approach, and no animal stirred.

Monte thought of nothing at all and started down the path.

The storm hit with a cold wet fist before they had gone two hundred yards.

A wall of wind smashed through the trees and a roar of metallic thunder exploded in the invisible sky. Great gray sheets of wind-driven rain pelted the trees and overflowed into silver waterfalls that drenched the forest floor.

Monte put his head down and kept going. He heard Charlie swearing steadily behind him.

The rain was cool and oddly refreshing on his damp back, and the storm seemed to clear the air in a way that was surprisingly welcome. In spite of the nerve-jangling bedlam of sound, he felt better than he had before. His nose stopped itching and even his sandpapered throat lost some of its rawness.

He kept a sharp lookout, but it was hard to see anything except the rivers of rain and the dripping bushes and the water-blackened trunks of the trees. The crashing thunder was so continuous that it was impossible to talk. Far above him, the branches of the trees swayed and moaned in the wind.

He was soaked to the skin, but it didn't matter. He shoved his streaming hair out of his eyes and kept on walking. He concentrated just on putting one foot before the other, feeling his feet squishing inside his boots, and he kept looking, looking....

There was still light, but it was a gray and cheerless light that was almost as heavy as the rain. It was a ghost light, fugitive from a hidden sun, and it had the feel of imminent darkness in it....

There.

A tremendous tree to the right of the trail, a tree that looked curiously like a California redwood, a tree that had a black opening in it like a cave....

And a frightened copper face staring out of the hollowness within; two dark eyes peering into the rain.

Monte held up his hand. "There he is!" he hollered.

Charlie came up beside him, his pudgy features almost obscured by countless trickles and rivulets of rain. "Let's grab him and run for it. We can make friends later where it's dry."

Monte smiled and shook his head. It might come to that eventually, but it would be a singularly poor beginning. He stood there with the storm howling around him and desperately tried to come up with something—anything—that would get across the idea that he meant no harm.

He had never before felt quite so keenly the absolute necessity for language. He was hardly closer to the man in the tree than if he had stayed on Earth.

Oh, Charlie had worked out a few phrases in one of the native languages and he *thought* he knew approximately what they meant. But none of the phrases—even assuming that they were correct—went with the situation. It wasn't the fault of the first expedition; they had planted their mikes and cameras well. It was simply the fact that you just don't *say* the right things in casual everyday conversations. A man can go through a lot of days without ever saying, "I am a friend." He can go through several lifetimes very nicely without ever saying something as useful as: "I am a man from another planet, and I only want to talk to you."

The closest thing they had was a sentence that Charlie thought meant something like, "I see that you are awake, and now it is time to eat."

That didn't seem too wildly promising.

"Why doesn't he ask us in?" Charlie hollered. "He's looking right at us. I don't need any engraved invitation. Let's barge on in and see what happens."

Monte stepped toward the tree.

The old man looked out at him with dark, staring eyes. Those eyes, Monte thought, reflected a lifetime of experiences, and *all* of those experiences were alien to a man from Earth. The man seemed somehow to be of another time as well as another world; a creature of the forests, shy and afraid, ready to panic....

"Charlie! Give it a try!"

Charlie Jenike cupped his hands around his mouth and bellowed a strange series of sounds; it sounded a bit like singing, although his voice was distinctly unmusical. "I see that you are awake," he hoped he said in the native tongue, "and now it is time to eat!"

The old man shrank back into the hollow of the tree, his mouth falling open in astonishment.

Monte took another step closer.

Instantly, without any warning, the man bolted.

He lunged out of his shelter, very fast despite his age, and ran awkwardly, his long arms pumping the air. He came so close that Monte actually touched him as he passed. He scrambled up a tree with amazing agility, wrapping his arms around the trunk and pushing with his feet on the wet bark. When he got up to where the limbs were strong, he threw one questioning glance back down at the two strangers and then leaped gracefully from one limb to another. He used his hands almost like hooks, swinging his body on his long arms in breath-taking arcs. The rain didn't seem to bother him at all; he moved so fast that he was practically a blur.

In seconds, he was gone—lost on the roof of the world. "Well, Tarzan?"

Monte stood there in the pouring rain. He was beginning to get a trifle impatient with this interminable game of hide-and-seek.

"I'm going inside," he said, taking out his pocket flashlight.

Charlie eyed the dark cave in the hollow tree. "That thing may not be empty, you know."

"I hope it isn't."

"After you, my friend—and watch out for Rover."

Monte walked steadily over to the opening in the tree and stepped inside.

5

There was heavy animal smell inside the chamber in the hollow tree, but Monte knew at once that the place was empty. He flashed the light around to make certain, but his eyes only confirmed the evidence of an older, subtler sense. The room—if that was the word for it—felt empty and was empty.

In fact, it was the *emptiest* place Monte had ever seen.

He moved on in, making room for Charlie, and the two men stood there in the welcome dryness, trying to understand what they saw—and what they didn't see.

The interior of the trunk of the great tree was hollow, forming a dry chamber some twelve feet in diameter. About ten feet above their heads, smooth wood plugged the tubular shaft, forming a ceiling that reflected their lights.

The place was a featureless vault made entirely from the living wood of the tree. Even the floor was wood—a worn, brownish wood that was porous enough so that the water that dripped from their clothes seeped away before it had a chance to collect in puddles. The curving walls were a lighter color, almost that of yellow pine, and they were spotlessly clean.

There was a kind of shelf set into one wall; it was little more than an indentation in the wood. The piece of raw meat that the wolf-thing had taken was on the shelf, and so was the cluster of berries.

That was all.

There was no furniture of any kind. There were no beds, no chairs, no tables. They were no decorations on the walls, no art-work of any sort. There were no tools, no weapons. There were no pots, no bowls, no baskets.

The place was absolutely barren. There were no clues as to what sort of a man might live there.

It was just a big hole in a tree: simple, crude, unimpressive.

And yet....

Monte looked closely at the walls. "No sign of chopping or cutting."

"No. It's smooth as glass. No trace of charring, either."

"How the devil did he make this place?"

"Like Topsy," Charlie said, "it just growed."

Monte shook his head. "I doubt that. I never saw a hollow tree that looked like this on the inside, did you?"

"Nope—but then I haven't been in just a whole hell of a lot of them."

Outside, the rain poured down around the tree and the wind moaned through a faraway sky. It was not unpleasant to be in the hollow tree;

there was something secure and enduring about the place, as though it had weathered many seasons and many storms.

But how could a man have lived here and left so few traces of his existence?

"Maybe he doesn't live here," Monte said slowly.

"Maybe this is just a sort of temporary camp—a shelter of some kind."

Charlie shrugged. There were dark circles around his eyes and he looked very tired. "I'd say that these people have no material culture at all—and that, my friend, doesn't make sense. You know what this place looks like? It looks like an animal den."

"It would—but it feels wrong. Too clean, for one thing. No bones, no debris of any kind. And I'm not at all sure that this is a natural tree."

"Supernatural, maybe?"

"I mean I think it has been *shaped* somehow."

Charlie sighed. "If they can make a tree grow the way they want it to, why can't they chip out a hunk of flint? It's crazy. This place gives me the creeps, Monte. Let's get out of here before we poke our noses into something we really can't handle."

Monte thought it over. It seemed obvious that the man would not return while they were in the tree. Nothing would be gained by parking here indefinitely. But he didn't like the idea of just pulling out. He was beginning to feel a trifle futile, and it was a new experience for him. He didn't like it.

He reached into his pack and took out a good steel knife. He carried it over and placed it on the shelf with the meat and the berries.

"Do you think that's wise?"

Monte rubbed at his beard, which was beginning to itch again. "I don't know. Do you?"

Charlie didn't say anything.

"We've got to do something. And I'd like to see what that guy will make of a real-for-sure tool. I'm going to get one of the boys in here and plant a scanner and a mike before he comes back. Then maybe we'll see something. I'll take the responsibility."

He cut in his radio and called the sphere. Ace sounded as though he were not exactly having the time of his life bucking the storm above the trees, but he wasn't in any serious trouble. Monte carefully dictated a report of what had happened, and arranged a rendezvous point at the edge of the forest.

"Come on," he said, and stepped back into the rain.

It was quite dark now, and the forest was hushed and gloomy. The rain had settled down into a gentle patter and the thunder seemed lonely and remote, as though it came from another world. They brushed their way through wet leaves and found the trail. The beams of their flashlights were small and lost in the wilderness of night.

Monte walked wearily along the path, his damp clothes sticking to his body. He was bone-tired—not so much from physical exertion, he realized, as from the strain of failure. Still, the night air was fresh and cool after the muggy heat of the day, and that was something.

All forests, he supposed, were pretty much the same at night. He knew that this one, at any rate, was less alien in the darkness. The trees were only trees, flat black shadows that dripped and stirred around him. Occasionally, he could even catch a glimpse of a cloud-streaked sky above him, and once he even saw a star. With only a slight effort of the imagination, he could feel that he was walking through the night-shrouded woods of Earth, perhaps coming home from a fishing trip, and soon he would walk into a village, where lights twinkled along the streets and magic music drifted out of a bar....

He blinked his eyes and shifted the rifle on his shoulder.

Steady boy. You're a helluva long way from Earth.

It was hard for him to get used to this world. Sirius Nine was just a name, and less than that; it seemed singularly inappropriate. He wondered what the natives called their world. He wished that he knew the *names* of things. A world was terribly alien, incredibly strange, until it was transformed with names. Names had the power of sorcery; they could change the unknown into the known.

Tired as he was, Monte was filled with a hard determination he hadn't known he possessed.

One day, he'd know those names—or die trying.

> EXTRACT FROM THE NOTEBOOK OF MONTE STEWART:
> This is the fourteenth night I have spent on Sirius Nine. The camp is silent around me, and Louise is already asleep. God knows I'm tired, but I'm wide awake.
>
> All my life I've heard that old one to the effect that when you know the right questions to ask the answers practically hit you in the face. I've even said as much to students in that other life of mine. (Space travel is a great cure for smugness. I feel pretty damned ignorant out here. I wonder if I wasn't getting a mite cocky, back home?)
>
> Well, I think I know some of the right questions. Here are the obvious ones:
>
> What was that man we chased doing in the forest by himself? And, if he lives in that hollow tree, does he live there alone? Wherever you find him, man is a social

animal—he lives in groups. Families, clans, bands, tribes, nations—the names don't matter. But a man alone is a very strange thing. And he isn't the only one, either; we've seen others. Where is the group he belongs to? And what kind of a group is it?

What are these people afraid of? The first expedition did nothing to alarm them. Presumably, they have never seen men like us before—we have given them no reason to believe that we're dangerous. I'm sure that old man wanted to talk to us—but he just couldn't make himself do it. Why not? Most primitive peoples, when they meet a new kind of men for the first time, either trot out the gals for a welcome or open up with spears and arrows. These natives don't do anything at all. Am I missing something here? Or are they just shy? Or what?

Why don't these people have any artifacts? I haven't seen a single tool or weapon of any sort. Don King hasn't been able to find any artifacts in archeological deposits. What's the answer? Are they so simple that they don't even know how to chip flint? If so, they are more technologically primitive than the men who lived on Earth a million years ago.

Why have they retained the long, ape-like arms of brachiators? Why do they swing through the trees when they can walk reasonably well on the ground? Is this connected in some way with their lack of tools? Are we really dealing here with a bright bunch of apes? And if we are, then how about the language? (Question: Is a bright ape with a language a man? Where do you draw the line? Or do we have to get metaphysical about it? And if they are apes, how are we supposed to contact them for the United Nations?)

What's the significance of that wolf-thing we saw? Charlie and I saw the man call Rover with a whistle. We saw Rover pick up the meat and carry it off. Later, we saw the meat inside the hollow tree. (Problem: Was the man going to eat it, or was Rover?) The man certainly seemed to control Rover. So is Rover a domesticated animal, or what? On Earth, man didn't domesticate the dog until after he'd used tools for close to a million years. Are there other animals they have domesticated?

How about the hollow tree? Is it natural, or do the natives shape the growth in some way? If they do, isn't this an artifact? If they can do that, why don't they have agriculture?

Those are some of the right questions.

I'm waiting for the answers to hit me in the face—but I'm not holding my breath.

Two days later, the watched pot began to boil.

First, the old man returned to the hollow tree and found the steel knife.

Then Ralph Gottschalk and Don King spotted a tree burial.

And, finally, Tom Stein—who was cruising around with Ace in the reconnaissance sphere—located an entire village that contained at least one hundred people.

Monte didn't know exactly what he had expected the man to do with the knife; he would hardly have been surprised if he had swallowed it. He and Louise stood by the scanner screen and watched intently as the man entered the hollow tree for the first time since Monte and Charlie had left.

The tree chamber was as Spartan as ever; nothing had changed. The knife was still on the ledge by the meat and the berries. Considering the probable condition of the meat by now, Monte was just as glad that the scanner did not transmit smells.

The old man stood in the center of the room, his dark eyes peering about cautiously in the half-light. His nose wrinkled in a very human way and he picked up the meat and threw it outside. Then he walked back to the shelf and looked at the knife. He stood there for a long time, a naked old man staring at a gift that must have seemed very strange to him, a gift that had been made light-years away.

Then he picked up the knife. He held it awkwardly, between his thumb and forefinger, as a man might hold a dead fish by the tail. He lifted it to his nose and sniffed it. He got a better grip on the handle and gingerly touched the cutting edge with the fingers of his other hand. He muttered something to himself that the mike didn't catch, then frowned.

He walked over to the curving wall and stuck the point of the knife into the wood. He yanked it out again, looked at it, and then shaved a sliver of wood from the wall with the cutting edge. His action left a single raw scar in the polished smoothness of the room.

"*Merc kuprai*," he said distinctly. It was the first time Monte had ever heard the man speak; his voice was low and pleasant.

"Charlie said that *merc* was a kind of polysynthetic word," he whispered to Louise. "It means something like: *It is a*——. So he's saying that the knife is a *kuprai*, whatever that is."

"Whatever it is," Louise said, "it must not be very impressive."

The naked man shook his head sadly and tossed the knife back up on the shelf. He did not look at it again. He yawned a little, stretched, and walked out of the chamber. The scanner still caught his back, just beyond the entrance to the tree. He sat down in a small patch of sunlight and promptly went to sleep.

"Well, I'll be damned," Monte said.

Louise shrugged, her brown eyes twinkling. "*Merc kuprai,*" she said.

"You, dear, can go to the devil."

She gave him a quick, warm kiss. "You seem to be oriented toward the nether regions today. Look up! Have faith! Remember that every day in every way—"

"Cut it out, Lise," he grinned.

That was when Ralph Gottschalk came lumbering in like an amiable gorilla. His face was flushed and he was smiling from ear to ear. Since Ralph was hardly the type to get excited over nothing, Monte decided that he must have found not only the missing link but quite possibly the whole chain.

"Monte, we've got one!"

"Swell. One what?"

"Confound it, man, a burial! We've got us a skeleton."

The man's excitement was contagious, but Monte held a tight rein on himself. It wouldn't do to go off half-cocked. "Where? You haven't touched it, have you?"

"Of course not! Do I look like a sap? But you've got to see it! Don and I just found it about an hour ago—it's not a quarter of a mile from camp. The son of a gun is up in a tree!"

"Are you sure of what it is?"

"Of course I'm sure—I climbed up and looked. The bones are in a kind of a nest up there—a regular flexed tree burial. Man, you ought to see the ulna on that thing! And I'll tell you this—that mandible may be heavy, but there's plenty of room for a brain inside that skull. In fact—"

"Anything in that nest except bones?"

"Nothing at all. No pots, no pans, no spears, no nothing. Just bones. But you give me an hour with those bones where I can really see 'em and I'll be able to tell you something for sure about these people!"

Louise touched his arm. "Come on, Monte! Let's go."

"I'd better have a look," Monte agreed. "Lead the way, Ralph."

Ralph charged off, still mumbling to himself. He ploughed through the scattered tents of the camp, crossed the clearing, and plunged into a stand of trees at an impatient trot. Monte was amazed at the big man's agility; the tug of the gravity and the enervating effects of the damp heat did not combine to make a sprint through the forest his idea of a swell time. Louise seemed to be taking it well enough, however, so he couldn't afford to say anything about it.

Don King was waiting for them at the base of a tall tree. Monte wiped the sweat out of his eyes and was annoyed to notice that Don looked as natty as ever.

"Hello, Don. Ralph tells me that you two have nosed out a burial."

Don pointed. "Right up there, boss. See that thing that looks like a nest on that big limb? No—the other side, right close to the tree trunk."

"I see it," Louise said.

Monte examined it as well as he could from where he stood. It looked very much like a nest that might have been made by a large bird, although it seemed to be made mostly of bark. He chewed on his lower lip. If he could just get his hands on those bones....

"Well, Monte? What do you say?"

Monte sighed. "You know what I have to say, Ralph. It's no go. We can't move those bones."

Don King swore under his breath. "It's the first solid lead we've gotten! What's the big idea?"

Monte put his hands on his hips and stuck out his bearded jaw. The accumulated frustrations of this job were beginning to get him on edge. "In case you haven't heard," he said evenly, "we are trying our feeble best to make friends with these people. It would seem to me that desecrating one of their graves would be a fine way of not going about it."

"Oh Lord," Don groaned. "Next you'll be telling me that those bones were probably somebody's mother."

"Not necessarily. They might just be somebody's old man. But I haven't got the slightest doubt that we're being watched all the time. I'd like to have those bones just as much as you would—maybe more. But we're not going to steal them—not yet, anyway. It may come to that. But it hasn't yet. Until I say otherwise, the bones stay there. Understand?"

Don King didn't say anything. He looked disgusted.

"I guess he's right," Ralph said slowly. "Sometimes we have a tendency to forget what those bones mean to people. You remember that joker in Mexico in the old days who tried to buy a body right at the funeral? He almost wound up in a box himself."

"Nuts," Don said.

Even Louise looked disappointed.

"Let's go on back to camp," Monte said, none too happy himself. "Those bones won't run away. They'll still be there when the time is right."

"When will that be?" Don asked, running a hand through his sandy hair.

"I'll let you know," Monte said grimly.

It was indeed fortunate, in view of the general morale, that the reconnaissance sphere landed when it did with the big news. The usually reserved Tom Stein popped out like a jack-in-the-box, just as excited as Ralph had been about the tree burial. His pale blue eyes flashed behind his thick glasses and he even forgot to be analytical.

"Ace and I found a whole bunch of 'em about ten miles north of here," he said. "It must be the main local village or something—at least a hundred of them. They're living in caves. We saw kids and everything. How about that?"

"That's wonderful, Tom," Monte said. "Maybe we can do some good with them. Maybe if we catch a lot of 'em in one place..." He thought for a moment. "Tomorrow we're going to take that recon sphere and set it down right smack in the middle of those caves. We're going to make those people talk if we have to give them the third degree."

"Hey, Janice!" Tom yelled to his wife, "Did you hear what I found? There's a whole bunch of 'em...."

Monte smiled.

Things *were* looking a little better.

An alien yellow moon rode high over the dark screen of the trees and the orange firelight threw leaping black shadows across the flat surfaces of the tents.

Monte, lying on his back on his cot, understood for the first time that the old saying about feeling invisible eyes staring at you was literally true. He knew that the camp was ringed with eyes, eyes that probed and stared and evaluated. It was not a pleasant feeling, but it was the way he had wanted it to be. Indeed, the main reason for establishing the camp in the clearing had been to give the natives a chance to size them up. He hoped they liked what they saw.

Ralph Gottschalk, his back propped up against a stump, was strumming the guitar he had insisted on bringing from Earth. He and Don King—who had a surprisingly good voice—were singing snatches of various old songs: *John Henry, When My Blue Moon Turns to Gold Again, San Antonio Rose, Wabash Cannonball.* As was usually the case, they didn't quite know all the words, which made for a varied if somewhat incomplete repertoire.

It was good to hear the old songs; they were a link with home. And, somehow, the whole scene was oddly reassuring. It was all so familiar, and at the same time so forever new: the dance of the fire, the distant stars, the singing voices. How many men and women had gathered around how many fires to sing how many songs since man was first born? Perhaps, in the final analysis, it was moments like this that were the measure of man; no one, on such a night, could believe that man was wholly evil.

And the natives of Sirius Nine? Did they too have their songs, and of what did they sing?

"It's beautiful," Louise said, sharing his mood as always.

Monte left his cot and went to her. He held her in his arms and kissed her hair. They did not speak; they had said all the words in the long-ago years, and now there was no need for words. Their love was so much a part of their lives that it was a natural, unquestioned power. There was too little love on any world, in any universe. They treasured each other, and were unashamed.

Tomorrow, there would be the caves and the natives and the curious problems of men that filled the daylight hours.

For tonight, there was love—and that was enough.

6

The gray reconnaissance sphere floated through the sky like a strange metallic bubble in the depths of an alien sea. The white furnace of the sun burned away the morning mists, leaving the vault of the sky clean and blue as though it had been freshly created the night before.

"There it is," Tom Stein said, pointing. "See? They're starting to come out now."

Ace Reid, unbidden, began to take the sphere down.

Far below them, Monte could see a panorama that might have been transmitted from the dawn of time. There was a sun-washed canyon that trenched its way through eroded walls of brown rock, and a stream of silver-streaked water that snaked its way across the canyon floor. Reddish-green brush lined the banks of the stream, and it looked cool and inviting. (Old habits and patterns of thought died hard; Monte caught himself wondering whether or not the fishing was any good down there.) At the head of the canyon, not far from the leaping white spray of a waterfall, there was a jumbled escarpment of gray and brown rock. The face of the rock was pockmarked with the dark cave-eyes of tunnels and rock shelters. There was even a curl of blue smoke rising from the mouth of one of the caves, which was the first real evidence of fire that Monte had seen among the natives.

He could see the people clearly, like toy soldiers deployed in a miniature world. There were men and women in front of the caves and on the steep paths that wound down to the canyon floor. Three or four kids were already down by the stream, splashing in the water. The people must have seen the sphere, which was plainly visible in the blue morning sky, but they didn't seem to be paying any attention to it.

"Look good, Charlie?"

The linguist smiled. "If they'll only *say* something."

Monte turned to Ace. "Set her down."

"Where?"

"Just as close to that cliff as you can get. Try not to squash anybody, but let 'em feel the breeze. I'm a mite tired of being ignored."

Ace grinned. "I'll park this crate right on their out house."

The gray sphere started down.

They shaved the canyon walls and landed directly below the cave entrances. Monte unfastened the hatch and climbed out. The brown rock walls of the canyon seemed higher than they had looked from above, rearing up over his head like mountains. The blue sky seemed far away. He could hear the chuckling gurgle of the stream and feel the gentle stir of the wind on his face. He stood there by the metal sphere and the others joined him.

Suddenly, he was almost overpowered by a feeling of strangeness. It wasn't this world that was strange, nor was it the natives who were all around him. It was himself, and it was Tom and Charlie and Ace, with their stubby arms and their layers of clothing. And it was the gray metal sphere they stood beside, a monstrous artificial thing in this valley of stone and water and living plants....

The people did not react to their presence. They seemed to freeze, neither coming closer nor attempting to get away. They just stood where they were, watching.

What was the matter with them? Didn't they have any curiosity at all? Monte began to doubt his own knowledge; he wondered whether all of his training and all of his experience had been any good at all.

Me, the expert on man! I might as well be a caterpillar.

Then, at last, a child moved a little way down the trail from one of the caves. He pointed at the sphere and laughed—a high, delighted giggle. The people began to move again, going on about their business—whatever that may have been. They were so close that Monte could practically reach out and touch them, and yet he felt as though he were watching them from across some stupendous, uncrossable gulf. He simply didn't *get* them, didn't understand what he was seeing. The natives had nothing; they lived in caves and hollow trees. Their activities seemed aimless to him; they didn't seem to do anything that had any purpose to it. They appeared unperturbed, and worse, incurious.

Yet somehow, they did not give him an impression of *primitiveness.* (He recognized that that was a weasel word, but he could only think in terms of the words and concepts he knew.) It was rather that they were remote, detached, alien. They lived in a world that was perceived differently, where things had different values....

An old man, considerably older than the one they had tracked to the hollow tree, walked with difficulty down the trail and stood there just above the sphere. He blinked at them with cloudy eyes and hunched down so that he supported part of his weight on his long arms. The wrinkled skin hung from his face in loose folds, almost like flaps. He was definitely looking at them, not at the sphere. Two young women drifted over and joined him. The child giggled again and nudged one of the wide-eyed girls.

Monte took a deep breath. He felt like a ham actor who had come bouncing out of the wings, waving his straw hat and doing an earnest soft-shoe routine, only to discover belatedly that the theater was empty....

Still, these people did not seem to be afraid. They were not so timid as the man in the tree had been. Perhaps, Monte thought, the people here did share one human attribute: they were braver in bunches.

Monte took a step up toward the old man, who frowned at him and blinked his faded eyes. Monte raised his hands, showing him that they were empty. "Monte," he said, and pointed to himself.

The old man muttered something and stood his ground.

Monte tried again, feeling as though he were caught up in a cyclical nightmare. "Monte," he said.

The old man nodded slowly and pulled at his ear.

"Larst," he said distinctly.

By God! He said something!

Charlie whipped out his notebook and recorded the single precious word in phonetic symbols. Monte smiled broadly, trying to look like the answer to an old man's prayers. "Charlie," he said, pointing. "Tom, Ace."

The old man nodded again. "Larst," he repeated. He sighed. Then, incredibly, he began to point to other things: the caves, the stream, the sky, the kids, the women. For each, he gave the native term—slowly, patiently, as though instructing a backward child. His voice was weak and quavering but his words were clear. Monte matched him with English, then eased himself to one side and let Charlie Jenike take over.

Charlie worked fast, determined to grab his opportunity and hold on tight. He tested phrases and sentences, scribbling as fast as his pen would write. He built up a systematic vocabulary, building on the words he had already learned from the tapes. The old man seemed vaguely surprised at his fluency, and patiently went on talking.

Tom Stein maneuvered two of the kids, both boys, down the trail that led to the stream. He took a length of cord from his pocket and made a skillful cat's cradle on his fingers. The boys were intrigued, and watched him closely. Tom went through his whole bag of string tricks—the anthropologist's ace in the hole—and tried his level best to make friends.

Monte was as excited as though he had just tripped over the Rosetta Stone—which, in a manner of speaking, he had. He stuck to the rules of the game; they were all he had to go on. *Begin with the person in authority.* How many times had he told his students that? *Find out what the power structure is, and work from the top down.* Okay. Swell. Only who *was* the person in authority?

Looking around him, he couldn't be sure. It could hardly be Larst, who was close to senility. It certainly wouldn't be one of the children. The women backed away from him whenever he tried to approach—one of them acually blushed—and they didn't seem to be very likely candidates. One difficulty was that many of the natives were not paying any attention to them at all; they simply went on doing whatever they were doing, and he was unable to get any clear impression of how they ranked. It was very hard, he realized, to size up people who wore no clothing; there were no status symbols to give you a clue. Except, perhaps, for the chest stripes....

He compromised by wandering around with his notebook and trying to map the cave village. The people did not hinder him, but he considered it best not to try to enter the caves themselves. He plotted the distribution of the caves and jotted down brief descriptions of the people he found in front of each one. He took some photographs, which didn't seem to bother the natives at all.

But they had made contact!

That was what counted; the rest would follow in time.

His one thought was to get as much done as possible. He lost himself in his work, forgetting everything else.

The great white sun moved across the arc of the sky and the black shadows lengthened on the floor of the brown-walled canyon....

Monte never knew what it was that warned him. It was nothing specific, nothing dramatic. It certainly wasn't a premonition. It was rather a thread of uneasiness that wormed its way into his brain, a subtle wrongness that grew from the very data he collected.

Long afterward, he told himself a thousand times that he should have seen it before he did. He of all people, moving through the cave village with his notebook and camera, should have caught on. But the plain truth was that he was so excited at actually *working* with the natives that he wasn't thinking clearly; his brain was dulled by the flood of impressions pouring into it.

And, of course, there had been no real cause for alarm in the weeks they had spent on Sirius Nine. Somehow, the human mind continues its age-old habit of fooling itself by moronic extrapolation: because there has been peace there will always be peace, or because there has been war there will always be war....

The thing that triggered Monte's brain back into awareness, oddly enough, was not a man—it was an animal. He spotted the creature sitting in front of one of the caves, apparently warming itself in the late afternoon sun. (If you habitually lived in a furnace, he supposed, it took a good bellows to heat you up a little.) Monte snapped a picture of the thing, then studied it carefully from a short distance away. It certainly was not related to Rover, the powerful wolf-like animal they had seen in the forest. In fact, unless he was very much mistaken, the animal was a primitive type of primate.

It was a small creature, no bigger than a large squirrel. It had a hairless tail like a rat, and its rather chunky body was covered with a reddish-brown fur. (It would have been practically invisible in the branches of the forest trees.) Its head, nodding in the sun, was large and flat-faced, with sharply pointed ears like a fox. The animal had perfectly enormous eyes; they were like saucers. When it looked casually at Monte, the animal resembled two huge eyeballs with a body attached.

Many features about the animal were suggestive of the tarsier. To be sure, the tarsier was nocturnal, and there was no sign that this animal was equipped for hopping. Still, the tarsier was the closest analogy that Monte could find.

It was the first animal that Monte had seen in the cave village and it prodded his thoughts toward the wolf-thing they had encountered in the forest. It was odd, he reflected, that they had encountered nothing like Rover in the village. As a matter of fact, now that he happened to think about it, it was odd too that...

He stood up straight, a sudden chill lancing through his body.

That was it. That was what was wrong about this canyon village. That was what had been bothering him, nagging at him. How could it be?

Monte walked as quickly as he dared over to the trail and scrambled down it. He had to fight to keep himself from running. He hurried over to where Charlie and Larst were still yakking at each other. The old man—he looked positively ancient now—was plainly weary, but he was still answering Charlie's questions.

Monte touched the linguist's shoulder. "Charlie."

Charlie didn't even look around. "Not now, dammit."

"Charlie, this is important."

"Go away. Another hour with this guy—"

"Charlie! We may not have another hour."

That did it. Slowly, reluctantly, Charlie Jenike got to his feet, stretched his sore muscles, and turned around.

There were shadows under his eyes and his shirt was soaked with sweat. He was controlling his temper with a visible effort.

"Well?"

"Think carefully. Have you seen any men here today?"

Charlie gave a sigh of exasperation. "Are you blind? What do you think I'm talking to, a horse?"

"I mean young men—or even middle-aged men. Have you seen any?"

Charlie shook his head, puzzled now. "No, I don't think I have. But—"

"But nothing. We've been idiots. *There's no one here except women and kids and old men!*"

Charlie's face went white. "You don't think—"

Monte didn't waste any more time. "Ace," he snapped. "Walk over and get inside the sphere. Call the camp at once. Hurry, man!"

While Ace started for the sphere, Monte eased his way over to where Tom was holding a group of kids enthralled with his string games. He squatted down beside him. "Tom. Try not to look alarmed, but I think we're in trouble. There's not a single solitary man of fighting age in this village. Ace is calling the camp now."

Tom stared at him, the cord forgotten in his hands. "Janice," he whispered. "She's back there—"

Ace stuck his head out of the sphere and hollered: "I'm sorry, sir. The camp doesn't answer.

The three men forgot field technique, forgot everything. As one man, they sprinted for the sphere.

As he ran, Monte's brain shouted at him with a single word, repeated over and over again.

Fool, fool, fool!

Ace had the sphere airborne almost before they were all inside.

They flew at top speed into the gathering shadows of a night that was suddenly dark with menace.

7

There was no fire; that was the first thing that Monte noticed. The camp clearing was gray and still in the early starlight. Nothing moved. The place was as lifeless as some forgotten jungle ruin, and the tents—there was something wrong with the tents....

Monte kept his voice steady. "Circle the camp, Ace. Let's have the lights now."

The sphere went down low and hovered in a slow circle. The battery of landing lights flashed on.

"Oh God," Tom Stein whispered. "Oh God."

Monte felt his stomach wrench itself into a tight knot. His mouth opened but no sounds carne out. His hands began to tremble violently.

The tents were ripped to pieces; they were little more than sagging frames. The clearing was littered with debris—pots and pans and clothing and chairs and bright cans of food. And there were crumpled, motionless heaps on the ground. They were very dark and very still.

Monte was a man of his time; he had no experience with the sort of thing that had happened down below. But he knew a massacre when he saw one. *Slaughter.* That was, the word. A word out of the past, a word that was no part of life as he had known it.

He wanted to be sick; but there was no time for that. "Land," he snapped. "Get your rifles ready."

The sphere dropped like a stone and hit the ground with a dull thud. Ace switched on the overhead lights and grabbed a revolver. The men scrambled out through the hatch.

There was an ugly smell in the warm air. Everything was utterly still, utterly lifeless. It seemed that nothing was moving in all the world.

The men advanced in a tight group, hardly breathing. The first body they saw was one of the wolf-things. His dirty-gray coat was black with blood. His white fangs were bared, snarling even in death, and his yellow eyes were open and staring. Monte shoved at the body with his boot; the muscles were already stiff, though not completely so.

The next body was also one of the beasts. His head had almost been blown off.

The third body, lying on its face, was Helen Jenike. Her back was clawed to shreds. Her fingernails were dug into the ground, as though she had tried to seek shelter in a hole. Charlie rolled her over and caught her up in his arms. He began to sob—dry, terrible, wrenching sobs that were torn from the depths of his soul. Monte stared at her face. Helen had always been such a dainty person; this was the first time he had ever seen her with her lipstick smeared and her hair in her eyes....

Monte and Tom and Ace went on. They found Ralph Gottschalk—or what was left of him—surrounded by four of the dead wolf-things. Ralph—big, gentle, Ralph—still had his rifle in his hands. His bloody face was frozen into an expression of incredible hate and fury. One of the wolf-things still had its teeth fastened in his mangled leg. Monte forced the jaws apart and kicked the thing aside.

They went on, across the scattered logs of the dead fire, toward the tents.

The last body they found was Louise.

She lay in the dirt, a red-stained kitchen knife in her hand. She seemed smaller than Monte remembered—a tiny, crumpled, fragile thing. He had never seen her so still. He picked her up and stroked her black hair. He didn't even see the blood. He stood there with his wife in his arms and listened to Charlie sobbing from across the clearing. She seemed so light; she didn't weigh anything at all.

He remembered: it had been a long time ago, on another world. She had turned her ankle in the Colorado mountains and he had carried her to the copter. "God," he had said, "you weigh a ton!" And she had laughed—she had always been laughing, always happy—and she had said, "You're getting old, Monte!"

Old? He was old now.

He sat down on the ground, still holding her. He couldn't think. Somebody's hand was on his shoulder. Ace's. He was dimly grateful, grateful for some small touch of warmth in a world that was cold, cold beyond belief. He shivered and wished vaguely that the fire was going. Louise had liked the fire.

"She's gone! She's not here!"

A voice. Stupid. Who wasn't here? She was here....

Tom Stein, pacing around like a crazy man. Why didn't he sit down? What was the matter with the man?

"Monte! Janice isn't here! She may still be alive."

Slowly, with a dreadful effort, Monte pulled himself back to awareness. It was as though he were far underwater, pulling for the light above him. But there was no light, there was no feeling. There was nothing.

"Monte, we've got to find her!"

He put Louise down, gently. He stood up, his face pasty white, his eyes wild. He looked around. The world was still there.

"Who else is missing?"

"Don isn't here. They may have gotten away. We've got to find her!"

"Yes. We've got to find her." He turned to Ace. "Call the ship. Tell them to stand by for boarding. Tom. Take your rifle and start firing into the air. One shot every ten seconds. Maybe they'll hear you."

Desperate to be doing something, Tom ran off and recovered the rifle he had dropped. He fired. The shot was small and lonely in the darkness.

Monte walked slowly over to Charlie Jenike.

"Let's build a fire. It's cold."

Charlie looked up at him with unseeing eyes.

"Come on, Charlie."

Charlie got to his feet, stricken and lost. He nodded wordlessly.

Together—closer in their grief than they had ever been in a happier world—they began to build a fire.

At the edge of the clearing, Tom Stein fired his rifle at the sky, once every ten seconds.

There was no warning at all that Don and Janice were near; they simply materialized out of the forest like two shadows. Tom almost shot his own wife before he recognized her.

"Why didn't you holler?" he asked fretfully. "Why didn't you shoot and let me know you were alive?" Then she was in his arms, clutching him as though she were drowning and only he could save her. "You're alive," Tom said over and over again. "You've alive. Are you hurt? You're alive!" He was so overwhelmed that he didn't even think of thanking Don King for saving her life.

Don was a far cry from the neat, handsome man he had been a few long hours before. His clothes were torn and his sandy hair was black with dirt. He was still bleeding from a gash in his left shoulder. He was trembling with the reaction to the ordeal he had been through, but he was probably the calmest man in the clearing. For him, the shock was over.

He sat down before the fire, his head in his hands. He didn't look at Monte or at Charlie. He said quietly, "I'm sorry. Sorry as hell. I did the best I could. They were already dead when I grabbed Janice and lit out."

Monte squatted down beside him. "Nobody's blaming you. We're just glad you're alive. What happened, Don?"

Don still did not look at them. He stared into the fire and talked flatly, as though he were describing something that had happened to someone else a long time ago. "It was still light, about the middle of the afternoon. We weren't doing much of anything, just waiting for you to get back. Ralph and I were kidding around about going back to that tree burial and poking into it a little. We didn't do it, though—we were afraid we might offend the little tin gods." He spat into the fire. "All of a sudden a pack of those damned dogs or whatever they are came busting out of the woods. They were on us before we knew what was going on. It was crazy, a nightmare. It all happened so fast we couldn't put up any kind of a defense. They seemed to be going after the women; I don't know why. They snarled all the time, like they had gone mad. I saw some of the native men in the trees. They didn't do anything—just watched. They never tried to help—I got the impression they had sent the dogs, but that doesn't make sense. We got our guns and did what we could—Ralph went after one of them with his bare hands. There were too damned many of them. I shot two of them that were after Janice and Ralph hollered at me to run. I couldn't see anything clearly, it was all chaos. I grabbed her and took off into the woods. I didn't know what to do, where to go. Those bastards in the trees could see me, and they could climb better than I could. I knew those dogs could trail us on the ground, and we'd never have a chance. I remembered that tree burial—I guess it was because Ralph and I had just been talking about it—and I headed for that. It turned out to be a good idea, but I don't take any credit for it—we were lucky. We climbed up to that damned nest and just sat there. The natives were all around us for a while, but they didn't do anything—maybe the place is sacred or something. The dogs followed us and I shot a pile of them—ten or twelve, at least. Then I ran out of ammunition; there hadn't been time to grab any spare clips. After a while the dogs went away, and so did the natives. When we heard you shooting we climbed down and came back. That's all. My God, what happened over at that village? Did you guys rape the chief's daughter or something?"

"Nothing happened. Nothing at all."

Charlie Jenike just shook his head; words were too much trouble.

Monte stood up, keeping his eyes averted from Louise's body. "You get the ship, Ace?"

"Yes, sir. They're standing by. Admiral York is about to blow a fuse. He says for you—"

"The hell with Admiral York. Look, Ace—this will take two trips, understand? Janice goes first; we've got to get her out of here. Tom will go with her, of course. And Don."

"I'll wait for you," Don said.

Monte ignored him. "When you get them stashed away, come and get us. Charlie and I will get the bodies ready—we'll use tent flaps to wrap them in. Take your time, Ace—there's no rush getting back here."

Ace hesitated. "They may come back again, Monte."

"Yes. I hope they do"

Ace looked at him and then headed for the sphere, rounding up the others as he went. The sphere lifted soundlessly into the starlit sky, and was gone.

Monte and Charlie sat by the fire, their rifles in their hands, alone with the dead. The night was utterly silent around them. It was not cold, but both men were shivering.

"Well, Charlie?"

"Yes. Let's get it over with."

They got to their feet and cut up what was left of the tents. Then they did what had to be done.

By unspoken assent, they took care of Ralph first, together.

Then each man did what he could for his wife.

When it was over, they built up the fire again. The damp wood hissed and sputtered, but the flames finally took hold and twisted up toward the sky in hot orange columns. Monte honestly didn't know whether the fire was to keep something away or to lure something in. He was sure that Charlie didn't know either.

Monte sat with his back to the fire, watching the black line of the trees. His vision seemed preternaturally sharp: he could trace the webbing of the branches against the stars. And his hearing was keener than it should have been: he heard each tiny stir of the leaves, every scrape of an insect across the forest floor, each distant night-cry of an invisible bird. He was aware, of course, of the fact that sensory impressions are sometimes heightened at moments of crisis but that datum was stored in a part of his mind that was not really functioning. He was surprised at his acute awareness, and that was all.

"Why did they do it, Monte? What did we do to them?" Charlie's voice was hoarse and ugly.

"I don't know. I thought we were very careful. Hell, maybe there *wasn't* any reason."

"There's always a reason."

"Is there? I'm beginning to wonder."

Charlie didn't say anything more, and the silence was hard to take. It was better to keep the night filled with words. When he didn't talk he began to think, and when he began to think....

"I guess we made the prize stupid blunder of all time," Monte said slowly. "We figured that because we meant them no harm they must necessarily feel the same way about us. We went in among the cannibal tribe with our hymn books and they popped us in the stewpot. We should have been more careful."

"They seemed so shy, so frightened. Was all that an act? How could we have known, Monte? *How could we have known?*"

"It won't help them to blame ourselves."

"But I do. God, I just went off and left her sitting here—"

"Cut it out, Charlie," he said harshly. "I can't take that."

'The silence came between them again, and this time they did not disturb it. They let the heat of the fire bake into their backs and waited for the sphere to return from the orbiting ship. The night around them was vast and filled with strangeness; it was more lonely than the stars that burned in the sky above them, and more filled with mystery...

They both sensed his presence at the same time.

"Monte?"

"Yes. Over there."

They got to their feet, their rifles in their hands. The light was not good, and at first they didn't *see* anything. But they both knew with absolute certainty that there was a native somewhere in the trees, watching them. They knew that there was just one native, and they knew approximately where he was.

Monte was as calm as ice. He squinted his eyes, waiting.

"There he is," Charlie whispered hoarsely.

Monte saw him now. He was up high, up where the branches began to thin out, up where he was outlined against the stars. A tall man, facing them, his long arms reaching up above his head....

The man seemed detached somehow, aloof and unworried. He was not trying to conceal himself. He was just standing there watching them, as though it were the most natural thing in the world to be doing....

Something in Monte snapped—literally snapped. It was as though a taut wire had been suddenly cut. The hate boiled up in him like searing lava; his lips curled back in a snarl.

He did not think, did not want to think. He let himself go. He was surprised at how easy it was, how steady his hands were, how clearly he could see. He even remembered not to hold his breath.

He lifted the rifle; it was as light as a feather. He got the motionless native in his sights. *Sitting duck.* He squeezed the trigger. The rifle bucked against his shoulder and a tongue of fire licked into the night. He was not aware of any sound. The slug caught the native in the belly. Monte smiled. He had wanted a gut shot.

The man doubled up in the tree, grabbing at himself. Then he fell. It took him a long time. He bounced off one branch, screaming, and hit the ground with a soft thud.

Monte and Charlie ran over to him. He was lying on his back, his long arms wrapped around his belly. His sunken eyes were wide with shock and fear. He tried to say something and a gush of blood bubbled out of his mouth.

Monte started for him, but Charlie pushed him aside. "He's mine," he whispered.

Charlie Jenike finished the man off with his rifle butt, and he took his time doing it.

They left the native where he was and went back to their fire. It was blazing brightly. Neither of them spoke.

When the gray sphere drifted down out of the sky, Ace helped them load the bodies of their dead. It didn't take long.

The sphere lifted again toward the invisible ship high above them in the starlit night. Monte looked down and watched the fire in the clearing until it was lost from view.

Then there was only the great night all around them, the great hollow night and the far cold stars. He closed his eyes. There was a terrible emptiness inside of him, an ice ache that cried out to him of something vanished, something lost...

Something that he had been and something that he could never be again.

8

The funeral was mercifully brief, and even had a certain dignity, but it was still a barbaric thing. Monte sat through it in a daze, his mind wandering. How Louise would have hated it all....

"When I die," she had told him once, back in those sunlit days when death was only a word and the had both known they would live forever, "I don't want any gloomy songs and weeping relatives. I want to be cremated and I want my ashes to be spread in a flower garden, where they'll do some good. You'll see to it, won't you, Monte?"

"Afraid I can't," he had said. "I've already promised you for a sacrifice to the Sun God."

Sirius?

Sacrifice....

There had been one consolation, he supposed, although that was hardly the word for it. Her body, stretched out in its makeshift box, was in space. It was drifting in the emptiness and the stars. Crazily, he wondered whether she was cold. At least she was not buried in the earth, with damp soil sealing her off forever from the light and the sun.

In time, she might even fall into the sun. A strange sun, to be sure, a white furnace of a sun, but still a sun. She might have liked that....

He could not believe that she was gone. Oh, he didn't try to kid himself about it. She was dead, and his mind accepted the fact. He couldn't console himself with any fuzzy notions that they would meet again in some Great Bye and Bye. But belief is something you feel, not just something your mind cannot reject. Even when he knew that Louise was in a box in space, he found himself listening for her voice, watching for her to come walking through opening doors, wondering why she stayed away now that he needed her so much.

It was unbearable. He shunned the room that they had shared, entering it only to try to sleep (Sleep? He had forgotten what sleep was.) He didn't drink much; drinking only made it worse. He knew that some men hit the bottle in an effort to forget, but that would never work for him. Alcohol only accentuated what he was already feeling; it had always been that way.

But there were times when he had to go into their room. There were times when he had to lie on their bed, and be alone in the darkness. There were times when he saw her clothes and the books she had been reading. There were times when he could smell her perfume, still lingering in the bare, tiny room.

Then he knew that she was gone from him forever.

Then he knew.

Admiral William York sat behind his polished desk and looked acutely uncomfortable. He was a tall man, tall and lean, and his gray hair was cropped close to his skull. He seemed to be at attention even when he was sitting down, but he was not an unduly formal man. He had warm brown eyes and a face that easily relaxed into a smile. In fact, Monte thought, he was the perfect officer—even to the slight limp that he had when he walked, a limp that hinted discreetly of past deeds of valor. He was a civilized man, and that didn't make the interview any easier.

Monte was aware of the contrast in their appearances. Monte's clothes didn't fit him the way they should; he had lost a lot of weight and was downright skinny. His beard was ragged and his eyes had dark circles under them. Monte was hard, harder than he had ever been, but he was too hard to be flexible any longer. He didn't bend and snap back. He—broke.

It didn't all show, of course; he was glad of that. He was still Monte Stewart, no matter what he felt like inside. But he felt oddly ill at ease, like a schoolboy summoned before the headmaster. He didn't belong here, in this room, with this man. The hum of the air vents bothered him, and the stale metallic smell of the gray ship. The air seemed cold and dead after the warm irritating atmosphere of Sirius Nine; he always seemed to be cold now....

"Drink, Monte?"

"Thank you."

Admiral York poured out a shot of whiskey for each of them. He sipped his, but Monte tossed it down like medicine. York made quite a thing out of lighting a cigarette, doing his best to make Monte relax. Monte didn't want to disappoint him, so he fished out his pipe and began puffing on it. The smoke *did* taste good. That, at least, had not changed.

Admiral York fingered a stapled pile of typewritten pages on his desk. There were fourteen pages, Monte knew, with his signature on the last one.

"Well, Monte?"

"You've read it. It's all there. There isn't anything else to say."

York leaned back in his chair, staring at his cigarette as though it were the most interesting thing in the world. "You realize, of course, that the safety of this expedition is my responsibility. I have to take most of the blame for what happened down there."

Monte sighed. "You're not a fool, Bill, so don't act like one. I made all the decisions with the natives. I was careful to make that clear in my report, in case there should be any question about it later. It wasn't your fault."

"Perhaps. But it *will* be if anything else happens, so nothing else is going to happen. We know what we're up against now."

"Do we? I wish you'd let me in on it."

"You know what I mean."

"That's what you keep telling me. But I *don't*."

York shrugged. "Look, Monte, I'm not trying to be difficult. I know that you've had a terrible shock; please believe me when I say that if there were anything I could do to help I would do it."

"I know that, Bill. Sorry."

"The fact remains, however, that I am not a free agent. I have the responsibilities of command here; I must do what I think best."

"And?"

"And I'm taking this ship back to Earth, Monte. I can't risk any further bloodshed. The decisions from now on will have to be made by higher authorities."

"You mean Heidelman?"

"I mean the secretary-general. Surely you realize the situation we've gotten ourselves into here? You do understand, don't you?"

Monte puffed on his pipe. He felt his hands begin to tremble and it made him mad. "You mean that we've failed. That it was all for nothing. That we're just going to turn tail and run."

York looked away. "Isn't that about the size of it? Think, man! You can't go back there. You must be able to see that. It was bad enough the first time. Now the natives have attacked us and killed some of our people. Worse than that, maybe, you've killed one of the natives. I'm not blaming you; I might have done the same. But we've got to draw the line somewhere. We didn't come here to start a war."

"What did we come here for?"

"That's your department, not mine. My job was to get you here and get you back. That's what I intend to do."

"Very fine, very noble. Maybe you'll get a medal out of it, huh?"

"There's no call to get sarcastic. I'm trying to be reasonable with you. You're being bull-headed, not me. It's always easy to blame the brass."

Monte got to his feet, his pipe clamped between his teeth. "Hell, I know I'm taking it out on you." He looked at York with weary eyes. "How do you think I feel? My wife is dead. Ralph is dead. Helen is dead. And I've flopped in the biggest job I ever had. Ever think of yourself as a failure? I never had. I always thought I could do anything. Maybe things came too easy for me; I don't know. I've had my nose rubbed in the dirt, but good. But I'm no quitter. I'm not through yet."

"But what can you *do?* I'm all for this hands-across-space stuff; I believe in it. But it's absurd to sacrifice yourself for the glories of anthropology.

You're not thinking straight—"

"To hell with anthropology! What kind of a jerk do you take me for? It's bigger than that and you know it. If we foul it up now there may never be another chance. The next outfit that comes out here—if there is a next outfit—will be a military expedition. Do you want that?"

"No. No, I don't."

"Okay. I loused up the first try. It's up to me to set it straight. It's my job. I want to do it, that's all."

"I can't let you risk the others."

"No, of course not. But who are we risking? There is no threat to the ship—they can't get at you here. Janice must certainly stay here, and I wouldn't want Tom to go back. I don't think Don would go anyhow. I don't know about Charlie—that's up to him. But I can go back."

"Alone?"

"Why not? The worst that can happen is that I'll get myself knocked off. What difference will that make?"

"Monte, I admire your guts. But I've seen it happen a thousand times—a man loses his wife and he thinks it's the end of the world. It isn't. You're still young—"

"Creeping crud! I've *got* to go back. I've got to live with myself, Louise or no Louise. Suppose you were sent out on a big assignment and you lost the first skirmish. Would you run for home? Would you?"

York hesitated. "Maybe. If I saw that there was no hope at all—"

"But you don't *know* that! We don't even know what happened down there, not really. We've got enough of the language now so that we can talk to them. We made some progress. Look, you're clear on all this. It's down in black and white that I'm in charge of all relations with the natives. We came out here to stay a year. I want that year. You can't just order me to go home, not when the ship is in no danger at all. That won't help what happened. We've got to try again."

York poured out another drink and handed it over. "Calm down. Just what do you propose to do? Go back down there with your popgun and start blazing away?"

Monte sat down and swallowed his drink at a gulp. "I swear to you that there will be no more killing. Not even in self-defense."

York looked at him and nodded. "I believe that. But where will it get you? You must have some sort of plan."

"I do. I'm going down there and I'm going to win their confidence. I'm going to find out what makes them tick. When I understand them I can deal with them. I'm going to give Heidelman his peaceful contact if it kills me."

"That's not a plan. That's an ultimatum. We can't trust those people— they've proved that. We've got to consider our own security."

Monte smiled. "That sounds pretty familiar, Bill. That's the old, old road that leads to nowhere. I can't trust him. He can't trust me. So wouldn't it be better to drop a big fat bomb on him before he drops one on me? Do you want to start that up all over again? Do you want that to be the history of Earth's first meeting with other men?"

"You gave them every chance to be friendly!" York was a little red in the face; this was a touchy subject. "You bent over backwards. What did it get you? There's no damn sense in it! I can't let you go back down there and get yourself killed. That *is* my responsibility."

Monte grinned; he was feeling better. "I didn't know you cared."

"Cut it out. I'll go this far with you—I'll give you a week. At the end of that time, I want a plan—a real plan. And you'll have to sell me on it, I warn you. I want a plan that gives a reasonable prospect for success. I want a plan that will ensure your safety. I want a plan we can show the boys back home that makes it dead certain that no more natives get hurt, no matter what good excuses we have. I want the works, in writing."

"You don't want much, do you?"

Admiral York permitted himself a smile. "As the man said, you buttered your bread—now lie in it."

Monte stood up and stuck out his hand. York took it.

"You've got yourself a deal, Bill. Thanks. I won't forget it."

"If this backfires, neither one of us will ever forget it. But good luck. And try to get some sleep, will you?"

"Sleep? Who has time for sleep?"

Monte turned and walked out of the room.

He hurried along the metal catwalks with the great ship, all around him, feeling more alive than he had felt in a long time. There were plans to be made. He stuck his pipe in his mouth and set out to find Charlie Jenike.

9

He found Charlie Jenike where he had known he would be: crouched over his notebooks and recording equipment in the cold little box-like room Charlie used for his linguistics lab. Charlie was so wrapped up in his work that he didn't even hear Monte come in.

Monte studied the man, seeing him with fresh eyes. He had never felt really close to Charlie until that fantastic night by the fire in the bloody clearing on Sirius Nine; there had always been a subtle antagonism between them. It was probably nothing much; they just rubbed each other the wrong way. And yet, somehow, he had been fated to commit a murder with Charlie Jenike. In a universe where strangeness lurked behind every commonplace facade, this was surely one of the strangest things of all.

(Oh yes, it had been murder when they had killed the native. Monte knew it and Charlie knew it. They had not even recognized the man. They had never seen him before. They hadn't known what he wanted or what he was doing. If you come home some night and find your wife has been murdered, you don't just charge out into the street and shoot the first man you find on the principle that one victim is as good as another. Maybe they had been a little crazy, but that didn't excuse them in their own minds. What was it that Don King had said in that bull session so long ago? *"We say we're civilized, which means that we have enough surplus to afford luxuries like high-minded philosophies. But if things got tough I'll bet we'd be right back where we started from quicker than you can say Cuthbert Pomeroy Gundelfinger; it'd be an eye for an eye, a tooth for a tooth, and a pancreas for a pancreas. That's the way men are."* Monte recalled that he had been rather self-righteous in that argument, talking learnedly about progress and ethics and all the rest. He had been pretty sure of himself. But then, it had been a very long time ago....)

Charlie certainly wasn't very impressive physically. He was a dumpy, sloppy man who was losing his nothing-colored hair; if he had ever glanced into the mirror, which was highly unlikely, he would have seen what looked disturbingly like a bulldog's face perched atop a penguin's rotund body. Charlie lacked all of the conventional virtues: he dressed badly, changed his clothes all too infrequently, had little visible charm, and didn't bother to cultivate the civilized buzz of small-talk which serves to cushion our dealings with our fellow seasick passengers on the voyage of life. Nonetheless, Charlie had something, something that was quite rare. Watching him at work, Monte realized that the man had a certain dignity, a certain integrity that had all but vanished from the contemporary scene.

The very words *dignity* and *integrity* were slightly suspect these days; like so many others, they had been corrupted by the politicians and the tri-di dramatists. It was a surprising thing to find such a man and to know him—it was something like finding a worm that could do algebra. Now that the chips were down, Monte found that he could turn to Charlie Jenike in a way that he never could with a man like Don King, or even with Tom Stein.

Charlie finally sensed his presence and turned around, his eyebrows lifted questioningly.

"I've been talking to Bill York. He wants to take the ship back to Earth."

"That figures. Will he do it?"

"Unless I can talk him out of it. I'd like to kick it around with you a little, if you don't mind."

The linguist fumbled for a cigarette and lit it. "I'll try to fit you into my list of appointments. Shoot."

Monte filled his pipe and sat down on a hard, straight-backed chair. The whisper of the air vents seemed very loud to him. It was odd that the noise didn't make Charlie's work more difficult than it was. He wondered suddenly why Charlie kept on working as he did. To keep himself from thinking about Helen? Work was a kind of opiate, but that was a feeble explanation. For that matter, Monte didn't know what it was that kept himself working. He smiled a little. He didn't understand Charlie, he didn't understand himself. How could he possibly hope to understand the natives of Sirius Nine?

"How much did you get from Larst?"

"Plenty."

"Enough to talk with them?"

"I think so. I already had a lot of stuff, and the old buzzard gave me enough of a key so that I can work out most of it. It's a curious language—very weak in active verbs. But I can speak it now, after a fashion."

Monte felt a wave of relief. That was one bluff he had pulled with York that had panned out. They had the words, they had a bridge. "What the devil do they call Sirius Nine?"

"That's a tough one. They think of the world in a number of different ways, some of them pretty subjective. They do have a word, though—*Walonka*. It seems to mean a totality of some sort. It means the world, their universe, and it has an idea of unity, of interconnections. It's the closest I can get. They don't quite think in our terms. You know, of course, that it's more than just a matter of finding different labels for the same thing—you have to dig up the conceptual apparatus that they work with. They call themselves *Merdosi*—the People. And they call those damned wolf things by a very similar term: *Merdosini.* A rough translation would be something like 'Hunters for the People.' Interesting, huh?"

"It makes sense. Did you get anything else suggestive?"

"I got one thing. One of the words that Larst applied to himself has a literal meaning of man-who-is-old-enough-to-stay-in-the-village-all-year-round. What do you make of that?"

Monte frowned. "It must mean that the younger men *don't* stay in the village all the time. And that means—"

"Yeah. When you noticed that none of the younger men were present, you were dead right. But it didn't necessarily mean what we thought it meant—that they were out on a war party of some sort. The attack on our camp might not have been hooked up with their absence at all. Those guys are out in the woods most of the time—maybe they all live in trees like the man we tried to contact."

"But they must come into the village *sometimes.*

"Obviously. There are kids running around. That would indicate at least occasional proximity."

"You think they have a regular mating season, something like that?"

"I wouldn't know. It's a possibility. But it seems a little far-fetched for such an advanced form of life."

"It wouldn't have to be strictly biological, though. Human beings do funny things sometimes. It might be a situation where there is some slight biological basis—females more receptive at certain times of the year—and then the whole business has gotten tangled up with a mess of cultural taboos. How does that strike you?"

Charlie ground out his cigarette. "Well, it might explain a lot of things. The attack on the camp, for one."

Monte got to his feet, excited now. "By God, that's it! How could we have been so stupid? And to think that I *planned* it that way—"

"You didn't know."

"But I did the worst possible thing! I set up our camp in a clearing, where they could watch us. I wanted them to *see* what we were like. And we had our women with us, all the time; We *flaunted* them. And then we went to the village with their women—"

"You couldn't have known."

Monte sat down again wearily. "Me, the great anthropologist! Any fool bonehead could have done better. I *should* have known—what was that guy doing in the tree by himself in the first place? We landed and the very first thing we did was to break the strongest taboo in their culture! It was just like they had landed in Chicago or some where and had promptly started to mate in the streets. My God!"

"It's something to think about. But that isn't the whole answer."

"No, but it's a lead! They don't seem quite so unfathomable now. Charlie, I *can* crack that culture! I know I can."

Charlie lit another cigarette. "You're going back there."

He said it as a simple statement of fact, not as a question. "Yes. I've got to give York a royal frosted snow-job to do it, but I'm going back."

"Don won't go. York won't let Tom and Janice out of this ship again."

"I don't give a damn. I'm going alone."

"You can forget that. Include me in. I'm going with you."

Monte looked at him. "You don't have to go, Charlie."

"Don't I?"

"You know what the odds are. I don't think we'll ever come back, to tell you the truth."

"So? Who wants to come back? What for?"

Monte sighed. He had no answer for that one.

"We're both crazy. But we've got to come up with a plan for Bill York. An eminently *sane* plan."

"Yeah, sure. Sane."

"Let's hit it. Got any ideas?"

Charlie smiled, relaxing a little. "I've got a few. I was afraid you were going to try to sneak off and leave me here. I was working on a small snow-job of my own."

Monte pulled his chair up to the table and the two men put their heads together.

An hour or so later, a passing crewman was astonished to hear gales of laughter behind the closed door of Charlie Jenike's linguistics lab.

EXTRACT FROM THE NOTEBOOK OF MONTE STEWART:

I've lost track of time.

Sure, I know what "day" it is and all that. It's easy to look at the ship's calendar. But it doesn't mean anything to me. (Funny to think of how much trouble a people like the Maya went to in order to invent a calendar more accurate than our own. And even their calendar was forgotten in time; it got to the point where it didn't matter. I wonder why? I wonder what really happened?)

It seems to me that Louise died only yesterday. That is the only past I know, the only past I have. There is a time when the pain is too much to bear. There is a time when the pain goes away—or so people tell me. Those are the two dates on my calendar.

I find it almost impossible to work on my official notebook. In this one, the one for myself, I can think.

A man can't think in terms of large abstractions like the United Nations and the First Contact with an Alien Culture. It gets to be a personal thing, a personal fight. There comes a time when a man must get up on his own hind legs and admit the truth. I'm doing it for me, for Monte Stewart. I'm doing it because I am what I am.

(And what am I? Cut it out, boy! You're not ready for the giggle academy yet!)

Well, a long time ago I asked myself some questions about the people of Sirius Nine. Or should I say questions about the Merdosi of Walonka? That is progress of a sort. And I think I've got some answers now; the questions must have been good ones. And, as usual, I've got some more questions.

But what do I know?

I know what that man was doing in the forest by himself. The Merdosi have a mating season of some sort. The men live out in the forest most of the time, and only come into the cave village with the gals at certain times of the year. This may be biological, or cultural, or—more probably—both. Question: What in blazes do the men do out there in those hollow trees? Question: How do the women and kids get by on their own in the village?

The Merdosi are afraid of us, and I still don't know why. Sure, we broke a powerful taboo by living with our women at the wrong time of the year—but that doesn't explain everything. They attack us because they are afraid of us; I'm certain of that. At other times they try to ignore us. It is as though we are a threat to them simply by being here. Why?

Obviously, there is a very close relationship between the people and the wolf-things—between the Merdosi and the Merdosini. The Merdosini are the Hunters for the People. The two life-forms are interdependent. Can we call this symbiosis? Regardless of the name we tag it with, we have a problem. It's easy to see what the wolf-things do for the natives—they do their hunting for them, and their fighting as well. But what do the natives do for the wolf-things? What do the Merdosini get out of the deal? It must be a very old pattern, but how did it start? How do the natives control those animals? On Earth, the dog probably domesticated itself—hung around the fire for scraps of food and the like. But that won't work here, because the natives seem to *get* their food—or some of it—from the Merdosini. What's the answer? (And we've got the same puzzle with those tarsier-like critters I saw in the village. Are they just pets, or something else?)

I'm convinced that the key to this whole thing is somehow mixed up with the fact that these people have no tools. We are so used to evaluating people in terms of the artifacts they use that we are lost when these material clues are denied to us. Making tools seems to us to be the very nature of man. The first things we see when we look at a culture are artifacts of some sort: clothes, weapons, boats, skyscrapers, glasses, watches, copters—the works. But most of this culture isn't visible. We can't see it, but it's there.

What can it be like? Is there a richness here that we are just not equipped to see?

And remember that they do have the concept of tools. They even have a word that means an artifact of some sort: *kuprai*. The old man knew what a knife was for, but he was not impressed by it. Well, we have a lot of concepts in our culture that we don't make much use of. I can remember hearing a lot of twaddle about how it doesn't matter whether you win or lose, but only how you play the game. Try telling that to a football coach. Try telling that to an honest man whose kids don't have enough to eat.

Take away all our tools, all the trappings of our civilization, and what do we have left?

What do the Merdosi have?

The gray metallic sphere came down out of cold blackness into warm blue skies. The white inferno of Sirius burned in the heavens like a baleful eye that looked down upon a red and steaming world.

The sphere landed in the clearing where the charred logs told of a fire that once had burned, and bright cans of food and broken chairs hinted at a meal that had never been eaten.

The hatch opened and two men climbed out into the breathless heat of the day. They moved slowly and clumsily, for their bodies were completely encased in what had been spacesuits a few days before. They looked like awkward robots who had somehow strayed into a nightmare jungle in the beginning of time, and they carried extra heads in their hands.

Supplies were unloaded and the sphere lifted again into the wet blue sky and disappeared.

The two men carried no weapons.

They stood for a moment looking at the dark and silent forest that surrounded them. They heard nothing and saw nothing. They were not afraid, but they knew that they faced a world that was no longer indifferent and unprepared.

They faced a world that was totally alien, and a world that was hostile beyond reason, beyond hope.

They were the Enemy. It was a fact of life.

Strange and unnatural in their stiff-jointed armor, already sweating under the great white furnace of the sun, they methodically began to make camp.

All around them, in the tall trees that reached up to touch the sky, long-armed shadows stirred and watched and waited.

10

Monte wiped the stinging sweat out of his eyes—no simple matter with his hand inside a spacesuit glove—and squinted up at the sun. The swollen white fireball was hanging just above the trees, as though reluctant to set. Its light turned the leaves to flame and sent dark shadow-tongues licking across the clearing.

It had been the longest afternoon of his life. The spacesuits, even with the air vents that had been drilled into them, were miserably hot and clumsy. He felt as though he were standing in twin pools of sweat, and the faint breeze that whispered against his damp face only made the contrast more unbearable. He thought of what it would be like with the helmets on and shuddered.

Still, it was the only way.

His throat was getting sore again from the irritants in the air, but his nose was clear. It was odd, he thought, how different things affected a man at different times on an alien world. Now that he was used to the way Sirius Nine looked, now that he knew that the name of the world was Walonka and its appearance was familiar, he was struck by the way the place *smelled*. Even if he had been blind, he would have known that he was not on Earth.

He smelled the acrid smell of sun-blasted canyons and the brown-rock smell of the mountains. He smelled the bubbling silver of the streams and the close, heavy smell of the trees. He caught the perfume of strange flowers and the greasy scent of vines that crawled up to the roof of the world. He smelled the slow wind that had flowed like oil over places he had never seen. He sniffed the rank odor of furtive animals that padded across the forest floor. He sensed the tang of seasons and woodsmoke and the great vault of the sky, and he smelled things that were unknown and nameless and lost.

How strange it was to smell things that conjured up no memories, brought back no nostalgia...

"Soup's on," Charlie said, looking more grotesque than ever in his bulbous spacesuit. "Get it while it's hot."

"I'll settle for a cold beer."

"Got to eat, don't we? Can't be a hero on an empty stomach, as someone once should have said."

"How about Gandhi? He was good enough to have York's ship named after him."

Charlie tried to shrug, but it was virtually impossible. "He wasn't lugging a spacesuit around on his back. Burns up the old calories, you know."

Monte took a self-heating can that Charlie handed to him and awkwardly spooned out a steaming horror that was supposed to be beef stew. He ate it standing up, for the simple reason that sitting down was too much trouble. He washed the stuff down with a canteen of cold water and was surprised to find that he felt somewhat better.

Sirius was below the rim of the trees now, although it was still flooding the sky with light. There were puffy, moisture-laden clouds on the horizon, and they looked black in the middle and crimson around the edges. It was still hot, but the evening breeze was freshening.

They built up the fire in the clearing until the logs sizzled and popped and white smoke funneled into the sky. They checked their tents and then they were ready.

"Do you see them?" Monte asked.

"No. But I *feel* 'em. They're all around us, up in the trees."

"Time for your speech, wouldn't you say?"

"Are you sure you wouldn't rather do it yourself? You can speak the lingo as well as I can by now."

"Not quite. Anyhow, you're more eloquent. Give 'em the works."

"It's useless, you know."

"Maybe. We've got to try."

Charlie Jenike walked stiff-legged to the other side of the fire. He stood there facing the trees. The fire hissed behind him. He looked somehow more alien than the world he faced: a squat mechanical man that had stepped out of a factory in a dark land beyond the stars.

The red-leafed forest was an abyss of electric silence: waiting, watching, listening.

Charlie Jenike took a deep breath and made his pitch.

"Merdosi!"

There was no answer; Charlie hadn't expected one.

"Merdosi!"

There were only the trees rooted in the hostile soil, only the immense night that rolled in from far away.

"Merdosi! Hear my voice. We do not come to you in anger. We carry no weapons."

(Monte smiled in appreciation; Charlie really *was* good with the native language. That last sentence was a marvel of circumlocution.)

"Merdosi! My people came to Walonka to be friends with your people. We meant you no harm. In our ignorance, we made many mistakes. We are sorry for them. The Merdosi too have made mistakes. It was wrong for you to send the Merdosini after our people. It was wrong to kill. We did not understand, and we too were wrong when we killed one of your men. This clearing has been stained with blood—your blood and our blood. That is past. We want no more killing. We will kill no more. Our only wish is to speak with you in peace."

The shadow-filled forest was silent. A log burned through on the fire and collapsed in a shower of sparks.

Charlie lifted his heavy arm. "Hear me, Merdosi! This is another chance for both of us. We are all people together. We must trust one another. On our world beyond the sky, many bad things have happened because people could not trust each other. Many times the first step was never taken, and that was wrong. Here and now, we are taking the first step. We have come in peace. We have trusted you. We have washed our hands of blood. Come out! Come out and let us sit by the fire and talk as men!"

No voice answered him. In all the darkening hush of the woods, no figure stirred.

"Merdosi! We have learned your words, and we speak them to you. There is nothing to fear! There is much to be gained. Do you not wonder about us, as we wonder about you? Will you not give us a chance, even as we have given you a chance? It is wrong for a man to hide like an animal! Come out! Come out, and let us be men together!"

There was no reply. He might as well have been talking to the trees themselves. Slowly, he let his arm fall to his side. He turned and rejoined Monte by the tents. There was a bleak sadness in his eyes.

"Well," he said, clearing his throat.

"It was good, Charlie. No man could have done any better."

"It wasn't good enough."

"Maybe not. We knew it was a long shot, didn't we? We gave it a try. What the hell."

Monte stroked his matted beard absently. He looked around the little clearing. The firelight seemed brighter now; the long night was near. He found himself looking at the exact spot where Louise had died. Quickly, he averted his eyes.

Charlie snorted. "We're nuts. They're nuts. The whole thing is insane. If we had all our marbles, we'd go back to Earth and forget there ever was a Sirius Nine."

"Think you could forget?"

"Maybe. I could try."

Monte laughed. "I'll tell you, Charlie: it's probably easier for me to come here than it would be to go home, and that's the truth. But the notion is not without its appeal. I could go back to Earth and file a classic report with the U.N. The intrepid anthropologist returns from the stars and gives the boys the word. *The natives are bloodthirsty jerks! I advise that they be obliterated for the good of mankind!* Ought to create quite a stir, hey?"

"Maybe that's just the report you should file," Charlie said soberly.

"There's another good one we could come up with; it would be very popular and would make everybody feel good. *The natives are poor ignorant dopes who don't know what they're doing. I advise that their culture be manipulated by the all-wise earthmen to make them smart like us. I propose an 'earthman's burden' for the good of the universe!* How's that sound?"

"Familiar. Stupid, but familiar."

"The devil of it is that most people would welcome a report like that. It's funny how many people there are who like to play God."

Charlie started to say something, then changed his mind. He walked over and managed to lift another log and toss it on the fire.

"Think we'll last out the night?" he asked casually.

"Maybe."

"Let's get with it. I'd just as soon try to make pals with the Devil as the Merdosi."

"We might have a better chance, at that. After all, the Devil is a product of our own culture a few millenniums back. He's one of the boys, even with his horns and tail. He even speaks our language, according to usually reliable sources. He makes deals."

"To hell with him," Charlie grinned.

"Exactly. Are you ready?"

"Yes."

"Put your helmet on and let me test it."

Charlie picked up his gleaming helmet, stared at it a moment, took a deep breath, and settled it on his shoulders. It clamped into place with an audible click, and Charlie locked the catches with gloved, puffy fingers.

Monte checked the helmet carefully. It was secure. Charlie's face, behind the thick glassite plate, seemed swollen and remote. Monte put on his own helmet and fastened the catches. All sounds from outside ceased. He knew a moment of panic when he felt as though he were smothering, but then the air came in. The doctored suits had breathing holes in the helmets, so that they did not have to depend on canned air.

He spoke into his mike. "All set?" His voice had a hollow sound to his own ears.

Charlie poked at the helmet and gave it a pull or two.

"Okay." His voice was tinny in Monte's ears. "You're sealed in like a sardine."

"This ought to be quite a night."

"Yeah. At least we won't die of boredom."

"We may roast to death, though."

"It's a thought."

They fell silent; there was nothing more to say. Monte felt oddly detached, as though his body belonged to someone else. It was already hot in the suit. The silence was overwhelming. The world seemed to have disappeared...

Side by side, like two cumbersome monsters who had lost their way, the two men moved into the sleeping tent. They lowered their, heavy bodies onto the protesting cots and lay quietly, their eyes bright behind their glassite plates.

"Now I lay me down to sleep," Charlie said.

Monte said nothing. He stared up into the hushed darkness of the tent and tried not to think.

Outside, the fat yellow moon would be rising. The old, uncaring stars would be looking down on the orange fire that burned in the little clearing. Somewhere, invisibly remote, the ship that had brought him from Earth would be floating in the dark silence.

Sealed in his anachronistic spacesuit, Monte Stewart was as alone as a man could ever be.

He closed his eyes.

Patiently, he waited.

They came out of the night and out of the stillness that lay beneath the silver stars. They came as he had known they would come, on great padded feet, with yellow eyes that gleamed in the close darkness of the tent.

He saw them coming; he was not asleep. They were phantoms, slipping like fog through the entrance to the tent. He could not hear them through his helmet, but he could see their glowing yellow eyes.

He imagined what he could not see: the dirty-gray coat with the long muscles rippling under a taut skin, the long sleek head with the crushing jaws, the saliva dripping from the pulled-back mouth...

He could smell the stink of them, hot and moist and heavy in the trapped air of the tent.

The wolf-things, the killers, the Merdosini.

They had come back to kill again.

"Charlie."

"Yes." The voice was tinny in his ear. "I see them."

He felt nothing, but he could see them nosing at his cot. He could see the black flowing shadows around Charlie's bed.

He lay very still, trying to slow down his breathing. His heart was pounding wildly in his chest. The sweat trickled down from under his arms and it was cold as ice in his hot suit. He waited, not moving a muscle.

Nightmare? Yes, this was what a nightmare was like. A nightmare was all terrible silence and the black shadows of death.

Incredibly, the punch-line of an ancient joke came to him: *Here comes old cold-nose.*

He fought down a mad impulse to laugh, to scream, to yell. These were the beasts that had killed Louise. These were the animals that had destroyed Helen Jenike. These were the killers that had torn Ralph Gottschalk apart.

These were the voiceless horrors of a fevered dream...

The wolf-things attacked.

Suddenly, with mindless ferocity, they were all over him. He couldn't see, couldn't move. The cot must have cracked under their plunging weight, for he felt himself fall to the ground. He was smothered under them, the stink of them filled his nostrils.

He waited, fighting down panic. They couldn't hurt him. He grabbed that thought and held onto it. *They couldn't hurt him.* That was what the spacesuits were for. If your defense is strong enough, you don't have to worry about the offense. The spacesuit was tough and it covered every inch of his, body. It would take more than teeth and jaws to tear through that suit. The natives scorned weapons. Very well. Let them try to open a can without a can-opener!

He felt nothing at all, he heard nothing but Charlie breathing into his suit mike. He could not see; one of the things was blocking his face plate. Flat on his back, he tried to move and failed. They must be all over him...

The stench was terrific. He lost track of time. Unbidden, his mind began to work. What if they blocked his air supply? Was the air getting stale? What if they found a fault in the suit, a weak spot, and white teeth began to gnaw at his bones? What if one of the natives came in and unlocked his helmet? What if the natives could direct the wolf-things well enough so that *they* could pry open his helmet, get at his head?

If only he could *see!*

There was some sound coming through the air filters—or was it only his imagination? A wet roaring, a growling, a slavering...

"Charlie!"

"I hear you."

"Can you move?"

"No."

"How long has it been?"

"I don't know."

"What if they don't stop, never stop?"

"You tell me. Calm down, Monte. This is your party, boy."

Monte flushed in hidden shame. Couldn't he take it?

What was the matter with him?

If only he could see.

If only he could move...

Suddenly, he *had* to move. He had miscalculated his own staying power; he could not endure this blind suffocation, this being buried alive. He tried to lift his arms and failed. He tried to bend his knees and failed. He tried to sit up and failed.

He began to cry, and choked it off as rapidly as it came. He gathered himself, sucked in fetid air. He *was* going to move. No stinking animal was going to stop him. He felt a strength pouring through him that was almost superhuman.

Now!

He wrenched and twisted to his right, felt the suit roll over. He was clear! He lurched to his feet, his eyes blazed. He stumbled out of the tent, pulling shadow beasts with him.

He could see! The fire in the clearing still burned feebly, and the moon was pouring silver down through the night. The wolf-things were all around him, circling him, moving in again. The muscles rippled on their lean flanks, their jaws were bleeding where they had tried to tear a hole in his suit.

Monte laughed wildly. "Come on, you devils! Come on and fight!"

"Monte! What are you doing?"

"Shut up!"

"Monte, remember—"

"Shut up, I tell you!" He was screaming, he had gone mad.

The wolf-things jumped him, trying for his metallic throat, trying to pull him down. There was no longer any thought in his mind of standing and taking it. He was clumsy in his suit, but he had a strength he hadn't known he possessed. He moved his arms as though they were pistons.

He caught one of the beasts in his gloved left hand, gripping it by the leg. He lifted it off the ground and smashed his right hand into its snarling face. The thing dropped like a stone when he let it go.

He picked up another one, staggering under its weight. He threw it at a tree, hard. He crouched down in his bulky armor, moved forward like a wrestler. His breath whistled in his teeth. He grabbed one that was trying to slink away, swung it in a great circle, and hurled it into the coals of the fire. It hit with a shower of sparks, rolled, and bolted for the safety of the trees.

His own laughter was maniacal in his ears. He seized a log and whirled it around his helmeted head like a scythe. He felt it crunch into something, and it felt good.

"Monte!"

Something had him from behind; he tried to shake it off but couldn't. He pulled free and turned, the log ready in his hands.

Charlie stood there, an impossible robot in the moonlight, waving his arms.

"They've gone!" The voice rang in his ears. "They've gone! Put the log down, you fool! What are you trying to do?"

He hesitated, and that was enough. Something like sanity came back to him. His arms were suddenly as heavy as lead and he dropped the log to the ground. He looked around. The clearing was empty. He saw one of the Merdosini dragging itself into the trees.

"You idiot! They couldn't hurt us. You know what we decided—"

That voice. He had to get away from that voice.

Trembling, he reached up and unlocked his helmet. He jerked it from his head, swallowed the fresh clean air.

Something inside him snapped. He leaned against a rock and was violently, desperately sick. He couldn't move, didn't want to move.

Charlie stumbled over to him, a gloved hand caught at his shoulder. He tried to brush the hand aside but he didn't have the strength. Charlie picked up his helmet and clamped it down over his head again. All sounds stopped except for the noise of harsh, labored breathing. His? Charlie's?

The tinny voice again. "You take that hat off again and I'll brain you with a rock. What got into you?"

"Don't know, don't know..."

He could hardly stand. Charlie steered him toward the tent.

There was a light. It came from Charlie's suit. He saw that his cot was smashed beyond repair. The tent was a shambles.

The anger poured through him again. He was glad that he had fought back, plan or no plan. He hoped that he had killed a few of them. Somewhere, in some dim corner of his brain, he knew that his thoughts were crazy thoughts—but it didn't matter.

The beasts had attacked them, hadn't they?

"Lie down, Monte. They won't be back tonight."

Charlie's voice sounded tired and hopeless, as though he had been let down from an unexpected quarter.

What's the matter with him?

Or is it me? What's the matter with me?

He was on the floor of the tent, on his back. He had no idea how he had gotten there, but it felt wonderful.

He was exhausted. Everything was far away, fuzzy.

"Charlie? Sorry, Charlie. Feel so strange..."

The voice came in from miles away. "Go to sleep. We'll talk about it in the morning."

"Yeah, go to sleep...."

He closed his eyes.

In seconds, he was asleep.

And that, really, was when it started.

11

Dreams?

Monte wasn't at all sure that they were dreams, which in itself was strange. Somehow, he had always known when he was dreaming. If the dream had been pleasant, he had enjoyed it. If it had been one of those terrible dreams that come welling up from the black pits of the mind—or from an improvident sandwich eaten too late at night—he had simply willed himself to wakefulness.

It's just a dream, he would think. *Wake up! End it!*

And he would stir and open his eyes and feel Louise's warm body next to his and everything would be fine.

But now his dream was very clear, very real. It was not at all complicated and it had a weird kind of plausibility to it. He was back home, and it was years ago. For some reason, he had killed a man—a featureless man, a man without a face. He had dug a hole out in the woods and buried the man. He had covered up the grave and forgotten about it. Long years had passed and nobody suspected that he was a murderer. He hardly knew it himself; he had buried his secret deep in his mind and kept it there. And then one day a hunter was building a fire. He cleared away the brush and found a decayed hand sticking out of the earth. He uncovered the rest of the body. The skin-shredded skull spoke the name of Monte Stewart.

They were coming for him, coming to get him. It was all over. The secret was out. He should have confessed years ago...

It's just a dream! Wake up! End it!

He fought his way out of the dream, peeling away the layers of fog and cotton. Sure, it was just a dream! A typical silly guilt dream, even. Calling Dr. Freud!

He stirred, opened his eyes.

He felt Louise's warm body next to his.

Good. It was over.

No! It could not be.

Why, Louise was dead. She couldn't be here. She was cold, cold...

And he had a spacesuit on, didn't he? How could he feel her warm body?

Dreams?

He moaned, not knowing whether he was asleep or awake. He tried to remember. He was in a tent with Charlie. Charlie Jenike. And they had been attacked by great wolf-things with yellow eyes. Why? What had they done?

Wait!

They were coming back again, out of the blackness that crouches just before the dawn. He could hear them padding into the tent. He could smell the animal stink of them. They were on top of him, their gaping jaws tearing at his chest...

He tried to move and could not. He was pinned down. His mouth opened, desperately seeking for the air that was no longer there. Cunningly, he tried to roll over. He didn't move an inch.

They can't get at me. I'm safe in my suit. Remember?

He relaxed. Safe!

But what was that, coming silently through the entrance to the tent? What was that long-armed naked shadow? It was bending over him, smiling...

It was unlocking his helmet, pulling it off!

Monte screamed.

A wave of blackness washed over him.

A metallic voice spoke in his ear, coming from far away: "Monte! Lie still! There's nothing after you! Wake up, wake up..."

He opened his wide, staring eyes. There was a robot bending over him. He saw the robot's face.

Charlie.

The gray light of morning was washing into the tent. He was alive.

After three cups of coffee, he was still shivering.

He stood with his back to the fire, knowing that it was foolish even as he did it. He could not feel the fire through his suit, and the early morning air was not really cold. It was damp and the ground was wet, but Sirius was greater than any man-made fire. It rose behind thick gray clouds and its heat was heavy and oppressive.

His eyes were tired and red-rimmed and his beard was a tangled mess. (Beards, he realized, were not ideal equipment inside spacesuit helmets.) He could not have slept more than two or three hours and he was bone-weary.

Still, his brain was working again. His sanity had returned, and he was grateful. Monte Stewart had never been a man to doubt himself before, but now he was unsure. He did not understand his own actions.

And those dreams, if dreams they had been. They were sick dreams. Tired as he was, they alarmed him.

"I don't get it," he said.

Charlie looked like he had not slept at all. He spooned breakfast mush out of a can and kept his distance. "You must have gone off your rocker."

Monte managed a wry smile. "I guess that man is not a very rational animal. We assumed that because we were deermined to be fair and peaceful the natives would be the same way. They weren't. And we assumed that I would always act logically. I didn't. Maybe we're two of a kind."

"But why? We made our big speech, we had our plan. We knew that the Merdosini would attack us, and we knew that they couldn't hurt us. All we had to do was to wait until they went away. We would have proved our point—we meant no harm even if we were attacked. And then you blow your stack and fight back. If that's the best we can do, we might as well quit."

Monte poured the dregs of his coffee into the fire. "I'm sorry."

"Swell, wonderful. You're sorry. What do we do now? Send them a making-up present?"

"I don't know. What do you think?"

"You're the big genius. This was all your idea. You tell me."

Monte rubbed his tired eyes. He looked at the mocking trees that surrounded the clearing. The plain truth was that he had no ideas at all. He had nothing but a hard knot of determination. He was too worn out to think.

"You won't win any good-conduct medals this morning yourself," he said irritably. "What's eating you?"

Charlie threw up his hands in despair. "He throws away the only chance we've got and then he asks me what's eating me. My God!"

Monte turned and faced him. "I said I was sorry. I'm not Superman. I make mistakes. I don't know what got into me. But I do know that if we start knocking each other we're through. Cut it out."

Charlie sat down heavily on a log. He cupped his chin in his gloved hands. He seemed infinitely weary. "It's everything, Monte. These damned suits. The miserable air. The whole stinking planet. I didn't sleep at all last night. Right now, none of it makes any sense. I don't even know what I'm doing here. I might as well be on the ship. I just don't care any longer."

Monte nodded slowly. "It would be easy to quit. It gets easier all the time. There just doesn't seem to be any logical reason for going on. I know all that."

"Then why not quit and be done with it?"

"I don't even know the answer to that one. But it's a hard thing to be defeated, Charlie. It's easy to quit, but you have to live with it a long, long time."

"Thank you, Friendly Old Philosopher. You've made it all as clear as mud."

"Maybe you'd better hit the sack for a while. I'll hold the fort. We won't get anywhere this way."

Charlie pulled himself to his feet. "You twisted my arm. I can't say that I'm anxious to stick my head in that blasted helmet again, though."

"Do it anyhow."

"Of course." Charlie looked at him strangely, but said nothing more. He picked up his helmet and disappeared into the tent.

Monte stood silently in the gray morning light. There was a smell of rain in the air. He studied the trees but saw nothing suspicious.

Dimly, in the depths of his mind, a thought nagged at him. He tried to pull it out into the open, but it was too much trouble.

He just stood there and looked at nothing, nothing at all.

Along about noon, when the cloud-smothered surface of Sirius Nine was a steaming jungle that threatened to melt Monte in his suit, the gray heavens opened up and a torrent of warm rain turned the clearing into a puddled swamp.

There was no thunder and little wind. The rain hissed down in shimmering sheets, effectively isolating Monte where he stood and masking the forest that surrounded him. It was a peaceful rain and he was slow in reacting to it. He was puzzled at his own feelings. The rain was pleasant against his face and even the slight trickle of water inside his suit was not unwelcome.

I want it to be a magic rain, he thought. *I want it to wash everything away. I want it to cleanse this world. I want it to make me clean again. I want it to make me forget, forget....*

Forget what? He shook his head. *I don't understand myself. Is there something the matter with me, something the matter with the way I am thinking?*

Sick? I must be sick. But what is it? What is it?

He stood for a long time in the strange shelter of the rain and then walked over to the tent. He pushed his way inside. He did not want to leave the rain, but he thought vaguely that if he were sick he should take some medicine and the medicine was in the tent....

He waited for a moment, letting his eyes accustom themselves to the darkness. His suit dripped in little puddles on the floor. He heard Charlie's labored breathing and realized that Charlie had gone to sleep without his helmet. That could be dangerous if the Merdosini came back. He started toward Charlie's cot.

Charlie sat up suddenly, his eyes wild.

"You!" Charlie pointed a trembling finger. "Keep away from me!"

Monte heard his own voice speaking. It was definitely his own voice, but it was alienated from him. It was very much like hearing a playback of his voice from a recording machine. It said: "Your helmet. You can't sleep without your helmet."

Charlie lurched to his feet, monstrous in his swollen suit. His breathing was harsh in the confinement of the tent. "Get out, get away! I know you now. You can't fool me any longer."

"You can't sleep without your helmet." (Why did he keep saying that?)

"Don't touch my helmet, let it alone!"

"You can't sleep—"

"Shut up!" Charlie tried to back away, but there was no place to go. "It's all your fault—everything is your fault! If it hadn't been for you, I wouldn't be here. If it hadn't been for you, we wouldn't have made so many stupid mistakes. If it hadn't been for you, Helen would still be alive!"

The words slashed through the fog in Monte's brain like a knife. "Charlie, I lost my wife too—"

"Clever! Oh, you're clever, no doubt about that. You wanted to get rid of her! You dirty murderer...."

"Charlie—"

"Get away! Get back, I warn you...."

Monte tried to run, but he was rooted to the spot. This was insane. If only he could think, if only he could free his mind from whatever it was that held him in thrall.

"I can't stand it!" Charlie crouched down: he was squat and ugly like some prehistoric beast with a scaly reptilian skin. "I won't just stand here and take it!"

"Wait, Charlie." (Charlie? No, surely this was not the Charlie Jenike he had known. What was happening?)

The thing that had been Charlie Jenike attacked.

The sheer hurtling fury of his rush knocked Monte from his feet. He fell heavily to the floor of the tent, he felt immensely strong hands closing about his throat, he heard Charlie snarling like a wild animal to his face.

"Kill you, kill you, kill you!"

Monte doubled his gloved fist and swung a short chopping blow at Charlie's exposed head. There was a crunching thud as he connected. The clutching hands relaxed their pressure against his throat. With a wild surge of power, he heaved the robot-body away from him.

Monte leaped to his feet, ignoring the weight of the suit he wore. His lips curled back in a smile. He walked over and kicked Charlie in the head with his boot.

Charlie began to scream. The sound was very unpleasant. Monte decided to cut it off. He knelt down beside Charlie, reached out, and got him around the neck. He started to squeeze.

The screaming stopped.

"Call me a murderer, will you? You miserable excuse for a human being…"

He tightened his grip. Charlie's eyes were bulging.

Then Monte heard his other voice, the one that whispered inside his brain—a voice miraculously insulated, protected, preserved.

Call me a murderer….

Miserable excuse for a human being….

A wave of revulsion washed over him. He jerked his hands away from Charlie's throat as though they had touched the fires of hell.

My God, what have I done?

Charlie! Charlie!

Charlie gasped for breath. He looked up with the most bewildered, tortured eyes that Monte had ever seen. The eyes were wild and stricken, but there was the light of sanity in them.

"Help me," Charlie whispered hoarsely. "Help me!"

Monte pulled him into a sitting position, then threw his arm across his shoulder and hauled him to his feet.

"Charlie! I don't know what's going on, I can't think. But we have to get out of here! Now, this minute!"

"Yes, help me…"

Together, they staggered out of the tent into the gray hiss of the rain. They didn't know where they were going, or why. They had lost everything, even their hope.

They knew only that they had to get away.

Fast. Before it was too late. Before it was all over.

They stumbled through the rain, two shapeless monsters spawned in a nightmare of desolation. They walked and crawled into the dark, dripping forest and disappeared.

Where the men from Earth had been, there was only an empty clearing in the rain.

An empty clearing and a dead fire and two sagging tents and two forgotten spacesuit helmets….

12

Run!

Monte felt the blood pounding in his head. The very air that he breathed seared his lungs; his chest heaved in shuddering gasps inside the prison of his suit. He slipped and fell sprawling in the mud. He lurched back to his feet and kept on going.

Run!

He had no destination: he was running away from something, not toward something. He was running away from the rain-soaked clearing, running away from the dark long-armed shadows of the Merdosi, running away from the wolf-things that prowled in the night.

And he was running away from himself.

Run!

The jungle of trees around him became an impenetrable wall; he had to fight for light, for air. Creepers and vines and thickets snatched at his boots. He could see nothing clearly. Even the leaden gray sky was invisible. There was nothing in all the world but the fury of flight, nothing but the mindless command to keep on going, always, forever.

Dimly, he was aware of the crashing of a heavy body behind him, a sound of boots sucking at the mud, a sound of shallow choking gasps for air.

Come on, Charlie! Don't give up! Run!

He crashed out of the trees into the half-light of the fading day. Through a screen of silver rain he saw a brown, swollen river. It gushed between eroding banks and foamed against glistening upthrust boulders. The water was as black as dirty oil, except where the surface was cut by rocks and the white spray leaped into the air. The booming of the river filled the world; there was nothing else.

He knew that he had to cross the river. It was desperately important to him that he get to the other side. But how? Swimming in the spacesuit was out of the question; he would sink like a stone. Even if he threw away the suit he could never swim in that rushing water.

Reluctantly, he stopped. He fell to his knees, fighting for breath. Charlie staggered out of the forest behind him and fell full-length on the ground, sobbing.

There *had* to be a way.

Somehow, he got to his feet. He walked upstream, staring at the thrust of the water. Behind the gray curtain of the rain, the boulders in the river bed glistened like naked primordial islands. A wan of sound beat at his ears. But every atom of his being was bent toward a single goal:

Run!

235

Get across the river!

He kept on going, his eyes narrowed against the rain. He hauled the senseless spacesuit with him as thoughtlessly as a turtle carries the shell upon his back.

There. He blinked his eyes. The river widened, fanning out between crumbling banks of yellow mud. Massive rocks loomed up out of the foaming water like a chain of battered islands that stretched from bank to bank. The river ran fast and rough in silver-laced rapids, but it was not deep. He could walk across on the boulders if he didn't slip. If he did miss his footing....

Well, that would be that.

He didn't look back; he simply assumed that Charlie was there. His boots squished through the sticky mud and he scrambled out upon the first rock. It was slippery with slime; he had to keep moving or fall. The spray drenched his face, making it hard for him to breathe. But the noise was the worst. The nameless river roared at him with an ancient chant of malevolent fury.

Like some misshapen, unrecorded beast from a forgotten era, he scrambled along from rock to rock. He could hardly see where he was going and he was driven on by a mad, unreasoning will that had possessed his body. He clawed at the slick rocks with his thick-gloved fingers, kicked at them with his boots, hugged them with his arms. He cursed them, reviled them, screamed at them.

He fell the last few feet, fell into dirty rushing water that rolled him over like a log. He crawled to the shore and flopped out of the water like the first amphibian groping for the land.

The river was behind him. He had crossed the river. He was too weak to stand. He lay in the mud, smiling insanely.

He heard someone screaming hysterically. He twisted around and saw Charlie's bloated body doing a crazy tightrope dance across the chain of boulders. He wanted to help him but he could hardly move. He slithered around in the mud until he was facing the river again and stretched out his hands. When Charlie fell from the last rock he caught him and pulled him out of the water.

Charlie lay face-down in the yellow mud, his body heaving convulsively. Gradually, his movements subsided.

He turned his mud-streaked face toward Monte and tried to smile.

"We made it," he whispered. "I don't believe it."

Monte took a deep breath; his demon was driving him on. "Can't stay here."

"Good a place as any. We're through."

"Find a dry place. Hole up."

"What for?"

Monte was impatient with talk. Didn't the man *know* that they had to keep on going? Couldn't he *see* that they had to get away from the river? Didn't he understand that they had to find....

What?

Monte pulled himself slowly to his feet. A part of him was amazed that he could stand, but another part of him knew that there were dark reservoirs of strength in his body that no machine could ever measure, no man could ever comprehend.

For a moment, he blacked out. Then the blood came back to his head and he swayed with dizziness. Despite the mud and the rain he felt hot.

Probably burning up with fever. But what does that mean? What is fever? Just a word. Words can't help me now. There are no words.

"Come on, Charlie," he said. "Get up."

"Can't."

"You can. Get up. It won't be far."

"We're beaten."

Monte reached down, caught Charlie under the arms, and heaved him to his feet. "You can't stay here."

Charlie shook his head. "I can't go on."

"You can. Just do it."

Monte turned and started away from the river. He concentrated on putting one foot in front of the other. He did not look back. He did not think. He just kept walking beneath a weeping sky, drawn as a metal filing is drawn toward a magnet that it cannot see.

The country was open now, exposed to the sweep of the rain. He walked through tall grass, trampling down the wet spears with his boots. He could feel the land rising under him, and far ahead, masked by the gray curtain of the rain, he saw the high horizon. A jagged and dark horizon that held the edge of the coming night.

Mountains.

He did not know how long it took him to reach the foothills; time had lost its meaning. He might have walked forever under the alien sky with the night wind in his face. But he did not stop. He simply endured. He kept on going.

It was quite dark and the rain still fell. He looked up at banks of cliffs and saw it there. A deeper blackness against the single shadow of the night. A doorway of darkness....

A cave.

He smiled. He had not known what it was that he was searching for, but he knew it when he saw it. A cave. That was it. That was the answer.

It *had* to be.

He climbed a twisting trail up the face of the cliff. He could hear Charlie behind him, dislodging rocks with his boots. He reached the mouth of the cave. He did not hesitate. He bent down and edged inside. It was black, black as midnight in a land that had never known the light of the stars, but it was warm and dry.

He was safe. He knew he was safe.

He moved back from the entrance and fell on the floor. He found a flat rock to use for a pillow. He closed his eyes.

He knew somehow that a cycle had ended. He had come full circle.

Charlie collapsed beside him, gasping with exhaustion. Monte's brain tried to tell him that he should not sleep, but it was no use.

It did not matter.

Nothing mattered.

He was safe, safe in the cave that was the beginning of all men, hidden from the world beyond.

He slept.

The strange, twisted dreams did not return. He slept the heavy sleep of complete and utter weariness. Gradually, his breathing became regular. The lines in his face smoothed and softened. His body relaxed.

When he woke up, Monte saw a golden haze at the mouth of the cave. The sun was up and the rain had stopped. Even inside the cavern, the air smelled fresh and fragrant. At first, he did not move. He just lay where he was, rejoicing in the simple pleasure of being alive.

No, it was more than that. He was not only alive. He was well. The fevered sickness that had chained his mind was gone, washed away. He felt cleansed and happy. It was perhaps the oldest and most fundamental of all human joys: *I have been sick, and now I am well. I have stood on the brink of the black pit, and I have come back.*

Sanity. It was something that Monte had always taken for granted. Madness had never been something that could happen to *him*. Others, yes. But not to him.

Now, he knew better. He was thankful just to be himself.

But what had happened to him—and to Charlie? Was it possible that they had been on Sirius Nine for just two nights? It seemed to him that those few hours had been an eternity, longer than all the rest of his life. He could not even remember them clearly. It was all so jumbled, so confused....

And there was something about the whole experience, something that he could not quite remember. A quality of desperate urgency, of testing, of menace. It had not been natural. It was somehow intimately bound up with the incomprehensible Merdosi, and with the wolf-things, and with the dark shadows of the unsuspected....

He got to his feet, moving quietly so as not to disturb Charlie. He crouched down and walked to the mouth of the cave. He stepped outside.

The white furnace of Sirius struck him like a blow, but he welcomed it—welcomed the heat and the light and the purity of it. He reveled in the sweep of the blue sky, the rain-washed green of the grasses, the flame of the red leaves on the trees. The fresh air kissed his face. Even the distant river was peaceful, winding its way between yellow banks, gleaming like glass in the hot rays of the sun.

He looked at himself, fingered the tangle of his matted beard. His suit was caked with mud. There was a great jagged tear in his left leg. His gloves were scratched and stiff. His body felt damp and infested with filth.

Slowly, Monte began to remove the spacesuit. The gloves went first, and he noticed that his hands were white and clammy, as though they had been too long away from the light of the sun. He struggled with the suit, taking it off section by section. It wasn't an easy job. When he had finished, the suit lay crumpled on the rocks like a discarded serpent skin.

He took off the rest of his damp clothing and stretched it out on a flat stone to dry. The heat of the sun felt wonderful, and it was with reluctance that he moved back into a shadow to get out of the glare. He knew that Sirius could blister his naked skin in a few short minutes. Still, it was a real temptation to linger awhile in the bright light.

He wanted a bath. A bath, he decided, was one of the great unappreciated blessings of civilization. A bath and a good meal and a cool drink....

Well, all that would have to wait. It was something just to get rid of the spacesuit. He looked at the thing with active dislike. The whole idea of the spacesuits, which had seemed so logical on the ship, was utterly wrong. It was wrong, and yet it was completely characteristic of the mistakes that he had made. How could you expect to contact a people by insulating yourself from them?

Somehow, he needed a new way of thinking. He needed a fresh approach. He needed to think the whole thing out with an uncluttered mind.

He sat down on a rock, cupping his bearded chin in his hands. He looked out at the panorama of the world below him. It was hard to believe that there was ugliness in all that beauty, hard to believe that evil could exist in such a place.

There had to be an answer somewhere. There had to be a path that he could follow, a path that would lead not only to an understanding of the Merdosi but also to an understanding of himself and what he represented....

That was when he heard the terrible sound.

He leaped to his feet, his reverie forgotten.

Inside the cave, Charlie was screaming.

13

For a moment a pang of despair shot through him and he abandoned himself to it. He had assumed that Charlie too would be free of the sickness, although there was no real reason for thinking so. It seemed to him that he was miserably alone, miserably helpless. He was faced with a task that was beyond his powers. He was making no progress at all.

The awful screaming continued. There were no words in it; it wasn't human. It was a naked animal cry of agony.

Monte pulled himself together. He didn't know how he did it, just as he didn't know what it was that had carried him through the past night of horror. He knew only that he was an actor in some vast and terrible drama and that he must play his part until he dropped.

He ducked down and went into the cave. There was plenty of light and he could see clearly. Charlie was on his back, his swollen arms sticking straight up into the air, his gloved fists tightly clenched. His dirty face was contorted and sweating, his mouth loose and trembling.

The screams filled the cave.

Monte knelt down, ready for anything. He felt as though he were caught up in some endlessly repeating cycle with no way out, no way to break the chain.

He slapped Charlie's face, hard.

"Wake up! You're dreaming. It's okay. You're safe. Everything's okay. Wake up!"

The screaming stopped. Charlie snorted and opened his eyes. The eyes were wild with terror, fined with a nameless fear.

"It's okay, Charlie. You've been dreaming. It's just me, Monte. Easy does it, boy. Relax. Take it easy."

Charlie looked at him. Gradually, the light of recognition dawned in his eyes. His arms dropped to his chest. He shook his head, licked his lips.

"It's all over, Charlie. Don't let it get you. Look—see the sun shining out there? We're okay."

Charlie stared at Monte's nakedness. Suddenly, he smiled. "What is this, a nudist colony? Now I know I'm nuts!"

Monte laughed with relief. Charlie seemed to be himself again. "I just couldn't stand that damned suit any longer. Come on outside and get yours off. You'll feel better. "

Charlie didn't move.

"Come on, get up. We'll get us some food...."

Charlie shuddered and seemed to withdraw into his suit as a turtle will pull its head back into its shell. Monte reached out and touched his shoulder, trying to pull him back from wherever he was going.

"There's nothing to be afraid of now. Don't let it get you again. Fight it!"

"No."

"Man, you can't give up! Look out there—the sun is shining—"

"Damn the sun. What difference does it make? Not *our* sun."

"What's wrong with you? What's the matter? Let me help."

Charlie closed his eyes. His breathing was very shallow. "I tried to kill you, Monte. Have you forgotten that?"

Monte waved his hand irritably. "We were sick. They did something to us. We weren't responsible. That wasn't *us* fighting. Don't you know that?"

"Words." Charlie opened his haunted eyes. "My God, the things I saw in my mind! The dreams I had! Am I like that?"

"Of course not."

"Those things came out of my mind. Things about you and Louise. Even about Helen. Slime! Sick? Lord, the sickness is inside us. I don't know myself. All the things you keep bottled up inside of you and then somebody takes the lid off. We tried to kill each other! And you say that everything is fine. Mad! We're both mad!"

"Maybe so. But this won't get us anywhere. We've got to fight!"

"Fight what? Shadows? Dreams? A planet? Ourselves? Go away. Let me alone. I don't want to do anything else, ever."

"Come on outside. The fresh air will do you good."

Charlie laughed—a bitter, hollow, broken laugh.

"Fresh air! That's funny."

"Dammit, I'm trying to help you! Charlie, we're all alone here. We can't quit. There's too much at stake."

"Garbage, garbage. Idiocy. We should have quit before we started. Helen's dead. Louise is dead. Ralph is dead. We'll be dead soon. And for what? For what? Hang the Merdosi! They're not like us, never have been, never will be. They're monsters. We're monsters!"

"You're contradicting yourself. Come on, now...."

A look of cunning came into Charlie's sunken eyes. "No. They're out there. All around us. I can feel them. They're after me, inside my head."

Monte was baffled in the presence of the sickness that he saw in the other man. It was like talking to a lunatic. "I've been out there. I've looked. We're all alone."

"I can feel them, I tell you! Do you really think you can get away from them by splashing across a river? This is their world, not ours. We're finished!"

Monte searched desperately for some magic words that would get through to him. There were no words.

Charlie sighed, closed his eyes again. He went down into the depths of some profound depression. He began to mumble, to whisper, to cry. "No good. I'm no good. The things I saw—in my own mind—I'm sick, so sick...."

"Do you want me to contact the ship?" Monte asked quietly. "You can't go on like this—it's asking too much of any man. Maybe it would be best—"

"No, no. Can't go back, nothing there. Can't leave you here. Just let me alone, can't you? Let me rest—think...."

Monte got to his feet. "You need something to eat. I'll get some."

"Don't go out there! Don't leave me! Stay here!"

"Starving never appealed to me much," Monte said firmly. "We have to get food. You wait here, do you understand? I'll be back."

Charlie began to cry again.

Monte walked out into the sunlight and put on his warm, dry clothes. He unhooked the spare canteen from the spacesuit and fastened it to his belt. He tried not to listen to the wretched sobbing from the cave.

He started down the trail toward the green world below.

The whispering grasslands surrounded him and the smell of the rain-washed air was sweet. The land sloped gently toward the river and the sky above his head was warm and blue and comforting. In spite of himself, in spite of everything, Monte felt a sudden surge of confidence.

He could take it. He knew that now, and it was a valuable thing to know. A man could go all through his life and never meet the final test that would tell him what he was. When all the horrors are behind you there is nothing more to fear.

How in the devil was he going to get his hands on some food? The water was easy; he could simply go on to the river and fill his canteen. But he had no weapons. He was not eager to go back to the clearing and pick up some cans, although it might come to that in the end. He might build a trap of some sort, but that was a slow and uncertain technique at best.

He remembered that Ralph had run some tests on a batch of red berries that he had picked. If he could find some of those it might help. But a man couldn't live on berries. Roots? Fish?

Well, first things first. He kept on toward the river, enjoying the walk, strangely at ease. The world of Walonka no longer seemed alien to him; it was even beautiful, once you got used to it. Perhaps all worlds were beautiful to appreciative eyes. Planets were not alien, at least not the ones a man could walk on without an artificial air supply. People were the problem. It was far easier to adjust to a new world than to a new human being.

He stepped out of the grass and saw the river gliding before him, quiet and peaceful in the bright sunlight. It was a far cry from the wild torrent of the night before; even the upthrust rocks looked dry and inviting. He stretched out on the cool bank and put his mouth in the water. He drank. It tasted clean and fresh. He filled his canteen and wished fervently that he had not left his pipe and tobacco back in the tent. He could do with a smoke. In fact, despite his empty belly, he would have been completely content with his pipe. He had always loved the land, any land that had not been spoiled by the stinks of civilization, and a man could ask for very little more than a clean river and a blue sky and a warm sun.

He felt completely at peace with himself.

Perhaps the river was the answer. There had to be fish in it, hanging in those dark pools by the rocks. As an old fisherman, he could almost *smell* fish. He could rig up a line of some sort, bait it with insects or even berries, catch himself a mess of fish....

And he suddenly remembered the birds. It should not be too difficult to locate some nests, swipe a few eggs. He smiled. If only that was all there was to life! Enough to eat, enough to drink, a fire to keep you warm, a shelter to keep you dry, a little love....

How did the lives of men get so complicated? Why did men insist on cluttering up their lives with all the little irritations that made a man old before his time? Why couldn't a guy just sit in the sun and fish and smoke his pipe?

He didn't know. But he was not simple enough to believe in his own lotus dream. He recognized it for what it was: a reaction to all the hell he had been through, a fantasy of all the Good Old Days that never had been. There was some truth in it, sure. Maybe even a little wisdom. But a man was what he was. He had a brain and he couldn't switch it on and off at will.

Louise was dead. Charlie was sobbing in a cave in some nameless cliff. He, Monte, had failed in his job. The Earth and Sirius Nine had touched across the dark seas of space, and their destinies were bound together forever—no enchanted Excalibur could cut the chains that tied them. There was a vast and intricate play of forces at work here and now, by this peaceful river, and they all centered on him. He had to do what he could, or forget about calling himself a man.

He got to his feet, then froze.

There was an animal drinking from the river not twenty yards downstream from him. It was a lovely creature, not unlike a deer, but it was small and its legs were short. It was not built for speed like a deer. There were no horns on its head. Its coat was a soft brown with flecks of white. It was very dainty, and it was—helpless.

The animal looked up at Monte, took him in with gentle liquid eyes, and did not move. It didn't seem frightened. It nibbled at the green shoots of a bush that grew along the river bank and twitched its short tail lazily.

Probably, Monte thought, the animal had confused him with one of the natives. The wind was blowing in Monte's face, and without the clue of scent the animal did not realize that he was anything strange. And the natives always hunted with the Merdosini....

If he could catch him, break his neck—or even stun him with a rock....

Monte took a step toward the animal. The animal eyed him curiously and continued to munch on the grass. Monte moved closer, careful to make no sudden motions. The creature sniffed the air. Its mule ears cocked forward along its head.

Monte held his breath. Fifteen yards to go. Ten.

The animal backed away. It gave a kind of whistling snort, turned, and trotted off through the high grass. It wasn't really running. Just keeping its distance.

Monte suddenly realized that he was very hungry. There was a lot of meat on that critter. He picked up a stone about the size of a baseball. If he could just get a little closer....

Monte broke into an easy run, bringing his feet down as softly as he could. The animal didn't look back, but matched his pace. Monte braced himself, deciding that a quick sprint was his only chance. He gripped the stone firmly. Now....

Just as he started to race forward, he saw it.

He dropped like a shot, hiding himself in the tall grass. He was not the only one hunting that animal. One of the wolf-things, belly low to the ground, swift and silent as death itself, was cutting across the trail.

Monte parted the grass and watched. How could he have been so careless? He was completely helpless without the protection of his suit—as helpless as that runt deer. But the wolf-thing didn't seem to be interested in him; he went after his prey with a single-minded concentration that was frightening to observe.

The little animal never knew what hit him. The Merdosini struck like a blur, like a soundless shadow. The great white fangs ripped at the jugular and there was a spurt of crimson blood that reddened the muzzle of the killer. It was all over in seconds.

That was when the man stepped out of the grass and whistled. Monte's eyes widened in surprise. He knew that man. He was an old man, tall and long-armed and naked with vertical stripes of vermillion on his chest. His skin was copper in the sunlight and the fine hair on his head was a fuzz of gold. And his eyes, those dark and tortured eyes—Monte couldn't forget them.

It was the same old man that they had first tried to contact after the landing on Sirius Nine. The old man who had fled from his hollow tree when they had tried to talk to him—how long ago? What was he doing here, on this side of the river?

The man called off the wolf-thing. The beast whined and rubbed up against the old man's legs in an oddly doglike gesture. The man patted his head absently, then reached down, gathered up the dead animal, and hoisted it to his shoulders. From where he lay in the grass, Monte could distinctly see the red blood trickling down over the copper skin.

Side by side, the man and the wolf-thing set off through the high grass.

They were headed straight for the cliff where the cave was. Coincidence? Monte hardly thought so.

He thought fast. It wouldn't do to make any foolish mistakes this time. The old man wasn't much of a threat to them as long as he was alone. And the wolf-thing was probably safe enough as long as the old man controlled him. If Monte let himself be seen, he might scare the old man away. He didn't want that. It was just possible....

He waited until they had a good lead on him. He waited until he was sure that the long grass would conceal his movements. Then he got to his feet and silently followed their trail.

He walked through the green world under the white sun.

Hope was reborn in him.

He followed the trail of the old man and the killer. Each step he took brought him closer to the foothills of the mountains where Charlie waited in the cave.

And each step he took filled him with wonder.

14

The old man walked steadily beneath his burden, the long muscles of his body seeming to flow as he moved. He did not stop to rest. The wolf-thing padded along at his side, occasionally even frisking in front of its master.

A man and his dog, Monte thought. A man and his dog packing out a deer. How easy it was to transpose this scene into an earthly parallel! Psychologically, it was a dangerous line of reasoning—and yet it had a certain validity to it. Offhand, to someone who had never been there, it might seem that the life-forms of Sirius Nine should be totally different in appearance from those of Earth. But wasn't that notion violently contradicted by all the facts of evolution? It was one of those insidiously logical ideas that suffered from one minor flaw: it wasn't true. Even a nodding acquaintance with terrestrial evolution should have been enough to puncture that particular bubble. One of the most arresting facts of evolution was the principle of parallelism or convergence. Life-forms that had been separate for millions of years often showed striking similarities. He thought of the classic example of the marsupials and the placentals. There were marsupial bears, cats, dogs, squirrels—everything. There were creatures that looked like elephants but weren't. And even the history of man illustrated the same idea. Man had almost certainly developed not once, but several times. There were types like *Pithecanthropus* in Java and China and Africa. There were classic Neanderthals living at the same time as *Homo sapiens,* and even interbreeding with them in Palestine and Czechoslovakia. There were many different groups of Miocene primates, such as the *Dryopithecines,* who were evolving in man-like directions. Perhaps there were only a limited number of solutions to the problems of survival. Perhaps a given type of life, such as a mammal, would of necessity develop along parallel lines, no matter where the evolution took place. Perhaps the twin mechanisms of mutation and natural selection would always ensure the survival of basically efficient types: fish and birds, turtles and rabbits, butterflies and men. Perhaps on all the Earth-like planets in the universe, given the proper conditions of air and sunlight and water, man would find only variations on a single master plan....

Alien? Sure, the life on a planet could be alien—Monte had found that out in the nightmare with the Merdosi. But wasn't it alien in its nuances, in its shadings, in its almost-but-not-quite quality? Wasn't it alien because it was subtly different? And wasn't that more truly alien, say, than something that looked like an octopus but had thought patterns just like a modern American?

Take that old man there, walking along under a white sun with a carcass on his back. His bodily proportions were different from Monte's, but so what? The puzzle lay elsewhere. Why was he doing what he was doing? What was he thinking about? What had motivated him to kill that animal and carry it toward the cave? What had it cost him in pain and worry and courage?

What *was* he doing?

Wait and see, boy. Wait and see.

Without hesitation, the old man started up the trail that led to the cave. There could be no doubt that he was familiar with the place; their sanctuary had not been as safe as they had imagined. Monte hung back, not wishing to show himself. He wanted to see what would happen. He listened carefully, but he could not hear Charlie. Asleep? Watching?

Moving quickly from rock to rock, Monte moved up the cliff. He angled off to the left so that he would come out just above and to one side of the cave.

Holding his breath, he wriggled forward and looked down. The old man was standing on the ledge just in front of the cave. The wolf-thing was whining and sniffing at the discarded spacesuit. The man put the dead animal down at the mouth of the cave. For the first time, he hesitated. He backed off a few steps. He folded his long arms across his vermillion-striped chest. He took a deep breath.

The old man spoke. There was a tremor in his voice. He was afraid, but he was determined to do what he had come here to do. He spoke slowly and distinctly, choosing his words with care. Monte had no trouble in understanding him.

"Strangers!" (Literally: "People-Who-Are-Not-Merdosi.") "I speak to you as once you spoke to me. I bring you a gift of food as once you brought me a gift of food. I speak my name: Volmay. There has been much trouble since you first spoke to me. Much of it has been due to my own cowardice. It is time for a beginning-again. I tell you my name: Volmay. Will you speak with me?"

He was answered by silence. Charlie said nothing at all. Monte cursed to himself. This was the chance they had been waiting for. Couldn't Charlie see that? He wanted to show himself, call down to Volmay. But if he startled him now...

"Strangers! Are you there? I speak my name again: Volmay. I have brought food to you. I am alone. Do you no longer wish to speak?"

Words! First it was the men of Earth calling out to the Merdosi. Then it was Volmay calling out to the men of Earth. And there were never any replies. The gap was never bridged.

Come on, Charlie! Give him a chance!

The old man stood alone on the ledge of rock, surrounded by the ancient mountains and the sweep of the sky.

The warm wind whispered in the silence.

"Strangers! It is not easy for a man to think against his people. I am only a man. My courage is weak. Soon I will go. Will you not speak with me?"

Silence.

Then—sound.

Movement.

Charlie hurtled out of the mouth of the cave as though shot from a cannon. He was screaming like a madman. His swollen suit was encrusted with filth, his face was contorted into a grimace of fury. He had a sharp rock in his hand.

Before Monte could move, Charlie had thrown himself on the old man. He knocked him down, leaped on top of him. He struck with the rock. The old man jerked his head away and the rock grazed his shoulder, cutting a red gash.

The wolf-thing snarled and circled, its belly low. The old man cried out to him, waved him away. Charlie lifted the rock to strike again.

There was no time to think. Monte jumped down from where he was hidden, fell, and scrambled forward. He grabbed Charlie's arm, twisted it.

"You damn fool! Let him alone!"

"Come to kill us! Get him, get him, don't let him get away!"

Charlie twisted free. He kicked the old man in the head with his boot, stunning him. The wolf-thing growled, fangs bared.

Monte leaped to his feet, threw a punch with his right hand. He connected with the chest plate of Charlie's suit, almost breaking his fist. Charlie swayed off-balance.

"Stop it! He came to help us!"

Charlie shook his head, his eyes wild. He lifted the rock. "Stay away! Keep out of it!" He turned toward the helpless man.

Monte felt as though he were back in the nightmare again, fighting his own kind, fighting himself. But he knew what he had to do.

"Let him alone, Charlie," he said quietly. "Let him alone or I'll kill you."

Charlie hesitated. He took a step toward Monte, then stopped. A look of utter bewilderment passed over his sweating face. The rock fell out of his hand. "No," he said. "I can't—I don't—I don't know...."

Then a strangled sob broke loose from him. He turned and ran down the trail, not even looking where he was going. It was a miracle that he didn't fall.

"Charlie! Come back!"

The awkward figure thrashed its way down the cliff, never pausing for a second. It ran full tilt into the grasslands and vanished.

Monte was caught in the middle. He didn't know what to do. He ignored the whining wolf-thing and knelt by Volmay's side. The old man's eyes were open. His naked body was trembling with shock.

"Are you well?" Monte asked, fumbling with the native language. "I am so—regretful. My friend—he is sick...."

"I know. I will live."

"I must go after him, bring him back. Will you wait?"

The old man spoke slowly. "It always comes to this, to sadness. I tried very hard."

"Yes, yes, I understand you. It is not too late—"

"Who knows? My dreams have been uneasy. We have both done wrong. We cannot trust one another. My dreams told me that we might have a beginning-again, but the dreams are so strange since you have come...."

"Volmay, will you wait? *Will you wait?*"

"It was not easy for me to come here. I do not know. I will try. I will try...."

Monte touched the old man's shoulder. "We are grateful for what you have done. I will be back soon. Wait for me."

"We will do what we must, all of us."

Monte couldn't wait any longer. Charlie was sick; there was no telling what he might do.

He left the old man where he was and ran back down the trail, toward the green world that had swallowed the man who had been his friend, toward the river.

Monte plunged into the tall grasses. It was easy to follow the trail left by Charlie's heavy boots—but it was not necessary. He knew where Charlie was going, knew it as certainly as he had ever known anything in his life.

He did not waste his breath in calling. It was too late for words and he needed to conserve what strength he had left. He was weak with hunger. The nervous energy that had sustained him was beginning to falter.

He was covered with sweat when he reached the river. He saw Charlie at once: a squat, bulbous figure on a rock in the middle of the stream. A pathetic, broken man smothering in the shell of his mechanical suit, looking down at the cool, clean water.

Why did he wait for me? Was it too hard to die alone?

"Charlie! Don't do it!" His voice was very small, lost in the immensity of the sky, drowned by the rush of the river.

Charlie Jenike looked back at him and said nothing.

Monte started across the rocks toward him.

Charlie smiled a little, a strangely peaceful smile, and jumped. He hit the water feet first and dropped like a stone. He came up again once, caught in the current. His clumsy body thrashed in the water. He seemed to be trying to swim.

Monte dove into the water, knowing that it was no use.

The river was swift and cold. He struck out for the struggling figure but he never had a chance.

Charlie went down again and stayed down.

Monte fished down from the surface, peering through the cool green depths. He stayed down until his lungs were bursting, surfaced, and went down again. He couldn't find him. There were deep pools in the river and the current was swift, swift....

He kept at it until there was no longer any hope and then fought his way to shore. He dragged himself out on the yellow bank and caught his breath. The river looked calm and untroubled under the arch of the sky. There was no sign of Charlie.

He felt empty, completely drained of all emotion. He was exhausted by everything he had been through. He tried to remember Charlie as Charlie had been: a brusque, unkempt man, a man devoted to his subject, a man of integrity, a funny little guy who looked like a penguin....

But that Charlie was far away, far away. He had died—when? Days ago, a lifetime ago. The sick, frightened, bewildered man that had thrown himself into the river had not been Charlie. He had been someone else, a broken man, a man who could not face the dark depths of his own being.

I brought him here. I brought all of them here. Charlie, Louise, Helen, Ralph.

And now I am alone.

And I too have changed....

He looked up into the cloudless blue sky. Somewhere up there a ship still sailed. A mighty ship that had crossed the gulfs between the worlds. A ship that held his people, wondering, waiting.... It always came down to human beings. Small, afraid, uncertain, powerless—but it was up to them. It was always up to them.

Monte turned his back on the river and began to retrace his steps. He was desperately tired. The white sun was dropping down toward the edge of the mountains and the day was hot and still and empty.

He climbed the trail that wound up the cliff. He reached the cave. He thought of it as his home; it was the only home he had.

The old man was gone. The wolf-thing was gone.

The dead animal was still there.

Monte sighed. He made himself go back down and gather wood. He built a small fire by the mouth of the cave and broiled a chunk of meat on a stick. The fat sizzled when it dropped into the fire. The smell of the cooking meat was a good smell. That, at least, had not changed.

He ate until the pain left his belly. He stood on the rocky ledge and watched the great night paint its shadows across the world of Walonka. He took a final swallow of water from his canteen and crawled into his cave.

15

The sunrise was a glory.

Light flooded the cave and Monte woke up instantly. There was no transition, no fuzziness. He was fresh and alert the moment he opened his eyes, as though just being alive was a great gift and there was no time to waste.

And I was the guy who always needed three cups of coffee to get going!

He stepped out of the cave, drinking in the beauty of the dawn.

The white ball of the sun was draped in clouds. It burned through the mist, shining like a rainbow. It reached down with fiery fingers and painted colors on the land: vivid green, flame red, jet black. It bounced its light off the mountains, making them gleam like glass. Its warmth sent a pleasant tingle through his body.

Monte hauled up more wood and built himself a fire. He took a long drink from his canteen and hacked out another chunk of meat from the dead animal. He used a sharp rock to clean the hide away and cooked an ample breakfast. The meat tasted like venison. It was tough and wild and juicy.

When he had eaten, he found a hard rock to use as a hammerstone and chipped out a reasonably good hand axe. He put a sharp edge on it, leaving the core of the original stone for a grip. He looked at it and grinned. He was making progress. Hell, he was in the Lower Paleolithic already! Another week or two and he could invent pressure flaking....

He went to work on what was left of the meat. He cut it into long narrow strips and put it in the sun to dry. He walked down into the grasslands and found some of the red berries. He pounded the berries into meat, melted some fat and poured it over the dry meat. He smiled with satisfaction. It probably wasn't the best pemmican in the world, but it would last him for a couple of days.

That was all he needed.

He sat cross-legged in front of his cave, looking down on the land below. The time had come. It was now or never.

He closed his mind to everything except the problem before him. He had all the facts he needed, all the facts he could possibly expect. He had all the pieces of his puzzle. All he had to do was put them together.

Only—where did you start?

Well, take it from the beginning. Go over it step by step. Think it through.

There must be a key.

There *had* to be a key.

Start with Mark Heidelman who had first told him about Sirius Nine. Was that the beginning? No—go back still further. Go back to the dawn of man on the planet Earth. Go back....

Suddenly, he got to his feet. He looked around him, his eyes staring. *I've been blind. Blind. Here it is, right in front of me!*

Yes.

A cave.

A fire.

And a chipped-stone tool.

He picked up the chunk of flaked rock that had become a hand axe. He held it in his hand, held it so tightly that his knuckles whitened.

A chipped-stone tool.

The beginning.

The key.

EXTRACT FROM THE NOTEBOOK OF MONTE STEWART:

This journal looks like something dug up out of a tomb. It's a miracle that it still hangs together. I suppose that no one will ever read what I write here, but somehow that doesn't seem to matter very much. Or does it? Maybe a man always needs to try to communicate—with himself, if necessary.

Communication.

In a way, that's what this whole thing is all about. I'm excited now. I think I see the answer. I must try to get it down. And then perhaps....

Once you see this thing in perspective, it's not difficult. The trick is to back off; take a long look down the corridors of time. Lord! Isn't it odd how a man can teach an idea for half of his life and then not apply it when the chips are down? I tossed it off every semester in my introductory lecture: "If you want to understand the human animal, you must go back to the beginning. Written records are very recent in the story of man—they only take you back a few thousand years. Man himself has been around for more than a million years. In order to get an insight into what he is like today, you must look back down that long road and see where he has been. You must go back to the beginning..."

The beginning?

After all, how do we know the story of man on Earth? How did we unravel the past?

We did it by digging up tools. Stone tools.

Paleolithic: Old Stone Age.

Mesolithic: Middle Stone Age.

Neolithic: New Stone Age.

We're so used to it we don't even think about it. It's a part of us. Of course! Who questions the basic dictates of his culture? It always seems so natural, so inevitable.

From the very first, as soon as man became man, he made tools. He chipped artifacts out of stone. This was how he lived. This was how he hunted, how he defended himself, even how he expressed himself. (Who can look at a Solutrean blade and not know that it is a work of art?)

Obvious?

Maybe. But consider this. When man on Earth first started down that trail, there was no turning back. When he chipped his first tool, he determined his destiny. All the rest flowed from that one creative act: spears, harpoons, bows and arrows, the plow, wheels, writing, cities, planes, bombs, spaceships....

It was a way of life, a way of thinking. It was man's path on Earth.

(It is not for me to say whether that path was good or bad. I don't know whether or not the terms have meaning in this context. But it is a fact, surely, that man saddled himself with a heavy load when he chipped that first stone tool. Only a fool can fail to read the lesson that is written in our story. An emphasis on external power causes a built-in penalty. Read our novels, listen to our music, look at our art. Visit an insane asylum. Count the suicides. Count the graves of all the wars. Weigh the boredom, if you can—the emptiness, the frustration, the weariness, the desperate search for diversions. We have power over things: we can build bridges, houses, ships, planes. But have we been fulfilled as a people? Have we even found a measure of happiness? Why do we need pills to ease the knot in our guts? Is our yearning for the stars only an expression of inner poverty? Was there a toll bridge on the path we walked? Was there a hidden joker in the deck we opened?)

A way of life, yes.

But was it the only way?

What if man on Earth had never taken that first step?

What if he had turned down another trail, a different trail?

What if he had never chipped that first stone tool?

What other path had been open to him?

Consider the Merdosi, back in the mists of dawn on Sirius Nine. See them with their long ape-like arms, their naked bodies, their dark and intelligent eyes. See them with the word-magic in their mouths, huddled together under a great white sun....

They had taken a different turning. They had started down a different trail.

What had it been?

Well, what were the key facts about the Merdosi now? How had they behaved? What techniques had they used?

Item: They had little or no visible material culture; they didn't make *things*.

Item: They had a close and pivotal relationship with some of the animals of their world, the Merdosini and the saucer-eyed creatures that looked like tarsiers. They seemed to control them.

Item: It was possible that they could influence growth patterns to some extent. For example, those hollow trees did not seem to be completely natural. And perhaps they could grow other things....

Item: They had been completely baffled by the men from Earth. They had not been able to adjust to a contact situation. They had been confused, upset, afraid. They had attacked, first with the Merdosini and then....

Item: They had attacked their minds. They had driven Charlie mad. While the men from Earth slept, they had induced a sickness into their brains. They had worked through their dreams....

Item: The baffling thing about their culture was the fact that there was nothing to *see*. All the visible clues were lacking.

Item: What had the old man said? What had Volmay told him? "We will do what we must, all of us. We cannot trust one another. My dreams told me that we might have a beginning-again, but the dreams are so strange since you have come...."

Dreams.

Yes, and was there not a parallel among many of the primitive peoples of Earth, the peoples who had not yet been smothered by the mechanical monster? Did not all of them place great faith in dreams? Did they not use dreams to see into the future, to give meaning to their lives, to touch the unknowable? Did they not trust their dreams as sources of deep wisdom? Did not some of them, like the Iroquois, develop the idea of the subconscious long before Freud, and recognize that illness might be caused by a conflict between the inner man and supposedly rational thought?

(And how about our own dreams? Did we not speak of dreams as symbols of hope and ideals? And were not our attitudes toward them very much like those of the Merdosi toward artifacts? Weren't we great ones for giving lip-service to dreams? "Never lose your illusions, my boy! Always keep your dreams before you! But of course we must be practical, take a good course in Business Administration....")

What did it all add up to?

Clearly, the Merdosi had developed a different aspect of the human personality. Their culture had centered on a different cluster of human possibilities. They had turned inward. They had tapped the hidden resources of the human mind. They worked in symbols, dreams, visions.

Telepathy? No, not quite. Rather, they seemed to have perfected a technique of projecting emotional states. That would account for their control over animals. That would account for what happened to Charlie—and to me.

But it must be more than that, far more. It must permeate every aspect of their lives. They must live in a world of symbolic richness, they must *see* the world in vivid colors, tones, shadings. They must be able to open their minds, share them. They must have techniques that we have never imagined—they must understand the growth of trees, the unfolding of life.

Yes, but the Merdosi were people too. They were not supermen. They were not idealized figments of the imagination. They were only different.

Wasn't there a hidden price-tag on their way of life too? What would the characteristics of such a culture have to be?

Obviously, there were certain advantages. There would be a closeness with other people, a harmony with life. Above all, there would be a kind of inner security, a peace. But the technique of dream interpretation depended in the final analysis on a static, unchanging society. Dreams did not come out of nowhere. As long as nothing changed, the old ways would work—you could understand the dreams, rely on them, trust the ancient commands they gave you.

But if you started to dream about a spaceship?

Or strange men with rifles?

Or men and women with alien customs?

Wouldn't the single basic fear of a secure society be the threat of insecurity, of change? What could you do when your dreams held no answers?

You would fear the coming of strangers with a dark, cold terror. They would strike at the very roots of your existence. How could you possibly trust them when all they offered were *words?*

Words were not enough.

Contact was not enough—indeed, it might be fatal. Protestations of friendliness were not enough.

I know what I must do.

The way is plain.

But can I trust myself, and all the things that have made me what I am? Is the bridge strong enough to hold us both?

It was no good trying to put it off. It had to be done. The next move was up to him.

Monte spent one last night in his cave, resting. Then he walked out into another of the glorious mornings of Sirius Nine, ate some of the pemmican he had prepared, and drank some water. He was ready.

He felt a certain affection for the little cave, and the symbolism of the place was not lost on him. Apart from that, he had always loved the high places. He was convinced that there were two basically different kinds of people—those who were drawn to the lowlands and those who found rest only in the mountains. If he could have his life to live over again, he decided, he would live more of it in the mountains where the air was clear and a man could touch the sky.

He looked down upon the green grasslands that rolled away to the darker green and yellow that lined the river. It *was* peaceful here, despite everything that had happened. Even the air seemed less irritating, and the rawness had left his throat. Could he not just once live up to the best that was in him, no matter what the cost?

Man had met man for the first time. The patterns of future history might well be determined by what happened here. And the universe was huge, swimming with islands of life. There was more at stake here than even the destinies of Earth and Walonka. There were other worlds, other men. Man had need of all the friends he could find, and one day he too would be judged.

Monte shrugged. It was a lot to ask of any one man. But perhaps it always came down to just one man, one decision, in the end....

He grinned at the crumpled pieces of the spacesuit, still heaped on the rocky ledge. He wouldn't be needing them any longer.

He started down the trail.

He was amused at his self-styled role as a man of destiny. He was well aware that he was not the ideal man for the part. It was too bad, he thought wryly, that he could not have walked naked from the cave. That would have been a dandy symbol, a real corker, the very stuff of legends.

Unhappily, he couldn't risk the sunburn; he needed his clothes.

A parboiled hero! There was one for the books.

He walked on through the tall grasses, stroking his beard, smiling to himself.

16

Monte crossed the river without incident. He retraced his steps to the clearing where he and Charlie had pitched their camp and was surprised to find it just as they had left it. Somehow, he had expected it to show the same changes he sensed in himself. That terrible day in the rain—surely that had been a million years ago, in another time, another age....

He stopped only long enough to pick up his pipe and tobacco. He clamped the pipe between his teeth and savored the delicious smoke. If they ever stood him against a wall before a firing squad, he thought, he would ask for a last pipe.

It was all very strange, just as life itself was strange. It hadn't been very long ago that he had given up his pipe for fear of frightening the natives. Now, when he was about to walk the same path he had walked before, the pipe no longer mattered.

He had learned something, at least.

The externals didn't count.

He moved into the forest. The great trees closed in around him, whispering with activity, but he ignored them. He went on to the field where he had first glimpsed Volmay so long ago—where he had offered him food and seen the first of the Merdosini. He found the path which led into the woods, the dark path that for him would always hold the echoes of blackness and rain and the wind that swept the roof of the world.

He located the hollow tree.

Volmay was sitting in front of it, his naked body gleaming in a fugitive patch of sunlight. His old head had fallen forward on his striped chest. He was asleep.

Dreaming?

As soon as Monte stepped into view, Volmay stirred and opened his eyes.

"Hello, Volmay."

"Monte. I speak your name. I dreamed that you would come."

"You did not wait for me."

Volmay smiled. "I waited here."

"I came as soon as I could."

"Yes. I knew that you would come. I wanted you to come. And yet I did not know—do not know—"

"What?"

"Whether it is good. I am an old man; I am confused. Nothing seems certain to me. I am very sorry about the other."

"That is done."

"Perhaps." Volmay frowned; deep lines stood out on his face. "I am sorry about all of the others. But I am only one man." He groped for words. He looked very tired.

"We are alike, you and I. We have both tried to do things that are hard for us to do. It is never easy to act alone. It is easier to flow with the tide, is that not so?"

"There are times when a man must swim against the current. I am ashamed that it took me so long. I was afraid."

"But you came to me. And now I have come to you."

The old man sighed. "It is not enough."

"No, we two can do nothing. I know that. I have come to—offer—myself."

The old man stood up. He looked at Monte with dark, sad eyes. "I do not understand your words."

"Sometimes a battle cannot be won by fighting. There are men of my people who found that out long before I was born. Sometimes a fight can only be won by a sacrifice, a surrender."

"That is a strange idea."

"Volmay, your people can see into my mind, is that not so?"

"If it is your wish. They cannot do it against your will."

"It *is* my will. I offer myself to them. I will hold back nothing. I want them to examine me. I want them to see for themselves what I am."

"And what are you, Monte?"

He laughed. "I am a man. I hope that is enough."

Volmay turned away. "How can you trust us, after what we have done? I can promise nothing. I do not know what will happen to you."

Monte sat down before the entrance to the hollow tree. It was warm in the sunlight. He refilled his pipe and puffed on it until the tobacco caught. "It seems to me that my people came here to you, not the other way around. We are the intruders. This is your world. It is only right that I should be on trial here, as you would be on trial if you came to our world. That is the way of things. I will accept your verdict."

The old man sat down beside him. "You will have no choice."

"I have already made my choice."

"I do not know. We are so very different...."

"Are we? I thought so, once. But the first step must be taken. One of us must have faith. Or else—"

"What?"

"I have not the words to tell you."

"There will be—unhappiness?"

"More than that, Volmay. There are forces at work here that we are powerless to stop, you and I. Our two peoples have met. We will never be entirely separate again; this I know. We two are the beginning of a long, long story. We will not live to see the end of it—perhaps it will never end. If we can trust each other, we can be friends. If we fear each other, we must be enemies."

"Perhaps it was wrong of you to come. We did not ask you here."

"Who is to say? It may be that one day your children's children will be thankful that we came to you. In any event, we are here."

"Do *you* think we will ever be thankful that you came?"

"I do not know. That is the truth."

"You are very strange. Why *did* you come here? It must have been a long, hard journey."

"Why do you dream in the sun? Why do you live in a hollow tree? We are what we are. My people, Volmay—they are a restless people. They have always been restless. To us, the stars were a challenge. Can you understand that?"

"The stars?" Volmay smiled. "The stars are the stars. They have always been there to light the darkness. But sometimes, at night, when the world is still, I have climbed high into the trees and looked at them and wondered...."

"You do understand."

"I am not sure. I have always felt closest to the stars when I was alone, not moving. I have always felt closest to the stars when the night wind touched my face. Can you get nearer to the stars than that?"

"I don't know. How can I explain—"

"Yes. Exactly. Words—they are nothing. But, Monte, I must ask something of you. I do not know so many things."

"I will try to answer you."

He smiled an old, tired smile. "How can you trust yourself? You know nothing of your own mind. How can you know what my people will see in you? Your dreams...."

"There is no other way."

Volmay looked at him. "There is hope. Yes. You survived an attack on your mind—you were strong enough to withstand it. That is surprising. There is something in you that carried you through. There is hope in that."

"I'd like to know myself what that something is."

"Yes. It is good for a man to know himself; I cannot imagine living otherwise. But my people are afraid. It will be very hard for them *not* to find evil in you. Do you understand that?"

"I understand. We are the same way, when we are afraid."

"And you are not afraid any longer?"

"I'm scared to death. But I'm more afraid of not trying."

"You will be very helpless, my friend. I would not want to be the cause of more harm coming to you."

"You have agreed that there is no other way."

"That is true."

"Then you must take me to the village and explain to them. Or if the time is wrong for the village, take me to the men."

Volmay looked at him with new interest. "You have learned about us."

He felt an odd thrill of pride, as though he had been given a professional compliment.

"Very well." The old man looked up into the trees. He squinted his eyes as though concentrating. He did not speak for a long minute. Monte followed his gaze and saw one of the little reddish-brown animals hiding in the branches, its huge eyes peering down at Volmay. He only caught a glimpse of the creature before it disappeared.

"I have sent a message," Volmay said. "All will be ready."

"Thank you."

The old man stood up and moved toward the tree. "We will eat together now. Then we will sleep. In the morning, we will go."

Monte followed him into the hollow tree.

It was high noon when they reached the village. The white furnace of the sun hung suspended in the middle of the sky, as though reluctant to move on. The eroded brown rock walls of the canyon reflected the light like smudged and ancient mirrors. The waterfall at the head of the canyon was an oasis of coolness, and the silver-flecked stream that snaked across the canyon floor looked familiar and eternal and inviting.

The cave-eyes of tunnels and rock shelters watched them from the gray and brown rock faces of the cliffs.

In a sense, everything was just as it had been before—and yet it was all different, completely different. There were no children playing down along the river, no people going about the seemingly aimless tasks of everyday living.

There was an air of taut expectancy in the village.

There was an aura of fear and suspicion and waiting.

The Merdosi had built a great fire on a ledge of rock that jutted out over the canyon. They had all gathered around the leaping flames in a circle of naked bodies and dark, staring eyes.

Monte followed Volmay up a twisting trail. He could not face the eyes that watched him. He looked at his feet and walked steadily forward.

He felt naked, exposed, alone.

He could find nothing in himself to cling to, nothing to help him.

He was beyond comfort, beyond science, beyond reason.

He was on trial, on trial before an alien judge and an alien jury. He did not know their standards of right and wrong, guilt or innocence. He did not even know what he had done, or had not done. He did not know what he was.

And through him all the people of Earth were on trial. Who was he to offer himself as the representative of a world? Surely, there were better men...

But if you really knew all there was to know about any man on Earth, would you invite him into your home?

He walked through the circle of eyes and stood with his back to the flames. It was very hot. He did not know whether or not he could stand it.

A young man with vertical blue stripes painted on his naked chest stood before him. He held out a gourd that was filled with a dark and fragrant liquid.

"Drink," the man said. "Drink and let your mind be open. It is the way."

Monte lifted the gourd to his lips and drank the stuff down. It tasted like heavy wine.

The fire blazed beneath him. The circle of eyes pressed closer, closer...

The sky began to spin.

I will not hide. I will let them in. I want them to know, to see, to share...

Black darkness and white light, all mixed up together.

Eyes.

They were in his mind, staring.

17

Knock knock.
"Who's there?"
Art.
"Art who?"
ArtIfact!
(Laughter.)
WHAT IS HAPPENING TO ME? WHO AM I?
There. There you are. See? You are still Monte Stewart. I am Monte Stewart. When the mind is confronted with something totally new it interprets it in terms of an analogue....
IS THIS AN ANALOGUE?
Call it what you will. Look. Listen.
Question: Is this what you have hidden all your life, kept sealed up inside you?
Answer: Yes. I am ashamed. I was ashamed.
(Laughter.)
Q: Don't you know how small it is, how trivial?
A: I didn't know.
Q: You know so much and so little. Are these the names you are trying to show us? Judas? Pizarro? Hitler?
A: Those are some of the names
Q: Einstein? Tolstoy? Gandhi?
A: Those are some of the names.
(Snapshot: An ugly mushroom cloud, shadows pressed into concrete.)
Q: That is the hydrogen bomb?
A: Not that one. Only an atomic bomb. We used it twice.
(Snapshot: A beagle puppy in an animal shelter. A kid with big round eyes. The puppy wags its white-flagged tail.)
Q: Merdosini?
A: Only a pet.
Music.
Q: What is that?
A: *Swan Lake. The Original Dixieland One-Step. Stardust. John Henry. Scheherazade. The Streets of Laredo.*
Q: What is anthropology?
A: The study of man.
(Laughter.)

Q. What is this Exhibit A you keep thinking about?

A: It is evidence in a trial.

Q: A trial?

A: In a court of law.

Q: Law?

CONFUSION. A MAN IS INNOCENT UNTIL PROVEN GUILTY! A MAN HAS THE RIGHT TO CONFRONT HIS ACCUSER! THEY USED TO CHOP OFF YOUR HEAD IF YOU STOLE A RABBIT!

Q: Why did you come here, to Walonka?

A: We have been searching for men like ourselves.

Q: Why?

A: I don't know. We gave each other many reasons. Perhaps because the universe is vast and man is small.

Q: You needed us?

A: That was a part of it. And there was the excitement....

Q: Like music?

A: Like music.

(A child's thought: "He's funny! He's funny!" And a mother-thought: "That's not nice!")

Q: Why do you smoke a pipe?

(Laugher. *His* laughter.)

Q: What is another world?

A: Earth is another world.

Q: Where is the Earth?

(Snapshot: Stars like fireflies in a great night. Empty miles lost in darkness. Round green islands floating, shining through necklaces of white clouds.)

A: It is far away.

Q: There were people like us on your world once?

A: No, not like you.

Q: But people who did not live as you live?

A: Yes.

Q: Why do you call them primitive?

CHAOS. TARZAN SWINGS ON A VINE, FLEXING HIS BICEPS. "ME MAN, YOU GIRL." A NEANDERTHAL SCRATCHES HIS HIDE AND PEERS FROM HIS CAVE. A MAN DRESSED IN SKINS, WORKING BY THE LIGHT OF A STONE LAMP, PAINTS ON A ROCK WALL DEEP BENEATH THE EARTH. AN INDIAN PRAYS TO THE SUN. AN OLD ESKIMO MAN CRAWLS OUT ON THE ICE TO DIE.

Q: What happened to these people on your Earth?

A: Some were killed, hunted down like animals. Some were put on reservations. Some were only—changed.

Q: Will this not happen to us, if your people come?

A: No! No! I don't think so.

Q: Why?

A: We have changed, we have grown up.

Q: Have you?

A: There are laws!

Q: Ah, we know that word! Who made the laws?

A: We did.

Q: What is progress? Your head is full of it.

A: I don't know. A word. Medicine. Ethics. Spaceships....

Q: What is it like not to know yourself, to be empty inside? What is it like to be uncertain and afraid?

A FLASH OF RED. ANGER. REBELLION.

A: Physician, heal thyself!

(Laughter.)

Q: You admire your people?

(Pause.)

A: Sometimes.

Q: You think they are good, your people?

A: Sometimes.

Q: When?

A: Your questions have no answers! We are not perfect. We have done the best we could. We have tried!

Q: You admire our people, the Merdosi?

A: Sometimes.

Q: When?

A: When you come out of your shells, when you take a chance, when you don't take the easy way!

Q: When we are like you?

A: Perhaps. But that is because I don't really know you! A man cannot admire what he does not understand. You have hidden yourselves from me!

Q: And if a man understands, then he admires?

A: Not necessarily. But if he truly understands, he may find compassion. He may even find love.

Q: Or hate?

A: That is possible. But there is hope....

Q: Ah! You would like to see into our minds, to understand us?

A: Yes! Of course! But I haven't finished telling you about my people. I have hardly begun! You don't know us yet. I haven't told you about Plato and baseball, poets and beer, Caesar and the Rocky Mountains, artists and Aztecs! I haven't told you about science—

Q: You are wrong. We have seen all these things. It is only that you don't remember—not all of our questions are shaped into words. We know you now. But would you like to know us?

A: Yes. But you can't possibly know my people yet! I haven't done them justice....

A knife in my brain, cutting them off. It is all changing. I am going out...

WAIT!

COME BACK!

IT IS OVER, IT IS OVER.

NO!

I CAN SEE, IT IS BEGINNING....

I am not myself, but I am a man.

(What long arms you have, Grandpa!)

Is this what freedom means?

I am standing on the roof of the world. There are leaves all around me, red leaves and green leaves, and they draw a line across the sky. There is a cool breeze kissing my face; the air is clean and spiced with the smells of living things. The big sky arches above me. The sun is white and near and friendly.

There are birds nesting in the high branches: brown and yellow birds that sing with the sheer joy of being alive. Every leaf is new-minted, every line in the bark of age-old trees is unique.

Nothing has changed. This is where peace reigns supreme. It has always been so, from the beginning of time. It will always be here, waiting for me.

I dive from the top of the world. The blood races in my veins. I smile; who could keep from smiling? I rush through the cool green air, reach out with my strong right hand, catch a branch. It gives under my weight, but I swing in a great arc-forward and down, so fast that I can hardly breathe! My left hand breaks my fall and I swing on my long arm, swing out and down....

(Look, Ma, I'm flyin'!)

I rest on a gnarled limb in the middle ranges, sealed off from the sky above and the land below. There is water here, standing in dark little hollows in the wood. And there is food: blue eggs in neat, round nests, red berries on thorny vines, combs of honey clouded in buzzing insects.

This is where a man belongs. This is where he finds his strength. This is where the good dreams are born.

There is no need to think, to analyze. It is enough to feel, to *be*. A man is not alone. He is a part of everything he sees; he shares in the harmony of the open sky and the budding land and the thrusting trees. He is in the crystal rivers that flow from dark mountain ranges, in the orange fires that warm the night, in the air that whispers over waving grasslands.

I love this place. I am grateful for what it is. I am grateful too that it was given to me, for the Sun Shadows built our world well, and built it to last forever....

It was long ago and it was yesterday. It was in the beginning and it is now.

The Sun Shadows looked down on Walonka and were sorry that it was lonely. They walked out on the Edge, where it is neither night nor day, and there they found the Moon Shadows. Together, hot and white and cold and silver, they danced beneath the stars.

They made the Merdosi, born of the sun and the moon in a shelter of stars. They carried them to Walonka. They gave Walonka to the Merdosi and Merdosi to Walonka.

"Live under the sun," the Sun Shadows said. "Look up and know that we are watching. Look down and see our Shadows walking across your land. That is the way it will be, forever."

"Live under the moon," the Moon Shadows said. "Look up and know that we are watching. Look down and see our Shadows walking across your land. That is the way it will be, forever."

The sun and the moon did not forget. They always watch us from our sky. The Merdosi did not forget. We have honored the Shadows of the Sun and the Shadows of the Moon, and we have kept Walonka as they gave it to us.

We have been careful....

A dream?

I am a man. A man spends half of his life with his eyes open and half of his life lost in dreams. The two go together. A man cannot live without his dreams and a dream cannot live until it is acted upon.

It is good to dream, to refresh myself. There is wisdom in dreams. If you dream in the afternoon, the Sun Shadows speak to you. If you dream at night, the Moon Shadows speak to you. And if you can dream on the Edge....

My dreams speak truth to me always. They tell me what I really want to do. And what I really want to do is *right*, for am I not a man?

Of course, sometimes a dream is not clear. It must be interpreted. There are Merdosi who are skilled in such things. And twice a year we all dream together....

It is dangerous to change. When the old ways are left behind, the dreams are confused. It is hard to know what is right.

It is wise to accept the world that was given to us. Our lives have been comfortable. Each of us in his time repeats a cycle that goes back to the Beginning.

And yet...

Sometimes the dreams are strange. There are longing dreams. There are dreams that speak of unknown countries. There are restless dreams. When a man wakes from such a dream, he is unhappy, he is filled with a sense of something missed, something lost...

It is better to ignore such dreams.

It is better to keep things as they are, forever.

(Ask me no questions....)

I am a boy.

I have lived my life in the village with the women and the old men. I have played down by the river. I have not told the Elders about *all* of my dreams, for I am ashamed. I have been happy, I suppose. But there are times....

I have seen the men come into the village. I have sensed the thrill in the air. I have watched, sometimes...

I have watched the men go back into the great forest, where the trees grow tall. How I have wanted to go with them!

My time is coming. I am *almost* a man.

They will build a great fire on the ledge that looks down over the river. They will bring us together, four boys and four girls. We will drink together, and the Elders will look into my mind. I hope they don't see everything!

If we are fit, we will be taken to the Place—four boys and four girls. There we will stay alone with the Sun Shadows and the Moon Shadows. We will stay alone until we are no longer boys and girls.

Renna has dreamed of me. I know she has, for she has told me so. And when the moon is full, and we are at the Place....

I am afraid, but I can hardly wait.

I want to be a man!

And later, much later, I can go into the great forest alone and find my tree....

I see—myself!

I come out of the sky in a round metallic thing that lands in a clearing. I step out into the air of Walonka. I sneeze.

How strange I look with my short arms and funny clothes, clutching my rifle! I am full of questions, full of strange smells. My mind is cold.

I am an alien.

I walk toward the forest. I never look up toward the roof of the world. I am busy with schemes, plans, subterfuges.

I am different.

I walk toward the Merdosi. I am something new, something unknown, something dangerous.

What do I want, with my cold, closed mind?
What do I want, with my words that are only words?
I am Change.
I am to be feared; I cannot be trusted.
I keep coming, keep coming, keep coming...
Go away, go away!
I keep coming, keep coming...
Go back, go back!
I keep coming, keep coming....

Knock knock.
    "Who's there?"
    BLACKNESS

18

Monte Stewart opened his eyes. At first, he was confused. The black nothingness of oblivion was gone, but it had been replaced by a gray, featureless gloom that was not much more informative. He felt a hard surface under him. He reached over with his hand and touched rock. He sat up, squinting. He felt dizzy and faint, but there seemed to be a lighter patch of gray to his right....

Of course! He was in one of the village caves. He had passed out during the trial, if that was the right word for it, and....

It all came back with a rush.

He leaped to his feet and ran toward the entrance to the cave. He stuck his head out, grinning like an idiot. The village was asleep around him, asleep and strangely beautiful in the first pale light of the dawn. The waterfall was a murmur of silver, the winding river a ribbon of glass. The forest was deep and dark and inviting.

He was on the Edge, where it was neither night nor day.

There was no fear in him now. There was no worry, no uncertainty.

He did not have to ask any questions.

He *knew.*

(Had he not seen into their minds, as they had seen into his? He knew the decision of the Merdosi as surely as they themselves did.)

He was free.

More than that, he had won—won for all of them.

He was frankly surprised at the outcome, and yet it had a certain inevitability about it. He was surprised and he was proud. He was proud of himself, proud of his people, proud of the Merdosi. And he was grateful, grateful for the meaning that had been given to his life.

He had lived his life in the conviction that understanding was possible between people. He had lived his life in the belief that hope was possible between men and women. He had lived his life in the belief that hope was not an obsolete word. How many men are given such a dramatic proof of the codes by which they live?

The verdict?

It was not a simple thing, not a matter of being guilty or not guilty. (What was the crime, what was the law?)

It was rather a matter of *acceptance.*

The Merdosi had accepted him as a man, as a human being that was neither all bad nor all good. They had accepted his people for what they were, seeing in them a fundamental kinship with themselves. They had recognized the differences and respected them.

Perhaps they would have preferred never to have met the men from Earth. But the men from Earth had come.

The Merdosi, at the very least, were prepared to make the best of a bad bargain.

They were willing to give the strangers the benefit of the doubt.

They loved their world the way it was, and yet they were big enough to know that they were not perfect. They had things to learn, just as did the men from Earth. It would take time, and the way would not be easy, but they were ready to try. They did not know where the new road might lead; there would be many new dreams. But surely, if all men walked the road together, it would be a good road....

Monte stood for a long time on the Edge, waiting for the night to end and the day to begin. He watched the stars winking out one by one. He sensed the silent thunder of the dawn.

The Merdosi had looked into his heart and mind, and they had trusted him. But what of his own people? What would they do to the world of Walonka in the years to come? Could *he* trust the men of Earth?

If the Merdosi could have faith in the aliens, could he have none?

But it would take more than faith.

There was work to be done.

He walked down the trail that wound down to the canyon floor, leaving the sleeping village behind him. There was no need to tell them he was leaving or where he was going; they already knew. He was free to go, just as he was welcome to stay.

He walked along the purling river.

Just as the great white sun flamed behind the mountains, he vanished among the trees of the waiting forest.

It was late afternoon when he reached the little clearing. The battered tents still stood. The blank-faced spacesuit helmets still lay where they had fallen. The charred black logs of the dead fire were still in place.

Monte shivered, despite the heat of the day. He was not alone here. He was surrounded by watching eyes, eyes of the living and eyes of the dead. He was engulfed in two sets of memories—his and those of the Merdosi. He was at once the explorer setting foot in a strange and unknown land and the native who stared and feared and wondered.

He sat down on a rock to rest, cupping his bearded chin in his hands. The problem, really, was the same as it had always been. The problem was communication, getting through to people. First it had been the Merdosi. Now it was his own people.

His own people....

A wave of homesickness swept through him, more intense than any he had ever known. This was not his world, could never be his world. He was hungry for the sights and sounds he knew, hungry for a sun that was not a white furnace filling an alien sky. He had done his job, hadn't he? Surely they could expect nothing more of him. He had only to signal the waiting ship, and go home.

(Home, the loveliest word in the language—in any language! See the shining snow on the Rockies, the green of the mountain meadow in spring, the friendly books that lined his office. Have a cup of steaming coffee, sleep in his own bed, have a classic bull session with the boys. And who was looking after the flowers that Louise had planted?)

That wasn't all, either. He would be famous, wouldn't he? He would be a big shot, a hero. Didn't every man have a hankering to be a wheel, even when he laughed at the wheels he knew? He would be a Success, a cornball dream come true. He could write his own ticket. He could be the top man in his field.

He got up, filled his pipe, and went to work. He straightened up the devastated tents, built a fire, and cooked a meal. Then he dug out the voice-typer and set it up by his cot. He lined up a supply of tobacco, arranged the portable light, and sat down to think.

This was going to be the most important piece of writing he had ever done in his life. Quite possibly, it was the most important piece of writing that *anyone* had ever done.

He tried to remember them, those people he must reach with his inadequate words. He tried to think of them as individuals. Admiral York—not an easy man to sell. Tom Stein and Janice; their memories of the Merdosi were anything but pleasant. Don King, a cynic with small use for dreams. Mark Heidelman. The secretary-general.

And there were so many others: politicians, reporters, hordes of self-styled experts.

How would he himself have received the story of the Merdosi if he had never come to Sirius Nine? He pictured himself sitting in his university office, his beard neat and trim, his eyes skeptical. He saw a student come crashing into his sanctum, all full of the wonderful story of the Merdosi. He could almost hear the biting sarcasm of his own comments....

He stared blankly at the voice-typer. Outside the lighted tent, he could feel the darkness of the world around him. Where were the words that could tell his story?

What could he say about the precedent he had tried to set, without sounding like a pompous idiot? How could he tell them what he had learned, without sounding like a romantic fool? How could he make it clear to everyone that this was a matter of life and death, a question of ultimate survival? How could he show them the enormity of the sacrifice the Merdosi were making by permitting the strangers to come among them? How could he explain the lesser sacrifice his people must make in return, a sacrifice of restraint, of wisdom, of humility?

He could only tell his story to the best of his ability. He could only use the feeble words he knew. He could only hope that the truth was good enough.

What was the story he had to tell? It was a simple story, really.

There were no primitive supermen. (Wasn't that what we secretly longed for? Didn't we want god-like beings who would shoulder our responsibilities for us? Didn't we want a benevolent sorcerer who might wave a magic wand over our world?)

There were no bestial savages. (Wasn't that what we secretly wanted too? A nice evil monster that we could handle, instead of the monsters we all had within us? A bug-eyed tentacled beast that we could focus all of our little hates upon?)

It was a shame. There were no supermen. (Lay my burden down!) There were no monsters. (Kill the witch!)

There were just people.

It was just a story of people who had taken a different turning on the pathway of life. Just a story of human beings—more advanced and less advanced, better and worse. Just a story of the Merdosi, who had been afraid to give their trust-until now. A story of a people ready to learn, and to teach. And a story of the Edge, of Sun Shadows, and Moon Shadows and a shelter of stars....

A story of how man met man, and wanted him for a friend.

He thought it was a good story, a story of promise, a story of beginnings. But he could not write the ending. That was up to the men of Earth.

He went to work.

It took him two days to tell his story.

When he had finished, he carefully arranged the machine cylinders and the manuscript on the table by the voice-typer. He took out his battered notebook and placed that on top of the pile. He had concealed nothing, held nothing back.

As soon as the time was right, he called the reconnaissance sphere on the portable radio equipment. It was there, as it was once each day, waiting for his call.

He talked fast, telling Ace what he had done and where the materials were. He told him what he was going to do and that he was in good shape. He made a few requests: tobacco, food, clothing. Then he cut the contact. He could not bear to listen to Ace's familiar Texas voice; it was too much like home.

And he couldn't go home, not yet.

He might never get home again.

He knew that if he ever returned to the ship he was through. Admiral York would never permit him to come back to Walonka, and he would never leave him behind if he had any choice. And Monte knew that it would be very easy to let himself be persuaded. Once he was on the ship it would be easy to convince himself that he wasn't needed here, that his job was done.

It wasn't done, of course. It was just beginning. It wasn't enough to blithely make contact with a people. What was needed was a bridge, a bridge of sympathy and understanding. He would have to be that bridge. There was no one else.

One day, the ships from Earth would come again. He had to be ready.

He changed his clothes and loaded his pockets with tobacco. He took nothing else. He left the tent, walked across the clearing, and entered the dark woods.

He did not look back.

There were open spaces in the forest where the blue sky showed through, but he averted his eyes. He did not want to see the gray sphere come down. He did not want to think of the great invisible ship that was his last link with home.

He walked on toward the hollow tree, where old Volmay would be waiting.

They had a lot of dreaming to do together.

After the Beginning

It took four years.

They were long years, and busy years. Monte, caught in the web of one culture, could well imagine what was happening in the other. It would have taken the spaceship about eleven months to reach Earth from Sirius Nine. It would take it another eleven months to come back again. Therefore the people of Earth had had two years and a couple of spare months in which to make up their minds.

That was about par for the course. How had the decision been reached? With cartoons and editorials and public debates? Or by secret discussions within the United Nations?

Well, no matter.

The men of Earth *had* to come back, that was certain.

But *how* they would come, and for what purpose....

That was something else again. That was the worry that nagged at Monte for many long days and nights.

It had been a strange four years. There had been the excitement, the thrill of exploring a new and unknown civilization. (He knew now how they had felt, those men who had first seen the ruins of the Maya, the hidden tombs of ancient Egypt, the Eskimo shamans in the long Arctic night!) And there had been the loneliness, the very special kind of loneliness that a man knows when he is cut off from his kind: He could never truly be a part of the Merdosi way of life; he was sealed away from it by years of alien experiences. He longed for the sights and sounds of Earth, and yet he was no longer quite a man of Earth either.

Change was always hard.

He had made new friends, and Volmay in particular was as remarkable a man as any he had ever known. But Monte missed his old friends, the men and women who had shared that other life with him. The loss of Louise was a hollow ache within him.

Perhaps he was just growing old. He was getting to the age where a man seeks a return, a link with his own past, a closing of the circle of life.

And there had been one real crisis.

It seemed very obvious to him now, and he wondered that he had not thought of it before. It was inherent in the situation. When the Merdosi looked into his mind, they saw more than his personality, more than a reflection of the character of his people. They saw the possibility of their own destruction—and they saw a new kind of knowledge.

Artifacts, for them, had always been a sort of confession of weakness. But they could not help recognizing their own weakness when contrasted with the men of Earth. They could see the advantages of weapons, just as Monte could see the advantages of a technique of projecting emotions. If you combined the two, you had a defense of sorts.

Just in case.

Some of the younger Merdosi men began to experiment. They were able to bypass millenniums through the medium of his mind. It was absurd to imagine that they could build themselves a missile with a nuclear warhead, of course; Monte could not have done it himself. But bows and arrows were something else again.

It was pathetic, but it had the seeds of destruction in it.

It made the situation just that much more critical. An arrow can kill as surely as a bomb or a bullet. And a death now could only invite retaliation. If that happened, Monte's whole life was reduced to an ironic joke.

Four strange and worried years....

It was with mixed emotions that Monte watched the coming of the ship, one spring day.

The monstrous ship filled the sky, blotting out the sun, making no attempt at concealment.

(A show of force?)

Landing spheres detached themselves from the mother ship and started down. Monte counted twenty of them. They glittered like ominous bubbles in the sunlight.

They landed.

With a sinking heart, Monte watched the soldiers climb out.

They lined up in little rows, like toy soldiers on parade. Behind them, in a protected pocket, stood six men who were not in uniform. That, at least, was encouraging. Monte would have given a lot for a good pair of field glasses.

Volmay smiled a tired old smile. "They have come to rescue you from the monsters, my friend."

"It looks that way."

"What will we do?"

"Will you go and speak to the other men, Volmay? Tell them to get ready. Tell them to have patience. Tell them that there has been a misunderstanding."

"I will do that. And you?"

Monte shrugged. "If they're so dead-set on doing it, I guess I'll go down there and let them rescue me."

"Alone?"

"That would be best, I think."

"Will they listen to what you have to say?"

"They'll listen. They'll listen unless they're prepared to shoot me on sight."

"You will be careful?"

"Yes."

"I wish you well. We will be waiting."

Monte clenched his fists and clamped his empty pipe between his teeth. He left the shelter of the trees and started across the field toward the soldiers.

The soldiers saw him coming. They stayed in formation, screening off the six civilians.

Monte walked up to them, his blood boiling. He put his hands on his hips, took a deep breath, and spat out of the corner of his mouth. He stood there, looking them up and down: skinny, ragged, bearded, his eyes as cold as ice.

"Get the hell out of my way," he said diplomatically.

One of the soldiers sneezed.

A colonel stepped forward. "Try to be reasonable, sir. We know you've been through a lot. But we have a procedure to follow here—"

"Great!" Monte was getting madder by the minute. "If I may coin a phrase, colonel, we can do without your particular bull in this china shop. Let's get something straight, shall we? The Merdosi are back there in the trees, watching every move you make. Right now they're friendly. More than that—they're trusting us. But you've got to get these soldiers out of here."

The officer flushed. He made a desperate effort to salvage his dignity, but a sneeze caught him unawares. "I have my orders—"

"Just a minute, please." A tall man in civilian clothes pushed through the line of soldiers. His hair was grayer than Monte remembered it, but he had the same smiling eyes. "Monte, is it really you?"

"Bob!" Monte laughed and clapped him on the shoulder. "Bob Cotton! My God, the last time I saw you—"

"The Triple-A meetings in Denver, wasn't it? It's been a long time, too long. Man, you look like a ghost. What have they been doing to you?"

"Bob, have you got some authority around here?"

Bob Cotton grinned. "Well, I'm the new anthropologist in charge of making contact with the natives. I guess I've sort of got your old job."

"For two cents I'd let you start from scratch. Boy, am I glad to see you! Can't you get this damned army out of here? Everything's okay if we don't mess it up now."

"You're sure?"

"Yes. You want me to sign it in triplicate?"

"That won't be necessary, Monte. Your word is good enough for me. But you'll have to talk to the big boys."

"Who'd you bring with you? The P.T.A.?"

"Not quite. The secretary-general sent along a committee of five. (We know how much you love committees, Monte.) They've got a big fancy title—something about Extraterrestrial Relations, which sounds highly immoral—but they're okay. One person each from the United States, Russia, England, China, and India. They won't give you any trouble, once they get a go-ahead from you. But the way things were left here, it's understandable that no one wanted to take chances."

"I told you everything's okay." Monte turned to the man in uniform. "If the colonel will be good enough to stand aside...."

The officer waved his hand. "Sure, sir. Glad to have you back, Dr. Stewart."

Monte shook his hand. "Sorry I was so cantankerous colonel. Buy you a drink later?"

The colonel sneezed and managed a smile. "I could use one."

Bob Cotton escorted him to the five waiting men.

They all had smiles of welcome on their faces.

Monte felt a great load lifting from his shoulders. He almost broke down and cried.

Everything was going to be all right.

Later that same afternoon, the first meeting took place between the two groups. It happened in a little clearing in the forest, not far from Volmay's tree.

On the face of it, the meeting wasn't very dramatic. It would have made a poor scene in a play, no matter how the music swelled behind it. Indeed, Monte thought, there were only two people left on two worlds who could really appreciate the enormity of what happened.

He himself was one.

Volmay was the other.

They stayed on the fringes now, gladly relinquishing the stage. But they were both remembering. Remembering that other meeting that had been only yesterday as worlds count time, and yet had been an eternity ago in some far lost age....

Volmay had been standing there, frozen with fear, and the wolf-thing had padded across the leaves.

Monte had walked toward him, meat in one hand and berries in the other.

"Monte," he had said, pointing at himself....

Had that been only yesterday, even as the worlds count time?

It was all so easy now.

Monte had led Bob Cotton and the U.N. committee to the clearing. They had left the soldiers behind and they were unarmed. The men of the Merdosi had been waiting, their bows and arrows tossed casually into the bushes.

One of the Merdosi men had stepped forward and shaken the hand of the man from India, smiling with pleasure at being able to show off his knowledge of the customs of Earth. "You are welcome among my people," he said in English.

"We have come in peace," said the man from India, proudly speaking a sentence he had learned in the Merdosi language. (Charlie's records, back on the ship, had been put to good use.) "I want you to meet my friends."

Simple.

Nothing to it.

Monte looked across at Volmay, and the old man solemnly winked at him.

That night, Monte slept alone in his tent. He was not quite ready to feel the steel of the ship around him. Outside, a small fire burned against the darkness of the hushed and silent world.

A light breeze began to blow, whispering through the trees its song of silvered rivers and sleeping grasslands and distant mountains. A fat yellow moon floated over the edge of the black forest.

Perhaps the Moon Shadows spoke to him as he slept; who can say?

For the dreams came to him again as they had come before into this tent in this clearing. The dreams came to him again, but this time they were different dreams: the dreams that come best when a man's work is done and he is alone.

Monte Stewart smiled in his sleep.

He was dreaming the best dream of all, the dream of the magic promise, the dream of going home.

Introduction - The Shores of Another Sea

Kingsley Amis, in his review of this novel, wrote that a six-foot, two hundred pound American anthropologist from Texas, dressed in a wide-brimmed hat, khaki shift and trousers, Ph.D. well hidden, was an unlikely hero for a science-fiction story; yet this was nothing more than a fair description of Chad Oliver himself. In his photos, Chad Oliver could easily have passed for John D. MacDonald's popular sleuth, the thoughtful yet adventurous Travis McGee. Amis's lapse into parochialism was odd in a critic who was a reader of science fiction, especially when he was discussing a novel about a first encounter with an alien civilization.

The first book I read by Chad Oliver was *Mists of Dawn*, a young-adult novel published in 1952 as part of a distinguished science-fiction program presented by Winston. These books set a standard for unpatronizing young-adult science fiction which, together with the books published by Robert A. Heinlein and Andre Norton, has rarely been bettered. *Mists of Dawn*, which I came upon in 1958, was also one of the first science-fiction novels I read. I remember being struck by the sympathetic account of the early humans depicted in the story; and the time-travel adventure enthralled me so completely that I read the book at one sitting. Chad Oliver became one of my favorite writers. And, I learned one of the joys of early readership--that there were other books by the same author!

Chad Oliver belonged to that distinguished group of science-fiction writers who are also scientists. The list includes Isaac Asimov, Gregory Benford, and Sir Arthur C. Clarke, among others; but Oliver was the only anthropologist in this group, and as such he brought a deeper sense of humanity into his writing. It was the qualities of compassion, attention to mood and thoughtfulness and character, together with a constant awareness of a larger horizon to human history looking back in time as well as forward into futures—that kept me reading Oliver's work.

283

When his first story collection, *Another Kind* (1955) appeared, Damon Knight noted that Oliver was "building up our field's most fascinating and comprehensive collection of anthropological science fiction." Anthony Boucher praised *Another Kind* as the "outstanding science-fiction book of the year." And this was only the author's third book. A comparable traversal of anthropological themes was not to be seen until the publication of Ursula K. Le Guin and Michael Bishop in the 1960s and 1970s.

The Shores of Another Sea, Oliver's sixth novel, was published as a Signet New American Library paperback original in 1971 and as a British hardcover in the same year; it received excellent notices in England. It followed *The Wolf Is My Brother* (1967), which won the Spur Award as best western historical novel of the year, given by the Western Writers of America. Oliver had every reason to feel encouraged, but the American paperback of *Shores* was not reviewed in any of the science-fiction magazines, not even in *Analog*, where Oliver was well known. One suspects that the printing was small and that few review copies were sent out.

The novel is set in Kenya, where Oliver spent some time doing anthropological research It's a novel in which personal experience is perfectly blended with the theme of first contact. Dean McLaughlin, a writer also noted for his anthropological themes, has called it "the most marvelously understated first contact story I have ever found. So quietly real you know it could have happened. Maybe it did."

As the novel unfolds, an unnerving analogy begins to emerge: we are to the baboons of the story as the alien visitors are to us. A subtle guilt begins to operate in the reader, recalling not only the horrors of the colonial white man's treatment of Africa but also our treatment of the planet's animal life. Only Arthur C. Clarke, in *The Deep Range* (1957), has given our treatment of Earth's animals the pointed consideration given the problem in Oliver's novel. It is a work rich in resonances and ironies, and Kenya's colonial past makes the reader tremble as the characters are overtaken by the full development of the central situation. The stresses and strains of the story, together with its deeply felt emotional core, involves the reader completely. Hemingway could not have written a better book with this theme.

The best and brightest of science fiction's critics and reviewers responded well to Oliver's two decades of science fiction. Anthony Boucher placed him in the front rank with Heinlein, Clarke, and Asimov. Gary K. Wolfe, writing in St James *Guide To Science Fiction Writers* (St. James, 1996), notes that Oliver's "real strengths lie in the construction of hypothetical anthropological problems and his graceful, understated style. *Unearthly Neighbors* (1960) may be the most carefully reasoned account of the problems of making contact with an alien culture in all science fiction." Wolfe credits Oliver as being solely responsible for introducing well-thought-out anthropological themes into science fiction. His work is "valuable both for the specific insights it offers and for the importance it holds in the developing sophistication of the genre." Damon Knight summed up Oliver's talent best: "Oliver has the kind of gift this field sorely lacks—the ability to touch the heart of the human problem."

One error about Oliver's writing career deserves to be cleared up: he never stopped writing fiction. Although his last science fiction novel was published in 1976, short fiction continued to appear in such anthologies as *Again, Dangerous Visions*, in the *Continuum* series, in *Future Quest* and *Future Kin*. In 1981, new stories were published in *Analog* and in Fred Saberhagen's *A Spadeful of Spacetime*. Another story, "Ghost Town," appeared in "Analog" in 1983. A work of nonfiction, *The Discovery of Humanity: An Introduction to Anthropology*, was published in 1981. He continued to write until his death in August of 1993, and published two award-winning historical novels in 1989, *Broken Eagle* and *The Cannibal Owl*, which received poor support from their publisher and should have new editions; both should be of interest to SF readers who know his work.

Chad and I became friends in the last decade of his life, when I edited the Crown Classics and included these three alien novels. We had a mutual friend, the writer Howard Waldrop, whom I had anthologized, and with whom Chad went fishing. Howard and I occasionally bring Chad back to life between us. When I told Howard of this NESFA omnibus of these novel about contact with alien humanities, he said: "Chad lost a year of life and school when he had rheumatic fever and spent nearly a year in bed reading air-war pulps and SF magazines and missing out on other kinds of stuff.

"Then he was taken—kablooie—from an upper-middle class white neighborhood in Cincinnati; and plopped down in the outskirts of Crystal City, Texas with blacks, native americans and latinos. If that wasn't disjunction enough, he lived in the Japanese-American internment camp during WWII, where his father was the doctor, next to the German and Italian POW camp. He had what we call a well-rounded introduction to other cultures, in a big hurry. And at the time he was a 78 pound weakling.

"'Football saved my scrawny ass,' is the way he used to phrase it. I don't know what this has to do with anything about Chad's career as a writer and anthropologist..."

"Everything, Howard," I said. "Read books while he was sick and later met a lot of different people. There are saints who started that way."

"Yeah—I knew that," Howard said, "but no one brought it up about Chad before."

We were silent for a few moments, holding Chad between us.

—George Zebrowski
Delmar, NY 2007

The Shores
of Another Sea

And if by chance you make a landfall on the shores of another sea
in a far country inhabited by savages and barbarians, remember
you this: the greatest danger and the surest hope lies not with fires
and arrows but in the quicksilver hearts of men.
— ADVICE TO NAVIGATORS (1744)

1

It began as a perfectly ordinary day—ordinary, that is, for the Baboonery.

Royce Crawford frowned at his crippled typewriter. He filled his pipe with tobacco from a yellow Sweet Nut tin, and lit it. It wasn't the best tobacco in the world, but it had one decisive advantage over all other brands: it was the only kind he could get. He could buy Sweet Nut for a few bob anywhere in Kenya, even at the *duka* in Mitaboni, and that made it extra special. He puffed on the pipe and stared at the bare plank walls of the little room he used as an office. The door was open and he could see into the main operating room across the hall. The clean white table was empty. The clamps were relaxed and waiting. They had been waiting for a long time now.

He had to finish his monthly report to Wallace, which was a chore he detested at the best of times. And this, emphatically, was not the best of times. Royce knew that something was wrong, but he had no solid facts at his disposal. He had an impression, a crawling sensation on his back, a feeling of unease. For three days he had felt that he was being...watched.

Royce was not an unduly fanciful man. He was singularly unworried by dreams. He wouldn't have known an omen if he tripped over one. In his scheme of things, premonitions were in a class with astrology and female vapors. At the same time, he was not a clod with a muscle for a brain. Royce had led an unusual life and he was no stranger to trouble. He had learned to trust himself when he could not rely on others. When he had a hunch it generally meant something. As far as he was concerned, if he felt that he was being watched it meant just that.

Something had him under observation.

A man cannot be a hunter without knowing what it is to be hunted.

He couldn't tell that to Wallace, of course. Wallace was a long way from the Baboonery. He was in another world.

Royce shifted in his chair and looked out the window. The window was open, as always, for the excellent reason that it could not be shut. It had a screen in it, but no glass. This alone marked the Baboonery as an American enterprise: most of the British-built structures in Kenya had glass windows and no screens. On the whole, he supposed, the system worked pretty well. The majority of the British houses—some still British, some not—were in the highlands where the weather was often chilly. It never got cold at the Baboonery.

Maybe that was part of the trouble, he thought without conviction. The weather *was* getting on his nerves. It was dry, bone dry, and it was hot. There was nothing green as far as the eye could see. The red dust was everywhere, like a crust of rusted iron. Even the elephants were a light reddish color, pink elephants for real; they would not be gray again until the short rains came. The baboons sat in their rows of cages and peered out along their snouts at a world that seemed too barren to support life. The parched dry banana leaves rustled in the steady arid wind like a mockery of rain. From somewhere around the main building, out of his line of vision, he could hear the tuneless song of Mbali, the shamba boy. It was a curious song: haunting but formless, it faded on the wind and could never be quite recalled when the singer stopped.

Royce's pipe went out and he lit it again. He pulled up the typewriter. Ben Wallace knew what the Baboonery was like. He had spent a lot of time there. He knew all about the heat and the politics and the men who could suddenly turn alien just when you thought you had them figured out. Royce thought of Wallace on the other end of the report he had to write, Wallace sitting there at his compulsively neat desk at the Foundation office in Houston. It was late September. The air conditioning would still be going full blast in Houston. There would be mobs at the Astrodome, watching the Astros limp valiantly through another season. Ben Wallace would be dressed in one of his sincere dark suits—wrinkle-free, lint-free, bulge-free. Wallace would want some facts, not impressions.

Okay. Royce typed the familiar heading: Kikumbuliu Primate Research Station, P. O. Mitaboni, Kenya, East Africa. He supplied the date and proceeded to confine himself to essentials. He had forty baboons on hand, fifteen of them female. He would ship twenty animals to Houston within three weeks, sending them by train to Nairobi and then putting them on the plane himself at Embakasi. The other twenty baboons were still undergoing tests of various sorts; he included information on the condition of each animal. The only unusual expenses—and they were becoming something less than unusual—involved repairs to the starter on the Land Rover and to the generator for the Baboonery electrical system. He added that he, his wife, and the two kids were all well, signed the report, and that was that.

Royce Crawford stood up, stretched, and glanced at his watch. It was after two. He would have to shake a leg. The men needed meat and he might have to go all the way to the Tsavo to get it. It had to be today; Donaldson would be coming in within the next day or two, and Donaldson did not take kindly to hunting when he was wet-nursing a safari.

Royce grabbed an envelope—already stamped and addressed to the Foundation—and walked out into the African sunlight.

It took Royce a good hour to do what he had to do. He sent the battered lorry into Mitaboni twenty-five miles away to air-mail the report and pick up some supplies. He checked the baboon cages to make certain they were clean and secure. He took his .375 out of the gun safe in the breezeway between the kitchen and his bedroom. He helped Kathy get the children down for their afternoon nap. He drank a cup of ferocious coffee.

Then he was as free as a man can be, and despite his nagging worry he was content. It was good to have a task ahead of him that was pure pleasure. There weren't many jobs like that left in the world.

The Land Rover, miraculously, started on the first try. It was a wide-wheel-base model with a tarp that stretched over a frame in back of the cab. In the dry seasons, the tarp wasn't used; the Land Rover, in effect, became a pick-up truck not unlike the ones Royce had used back in Texas. When he hunted, Royce rode in back with Mutisya. Kilatya, God help him, did the driving.

There were three dirt roads, little more than trails, that led away from the cluster of buildings that was the Baboonery. One, straight as a drunken snake, went ten miles through the bush to join the main road that connected Mombasa on the Indian Ocean with Nairobi in the heart of Kenya. A second road more or less followed the railway, crossed the Tsavo River, and ultimately—if you were lucky—led into Mitaboni. It was shorter than going to Mitaboni by way of the main road, but it was so rough that it took twice the travel time. The third road, impossible for anything except a vehicle equipped with four-wheel drive, went straight into the bush. It was strictly a hunter's trail; it did not lead to anything except a bluff overlooking the Tsavo River. To Royce, it was the most pleasant road in the world. There was something to be said, after all, for the old roads—the winding country lanes, the gravel farm roads he had known at home, the packed brown ruts that led to pastures and barns and weathered frame houses. It was a loss that all the roads back home had turned to ribbons of cement. A man could move in a hurry on those roads, but there was nowhere worth going.

They took the third road.

Royce balanced easily in the back of the Land Rover, one hand holding the .375 and the other resting on the metal frame. His wide-brimmed Texas hat shielded his eyes from the sun and the jolting vehicle could not go fast enough on that road to make the wind a problem. He felt no compulsion to speak, and neither did Mutisya. They knew their jobs.

For a moment, it was not very different from setting out on a whitetail hunt back home. Royce had ridden in a thousand pick-ups on a thousand days like this one: hat clamped on his head, the feel of the rifle in his hand, the always-new sense of peace and expectancy in his heart.

In less than a minute the Baboonery was invisible behind them, screened by the bush and a slight dip in the land. It was an astonishing transition; Royce never got used to it. Within a few hundred yards he was in another world, an older world, and—perhaps—a better world.

He knew that he could never describe it to anyone, not really. He had tried, in some of the hunting articles he had written, but he had never come close. It had to be experienced. It had to be seen and smelled and heard. A man had to bring something of himself to it. Some men, the dead ones that still walked, never could feel it. They were the men who might glance at a trout stream in the Rockies and see just another creek.

There was the sky, that immense African sky that was like no other sky on earth. There was the land, now choked with thickets of thorny brush, now opening up into great meadows dotted with graceful flat-topped acacias and grotesque swollen-trunked baobabs. There were the colors, subdued now after the drought: long tawny grass the color of lions, red dust that powdered the earth, the dead gray-green of what was left of the vegetation. There were the birds, countless birds, birds on the ground and in the trees and darting through the clean air. Most of all, there was a feeling that time had no meaning here; time was somehow suspended. It was an illusion, of course, but it was a good illusion.

The Land Rover pushed its way through a thick clump of brush. The tsetse flies came out in a cloud; they were always there, at that particular place, waiting. They settled on Royce and Mutisya, going for the patches of exposed skin. The devils hurt. It wasn't just a matter of worrying about the sickness the flies sometimes carried. They were long, tough flies, and they bit until they drew blood. It was impossible to brush them away. You had to pick them off your skin and kill them one by one. Flies, Royce thought, were the curse of Africa. Flies and ants. The pretty picture books always left them out, but they were ubiquitous. He had seen the ants so thick that bedposts had to be placed in cans of gasoline before a person could sleep in safety. He had seen tsetse flies go after a herd of skinny cattle and turn their hides into raw sores. He had seen common flies so numerous in African villages that children would sit with flies in their noses and ears and eyes and refuse to make the hopeless effort to chase them away.

Fortunately, the tsetse fly cannot live in open country. As soon as the Land Rover emerged from the thick brush the flies were gone. Royce didn't expect to encounter them again until they passed through the same clump of brush on the way back to the Baboonery.

He felt a wonderful sense of freedom, as though he had just been released from prison. Royce had never been a city man when he could avoid it, and this was a world where the city was only a faded memory of thronging unhappy people and jangling noises and filth that had once been air. Life could be dangerous here but it was not complicated. A man would win or lose on his own personal ability. He was not just a puppet jerking on a string.

The Land Rover bumped to a stop as Kilatya engaged the low-ratio four-wheel drive. They went over the edge of the cut made by the Kikumbuliu River—little more than a trickle of water now—and splashed through the bed of the stream. The other bank was steep and it was hard to hang on as the Land Rover churned its way back up to level ground.

The land opened up before them in a vast level plain. The trail ran along in a reasonably straight line that roughly paralleled the Kikumbuliu on their right. On the far side of the river there was a rocky ridge. On the near side there was only a sweep of sun-drenched miles that led away to the Tsavo. There was a light breeze blowing and it was cool and comfortable.

Mutisya watched to the right and Royce to the left. There was nothing to it; the game was thick. In less than a minute Mutisya caught his arm and pointed. Royce caught a glimpse of gray with vertical white stripes. Kudu.

Royce knocked with his fist on the top of the cab. Kilatya, as usual, kept on going. Royce leaned forward and hollered into the open window. *"Simama!"* he said. "Stop!"

The Land Rover jerked to a quick halt as Kilatya hit the brakes, driving with his customary delicacy of touch. Royce was thrown forward almost over the cab. He grabbed his field glasses. It took him only a few seconds to pick the animals up. There were four or five kudu out there.

He considered trying a shot from the Land Rover, where he could use the top of the cab as a rest for his heavy rifle. But even as he watched the antelopes moved away from him, screening themselves with brush. They were a good two hundred yards away.

He jumped down to the ground. *"Haya!"* he said. "Come on!"

Mutisya did not need to be told what to do. He had hunted kudu when Royce's only knowledge of Africa had come from Tarzan books. Still, he smiled. He rather liked Royce, and he was used to redundant orders from white men.

They struck off through the bush, keeping downwind from the kudu and making use of what cover there was. They moved fast; it was not difficult country in the dry season, and there was no particular need for caution. Royce had a healthy respect for mambas and puff adders, but they were no more common in Africa than rattlesnakes were in Texas and it was absurd to go about in constant fear of them. As for the dangerous animals—lion, elephant, rhino, water buffalo—a reasonable prudence was all that was necessary.

He could not see the kudu but he knew where they were. They would not move very far unless they were seriously alarmed. They had a trick of running off for a short distance and then stopping. They would often stand quite still and look at a hunter until he fired.

Mutisya spotted them first. He crouched down behind a bush, saying nothing. Royce dropped to one knee. He could see three of them clearly. One ram had his head up, listening. He was not over one hundred yards away.

It was a piece of cake. Royce lifted the heavy .375 to his shoulder and peered through the scope. The kudu presented a natural target; Royce drew a bead just between the first two vertical white stripes. He squeezed the trigger. The big rifle bucked against his shoulder and the flat sound of the shot shattered the afternoon silence.

The kudu dropped with the startling suddenness of a man clubbed with an iron crowbar. They wouldn't have to track that one. The other animals ran off with the shot, bounding away with the white undersides of their tails showing curved up over their rumps.

Royce was shaking a little, but he was grinning from ear to ear. It had been a clean shot. The regret would come later. There was still something in a man that responded to a kill—something, perhaps, that dated from a time when there was no latitude for sentiment.

"Mzuri," Mutisya said quietly. "Good."

Royce sent Mutisya back to tell Kilatya to bring up the Land Rover. Then he walked over and looked at his kill. The antelope was beautiful, even in death. The gray coat with the white stripes was dusty but sleek. The graceful horns were in good shape. It was a so-called lesser kudu, of course; Royce had never even seen the greater kudu. Nevertheless, it was quite an animal.

It had the soft, sad eyes of death.

The Land Rover pushed up through the brush like a tank. Royce opened the tail gate, and the three men wrestled the kudu into the back of the vehicle. It wasn't an easy job; the kudu was over two hundred pounds of dead weight. When they got him inside, Royce put up the tail gate again.

That was all there was to it.

Royce pulled out his pipe and lit it. He glanced at his watch. It was only four-thirty. A good two hours of daylight left.

Plenty of time. He did not want to go back to the Baboonery. He felt secure here, at ease. The feeling of being watched was somehow diminished. It was as though it was the Baboonery itself that was under observation, and when he moved away from it he moved outside a zone, like an animal stepping beyond the area swept by field glasses....

If he went on, he might see Buck again.

He told Kilatya to push on to the Tsavo and climbed in next to the dead kudu. The flies were beginning to gather around the darkening blood on the animal's shoulder. He could smell the blood.

He felt better when the vehicle started and he could drink the cleansing wind.

The land was softer now, and more mysterious. Much of its naked harshness was gone. The shadows cast by the lowering sun broke up the stark outlines and created depths, as though a flat picture had suddenly become three-dimensional. The world was very still except for the whine of the Land Rover's engine.

The trail angled away from the Kikumbuliu and stretched out in an easy descent across the sloping plain that led to the Tsavo. There was not much brush here and Royce could see for miles. There were elephant droppings along the pathway that looked fresh, but he could not locate the elephants. He saw a small herd of zebra in the distance, and that was all.

He wondered what Mutisya was feeling, standing next to him in his old khaki shorts and a torn white undershirt. Mutisya did not know exactly how old he was, but he figured his age as about forty. His black face was smooth and unlined; the muscles in his bare legs were long and powerful. There was something enduring about Mutisya: he had been here before Royce came and he would be here after Royce was gone. He was a Kamba, as were all the men who worked for the Baboonery; his incisors were filed down to points in the old tribal fashion. He was a good man, with the gift of dignity. Royce wished him well, whatever the future might hold for him.

The Land Rover approached the drop-off that masked the valley of the Tsavo. Kilatya stopped without being told. It was possible to drive all the way to the river when the country was dry, but the game there spooked easily. It was better to walk.

The three men walked quietly to the rim of the valley. The river seemed very near; it was in fact no more than three-quarters of a mile away. It looked placid and still from where they were, like a dark ribbon of oil. Actually, the water in the Tsavo was clear and the current was fairly swift. Africans drank from it all the time, but Royce had never tried it. He stuck to water that had been boiled and filtered.

Royce lifted his glasses and surveyed the valley. There was a good deal of vegetation and there were even patches of green here and there. He picked up the giraffes first, off to his right. There were a lot of them, sixteen or seventeen that he could count. He swung the glasses and saw a troop of baboons out on the rocks by the river with one big old male standing guard. He wasted no time on them. He saw all the baboons he needed while he was working. He moved the glasses to his left.

There they were.

Four of them that he could see.

No, five. Waterbucks. He studied them closely, his palms beginning to sweat. They were all males. There was something about waterbucks that got to him; it was just one of those things. They weren't very good eating and most hunters thought little of them. But the waterbuck was a majestic animal. They were big fellows; there wasn't an animal in the group that was much under four hundred pounds. They held their heads erect with their annulated horns almost motionless. They had a white ring around their rumps and patches of snowy white at their throats and eyes. Their coats were a gray-brown with a pronounced reddish tint.

He looked at them intently but he did not see Buck. Buck was one in a million, an old bull that moved with the grace of a legend. He would hit five hundred pounds easily. Buck would be a record if he could get him, but it wasn't the record that challenged Royce. Buck was...special. There is always one animal that stands as a symbol for a hunter, one animal that consummates the dream. For Royce, it was Buck. He had only seen him twice. Buck did not run with a herd, but he had been near groups of males when Royce had seen him.

There was always a chance.

"Come on," he said.

He started to walk into the valley. Mutisya came along without comment, but Kilatya hesitated. Royce turned and beckoned. Kilatya was a good tracker. Kilatya held back but finally came after them. He seemed very nervous.

They walked down into the shadowed valley of the Tsavo, bearing to the left. It was very still. The soft call of a dove accentuated the silence. The dove called in a regular pattern, first two short calls and then a pause, and then four slightly longer calls with an emphasis on the next to last one. It sounded almost like an owl: hoo hoo…hoo hoo *hoo* hoo.

Royce checked his watch. Five-thirty. They didn't have much time left now.

It was the killing time for the big cats.

In fifteen minutes they were out on the valley floor and the ridge from which they had come was dark behind them. Royce had seen nothing: nothing had moved. He could not see the waterbucks now. He could see the heads and stalk-necks of the giraffes in the distance and that was all.

Then, quite suddenly, he heard something.

The sound was not loud but it was…disturbing. It was out of place. It did not belong.

A humming noise, like a great generator. A faint whistling roar, not an animal's cry, almost beyond the threshold of hearing…

He looked up, trying to find the source of the sound. He saw, or thought he saw, an arc of white in the cloud-shadowed sky. It was like a phantom vapor trail but it did not persist. He had just a glimpse of it, curving down toward the earth, and then it vanished.

He held his breath and listened. There was nothing. No sound of a crash, certainly. Even the humming was gone.

The fading sun lost its warmth. Royce felt cold. The thing might have been a jet, certainly; the big planes sometimes passed over this area. And yet, somehow, he could not believe it. He had seen and heard plenty of jets and this one was *wrong*.

Whatever it was, it had come down near the Baboonery. If it had been anything at all…

Buck had been shoved out of his mind. It was getting late. Night would fall before they could get back to Kathy and the kids.

He led Mutisya and Kilatya back up the ridge to the Land Rover, moving almost at a trot. All three men got into the cab. It was crowded but Royce was grateful for the nearness of the other men.

Royce punched the starter. The engine caught on the second try. He switched on the lights and turned the Land Rover around. He picked up the trail and got moving. He hit forty, which was too fast for the road.

It was pitch dark when they reached the steep Kikumbuliu crossing. Royce had a bad moment going up the bank but the four wheels dug in and pulled the vehicle over. He yanked the red-knobbed lever and went back into two-wheel drive. The worst was over now.

He drove through the thick bush and he could feel the darkness pressing in around him. The twin beams of the headlights were like toy flashlights in a sea of black. He felt a momentary sense of panic, a drowning in an ocean of night, a sensation of shadows that were reaching out for him, swallowing him….

They came out of the bush. The clearing was startling in its openness, its familiar solidity. He saw the warm lights of the Baboonery ahead of him.

He knew at once that nothing was wrong. He shook his head. He was getting jumpy, acting like a child afraid of the dark. Maybe he had been out here too long.

He drove the Land Rover past the baboon cages and stopped it under a floodlight that was some forty yards behind the barracks where the African staff lived. They unloaded the stiffening kudu and Royce gave Mutisya instructions to relay to Elijah, the foreman. The kudu had to be butchered without delay and the meat stored in the freezer.

Royce moved the Land Rover to its usual parking place at the back of the main building. He got out and took the keys with him. He was very tired.

He didn't know what to tell Kathy. Had anything really happened? Kathy was not the nervous type, but he did not want to alarm her over nothing. Better wait, he decided. If she had not noticed anything peculiar he could take a look around tomorrow. For what, he did not know.

He looked up at the stars blazing in the great night sky. Then slowly, almost reluctantly, he looked out into the bush. The lights of the Baboonery were only a fragile island in a sea of darkness. The vastness of the African night lapped at the edges of the light, trying to get in.

Royce felt very much alone.

Even as he stood there, the drums started up from somewhere near the railroad. Royce smiled a little. It was nothing more than a dance over at Kikumbuliu Station. Still, he could have done without the drums tonight. The world did not seem as neatly predictable as it once had.

He took a firm grip on his .375 and went inside to eat his dinner.

2

Royce woke up the next morning to the sound of excited voices. There was no shouting, nothing alarming. Just a babble of voices drifting through the open window. Ordinarily, the sound would not have been enough to awaken him. He must have been tense, he thought, sleeping on the edge…

He sat up straight in the bed, instantly alert. Kathy stirred drowsily at his side.

"What's going on?" she muttered into her pillow.

Royce strained to make some sense out of the voices. Everyone seemed to be talking at once. They were all speaking in Kamba, which didn't help any. Royce's knowledge of Swahili left something to be desired but his Swahili was better than his Kamba. He did catch the word *nguli*. Baboon.

"Just some problem with the monkeys," he said. "Go on back to sleep. The kids are still out cold."

He piled out of bed, jerked on his pants and a shirt, and slipped his bare feet into some scuffed loafers. He left the bedroom at a moderately civilized pace and closed the door behind him. He hesitated a moment at the gun safe on the breezeway, decided that he did not need a weapon, and ran outside.

The men were all gathered in a knot over by the baboon cages. The baboons had caught the air of excitement and were very active, banging around in their cages and making explosive coughing noises. Royce had heard that sound many times in his work with baboons—it sounded exactly like the noise a man would make if you crept up behind him and stuck a big, dull knife in his back. There was a strong smell of urine.

Royce joined the men. The reason for all the commotion was plain enough. Two of the sturdy baboon cages had been ripped open. One cage was empty. In the other one there was a male baboon—a big fellow weighing some fifty pounds—dead on the floor of the cage. His great white teeth were exposed in a snarl of pain. He looked as though he had been torn apart. One leg had been wrenched from its socket; it was attached to the animal only by a strip of bloody hide.

Royce reached into the cage and dragged the body out. The animal lay stiffly on the hard-packed earth. The baboon was not a lovely animal at best, and he looked worse in death. He was somehow an obscene, snouted, four-footed caricature of a human being, and the analogy was not lost on Royce.

"Well, Elijah, what do you make of it?"

Elijah Matheka, the headman, shrugged. His eyes, behind the tinted glasses he always wore, were very wide. "One is dead, one is gone. That is all I know, Mr. Royce."

"You heard nothing?"

"None of us heard anything. When we got up it was just as you saw it."

Royce crouched down and fingered the body. There were no puncture wounds that he could see. The skull was intact; there was no fracture. The animal looked as if something had grabbed it and literally pulled it apart. And something—or someone—had forced the cages open.

A man? It would take a man of extraordinary strength, to say nothing of stupidity. Royce would no more have gone after a baboon with his bare hands than he would have wrestled an elephant. No one from outside would have bothered, unless he had been dead drunk. Baboons were worthless except for research. The men on the place had no great love for baboons, and the feeling was reciprocated. They were not above poking a stick at a troublesome animal, or even shaving a patch of his hide when he was out cold so that the bugs could get at him better. But they had never killed a baboon here. It was senseless. If they lost one they had trapped they just had to trap another one, and that was too much like work.

"Mutisya. Any tracks?"

"I did not see any. The ground here is very hard."

Royce stood up. He felt quite calm, which he recognized as his reaction to trouble. He knew that this incident, whatever its meaning, was only the beginning. There had to be a reason behind it. It could not be written off as just one of those things. He had to find that reason. If troubles were coming, it was bad policy to get the men all stirred up.

He had not forgotten what he had seen and heard the day before. He could think of no connection, but it disturbed him.

"Okay," he said. "We'll have to keep our eyes open for awhile. Elijah, please take that baboon and put it in the freezing compartment in the operating room. Don't forget to switch on the freezer. The police may want to have a look at it. Mutisya, take Kilatya along with you and see if you can find any tracks out along the edges of the bush. Just walk in a big circle, understand? If you don't find anything, we'll check the traps as usual later. All clear?"

The two Africans nodded.

Royce turned and started back to the main building. He eyed it with a strange sensation of never having seen it before. It was a long rectangular structure built on piles. The walls were of unpainted boards, slightly golden in the morning sun. The roof was gray thatch. At one end was his bedroom, where Kathy and the children were asleep. Next came the screened breezeway, with the concrete gun safe set against one side. The next room was the kitchen, the biggest room in the building. It was a pleasant place, with its great wood-burning stove and gleaming white refrigerator and freezer. He noted with approval that there was a curl of blue smoke drifting up into the pale sky; Wathome would have the coffee ready soon. After the kitchen came the combined dining room and sitting room: a long plank table with wooden chairs, some uncomfortable leather-covered furniture, a radio, a pocked dart board. Finally, at the far end of the main building, next to the dirt road, there was a guest bedroom.

It was all very familiar, and very odd. Africa was like that, he thought. It was a real place, not just a squiggle on a map. Like any real place, it had its share of monotony, of boredom, of the commonplace. There were times when he had to remind himself of where he was. *Hey, I'm in Africa!* There were times when he had to look up and out, look far to the westward, where he could sometimes see the snow-capped twin peaks of Kilimanjaro suspended in the clouds.

And there were times when he sensed sharply where he was, and what he was. A stranger in a land that could be suddenly alien. A man surrounded by a world that was not always what it seemed, a world still half understood.

Well, the baboons had settled one thing.

He would have to tell Kathy.

Kathy looked up when he came in. She was still in bed, but the kids were awake. Susan, who was eight, was already dressed. Barbara, who had just turned five, was tugging on her shorts.

"What was that all about?" Kathy asked.

"That's a good question. Tell you all about it after breakfast, okay?"

"But what happened? Did a baboon bite Elijah or was it the other way around?"

"After breakfast."

She caught the note of strain in his voice. "Okay. You're the *bwana.*"

He gave Susan a pat on her close-cropped hair; they had to keep the kids' hair short to frustrate the bugs. "You and Barbara run along to the kitchen and ask Wathome to give you your breakfast. Daddy's going to shave."

The children ran out happily enough. They got a big charge out of eating with Wathome, and already their Swahili was better than Royce's.

There was a silence in the room after the kids had gone and Royce didn't break it. He went into the bathroom and took his time about shaving. There wasn't any hot water yet; the water was heated in a pipe attached to the kitchen stove and it didn't really warm up until around noon. Royce was in no hurry. He needed time to think. He came out, sat down on the bed, and kissed his wife. Her body was still warm with sleep.

"What was that for?" she asked.

"Just felt like it."

She looked at him. "There *is* something wrong, isn't there?"

"Maybe." Royce hadn't gotten married yesterday. There was a right time for discussing problems, and that time was definitely not in the morning before your wife was fully awake. "Let's get some coffee in us and we'll hash it out. I'll go and ride herd on Wathome—I don't want any of that pineapple and mush for breakfast this morning."

Kathy slipped out of bed. "Be with you in a minute."

Royce went into the kitchen, checked to see that Susan and Barbara were messing gleefully with their corn flakes, and told Wathome to fry up some bacon and eggs. He poured himself a cup of black coffee from the big pot on the stove and took it into the dining room.

He finished the coffee before Kathy joined him and had another cup with his breakfast. The eggs were greasy and the bacon was tough and on the rancid side. He said nothing of consequence until Kathy had finished her second cup of coffee.

"Well?" she said.

Royce fired up his pipe and chose his words with some care. He told her exactly what had happened. He neither exaggerated nor minimized it. He told her about his feeling of being watched, the thing he had seen and heard in the sky, and the two baboons, one missing and one dead. "I don't know what the hell is going on," he said. "Some of it could just be my imagination. But that baboon is real enough. I'm worried, and *that's* real enough."

"I don't like you spending so much time out there in the bush," Kathy said slowly. "If something is really happening, you could just disappear and I'd never know what became of you."

Royce knocked out his pipe. "I can take care of myself. But I can't stay here all the time and do my job. That's the problem. What happens if there's trouble here while I'm gone?"

"I'm not alone here. The men would take care of me."

"Maybe. I hope so."

He studied his wife. Kathy had been a pretty girl when he had married her ten years before, but now, at thirty, she was more than pretty. Not beautiful, if by beauty you meant the blank-faced androids that sleepwalked through the movies or the curious mammals that posed in the boys' magazines. Kathy had been marked by living. Her body was a bit softened by the two children she had carried. There were tiny wrinkles at the corners of her brown eyes, but the eyes were still alive; the fun had not gone out of them. Kathy flew off the handle sometimes, but never over big things. Like many women, she was at her best in a crisis.

"Honey, I'm wondering if you shouldn't maybe take the kids and fly home, just for a few months. Until we find out what the score is."

Kathy laughed. "For a dead baboon? Leave you here all alone? You'd forget to take your malaria pills. You'd marry a Kamba girl and I'd never see you again. That's out. If I go, you go."

"Damn it, this isn't funny."

"I didn't say it was. But if it's serious enough to send me away then you haven't got any business being here either. You can't have it both ways."

"We've got to be practical. I can't leave. This is one of the most isolated spots on the face of the earth. If there is trouble I might not be able to get you out in time."

"Has anyone threatened you? Or me? Or the kids?"

"No. Not yet."

"Then why can't we just wait and see? We talked this all out before we came here. I'm not going to run home at the first sign of trouble. Isn't Donaldson coming in with a safari today?"

"Today or tomorrow."

"He'll camp right down the road there, won't he, like he always does? That should give us some protection, if we need it."

"I'd hate to trust my wife to the tender care of Matt Donaldson. He's a peculiar guy, Kathy."

"You've got romantic white hunters on the brain, dear. I couldn't care less about Donaldson as a man—but he knows this country and he knows guns. He'd be a good man to have around if anything happened."

Royce stood up. He felt vaguely annoyed that Kathy did not share the unease he felt. He could not put the thing into words. Something in the sky, a dead baboon, a missing baboon. It was absurd. And yet…

"Okay," he said. "We'll let it ride awhile. But I want you to take the .38 out of the gun safe and put it in the bedroom. If something happens, you take the kids, go in there, and lock the door. If you have to shoot, shoot to kill. Don't close your damn eyes."

"What am I supposed to shoot? A baboon? A Mau Mau?"

"Or Frankenstein's monster. Or a lust-crazed white hunter. Hell, *I* don't know. But I'm not kidding, Kathy. You take that .38 and you get it ready."

"Yes, *bwana*. I love you when you're masterful."

"Good. After I run the trap line, I may stop in and have a talk with Bob Russell. Maybe he has some ideas. I'll send Elijah into Mitaboni to notify the police. They won't do anything but maybe they'll send a man out here to look at that baboon. I'll be back before dark."

At that moment, Susan ran in. She jumped up and down in great joy. "Barby just had a BM in her pants," she announced proudly.

Kathy got up. "Life goes on," she said.

Royce went to get his rifle out of the gun safe. He supposed that kids had gone on having bowel movements in the middle of Mau Mau raids, or Indian raids for that matter, but it certainly seemed inappropriate.

He forced himself to start thinking about the traps he had to check.

It was a strange world. At a time like this his wife had to change Barby's pants and he had to go off to hunt baboons.

Still, as Kathy said, life went on.

Royce took Mutisya with him in the Land Rover. Mutisya had found no tracks in his search around the Baboonery. In itself, that was not too peculiar. The land was very hard after the long dry spell and it did not take tracks easily, not even elephant tracks.

They took the back trail, the one that ran along the railroad for a few miles, crossed the Tsavo where the river was low enough, and wound up in Mitaboni. The traps were on the far side of the Tsavo; Royce wanted to work that area before the rains came. Nobody could get into that place during the rainy season.

Even if there had been no traps, Royce would have taken this trail. If something *had* fallen from the sky, it must have been in this general region. The thought crossed his mind that it might have been a space capsule of some sort. He had been told that some of the early astronauts had passed right over the Baboonery. Even the moon shots involved some earth orbits. He had not heard of any new launchings, but he supposed that there were experiments with both manned and unmanned craft that were not announced to the public. Surely, though, if there had been trouble the area would be crawling with people. He hadn't even seen a search plane.

He kept his eyes open nevertheless.

Unhappily, there was little to see. The land was flat under the great blue sky, flat and red and parched. No Kamba lived here and there were few animals visible. The monotony was broken only by the gray baobabs, looking like Disney trees with their fat trunks and spindly branches, and by the euphorbia plants, which were cactuslike and always reminded Royce of the sort of thing people expected to see in Texas but which would have been more at home in California or Arizona. The sun was hot and the Land Rover kicked up thick clouds of red dust. The dust was half an inch thick on the floor of the Land Rover before they had gone two miles.

They crossed the Tsavo at the ford with only the usual difficulties of slipping wheels and water through the floorboards. Royce had been informed that there were crocodiles in the Tsavo, but apparently they were not as mindlessly aggressive as they were in the movies. He had never seen one. On the far side of the river the vegetation was thicker and the flies and mosquitoes were a nuisance. Royce remembered that he had forgotten to take his daraprim that morning and made a mental note to swallow the pill when he got back. Once a week, and it was all too easy to forget. Malaria had a way of reminding a man if he forgot too often.

It was early afternoon when they reached the clearing where the traps were set. Baboons were all over the place when they arrived, even climbing on the traps themselves. The animals pulled back at the sight of the Land Rover but they did not go far. There were about fifty of them and most of them took to the trees. This had surprised Royce the first time he had seen it; baboons were ground-dwelling monkeys and they liked open country and rocks. The books all said that they weren't much good in the trees, but evidently the baboons had read the wrong books. They frisked about like so many giant squirrels, and they made a fearful din.

Royce ignored them. He knew from experience that the troop would stay close and holler in an attempt to frighten him away from the trapped animals, but the baboons would not attack. It was strictly a bluff.

He pulled the Land Rover up to the first traps and stopped. He climbed out, leaving the rifle in the vehicle. He took the gadget he always thought of as a prod pole with him. It was not actually a prod, being basically a syringe attached to a wooden pole about four feet long.

There was no need to speak. He and Mutisya had the routine down pat by now.

There were three traps in the first series and two of them held baboons. The third trap was sprung but the animal had gotten away. Royce studied the empty trap with some care. The traps were quite simple. They were just big cages made out of wood and wire with a raised platform in the center. The bait, usually pineapple or maize, was fastened to the platform by a cord. When the baboon climbed up and moved the food, a trigger was released that dropped the door of the cage. That was that, unless the baboon managed to force the wire enough to get out. A large baboon was a powerful animal; there had been escapes before. Royce could not tell whether the empty trap had been opened from within or without. He saw nothing suspicious, but it did seem to him that if someone were swiping baboons this would be the place to come. Why go to the Baboonery where there were people around?

The two caged baboons were alarmed and wary. They were also dangerous. They rushed around the cages in a panic, lunging at the wire and snapping their impressive jaws. They made very rapid coughing noises and thoughtfully dropped sticky dung all over the cage floors.

Royce eliminated one right away; she was a female, and his current orders called for only males within a weight range of thirty to fifty pounds. She would have to be released, but not until they had gotten the baboons they needed.

The other one was okay.

"Friend," Royce said, "how would you like to visit the United States?"

The baboon did not seem enthusiastic.

Royce approached him with care. A trapped baboon was a formidable animal. They were very large for monkeys, bigger than the smallest ape, the gibbon. They had nasty dispositions when they were crossed, and they were tough. Royce had seen war dogs in action, but he had often thought that they couldn't hold a candle to a war baboon if there had been such a thing. Unlike most monkeys, the baboon was not flat-faced. Possibly because of his terrestrial habits, he had a tremendous projecting snout. He had powerful jaws liberally supplied with strong white teeth, and he knew how to use them. Once a baboon caught hold of an arm or a leg it was almost impossible to pry his jaws open. There had been accidents at the Baboonery, and Royce had learned to keep his mind on what he was doing.

He filled the syringe on the end of the pole with sernyl. Mutisya went around to the back of the cage and attracted the animal's attention. Royce made one quick lunge, got the needle in the baboon's rump, and rammed the elongated plunger home. The baboon shrieked, whirled, and rushed across the cage. Royce stepped back out of range.

There was nothing to do now but wait. Knocking out a freshly trapped baboon was not particularly difficult. It was a nightmare, though, when you had to knock them out a second time at the Baboonery, or if you chanced to catch a baboon that had been stuck before but had escaped. The animals were quick to learn, and they wanted no part of that needle a second time. They would grab at the needle when it came into the cage and they were so fast that they could twist the needle off before you could get it out of range again. Royce had once spent three solid hours trying to stick a baboon in a small cage without success.

The animal showed no instant effects from the sernyl, but he gradually slowed his desperate lunging. Within minutes, his eyes turned glassy and he began to stagger. The snarl on his face relaxed into what closely resembled a bemused smile. He hauled himself up onto the platform, wobbled on rubber legs for a moment, and fell in a heap to the floor of the cage.

Royce gave him another minute, then opened the cage. He dragged the inert body by the legs to the Land Rover and dumped the baboon into the back of the vehicle. The animal would be out cold for several hours, and they could give him another shot if necessary. Occasionally, they miscalculated and a baboon revived ahead of schedule. Royce had fond memories of the day when a big animal had come to in the market at Mitaboni and had staggered out on a tour of inspection. It had been great fun for awhile, but it was not really dangerous. The baboons had a bit of a hangover when they first revived, and they were slow and easy to catch.

They checked all of the traps in the clearing, and when they were through they had four baboons sleeping the good sleep in the back of the Land Rover. They released eleven animals, all of them females or immature specimens. They repaired and reset the traps. Next time, Royce knew, they would be less successful. Most of the baboons would be wary now and stay clear of the traps. Soon, Royce would have to bring in a crew and shift the traps to a new location. That was a hard job and he was not looking forward to it.

The two men climbed back in the Land Rover and Royce continued along the trail to Mitaboni. He saw nothing that was in any way unusual but the nagging sense of unease persisted. Royce knew that he was driving too fast; the limp baboons were bouncing in the back.

There was something very funny going on, something he could not understand. The unknown was always a potential threat. Whatever it was, it could be dangerous.

It would not just go away.

He wanted to talk to Bob Russell.

If anyone could help him, it would be Russell.

3

He drove through Mitaboni without stopping, a process that took less than thirty seconds. Mitaboni didn't amount to much, and the first time Royce had seen it he had reacted with something close to despair. With time, however, Mitaboni took on a certain charm.

Mitaboni was like a lot of the little towns that had grown up in Africa during the past fifty years. It was a shipping point for the railroad, with a series of large cattle pens strung out along the track on the northern end of the settlement. It was a minor stopping place on the main road from Nairobi to Mombasa, boasting two petrol stations. One was Shell and the other was Ozo, and both of them ran a kind of general store on the side. There were no Europeans in Mitaboni, and most of the shops were still run by Asians. The ubiquitous Patel boys controlled the Shell station, and one Dalip Singh was the Ozo impresario. The buses used Mitaboni as a watering stop, pulling in several times a day to disgorge loads of sweating and irritable passengers in search of soft drinks. There was a small open-air African market, a shack called the Corner Bar which did a fair business in Tusker beer, a rather pretty old mosque, and a shed that served as a post office. It was one of the miracles of the ages that a letter mailed in that post office eventually reached the United States; Royce had never lost any mail, coming or going. There was a grim-looking hotel that had been patronized mainly by Asians whose cars had broken down on the punishing road; now that the road had been paved after a fashion it had lost most of its business. Europeans who wanted to stop on the road between Nairobi and Mombasa always stopped at the oasis of Hunter's Lodge, some twenty miles away on the Nairobi side, or at Mac's Inn, about thirty miles distant toward Mombasa. Mitaboni also boasted a tiny whitewashed police station, staffed with three African members of the Kenya Police who spent most of their time cruising about with great dignity on bicycles.

Royce relaxed a little when he had cleared Mitaboni and was out on the main road. It was a genuine pleasure to get away from the thick dust and the jarring jolts. He could hit sixty with safety now that he knew where the worst holes were.

He drove eight miles toward Mombasa—and also toward the Baboonery—and then turned off to the left down the well-kept dirt road that led to Russell's house. One nice thing about the main road was that you always knew exactly where you were. There were stake markers placed every mile along the way. On one side they gave the mileage to Mombasa, and on the other the mileage to Nairobi. Russell's turnoff was at mile 140 on the Mombasa side.

It took him several minutes to reach the house and he could hear the dogs barking long before he got there. Russell's land was mostly planted in sisal; it was too dry to grow most of the profitable cash crops. It was not lush and green like the farms in the highlands—those that were left—but Russell made up the difference in quantity. He had thousands of acres and he used them well.

The house was a substantial one, a low rambling structure of white stone and stained wood. A great porch lined one whole side of the building, and Russell had screened it in against the bugs.

Royce stopped the Land Rover and before he could get out, Russell had come outside to greet him. Royce asked Mutisya to check the baboons and give them another shot if they started to come around. Then he went on alone to talk to Russell. He could have taken Mutisya with him, but it would have been awkward with an old settler. Russell's men would see to it that Mutisya got something to eat and drink. The system was changing, but it still made Royce uncomfortable. While he was Russell's guest he would have to play it Russell's way.

Bob Russell was a short, chunky man, but he was not fat. He was as hard as though he had been cast from iron. His broad face was very red, partly from sunburn and partly from many years of close attention to a gin bottle. His hair was long and straight and jet black, and he brushed it back without a part. His eyes, under bushy black brows, were shrewd and very dark. He was dressed in the standard Kenya uniform: white shirt with the sleeves rolled up, khaki shorts that were baggy by American standards, sturdy black shoes with tan socks that came almost up to his knobby knees.

He stuck out his broad, hard hand and Royce took it. "Well, Crawford," he said. "Good timing, if I may say so. I was just about to have tea. Hope you can join me?"

"Thanks. I'd appreciate it very much."

"Not at all. Always glad to see you. Gets a bit lonely out here, you know. Come in, come in."

Royce followed him across the porch and into the main sitting room. It was wonderfully cool in the house and spotlessly clean. The room was big and comfortable. It had no frills, but it was as solid and pleasant a room as Royce had ever been in. There were worn zebra-skin rugs on the red tile floor and a very fine kudu head was hung on the wall over the great fireplace. The couches and chairs were faded but substantial; they looked like they were good for another fifty years. There were only three pictures in the room, photographs that stood in matching frames on a long side table. One was of Russell's wife, who had died nine years ago. The others were of his sons, both of whom were in England. Shelves lined two walls and they were filled with books. The books were a wild assortment ranging from British paperbacks to large leatherbound works on African exploration in the old days. Most of the Kenya settlers had been great readers, there being very little else to do on the remote farms when the day's work was done, but Russell was exceptional. He read omnivorously and he could discuss anyone from Shakespeare to Sartre. There was an ancient grandfather clock in one corner, taller than a man, and its unhurried ticking filled the room with the measured beats of eternity.

Russell's houseboy, a lanky African dressed in the traditional *kanzu* that looked like a cotton nightshirt, padded in on bare feet and waited for instructions. He knew perfectly well what the order would be, but that was part of the ritual.

"*Chai kwa mbili,*" Russell said. "*Upesi!*"

Royce stifled a smile. He had a vision of a couple of straw-hatted soft-shoe men dancing out on a stage while the band struck up that old favorite, "*Chai kwa Mbili*"— better known in some quarters as "*Tea for Two.*"

The two men made small talk until the tea arrived, and Royce found it heavy going. Unlike most of the Englishmen he had known, Russell made him feel somewhat uncomfortable. The man was cordial enough in a superficial sort of way, but he had a trick of keeping his distance. Royce had a notion that Russell resented him, resented his presence in Kenya. The feeling was understandable enough. Bob Russell had been here, on this farm, for thirty-five years. He had built this house. He had carved his sisal plantation out of the bush, and he had fought rhinos and elephants and malaria and God knew what to do it. He had lived through the time of the Mau Mau and the difficulties that had come with independence. He had lost his wife to this land. His future was uncertain. And now an American breezed in on a jet, took a cushy job trapping baboons, and made more money than he did. It gave a man food for thought.

Still, most of the English were not like that, not the ones Royce had met. Whoever had dreamed up the stereotype of the cold reserved Englishman had not spent much time in Kenya—or in England either, for that matter. Perhaps he was not being fair to Russell. The man had had a tough time of it. In any event, he was the only settler who lived anywhere near the Baboonery. If Russell couldn't tell him what he needed to know, then he was not likely to get the information anywhere else.

Tea time was a ceremony, of course, and it could not be rushed. The African brought out a silver tray with two small pots of tea, two fine china cups and saucers, sugar, a pitcher of milk, cakes, cookies, and a variety of tiny rectangular sandwiches—cheese, cucumber, and lettuce. It took Royce half an hour to do justice to the ritual. He pulled out his pipe and lit it. Russell fished out a cigarette and inhaled deeply. He smoked Rex, a local brand of filter-tips.

Royce could now come to the point.

"I've run into something strange at the Baboonery," he said. "I'd appreciate getting your advice on it."

"Ah. Well, lets have a crack at it."

Royce told him what had happened. The story seemed overly familiar now; it was the second time he had gone through it that day. It was difficult to communicate a sense of urgency.

Russell lit another cigarette, watching Royce intently.

"That's all there is? You have left nothing out?"

"That's it."

"Well, now. You have two problems, it seems, or maybe three. What was it that you saw in the sky? What could kill a baboon like that? And what would want to steal a baboon? It sounds rather like something out of Conan Doyle."

"You know this country. Does any of this ring a bell?"

Russell thought it over carefully. "It *is* strange. It's a big sky we have here, you know. I've seen things in my time. Meteorites, fireballs—something of the sort most likely. As for the baboons, I haven't a clue. Fifteen years or so ago, yes. You weren't here during the Emergency, of course. That sort of thing wasn't at all uncommon then. Dogs skewered on gateposts, cattle with their heads cut off, all that sort of rot. But there aren't any Mau Mau these days—they're all in the bloody government." His voice was edged with bitterness, the helpless anger of a man left behind by the retreat of empire. He paused a moment and went on more calmly. "That's all over and done with. Things have worked out better than I thought they would, I'll give Kenyatta that. Doesn't help with *your* problem, though. Almost has to be a man. What else could it be?"

"How could a man tear a baboon apart that way? And why bother? Why not just shoot an arrow into him?"

"I've no idea. Why do Africans do anything? I'll tell you this, Crawford. This is an old country, Africa. Birthplace of man and all that, if old Leakey is right about those skeletons of his. Empires rose and fell on this continent when England was just a pack of wild men. There are ancient currents here, currents that you and I will never understand. You take our Kamba friends. They look harmless enough now, and some idiots even find them comical. But these people fought the Masai to a standstill, and they once had a trading network that controlled a territory all the way from the Indian Ocean to Lake Victoria. People don't change completely overnight, Crawford. I know all about the schools and the ministers and the judges. I give them their due. But I know all about the witchcraft and the killing oaths and the poisoned arrows, too. These people have one foot in another world. You can't figure them out. Don't try."

"But look, Bob. You don't rip a baboon apart with witchcraft. Maybe the Kamba were responsible. There's some resentment toward the Baboonery.

It probably won't be many years before the government has to chop it up into farms. But what kind of a Kamba is it who can do that to a baboon with his bare hands?"

"A drunk one," Russell suggested.

"I just can't believe it," Royce said reluctantly. "I wish I could."

Russell shrugged. "You haven't been harmed yet. Stay out of it. Keep your eyes open. Look out for your own business, do your own job. You asked for my opinion. I'm afraid that's it. Not very helpful, I suppose. You don't have to go out of your way looking for trouble in this country. It will find you if it's headed your way."

Royce stood up. "I appreciate your advice. I'll think on it. I'd better be getting back now."

"Care for a quick one before you go? Dusty road ahead of you, you know."

"Thanks, but I don't want to leave Kathy there after dark alone. Another time, if I may. You must drop in and see us soon. Donaldson should be in with a safari shortly. Drive over and we'll break out a fifth."

"Sounds good. I might do that." Russell extended his hard, blunt hand. "Be careful. And keep me informed, will you?"

"Right. Thanks again."

Royce hurried out to the Land Rover. "Okay, Mutisya?"

"Okay, Mr. Royce."

Royce drove back to the main road and pushed the vehicle as fast as he dared toward the little trail that angled off to the Baboonery. He covered the nine miles in eight minutes, which was pretty good. He turned off to the right where the old white sign was nailed to the baobab tree: *Kikumbuliu Station.* There was no mention of the Baboonery, which was beyond the station on the other side of the railroad track.

He had to slow down to a crawl. It was ten miles to the Baboonery and the road was nothing more than a rough dirt track hacked through the bush.

The sun was low in the red-tinged sky. The desiccated bush was hot and still. The gritty red dust was everywhere, like the patina of ages covering a landscape of the dead. There was no sign of life except for a single dik-dik, no larger than a dog, that sprang up in the middle of the road and ran away at the sound of the Land Rover's approach.

He passed the deserted loading shed that marked the station and bounced across the railroad track, those incongruous strips of battered metal that lanced an improbable hole through the African wilderness. It had taken more than a few lives to lay those tracks. The so-called maneaters of Tsavo sounded rather melodramatic by today's standards, but the big cats had been real enough. He pushed on toward the Baboonery. The road was even worse now, if possible. It had taken him nearly an hour to cover the ten miles from the main road.

He saw them as soon as he reached the edge of the clearing.

Kathy was sitting on the wooden steps outside the main sitting room, watching Susan and Barbara playing in the dirt.

She waved to him.

Royce felt a sudden stab of relief and noticed that his hands were trembling on the wheel.

It had been a long day.

4

The next morning started out like a repeat of the day before. One of the cages had been broken open and another baboon was gone.

At first, Royce was more angry than worried. The theft seemed a calculated affront, an insult rather than a threat. He had set up a watch during the night and the loss of another baboon was galling.

"Well, Elijah," he said to his headman. "This was your responsibility. Who was on duty last night?"

"Kilatya, Mr. Royce." Elijah's eyes were invisible behind his tinted glasses.

"And where is Kilatya? What does he have to say?"

"Kilatya, he says nothing. He is not here."

"Where the hell is he?"

"I do not know. He is not here."

Royce put his hands on his hips. "That's just great."

He knew that there was no point in questioning the other men. Even if they knew where Kilatya was they would not tell him. It was not unusual for a man to disappear for a day or two and then show up again with some unlikely but immensely detailed explanation. Royce had learned to accept the stories with good grace and simply dock the man a day's wages. The alternative was to have no crew at all. Kilatya was a fine tracker; Royce needed him.

In this case, it was not difficult to figure out what had happened. Kilatya had been standing guard and he had lost a baboon. Rather than face the music, he had gone home to hide. He would probably be back eventually.

The fact remained that another baboon had been taken. Royce spent the morning checking for signs. He found one place with some broken brush and a sharp-edged depression that looked as though it had been made by a heavy object—the sort of mark that might be made by a man taking a large post and ramming it hard against the earth. That was all. There was no trail that he could follow and he was no nearer an explanation than he had been before.

Something was after his baboons. That was the only solid fact that he had, and it made no sense.

Royce had just finished lunch when he heard the trucks coming. He pushed back his plate, which contained the remnants of one of Wathome's favorite concoctions, a grisly mixture of bacon and spaghetti.

"Here comes the great white hunter," he said to Kathy. "Two cheers."

They walked outside and stood on the steps. The trucks were very close. He could see the billows of red dust that marked their passage. The sun hammered down on the land as though it had a grudge against it. It was hot and still and Royce's shirt was sticking to his back. Nothing green showed anywhere. There was not a cloud in the vast blue sky. The great dry leaves of the banana trees rustled very faintly, reminding him mockingly of the rain that would not come.

The three dust-covered trucks, loaded down with equipment, jolted around the bend in the road. They went on through the Baboonery grounds, showering dust, and turned right toward the Tsavo. Donaldson always camped on the near side of the Kikumbuliu, where the bush opened up after the tsetse fly-infested area.

Royce waited. The Land Rover came along in about five minutes, hanging back to keep free of the dust kicked up by the trucks. Donaldson was at the wheel and he stopped when he saw Royce and Kathy. He jumped out, leaving his clients to stew for a moment in the sun.

"Ho!" he called. "Good to see you again."

He shook hands with both of them. His lean hand was as hard as a rock. Royce stifled his dislike and welcomed him.

Matt Donaldson stood an even six feet but he looked taller than he was. Royce, who topped six feet by three inches, felt short in his presence. Donaldson was lean and sinewy and he moved like a cat. His long hair was the color of straw and his eyebrows were burned to the shade of white gold by the sun. He exuded vitality like a healthy animal. His thin face and his watery blue eyes could be cruel, but he knew how to turn on the charm that was so necessary in his business. He was dressed casually but neatly: khaki shorts and shirt, heavy boots, and a floppy brown hat that he carried in his left hand. The hat was battered with wear and it was not equipped with a leopardskin hatband. The dashing hatband was strictly for the hunters who did their stalking in the bars of Nairobi.

"I have a bit of a favor to ask of you, Royce."

"Ask away."

"You remember old Wambua?"

"The political hotshot? I'm not likely to forget him."

"Well, it's like this. The old boy has got wind of the fact that I have a couple of rich American clients out here. He has decided to honor us with his august presence."

Royce groaned. "Another dance?"

Donaldson grinned. "Bang on. He can't be far behind me with his merry men. I have a camp to set up. Will you stop them here and let them get

their drums heated up in the clearing in front of your baboon cages? Then
we'll come back in a few hours and we'll all watch an exciting, authentic
native dance. How does that strike you?"

"You really want to know?"

"I knew you would respond with your customary enthusiasm." Donaldson looked at him closely. "I say, you don't really mind? I *am* in a bit
of a spot...."

"Of course not, Matt. Glad to help."

"Thanks so much. Back shortly!"

He trotted back to the Land Rover, climbed in, and gunned the vehicle
after the vanished trucks. Royce managed a smile for the two Americans
sweating in the front seat.

"There goes a day's work," he said sourly.

"We owe him a few favors," Kathy said. "And we've got to stay on the
good side of Wambua. Especially now."

"I'll buy that. Look, I'll tell Elijah to get ready and I'll keep an eye
peeled for the *corps de ballet*. You better put the kids down and see if they'll
go to sleep this early—they won't be taking any naps once the drumming
starts."

He walked off to find Elijah. He was not happy about the loss of time,
but he was glad that Donaldson had arrived.

There were times when it was better not to be alone.

The two battered trucks, filled to overflowing with young laughing Africans,
clanked into position in front of the baboon cages. The trucks were usually
used in hauling produce to various local markets, but Wambua borrowed
them occasionally for his dancers. Since Wambua was something of a
wheel in the government, the owners of the trucks tended to give them
up without undue protest.

The trucks disgorged Africans. All of them, male and female, were
quite young. None of them looked over twenty, and some of the girls
couldn't have been more than thirteen or fourteen. They were an attractive, healthy-kooking group. The men wore shorts, in deference to their
European audience, but were barefoot and naked from the waist up. They
had on some beads—necklaces, armbands, anklets with rattles—but they
weren't dolled up like the girls. The girls wore short black skirts and little
beaded bras—again in consideration of what they felt to be proper for
a European audience—and they were bedecked in bright-colored beads
and rattles. All of the girls had small silver whistles suspended on finely-
wrought chains around their necks. Their hair, of course, was cut shorter
than the men's.

The dancers went right to work. They got two fires going almost as soon as they left the trucks. The fires weren't just for local color; they needed them to heat the drumheads on the long cylindrical drums, to get them tight enough for proper playing.

Old Wambua came out last and advanced toward Royce. He was a heavy-set man, dressed in a baggy brown European suit with a stained red tie. He carried a fly-whisk as a symbol of his status. He was not really old in years—fifty or sixty perhaps—but he gave an impression of having been around. He bowed slightly and grinned. His front teeth had been filed to sharp points in the old Kamba style.

"Jambo, Bwana," Wambua said. He was kidding, of course; he spoke perfectly good English, and the old deferential Swahili greeting to Europeans was a kind of a joke now.

"Jambo," Royce said, going along with it. *"Karibu, Mutumia."*

Wambua laughed aloud. Royce had mixed Swahili and Kamba in his reply, telling a tribal elder that he was welcome.

"The two Americans," Wambua said, switching to English. "They are here?"

"In the safari camp with Mr. Donaldson. They'll be along shortly."

Wambua chuckled. "They have much money, very rich. They pay us well for our dance. We make friends for Africans and they see something new. How do you say it? Everyone is triumphant."

"Everybody wins." Of course, they could have seen dancing for nothing almost any night out in the bush. But you had to know where to go, and you had to be careful about cameras. The Africans had the notion that tourists could go back home and make vast sums of money out of their photographs of African dances, and they wanted their cut. Civilization had many facets.

"They come now," Wambua said, nodding.

Royce looked up and saw Matt Donaldson walking along the dirt road from the safari camp. His men apparently had set up the bathing facilities in record time, since the two people with him were no longer covered with trail dust. Royce eyed the Americans without pleasure. Somehow, he always wanted Americans to make a good impression here. The man was young and scrawny, dressed in very tight blue jeans, a fancy new bush jacket of the sort sold at Ahameds in Nairobi, and a hat with a leopard-skin hatband. The woman with him was a rather striking blonde in a green frock and open-toed sandals. She was puffing on a cigarette in a long black holder.

Donaldson made the introductions and chatted away glibly about the coming dance, going into his white-hunter-with-incredible-experience routine. "Jolly good, actually. Not up to your Kipsigis, of course, or your Masai. But fascinating, no doubt of that."

Royce managed to swallow that with a straight face. The Masai weren't any great shakes as dancers, and he knew that Matt loathed Kamba dancing. But a hunter had to be more than a crack shot. A good one was a talented bull slinger as well, and Matt Donaldson was one of the best.

Elijah slipped unobtrusively up behind Royce.

Royce turned. "What is it, Elijah?" If the man would only take those tinted glasses off, he thought. It was like talking to a mask.

"I thought you should know, Mr. Royce. Some of these men, these dancers, they are from the place where Kilatya has his wives and his cows. They say he is not there. He has not come home." Elijah waited, shifting from one foot to another—waiting for praise, for instructions, for some indication of what he should do.

Royce could not help him out. He felt chilled by the news; he did not know what it meant. "Thank you, Elijah. There is nothing we can do now. The dance is about to start; you and the rest of the men might as well watch it. We won't be working this afternoon."

"*Ndio*, Mr. Royce." Elijah looked troubled, but he did not press the matter further. He walked away to join the rest of the African staff, all of whom were already standing in a line to watch the proceedings. Royce's permission to take the afternoon off had been a trifle redundant.

Royce's sense of unease returned very strongly. Something was wrong at the Baboonery....

The Europeans took their seats on folding wooden chairs. (In East Africa, virtually all white men were lumped together as "Europeans." It made little sense to Royce, but that was the way it was.)

The dance began.

To Royce, the most amazing thing about the whole business was the speed with which he had adjusted to it all. He had been at the Baboonery for less than two years, and already he could take the scene before him almost for granted. It took a conscious effort on his part to see the strangeness.

The African bush was all around them, dry as tinder, flaked with red dust, enfolding its secrets under the vast afternoon sky. The world here had been old when man was young, and the animals that prowled through the dead grasses and the sleeping river valleys were very like the ones that men had known thousands of years ago. They were surrounded by miracles of life—the elephant, the lion, the rhino—that were making their last stand against the swelling growth of civilization.

And here, right before their eyes, was a bizarre collection of buildings and people and animals—a cluster of unlikely combinations thrown together as though in defiance of the laws of place and time. Thatched roofs and electricity, drums and radios, trucks and baboons. A professional hunter from England, Americans as different from one another as a Kamba from a Masai, Africans of all kinds: a cook in a *kanzu,* a headman in tinted glasses, a politician in a red tie thinking about an Africa newly born, young people with bare skins gleaming in the sun dancing a traditional dance for money.

There were three drummers, standing on the far side of the dancers. Each had a cylindrical wooden drum about three feet long which was suspended from a thong around the neck and supported on one bent knee. The drumheads were of cowhide or snakeskin, and the drummers played on both ends with the fingers of their hands. The beat was staccato and very fast, rattling out like rifle fire, reaching a crescendo, stopping, and starting again.

The dancers formed two columns with the men on one side and the girls on the other. They did not touch one another. One man faced the dancers, his back to the audience, and shouted out commands like a drill sergeant.

For half an hour or so, the dance was more like a series of rapid marching drills than anything else. The leader would call out his instructions, the drummers would hammer away with a sound like marbles poured out on a hard table, and the two columns would whirl and rush forward and backward with a fair amount of precision. Occasionally, the dancers would raise their hands and make barking noises as though firing imaginary rifles. Each drill was very short, lasting only a few minutes, after which the drums would stop and Wambua would smile benignly and the audience would dutifully applaud.

It got more interesting as the dancers warmed up. The military orders disappeared and the dancing reverted to an older style. Individuals stepped out of the lines and improvised dances based on the movements of animals: leaping antelope, pacing ostriches, lumbering rhinos, trumpeting elephants. The rhythm of the drums became more complex, with drums beating out counter-rhythms. The shrill whistles pierced the warm air and the rattles on the stamping feet added a fourth pattern to the beats of the drums.

Royce watched, caught up in it now almost in spite of himself. The Africans in the audience broke up into knots and began to perform dances of their own.

The dancing girls started to ululate, throwing their heads back and giving long liquid cries that trembled through the pulsating noise. The dust thickened and streaked the gleaming bodies with rivulets of rust.

The dancers paired off, male and female, and the style of the dance became explicitly sexual. The dancers still did not touch, but they came very close. First a man would dance before the girl, then the girl before the man, and then they would face one another, breathing heavily, stamping their feet, jerking their heads like turtles back and forth over the shoulders of their partners.

Money had been the cause of the dance, but money was forgotten now. The dancers ignored their audience. They were in a world of their own, a world Royce could never enter. This was an older Africa, an alien Africa, an Africa divorced from the world outside. The dance went on and on until it seemed that the dancers must drop from sheer exhaustion. The sun dipped into the west and long shadows crept across the land.

It was dark when the drums stopped. The lights of the Baboonery were feeble sparks in a night that stretched away to infinity. The sudden silence beneath the emerging stars was taut and explosive.

Royce was emotionally numb. The noise and the dust and the strain had gotten to him. He was dog tired. He kept going somehow until all the visitors were gone. He arranged with Elijah to set up a watch for the night. He ate a cheese sandwich, washed it down with a bottle of beer, and was in bed by nine o'clock.

He slept instantly, but it was a light and troubled sleep.

The drums started up again, somewhere lost in the great African night.

He reached out for Kathy and pulled her close.

Kathy lay awake in his arms, watching the blowing white curtains that fluttered like ghosts on the open windows, listening to the distant drums.

Royce slept late the next morning and he woke up feeling drugged and fuzzy. When he joined Kathy at the breakfast table it took him three cups of violent coffee to get the cotton out of his head.

He noticed that there was something different about the light. He walked to the door and stared out. There were heavy black clouds in the sky, blowing in from the coast of the Indian Ocean. There were still patches of blue and the sun was shining, but the vast vault of the African sky was broken by the drifting mountains of clouds. The wind had freshened, kicking up the red dust, and the air was cooler than it had been for a long time.

"By God," he said. "Look at that."

"It's too early for rain, isn't it?" Kathy asked.

"That's what they say back home just before one of the frog-chokers hits. You're right—the short rains shouldn't start before the end of October. But nothing else in this country operates on schedule. Maybe the short rains are coming three weeks early."

"I don't believe it. It *never* rains here."

"I wouldn't bet on it, sugar."

He stood there, staring at the sky. Unbidden, the memory of what he had seen in that sky crept into his mind. Fireball? Meteorite? Way down deep, he couldn't accept it. It had been something else....

He stepped outside and shaded his eyes. He looked away at the sky, off in the direction of the trapping trail that led to Mitaboni. The lines around his mouth tightened.

"Look at that!" he said.

She joined him and followed his pointing finger. She saw them at once and felt a stab of irrational fear she tried to conceal.

The sky was stained with the black dots of birds, hundreds of birds, wheeling in great lazy circles on the wind. The birds were miles away but there was no mistaking them. They were buzzards.

"Maybe Matt took his clients out hunting this morning," she said.

Royce shook his head. "Not there, baby."

He went in and took the .375 from the gun safe. He checked the rifle, stuck some extra shells in his pocket, and climbed into the Land Rover. He picked up Mutisya and drove as fast as he dared toward where the buzzards were circling.

Speed was important. Scavengers were notoriously efficient in Africa.

Something was dead out there. Royce wanted to get a look at it before it was too late. He tried not to think beyond that.

It took him nearly an hour of rough, jolting driving. He had to leave the trail finally and cut across open country. It was high noon before he reached the kill.

The buzzards took off at his approach, flapping into the sky with their naked turkey-necks extended like snakes. He drove right up to the thing on the ground. There were some twenty obscene marabou storks tearing at the dark dead figure; they rose heavily into the air, like deacons with wings, as the Land Rover jerked to a halt. The smell of death was thick in the sunlight, a smell of meat and blood and bloated flies.

Royce and Mutisya climbed out of the Land Rover. They did not speak. They walked over to the body in the dirt and looked down. Royce's eyes widened in horror. He swallowed hard to choke back the impulse to vomit.

"Kilatya," he said.

"Yes, Mr. Royce. We have found him."

Royce stared at the thing that had been a man. The eyes had been pecked out of the skull. One leg was nearly gone, with the greasy white bone showing through the strings of flesh. Kilatyas chest, naked to the sky, was bloody pulp.

An inane phrase kept repeating itself in Royce's stunned mind. *How about that, sport fans. How about that....*

"Get the tarp from the back of the Land Rover," he said. "We can't pick him up the way he is now."

Mutisya got the tarp. The two men managed to slide the body onto the thick canvas. There was no way to get rid of the flies. They folded the tarp over Kilatya, hiding him, and lifted the body into the back of the Land Rover.

"Mutisya. We must take great care. If there are tracks, we must find them. Understand?"

"*Ndio,* Mr. Royce."

The two men separated, searching the ground. There was no point in looking for signs where the body had been. The birds had messed the place up too much for that. They had to backtrack, find the trail. *Something* had found Kilatya here, and *something* had gone away again....

They were lucky. The dust was thick enough to take a track. Mutisya found where Kilatya had come on foot, walking from the Baboonery. That was easy. They fanned out from that point, working both sides of a circle.

It took them a long time. They studied every inch of the ground. They came up with three kinds of fresh tracks. One set of prints probably came from a jackal. They ignored that sign.

There were other tracks that were unmistakable. Royce had seen them a thousand times; they were one of the few tracks he could recognize on sight. They had been made by baboons. He could tell by the different sizes that there had been at least two of them.

The remaining tracks—if tracks they were—sent a chill down his spine. He had seen them only once before. Sharp-edged depressions, deep prints. Made by something heavy. As though a flat-bottomed post of hard wood or metal had been slammed into the earth....

They found one other thing. A tuft of baboon hair caught in a thorny bush.

The evidence was clear. It was even possible to reconstruct what must have happened. Kilatya had been on guard at the Baboonery. Something had taken one of the baboons. Kilatya had followed that something into the bush. He had caught up with it here. And that had been the end of Kilatya.

It was clear, but it made no sense. Baboons did not kill human beings. They were capable of it, no doubt of that, but they just didn't *do* it. Certainly, one or two baboons would never attack a man. A whole troop might do it, although Royce had never heard of such a thing, but not a couple of animals on their own.

That left the other thing, the thing that made the deep prints. An elephant? The idea was absurd.

The facts were simple enough. The baboons and whatever had made those sharp-edged prints had come together here, just as they had at the Baboonery. Two baboons were missing. A baboon was dead, the body still in the freezer. And now Kilatya was dead.

Facts were fine, but facts alone were never enough. What did they mean? What *could* they mean?

The two men got back into the Land Rover and Royce drove the rough trail to the Baboonery. He took it easy, concerned for Kilatya's body. Whenever he hit a hole in the road the corpse thumped soddenly in the tarp.

It was afternoon when he reached the thatched buildings in the clearing. It was hot again despite the dark clouds blowing across the sky. The caged baboons coughed out a greeting. Royce stared at them, his hackles rising.

Welcome home, he thought.

The Baboonery seemed very small and very lonely and very isolated.

When the Land Rover stopped, there was a smell of fear and death in the air.

5

There was no telephone at the Baboonery. There was no radio transmitter.

Royce told Kathy what had happened. He instructed Mutisya to stay with her and to make certain that the children did not stray from the main building. He climbed back into the Land Rover and made the short run to Matt Donaldson's safari camp—five neat green tents in a clearing located just before the trail crossed the Kikumbuliu. Matt's American clients were asleep in their tent, which simplified matters somewhat. Royce quickly explained the situation and Matt glanced at Kilatya's body.

"Get that bloke out of here, will you?" Donaldson said in a low voice. "You'll frighten my clients right out of their new safari boots."

"I'm taking him in to the police at Mitaboni."

"Want a bit of advice?"

Royce shrugged, wiping the sweat out of his eyes.

"Take old Kilatya out in the bush and plant him. Save you all sorts of trouble. The local Sherlocks will swarm over this place like flies. They won't find out anything, you can bank on that. They'll muck up my safari and you'll be filling out forms until your arm drops off."

Royce shook his head. "Can't do that. You know the law. Dammit, a man has been *killed.* I've got to find out what the hell is going on."

"You won't find out from the police. In the old days, maybe. Not now. Royce, these people are forever killing one another. Or maybe it was an accident; I don't know. I say forget it. Get yourself another driver."

Royce felt a flash of anger. "It's not that simple. I'm taking him to Mitaboni. Will you look in on Kathy if I'm delayed?"

"Certainly. No offense, Royce. You do what you think best. It's your *shauri.* Just remember, I warned you. Now please get that body out of here before our friends emerge to sample the wonders of the African afternoon."

"Right. Thanks, Matt."

Royce turned the vehicle around, went back past the Baboonery, and headed toward the main road to Mitaboni. It was slow going and he could hear the tarp-wrapped body thumping behind him. When he finally emerged on the paved road he gunned the Land Rover with a sense of relief.

He still had a couple of daylight hours left when he got to Mitaboni. He pulled up in front of the ramshackle post office and got out into the sultry air. The flies began to settle on the tarp in the back of the Land

Rover. He stepped into the public telephone booth outside the post office and closed the door. It took him half an hour to get a call through to the district headquarters at Machakos, a distance of a little better than one hundred miles. It took him another fifteen minutes to talk his way past a battery of officious clerks and get the ear of a captain in the Kenya Police. The captain told him that this was a very serious matter, which he already knew. The captain said that he was sure the local police could handle the situation, which Royce doubted. The captain thanked him for calling.

Royce left the telephone booth in something less than high good spirits. He was drenched with sweat. He drove across to the Mitaboni police station, carried Kilatya's body inside, and placed it on the long counter.

"I have a dead man here," he said to the building's only occupant.

The African policeman, dressed in a crisp blue shirt, shorts, and heavy shoes, thoughtfully unwrapped the tarp. "This man, he is dead."

"I know that."

"This matter is very serious."

"I know that."

"I will have to notify Machakos."

"I've done that."

The policeman eyed him suspiciously. "We will see."

Royce sighed and sat down. He stared at the fly-covered body on the counter while the officer attempted to contact Machakos. Another forty minutes went by. The policeman returned from his labors and confronted Royce. "I am in charge. This is a very serious matter. There must be an investigation."

"Good. That's why I'm here."

It took Royce two hours to relate what had happened while the policeman took laborious notes. The body remained on the counter the entire time. Nobody came into the station and nobody left it. The policeman informed Royce that he would be out the next day to search for "clues." Royce thanked him and left.

Darkness had fallen and the air was cooler. Stars gleamed through the broken clouds. Royce was tired, hungry, and disgusted. He made a quick detour on the way home to tell Bob Russell what had happened. He refused Russell's offer of food and pushed on to the Baboonery.

It was late when he got there. All the lights were on and Mutisya was sitting on the front steps.

"Everything okay, Mutisya?"

"Okay, Mr. Royce."

"Thank you. Go and get some sleep, Mutisya. Tell Elijah to post a watch."

Royce went on inside. He was too tired to think.

He knew one thing.

Everything was definitely *not* okay.

The police arrived the next morning—all three of them, comprising the entire Mitaboni police detachment. They proceeded to launch their investigation, and they soon had the place in a state of total confusion.

Royce held himself under control; there was nothing else he could do. The scene before him was something between a Marx Brothers' movie and watching a man trying to empty the ocean with a bucket. The police checked everything they could think of, including driver's licenses, passports, and trapping permits. They examined the dead baboon in the freezer. They grilled the African staff. They studied the baboons in the cages. They marched down to Donaldson's camp and looked at the tents. After a two-hour break for lunch—cooked by Wathome—they actually had Royce drive them out to where Kilatya's body had been found. They studied the tracks and scribbled away in notebooks.

When they were all through they went into a huddle. The officer in charge called Royce to him.

"This matter is very serious," he said.

Royce couldn't think of anything to say to that.

"You will not be charged," he said.

Royce couldn't think of anything to say to that either.

"It is our decision," the policeman said solemnly, "that this man was killed by baboons unknown."

Royce bit down hard on his pipe. He had the distinct feeling that wild laughter would not be appreciated.

"Wild animals in cages are very dangerous. Be more careful in times to come. If there is more trouble we will have to think again about the matter of trapping permits."

The policeman saluted and took his leave.

Royce watched the police Land Rover disappear in a cloud of dust. He put his hands on his hips. "Well, I'll be damned," he said.

He went into the kitchen and got a bottle of beer. He needed it.

He sprawled on the uncomfortable leather-covered couch, waiting for dinner, staring at nothing. Kathy was busy with the kids back in the bedroom, which was just as well. He didn't feel much like talking.

Somehow, he had to organize his thoughts.

The police had been a waste of time, but he couldn't blame them. This thing was completely outside the range of their experience. They knew their business when it came to accidents on the Mombasa road or cattle rustling or witch killings, but this....

A sound in the sky. A baboon torn apart with superhuman strength. Mysterious tracks. A man killed trailing a baboon….

Was there a cop in the world who could have made any sense out of all that?

Royce himself did not know what to think. The comic-opera interlude had done nothing to ease his mind. He knew that he was in danger even if he did not know exactly what the danger was. He was isolated here, vulnerable. He had a wife and two children to consider.

He also had a shipment of baboons to get out. He had men to feed and pay, equipment for which he was responsible. He could not just lock the door and walk out.

He fired up his pipe. His mind kept wandering. It was all so strange, so strange that he was here at all….

Two years ago, Africa had been little more than a splotch on a map to Royce Crawford. It was halfway between Edgar Rice Burroughs and actors shooting lions on TV—lions that were invariably "man-eaters terrorizing the native villages."

Royce had settled into a comfortable rut. It was a more interesting rut than most and he might have remained in it for the rest of his life if it had not been for Ben Wallace. After Royce had graduated from the University of Texas and served his time in the army, he was too restless to spend his years parked in an office by day and stuck in a tract house by night. There were two things that Royce liked. He enjoyed hunting and fishing, which kept him outdoors, and he liked to write straightforward prose that bore some relationship to the English language. In both of these activities, he was terribly old-fashioned. His country had become an urban land; most Texans lived in cities now, and their most violent form of exercise consisted of carrying beer from the refrigerator to the backyard barbecue pit. The writing that was currently much admired seemed to deal exclusively with sex hang-ups and the feeble joys of drug addiction.

Royce made the happy discovery that there was a market for more or less factual stories about hunting and fishing. He taught himself to take passable photographs, and he made an unspectacular living writing for magazines like *Field and Stream* and *Outdoor Life*. It was fun, but it got tougher as time went on. There were only so many basic variants on how to fish for bass in stock ponds and how to pot Texas deer in the wilds of Kerr County. He had to keep on the move, looking for unusual ideas, and living began to get complicated.

Then Ben Wallace had called.

Royce went to Houston to talk to him. He knew in a rough kind of way about the Foundation's medical research work in Africa, and he figured that Wallace wanted him to do an article on baboons. Instead, Wallace offered him a job in Africa.

"Why me?" Royce asked. "I'm not a doctor. I don't know anything about Africa."

"We don't want a doctor," Ben Wallace said. "*You* are not going to experiment on the baboons. We fly doctors in sometimes for work on the spot, but mostly we are concerned with getting the baboons out to the doctors—it's more economical that way. We want a man who knows something about animals. You do. We want a man who can hunt for meat. You can. We want a man who can get along in somewhat primitive circumstances. You do that all the time. We want a man who can get along with people. We think you can. We want a man with some education. Your college record was a good one. Don't sell yourself short, Mr. Crawford."

"Okay. I'm the answer to the Foundation's prayer. Why is the Foundation the answer to mine?"

Ben Wallace smiled. "May I speak frankly?"

"This would seem to be the time for it, Dr. Wallace."

"Very well. I've checked you out very carefully indeed. You're making a living out of your writing and that's about all. You don't have any compelling ties to keep you here for the next few years. Your oldest daughter—Susan—will be starting to school, but your wife can teach her the first-grade stuff. Susan will get far more out of a year or two in Africa than she's likely to get around here. You *could* go."

"Maybe I could. Why should I?"

"Look at it this way. We'll pay you ten thousand dollars a year to manage the Baboonery. That's about what you make in a good year here. The thing is, almost all of that will be clear profit. You will have no living expenses. We'll pay your passage over and back. Your quarters will be provided, and your food and a reasonable liquor allowance. We'll supply the ammunition for your hunting. Your job won't take more than five or six hours a day. You'll be sitting right smack in the middle of some of the best game country left in the world. You can do plenty of hunting and take all the pictures you need. You should be able to sell as many stories from there as you could poking around shooting jack rabbits in Texas. You can even take some time off and go fishing—there are some fine trout streams on Mount Kenya, you know, and there is good Indian Ocean fishing at Malindi. You'll have some interesting years at the Baboonery, and you'll wind up with two or three times the money you could make if you stayed home. That's why you should go. If you've got any arguments against that, I'd like to hear them."

Royce hadn't been able to think of any arguments.

That was how he had wound up at the Baboonery.

Of course, Ben Wallace had left a few things out of his description of paradise. Little things like fear and isolation and death....

Royce refilled his pipe. Houston seemed more than a world away.

Perhaps Kilatya *had* been killed by a baboon—or by baboons—unknown. Except that *unknown* was the wrong word. The right word was *alien.* Face it. Something had come down out of the sky. Something was walking through the bush that left an unearthly track. Something was *changing* the baboons....

How? Why?

Royce did not know and could not know. But even if his imagination was playing tricks on him, one thing was obvious: he ought to get Kathy and the kids away from the Baboonery. He could take them to Nairobi, put them up in a hotel whether they wanted to go or not. Then he could come back alone. Find out for sure what in the hell was going on. Then make a final decision....

Wathome stuck his head in from the kitchen and announced that dinner was ready. Kathy came in with Barbara.

"Where's Susan?"

"She's not feeling well. I don't know what's wrong with her. I put her to bed; she says she doesn't want any dinner." Kathy looked worried.

Royce joined them at the table. "Well, let's eat our dinner anyway. Maybe we'll all feel better later."

He hardly tasted his food. Kathy seemed so distracted that he did not try to talk to her. Perhaps it would be more sensible to wait until Susan was over her cold or whatever it was. He had a lot of work to do. As long as Matt Donaldson was camped down the road they were not alone.

Better to wait....

After the dinner dishes had been cleared away and Wathome had gone, the night seemed suddenly very large and very still. The moon, like a coin of old silver, was high in a cloud-shrouded sky. The air was chilly and a small breeze stirred through the leaves of the banana trees. The baboons were restless, coughing and grunting in their cages. Somewhere, far away in the depths of the night, a solitary leopard gave a harsh cry of anger at a missed kill.

Royce sat on the edge of the bed, puffing on his pipe. "Hear that *chui?* I know just how that old leopard feels. I thought we might get someplace with the police in here, but we're right where we were before. I really think we ought to get you and the kids to Nairobi. A couple of weeks at the Norfolk would do you good."

Kathy took off her dress and hung it in the closet. She went over to check on Susan and then sat down next to Royce, smoothing her slip over her knees. "Let's wait until Susan is better. She feels hot to me. Then we'll talk about it."

Royce kissed her, gently at first.

"Sex fiend," she whispered. "You might at least turn the light out."

"I was just being friendly."

"Be a little less friendly. But put that stinking pipe away. I have to draw the line somewhere."

Royce got up, turned off the light, undressed, and went to his wife.

Later, when he thought Kathy had gone to sleep, he got up again and pulled on his clothes.

"Where are you going?"

He bent over and kissed her lightly. "Just going to have a look around. I won't be long. Go back to sleep."

"Be careful," she said drowsily. "I love you."

"I love you," he said quietly. *Lord,* he thought, *I really do. I'm an anachronism. If anything ever happens to her or the kids…*

He picked up his pipe and the long flashlight he kept on the dresser. Closing the door behind him, he took the rifle out of the gun safe and checked its load. He went into the sitting room, filled his pipe, and lit it. It was bitter with too much smoking.

He did not turn on any lights.

He stepped outside, closing the door softly behind him. He could see fairly well by the light of the moon and stars. It was a strange world, a world without colors, but it was not difficult to orient himself. Objects had sharp outlines in the night; everything was either a luminous gray or a jet black, with nothing in between. It was almost cold. He wished that he had worn a jacket.

He started walking, circling the buildings, not using his flashlight. He was challenged once by Nzioki, one of Elijah's men. He was faintly surprised to find that the watch was actually being kept. He identified himself and kept walking. He was not looking for anything in particular. He was just looking.

At the very least, he could prowl around and satisfy himself that there was nothing lurking under the bedroom window. *I'm like an old maid checking under the bed,* he thought. *What do I do if I find someone—or something?*

He went all the way around the main building. He saw nothing unusual and heard nothing. He repeated his effort on the building that housed the operating rooms and his office. Nothing there.

He stood for a long time and watched the quarters of the African staff. There were no lights showing. Everything was quiet. He walked along the line of baboon cages, not getting too close. The animals stirred and grunted sleepily. That was all.

Royce knocked out his pipe against his shoe, refilled it from the tin he had put in his hip pocket, and lit it with a match. The flare of the light seemed very bright. It took his eyes a long moment to adjust again after the match went out.

Little man, what now?

He started off along the dirt road that eventually skirted the railroad track. This was the way that Kilatya had gone. He walked almost silently, flashlight in his left hand and rifle in his right. He did not intend to go far. Once he left the cleared area of the Baboonery and the smell of man, there was always the chance of running into animals. He did not fancy running into a big cat in the middle of the night, with or without a rifle. He smiled a little, remembering those ads that filled the magazines he wrote for. *Attacked by a killer lion, I would have been lost without my Little Dandy Hotshot Flashlight Batteries! Blinding the beast with my flashlight's titanic glare, I whipped out my pipe and blew smoke in his nose until he fell to the earth....*

The whistle of an oncoming train startled him for a moment. The thing always took him by surprise, although it was a soft whistle, the sort of sound he always associated with a model railroad. A train just seemed so unlikely here.

It was even quieter once the train had gone by. There wasn't a sound in the bush. It was a land of the dead.

He was ready to turn back when something caught his eye. Off there in the distance to his right. At first, he thought it was a light from the train. But the light did not move and the *quality* of it was wrong. It was a soft, pale glow, almost like moonlight. It was steady and utterly silent.

Royce took a deep breath. That glow was coming from the area where that thing from the sky had come down. It couldn't be more than a couple of miles away.

He did not pause to consider a plan of action. He wanted to get a look at whatever was producing that eerie light. He headed toward it.

There was no trail. He walked directly into the bush, moving as quietly as possible, using his flashlight sparingly. The glow ahead of him seemed to intensify that darkness. Thorns ripped at his clothing. Twice he had to backtrack to get around thick clumps of brush. He was worried about snakes. Nesting birds fluttered up before him. His hands were wet with sweat in the cool night air.

The glow was a little closer. He figured he had covered half a mile, maybe more.

Then, quite suddenly, the glow…stopped.

It wasn't there.

There was only the moonlight and the stars and the hush of the night.

Royce stood stock still and waited. Long minutes crept by. The glow did not return.

He finally turned and began to retrace his steps. There was nothing else to do. Without the light to guide him it was madness to search the bush in the middle of the night. He made his way back to the trail and almost ran toward the dark Baboonery.

He was very tired but his mind was churning. He went into the cold kitchen and drank a bottle of beer, standing at the window and looking out at the cloud-shadowed stars. The beer helped a little.

He walked silently into the bedroom and checked his sleeping family. He put the rifle under the bed. He undressed in the dark and slipped into bed next to Kathy. She stirred but did not awaken.

Royce lay in the silence staring at nothing. His mind was filled with questions that had no answers.

6

The days drifted by, one by one. Royce was not lulled by the routine of running the Baboonery, but he was preoccupied. He had a lot to do, and he made the mistake of postponing the decisions he had to make.

Each day the dark clouds rolled through the great sky, throwing racing shadows across the parched land. It was hot again, hotter than ever with a dry wind that picked at the naked trees and piled the red dust in gritty drifts that rippled like sand dunes. The animals were pink-eyed and irritable, sticking close to the lowering streams. The white termite hills, taller than a man, stood out like sentinels in the barren plains. The promise of rain was worse than the blue skies and blazing sun had been; day after day the arid earth stared up at the tantalizing swollen clouds, waiting, waiting, forever waiting....

Susan seemed to be getting better, but she had a lingering fever. Her temperature shot up briefly to 102, then dropped down to around 99 and stayed there. She rested comfortably; she slept a lot and was very quiet. At least she was not getting worse. Royce was afraid to take her to Nairobi until she recovered some of her strength.

Kathy doctored Susan from the suitcase full of medical supplies she had insisted on bringing with her. She stayed with her day and night, and Susan was pleased with all the attention. Barbara was left to young Mbali, the shamba boy, which suited her fine. Royce was amazed at the patience shown by Mbali, who was little more than a child himself. Barbara adored him. Every night she would tell Royce with shining eyes of some wonderful new thing that "Bally" had done with her. Royce was deeply grateful to Mbali, and told him so. Mbali just smiled, looking down at his bare feet, and shyly said that he liked the girls. He said that he prayed for Susan at night, and Royce believed him.

Royce made no further attempt to search the bush. It was too much like asking for trouble. He did not see the strange glow in the night again.

They built strong wooden shipping crates for the baboons. The generator broke down and Royce spent a day repairing it. Royce and Mutisya found a good new area for the traps and salted it with maize and pineapple to bring in the baboons. They went out with a crew of men and finished the dirty job of moving the heavy traps.

The trapping went slowly, and Royce needed some big males for his shipment. It seemed to him that the ratio of trapped males to females was unusually low. There were a lot of empty traps. He examined them carefully. Sometimes, the bait was gone but nothing was caught in the trap. Baboons did escape from the traps occasionally, but he could find no sign that the traps had been forced from within. If something were releasing baboons from the traps, then that something had learned to open the traps properly. There were no damaged traps. At the Baboonery, the cages were undisturbed.

Royce saw baboons lurking at the edge of the clearing around the Baboonery several times. It had happened before; even elephants had been known to parade along the trail right by the front door. The baboons bothered him now, though. They seemed to be *watching* him. He knew that he was jittery but he saw no point in taking chances. Whenever he spotted baboons near the clearing he took his light rifle and drilled them neatly through the head. The buzzards did the rest.

The day finally came when Matt Donaldson loaded his clients into his Land Rover and carted them back to Nairobi to catch a plane for home. Matt left his camp intact, explaining that he intended to return shortly with some new hunters he was expecting.

Royce's sense of uneasiness increased sharply when Matt had gone. He was afraid to make his trapping run and leave Kathy and the kids alone. Susan was definitely getting better. She was stronger now, almost her old self again. Surely, the trip to Nairobi would not harm her in a day or two….

He decided to tell Kathy to pack her gear.

He stood on the steps of the Baboonery, staring up at the cloud-darkened sky. He felt as though he were trapped in a dream, marking time.

The hot, dry wind plucked at his shirt.

If only it would rain, he thought crazily.

If only it would rain.

Royce woke up early in the morning on the first day of November. He was fully awake but he did not move for a moment. Kathy had been up during the night with Susan and she was still sound asleep. He looked at the white curtains on the windows. They were hardly moving at all; the air was still. He could see the light of the sun behind the curtains.

The cloud cover was breaking, then. The rains were already late. Some years, he knew, the rains never came….

There was a curious heavy smell in the air. Royce couldn't quite place it. He got up quietly, pulled on his clothes, and went into the empty kitchen. He took out the electric coffeepot that Wathome never used and plugged it in.

He stepped outside to have a look around.

He saw him at once, sitting under his bedroom window. A big male baboon. The animal just sat there, staring at him. Its red-rimmed eyes were challenging and unafraid. There was white saliva on his snout.

Royce felt a stab of fear. For a moment, he could not move. He had seen plenty of baboons in his time, but this one was…different. There was a cold intelligence looking out through those animal eyes. The beast was *studying* him.

"Okay, Big Daddy," Royce whispered. "You just sit there for ten more seconds."

Royce whirled and started back inside to get his rifle. He stopped before he got through the door. That smell. It was much stronger now. The baboon, yes, but there was something else.

The baboon still made no move.

Royce looked down the trail that led to the main road. The fear came again, a fear that was close to horror.

He ran into the house, trying to think, trying not to panic.

It would take more than a rifle to help him now.

Royce hesitated for a long minute in the kitchen. It would not help matters any to go flying off in all directions at once. He had to get things organized, and he had to do it fast. His senses were suddenly sharp: he was aware of the coffeepot bubbling on the table, the hum of the refrigerator, the nervous stirring of the baboons outside in their cages….

He strode quickly into the breezeway between the kitchen and the bedroom and opened the gun safe. He took out the .375 and a box of cartridges.

He went into the bedroom and bent over his sleeping wife. He touched her shoulder, gently.

"Kathy. Kathy, wake up."

She stirred and opened sleep-fogged eyes.

"Kathy honey. Come on, wake up. We've got trouble. I need your help."

She sat up, coming back to consciousness with a visible effort. "What is it? Is Susan…?"

"Susan's okay. She's still asleep. Are you awake enough to remember what I tell you? I haven't got much time."

Kathy rubbed her eyes. "I guess so. What's going on?"

"Come over here to the window." Royce kept his voice steady.

She climbed out of bed and followed him to the window. He pulled back the curtains. The baboon was gone, but that was a minor problem now. He pointed. "Look at that."

Already, it was worse. Away across the red-brown earth, not over four hundred yards from the Baboonery buildings, a wall of dirty smoke boiled up into the morning sky. A jagged line of orange flame blazed under the smoke. It was a big fire, a very big fire, and even as they watched it seemed to move closer. A kudu bolted out of the bush, ran across the clearing, and vanished behind the main building. The sky was full of birds.

"Jesus H. Christ," Kathy said.

"Get the picture? Just another humdrum episode of *Breakfast with the Crawfords.*"

Kathy managed a smile and Royce found himself smiling in return. Kathy had a strength in her that always surprised him. Whatever his problems, she wasn't one of them. "Okay," he said. "You get the kids up, take them into the kitchen, and give them something to eat. There's time for that. Make sure Susan gets her medicine. There's coffee ready in the pot. Take the .38 with you and keep it with you—it's in the dresser. When you finish in the kitchen, you and the kids go and sit in the Land Rover. I want to know exactly where you are. If we can't lick this fire—and our chances are not too bright—we'll take off down that back road to Mitaboni. How was Susan last night?"

"About the same. When you called me I was afraid…"

"I'm scared right now, I'll tell you that. Dammit, Kathy, something is trying to burn me out of here."

"Maybe you ought to take the hint."

Royce realized with a kind of wonder that he hadn't really considered quitting, not yet. Getting Kathy and the children out was one thing, running him off was something else again. "If I'm licked, that'll be the time to run away. I'm not licked yet."

She didn't argue. "We're wasting time. Do what you have to do. But for God's sake be careful. I'm not ready to be a widow yet."

Royce grabbed the .375 and ran out the back door of the breezeway. The sharp smell of the fire was stronger now. The baboons in the cages were pacing and grunting. Behind him, the great cloud of smoke rose like a seething brown mountain into the still air.

He had time for some fleeting thoughts even as he ran; all of his senses had speeded up to the point that he could look back on his usual self as though he had been a slow-motion zombie. A man never realized how much he took for granted until it was all taken away. In the world Royce had known, when someone in your family got sick, you called the doctor. If someone threatened your life, you called the police. If fire broke out, you picked up the phone and hollered for the fire department.

It was different here, worlds and centuries different. He began to appreciate what a people like the Kamba were up against. Plagues, famines, fires—what could a man do? A fire in a dry land was not just an annoyance, not just an insurance-covered curiosity staged as a passing entertainment—it was a blazing monster, an all-devouring horror, an implacable wall of destruction.

It was a killer, and his weapons against it were a joke.

And if the baboons turned on them…

"Elijah!" he hollered, beating on the door of his headman's quarters. "Mutisya! Wathome! Come out quick, hurry! *Mota!* Fire!"

He waited impatiently as the men tumbled out. He did have water; that was something. But the pressure was nothing much, and he had only the one hose that Mbali used for watering the garden and keeping the dust down. He couldn't stop that fire with a garden hose, that was for sure. He had shovels and axes and rakes, but he didn't have enough manpower….

And he didn't know enough, either. He had never fought a big fire in his life.

Well, this was a good time to start learning.

The Africans stared at the smoke and sniffed the air. They did not panic. They simply waited for instructions. Their confidence in him was touching but not very helpful.

"Elijah. What should we do?"

Elijah examined the smoke solemnly through his tinted glasses. "It is a very large fire, Mr. Royce."

Royce waited. Elijah said nothing else.

"In the place where the doctors cut on the baboons," Mutisya volunteered, "there is a machine for putting out fires."

Royce had forgotten about the fire extinguisher—not that it made any difference. One fire extinguisher for a forest fire—it might have been funny under other circumstances. It wasn't particularly hilarious now.

"Okay," he said. "This is what we'll do. Mbali, you take the hose and put the water on everything you can reach. Try to get the thatch on top of the buildings as wet as you can. Do you understand?"

"Ndio." The boy, pleased to be trusted with important work, ran off to get the hose.

"Elijah, take all of the men and supply them with tools—shovels, rakes, axes, pangas if you've got some. Get between the fire and the buildings and clear that area of anything that will burn. Then we'll try to dig some kind of a trench—at least get the grass turned under. I'll go down to Donaldson's camp and round up the men there. I'll join you as soon as I can. Any questions?"

Elijah shook his head. He looked dubious. "It is a very large fire, Mr. Royce," he said again.

"Do your best. That's all I ask. I'll be back in a minute."

Royce didn't wait to check up on them. There was no time. He piled into the Land Rover—Kathy and the kids were still inside the building—and jolted down to Donaldson's camp. He found four men there and some good tools. He drove them back to the Baboonery, parked the Land Rover in a reasonably shady spot for Kathy, and ran for the fire.

As soon as he got close to it his heart sank. The fire was an inferno—a solid wall of blistering heat and choking smoke. It was moving, not fast but inexorably, toward the Baboonery. It was a noisy fire: it hissed and crackled and roared at him, telling him things he did not want to know.

He had a couple of things in his favor, he figured. He tried to concentrate on them. There was no wind at all. That was a real break. Once that fire got a wind behind it they were through. And they had kept the land around the buildings fairly clear of brush; there wasn't much to burn in this area. If they could keep the flames from jumping to the buildings…

Don't think. Work, dammit. Set an example.

He uprooted small, dry bushes and ran with them away from the fire. He scooped up sticks and twigs and tufts of brown grass. The sweat poured from his body in drops and trickles and streams. Smoke reddened his eyes and clogged his throat. The fire roared at him, punched at him with fists of heat. He lost all track of time; he was trapped in an eternal *now,* a moment that stretched on forever, a moment where nothing changed, nothing made any difference….

He ran back and Mbali hosed down his hot skin with water. Even the water felt hot. He went on working in a kind of madness, his eyes wild and bloodshot.

The fire drove them back. They couldn't get close to the flames; the searing heat reached out for them, hammered them with a wind from hell. Mutisya's hair began to smolder and he ran screaming for the hose, beating at his head with his raw and bleeding hands.

There were snakes, too many snakes, driven from cover by the crackling heat. Royce saw a six-foot green mamba, its thin body writhing in agony in the dirt. He reached for his rifle, picked it up, and tried to take aim. His hands were shaking so badly he couldn't draw a bead on the snake. Wathome ran up and sliced off its head with a panga.

They were losing their fight. Dimly, Royce knew that they could not win. The fire was too big, too fierce, too totally overpowering.

One more effort….

"Stop!" he yelled. No one heard him. "Stop!" he screamed at the top of his voice. "The trench! Dig the trench!"

He grabbed a shovel and retreated away from the heat. The smoke was so thick he could hardly catch his breath. He began to dig, trying to make a wide furrow the fire could not jump. The crust of the earth was as hard as rock. He jammed the shovel into it, cursing it, fighting it. The handle of the shovel was slippery with his own blood. He was so weak that his knees were trembling. His mind began to spin.

He sensed an animal running by him. Heard the thuds of hooves on the unyielding ground. Saw stripes. A zebra....

He fell. He could not get up. He started to crawl away from the fire. His throat was a parched ache. He could not swallow.

He had failed. They had to get out before they were all killed.

"Give it up!" he tried to yell. His voice was little more than a croak. "Get the lorry, get the men out. Elijah..."

Then he heard it. He heard it before he felt anything at all. A hissing sound, a strange hissing, a new hissing that cut through the roar of the fire.

It sounded...

What did it sound like?

He shook his head. It was like a campfire when you poured what was left of the coffee on it. A wet hissing, a hissing like water on flame....

He rolled over, turning his face up to the sky.

He felt it then. Water. Big fat drops of water. Rain!

He said it aloud, tasting the word, tasting the cool drops that splashed on his parched lips. "Rain, rain, rain...."

It came down harder, dripping through the dense clouds of smoke.

He threw out his arms and let it come.

It poured. It rained buckets and lakes and rivers. It soaked him. His skin drank it in like a blotter.

He began to laugh.

He laughed like a crazy man, letting the rain pound him into a growing sea of mud.

Suddenly, incredibly, the whole world was laughing.

He pulled himself to his feet, grabbed his rifle, and staggered for shelter. He couldn't stop laughing. He didn't want to stop. Everyone was laughing. Rain!

"Come on, rain!" he muttered. "Don't quit. Don't ever quit. Rain like you've never rained before!"

He jerked open the breezeway door and stepped inside. He stood there, swaying. Kathy had come in and she stared at him almost without recognition. His clothes were torn, his hair singed. His face was black and greasy with smoke. His arms were smeared with blood and dirt.

"It's raining," he said inanely.

Then he collapsed in a heap on the floor.

When he came to, he could hear it before he opened his eyes. A wild wet drumming on the roof. He could smell it. A fresh clean damp smell, the sweet smell of water, a smell of oceans of rain pouring down on a thirsty earth.

Royce knew the thrill of rain in a dry land. He was no stranger to the electric excitement of a cloudburst after long months of dry, searing heat. But he had never felt it this keenly before. This was more than rain. This was...

Well, hell.

This was life itself.

He opened his eyes.

"The fire?" His voice was a painful rasp.

Kathy handed him a glass of water. He choked it down. It was cool on his throat, cool and wet and soothing.

"There isn't any fire. There's nothing out there but a puddle as big as the Indian Ocean."

Royce tried to get out of bed, failed, and tried again. This time he made it. His body was one dull ache from head to toe. He stumbled over to the window and looked out.

It was a new world. The earth was gray under leaden skies that poured down silvery sheets of rain. Where the fire had been there was an ugly carbon-black scar. The naked land around the Baboonery was splashed with miniature lakes. Rain beat a tattoo on the roof and dripped in a steady stream from the thatch. In the puddles, the big drops hit like bullets, throwing up little geysers of spray. A wet smell filled the air with a heavy, tangible scent.

He took a deep breath. "What time is it?"

"About eight in the morning. You've been out for around fourteen hours. I figured you could use the sleep."

"Where did it come from?"

"It started to cloud up around noon yesterday. I guess you didn't see it because of the smoke. At first I didn't think anything of it—we've had the clouds before—and then I couldn't get through to you. You were...well, I've never seen you like that before."

"I hope you never see me that way again. Did you catch the news last night?"

She nodded. "The rains have started all over southern Kenya. It was raining in Nairobi when the news came on. I guess this is it."

Royce sat down on the bed again. He felt like hell. Everything hit him with a rush. He'd seen that crazy baboon and something had tried to burn them out of the Baboonery, and he had cleverly passed out and left his wife alone. If anything had happened...

"The kids?"

"They're having breakfast with Wathome."

"Susan?"

"She's better, I think. Maybe this rain has helped her, somehow. There was no fever this morning." She sat down next to him and took his hand. "Stop worrying. You're in no shape to wrestle with any problems yet. We're all safe and the fire is out."

"But…"

"After breakfast, okay? You didn't get around to eating yesterday—it's not like you to forget *that*."

"I don't have time to eat…."

"Royce. Look at me. If you get sick and conk out on us, what happens then? You go take a shower—the water's a little muddy but not too bad yet—and get some clean clothes on. I'll fix breakfast. *Then* we'll worry. Deal?"

"Deal."

Royce peeled off his pajamas—Kathy had somehow managed to get his dirty clothes off after he had passed out—and stepped gingerly into the shower stall. He turned on the taps and waited. The water got lukewarm but not hot. Maybe that was just as well; there never was any really hot water until the cook stove had been going for two or three hours. The water was brownish and gritty but it felt good against his skin. He let it soak in for ten minutes or so and then shaved and dressed. He felt better. His hands were cut and blistered and his hair and eyebrows were singed, but otherwise he seemed to be okay except for a persistent ache in his shoulders.

He had been lucky, very lucky. But it would not do to push his luck too far. He had been warned. The fates would not likely intervene on his behalf again. He had to get Kathy and the kids away from this place.

He stepped out of the bedroom into the breezeway. The rain was coming down in solid sheets and the plank floor was slick with moisture. The dry warmth of the kitchen was suddenly very welcome.

He shook hands with Wathome and thanked him for all he had done the day before. Then he greeted the kids. Barby was bright-eyed as usual, and eager to go play in the rain. Susan looked better, much better. He gave her a kiss. Surely, she could stand the trip to Nairobi now.

He seated himself at the wooden dining table in the main room and discovered that he was famished. He put away a pile of Kathy's scrambled eggs and six slices of fried Spam—available at the curiously named Supermarket in Nairobi, an edifice that contained everything from groceries to a tearoom, and an institution that endeared itself to visitors by stocking such exotic foods as hamburger and Chef Boy-Ar-Dee spaghetti. As far as Royce was concerned, Spam was considerably better than Kenya bacon, and it hit the spot this morning. He drank three cups of coffee and began to feel almost human.

He pushed his cup back. "There," he said. "Now we can attend to our worrying."

"Okay." Kathy lit a cigarette. She looked fresh and relaxed, as though she had been enjoying herself on a carefree vacation. "Worry away."

Royce considered. "I'm not much for giving orders," he said slowly, "but I'm giving one now. It's time for you and the kids to get out of here. Susan is well enough to take the trip to Nairobi. We can put you up at the Norfolk. I can come back here and do what has to be done. I can take care of myself, but its too dangerous for *you* to hang around here. I...what the devil are you laughing about?"

Kathy's laughter had an edge of hysteria to it; she wasn't as relaxed as she looked. "I listened to the news while you were taking your shower. I'm afraid your plan won't work."

"Why the hell not?"

"You hear that rain out there?"

"I'm not deaf."

"Well, old sport, we've had better than six inches of rain since yesterday. There's no end to it in sight, either. We could never make it through that gunk to the main road. Even if we *did* make it we couldn't go anywhere."

Royce felt a sudden cold knot in the pit of his stomach. He hadn't been thinking. This was Kenya, not the United States. The main road to Nairobi was paved after a fashion, but the bridges...

"There are cars stuck all along the road," Kathy said. "Every last crossing between here and Nairobi is under water, and it's the same way between here and Mombasa."

"The train?"

"They're holding them at both ends of the line. Same deal—tracks covered with water and a couple of the bridges too dangerous to cross."

Royce stood up. "That's just great."

He listened to the rain pounding down on the thatch roof. He should have known. Everything stopped when the rains came. Even back home, all through the southwest, a good gully-washer could knock out a road. And here...

"How are we fixed for food?"

"Pretty good. Enough for a couple of weeks, anyway."

Royce pulled at his ear. He had plenty of petrol on hand; he could keep the generator and the pumps going for a month if he didn't use the truck or the Land Rover. And he wouldn't be using the vehicles in that soup out there. They were in no immediate danger from the rain. Unhappily, the rain was the least of his worries.

"We'll just have to wait until the water goes down," he said, trying to get a confidence into his voice that he was far from feeling. Kathy had

had enough shocks. She wasn't Superwoman. He had to be careful, very careful. "It can't keep on raining like this for long. It doesn't rain *continuously* during the rainy season. If the sun comes out for a day or two we'll be able to make it."

"If the bridges hold."

"We'll worry about crossing the bridges when we can get to them, to coin a phrase. I'd better go out and check things over. We may have a flood on our hands if this keeps up."

"Royce?"

He knew what was coming. He did not know what he could say. He waited.

"Royce, what *is* it? I mean…what's happening? Is there something *after* us?" Kathy laughed nervously, almost in embarrassment. There had been no melodrama in the world she knew. They had all been conditioned to a different kind of life. Indian raids, ghosts, outbreaks of plague—those things were over and done with, dead as the dinosaurs. Even here, linked by an umbilical cord to the world outside, such things were anachronisms. They just couldn't happen. The fabric of their lives, the assumptions they took for granted—they could not simply *disappear.*

Royce hesitated. The words were hard to say. There was a kind of magic to words. If you did not put a name to a thing, it was not quite real. It might go away, it might be nothing at all….

Say it. Spit it out. She has a right to know.

"It's just a guess, Kathy," he said. "I may be wrong. I hope I'm wrong. But I think we have visitors. And I don't think they come from…well, anywhere on this earth."

She stared at him. She seemed shocked not so much by what he said as the fact that *he* had said it. "You? Things from another world? You always said those people—people who believed in that stuff—you always said they were a bunch of nuts."

He shrugged. "I said I'd believe it when I saw it with my own eyes. I think I have. I don't give a damn about theories. I don't care if a million lunatics saw visions in their backyards. All I know is that I'm faced with a situation and I have to deal with it as best I can. I can't refuse to face it just because of some stupid name tags. Call that thing I saw a glotz if you want to. I think we've got one."

"But here? In the middle of nowhere? It's crazy. What would they want here?"

"Facts aren't crazy just because we don't happen to understand them. Let's assume they want baboons, for openers. That's what they've taken. Let's assume they want us. We're the ones who are here—you and I and the kids and Wathome and Mutisya and Elijah and the rest."

"But *why?* It doesn't make any sense."

"It doesn't make any sense to *us*. Why should it? If there really are beings out there somewhere, and if they did decide to pay us a call, their motives might be absolutely alien to us. Maybe they came all this way to do the equivalent of throwing a pie in our face. Maybe they came here because they have a passion for snails or butterflies or baobab trees—how in the hell would I know?"

Kathy, strangely, looked relieved. The unknown was a fearful thing. But this sort of notion—something that rational people had laughed at for years—this couldn't be *serious*. "This will all seem funny in a day or two. There must be some perfectly reasonable explanation for it all. The fire could have started naturally—a spark from the train, an African tossing a cigarette into the bush. Maybe the baboons are just sick or something."

"Maybe." Royce managed a smile. "Maybe I'm just tired. But it is raining, and I've got work to do."

He walked into the bedroom to get his raincoat and boots. The rain was coming down in buckets. There was half an inch of water on the floor of the breezeway.

He listened to the rains with new ears. The rains had saved the Baboonery, no doubt of that. Probably, the rains had saved his neck as well. But there was a bitter irony in those driving rains.

They were completely isolated now. There could be no help from anyone. The rains could not alter the basic fact: someone—something—was out to get them. He did not believe for a moment that there was no logic or reason to *their* actions, whoever or whatever *they* might be. He was ready to take them at face value. They had come. They had taken baboons. They had killed. They had threatened the Baboonery.

And here he was, with his family.

Sitting ducks.

He was cut off as surely as though he had been trapped on the moon.

7

Royce stuck the .38 in his jacket pocket where it would stay dry and stepped outside. It was incredible how much everything had changed. The very air had a new smell to it, an underwater smell, a smell of sand on the beach when the tide ran out. His boots sank into gummy mud that was inches thick. There was a solid sheet of water beginning only thirty yards or so back of the baboon cages. The gray sky was thick and close and the rain poured down with numbing force.

He stood in the driving rain and tried to think. It was at least possible that the beings who had come out of the sky might be slowed up in their activities by the rain. It was also possible that they might welcome it; he could not know. In any event, there were three things that had to be done without delay.

He slogged around to the men's quarters and rapped on Elijah's door. *"Hodi?"* he shouted.

There was a moment's pause. Then he heard Elijah's voice. *"Hodi."*

Royce shoved the door open and stepped inside. Elijah was sitting on his bed, warming his hands over a small charcoal stove. He still wore the inevitable tinted glasses.

Royce stood there dripping. "Elijah, I know you're tired. I'm tired too. But there's a lot of work to be done."

Elijah sighed. "We cannot stop the rain, Mr. Royce."

Royce felt a brief irritation. He stifled it. "You have all done very well. I appreciate it. But we have to protect the pumps and the generator. The baboon cages have to be moved. We can't just sit in our houses and wait for better days."

Elijah said nothing.

"I want the men out, Elijah. I want you on the cages—we'll have to move them into the shed. I want Mutisya to take charge of getting some runoff ditches built around the pumps and the generator. Have Mr. Donaldson's men gone back to their camp?"

"They are not here, Mr. Royce."

"Well, they'll have their hands full with those tents. I'll check later and see if they need any food. Let's get with it, Elijah."

Elijah moved slowly, but he moved. He shrugged into a plastic raincoat that had been supplied by the Baboonery and stepped out into the rain with obvious reluctance. Royce followed him out.

It was a bad day.

The men were tired and they worked in a kind of stupor. Royce had to ride herd on all of them, directing each job in time-consuming detail. Only Mutisya and Mbali showed any initiative at all.

Royce kept his temper under control. There were times when the Africans drew away from him, retreating into their own values and their own ways. It did no good to shout at them. Of course, their own jobs were at stake in keeping the Baboonery operational, but he refrained from pointing this out. They had their own problems; he could not expect them to view things through his eyes. He kept a smile on his face and did the major share of the work without complaint. They needed each other. He would be up the creek if the men turned surly. They would be in trouble if the power failed and they just sat in their rooms waiting for something to happen. Royce ducked in and told Wathome to fix an unusually hearty dinner, and he set aside a case of precious beer to give the men with their evening meal.

Somehow, he got the job done.

The baboons were moved into the shed. Baboons, like all large primates, were very susceptible to respiratory ailments. He couldn't leave them out where the rain swept through their cages. It took four men on each cage to lift them. The wet, angry animals kept trying to grab the shoulders of the carriers, which didn't help any. That was normal, though. Royce examined the baboons closely but saw nothing unusual about them. They were just baboons—unlovely, ill-tempered, nasty, but not alien in any way.

They dug drainage ditches around the pumps and the generator and used empty shipping crates to shore up the weak points. It was hard, back-breaking work. They were all soaked to the skin before nightfall. It made little difference whether a man kept his raincoat on or took it off. If he kept it on, his sweat drenched him from inside. If he took it off, the rain pelted him unmercifully. Royce took his off by early afternoon. The rain at least was cool.

All that day, he forced himself to keep alert. He did not know exactly what he was watching for, but he was confident that he could recognize anything unusual if he saw it. He spotted nothing suspicious.

When it was too dark to work further, he stumbled into the main building. He was very tired; the last two days had taken their toll. He didn't really want any dinner but he made himself change into dry clothes and eat something.

"Daddy," Susan said happily, "the roof is leaking."

"Daddy will fix it tomorrow," he said.

He fell into bed before the after-dinner coffee came.

He knew that he was courting disaster by going to sleep before he had established any sort of a guard, but he had to take a chance. He could not stay awake himself. The men were as tired as he was. It was raining so hard that visibility was close to zero.

He slept instantly.

Once, deep in the night, a sudden stillness awakened him. For a moment, he couldn't figure out what it was. Then he realized that the rain had stopped. Moonlight was streaming in through the curtains. He could hear a distant roaring over the light drip of the water from the sodden thatch on the roof. Sleep-fogged, his tired brain puzzled over the strange sound. It came to him that the roaring must be the Kikumbuliu River. Only a few hours ago, or so it seemed, the Kikumbuliu had been a narrow trickle of water that he could drive a Land Rover through. It must be a raging torrent now.

He stared at the moonlight. Maybe the rain had stopped for good. Maybe, in the morning, the sun would shine.

He knew that he should get up and take a look around. He started to sit up in the bed. Kathy pushed him down again. "I'm awake," she said. "I'll call you if there's any need. Go back to sleep."

Exhausted, he slept again.

He dreamed no dreams.

Royce slept until nearly ten o'clock the next morning and when he woke up it took an effort for him to get out of bed. It was raining again; he could hear it thudding on the roof thatch. It didn't seem to be coming down quite as hard as the day before, but it was raining steadily. The whole room had a damp smell to it.

He listened for the thumping of the generator and was faintly reassured when he heard it. At least they still had power.

He went in to eat his breakfast.

"Welcome to Noah's Ark," Kathy said.

"We've got the baboons," he said. "That's a start."

He ate his breakfast slowly. Each item of food had now become a thing to be appreciated and savored. Coffee, cream, eggs, bacon, bread—when they were gone, that was it. A man could hunt in that swamp out there for a long, long time without finding a chicken or a pig, to say nothing of coffee or wheat. He might find a cow if he were lucky, but it wasn't likely. The Kamba would keep their herds close to home; there was no need to search for water now.

It was curious, Royce thought. The Baboonery had always seemed a lonely kind of place to him, stuck out in the middle of the African bush. By most standards, it had been isolated from the first. But it was different now, very different. There was no lifeline to connect him with the outside world. He could not pile in the Land Rover and go to Mitaboni for tobacco or milk. He could not depend on the train to bring in needed supplies. He couldn't even get a letter out.

He was beginning to understand the meaning of true isolation. He didn't like it, but it did not panic him. He told himself that a century ago things had not been so very different for some of his own ancestors in Texas. There had been small settlements and farms and ranches in his own state as remote as the Baboonery was now. There had been fires and floods and sickness and Comanches. Whatever it was that had come down out of the sky to threaten him, it was not more mysterious or more deadly than the Indians had seemed to his own people less than one hundred years ago. It was a strange thought, and an oddly comforting one.

If his ancestors had endured, he could do the same. Surely, he had not become that much less of a man in a mere hundred years.

"Did you catch the news?"

"I caught it. You can see most of it outside. It's raining all over Kenya. The roads are all knocked out and a lot of the bridges are already gone. It's a real dilly."

"How's the roof holding out?"

"Not bad, considering. We've got about a dozen leaks."

"I'll see what I can do. I have a sneaking sort of suspicion that we won't be going anywhere for a spell."

"Just try to take it a little easy today. I'd feel a hell of a lot safer if I didn't have a dead man in bed with me at night."

"There's some life in the old boy yet."

"See that it stays there. You know how we modern women are. Restless, unsatisfied, pampered—I may take up with a baboon."

"You won't find them very effective."

"Maybe not. But I can write my memoirs and make a fortune."

"Not a chance. *Beauty and the Baboon*—it'd be so tame these days that nobody would pay any attention to it."

"We could make it a female baboon, a crazy mixed-up baboon girl with a grudge against the world, a baboon raised from infancy by a Chinese spy...."

Royce grinned. "Knock it off. I'm going up on the roof and dig in the thatch."

"Very symbolic," Kathy said.

Royce went out into the rain, feeling better than he had any right to feel. Everything looked normal, aside from a certain bottom-of-the-sea impression. It was possible, he supposed, that *they* were hampered by the rain just as he was. It couldn't be easy for them to maneuver in an alien environment. They had shown that they could opeate under dry conditions, but perhaps the mud and the water would slow them down. Baboons, too, did not take well to heavy rains....

He checked the generator and the pumps and got Elijah to do some more work on the drainage ditches. He found Mutisya and told him to keep an eye out for game. If they were going to be cut off for any length of time, they had to have meat.

Then he went to work on the roof. He plugged the leaks as quickly as he could, not taking the time to do the job properly. There was other work to do before nightfall.

He needed more lights. The hours of darkness were long and dangerous. The baboon cages had been tampered with at night, Kilatya had been killed at night, the bush had been fired at night. He had a light on a pole next to the generator, another one over the door to the building that housed the operating room, and a third light between the kitchen and the men's barracks. The area in front of the Baboonery depended on the light that filtered through the windows of the main building, and that wasn't good enough. There was a guest house out there, a square thatched structure that was little more than a bedroom and a bathroom. It was already wired for electricity. If he could rig up a light socket above the door, keep a bulb burning there at night…well, it might be useful.

He had to do *something*.

He collected the necessary gear from the supply room, which was next to his office, and walked through the pelting rain to the guest house. He hadn't been in there for a long time. It was never used except by the visiting doctors, and there hadn't been any doctors around for quite a spell. The little house was damp but oddly stuffy despite the open windows. It had a smell of loneliness and disuse about it. A great king-sized bed that stood several feet off the floor dominated the room. It was neatly made up, ready for a giant. Kathy always referred to it as the Orgy Bed, but Royce had never tried it out.

He went to work, and the job proved to be easier than he had anticipated. He had plenty of time to think.

The rain mocked him as he worked. There was nothing dramatic about it—just a steady rain drumming on the thatch over his head and splashing into the muddy earth outside. There was no thunder, no lightning, no high wind. There was just a constant reminder that he was trapped, trapped by a combination of the most ancient of the elements and something so new that his world lacked even the words to discuss it sensibly.

Of course, his whole evaluation of the situation might be faulty. He recognized that. He could not *prove* that something had come down out of the sky and landed out there in the African bush. He could not *prove* that the strange events around the Baboonery had been connected with that landing, assuming that the landing had really happened. On the other hand, he could not prove that the sun—however obscured by clouds—would rise tomorrow either, or that the lights in the night sky were stars. The best that any man had to go on was a very high degree of probability. It was folly to act on any assumption except the one that seemed to fit the facts best. *All* explanations had once been fantastic guesses. There had been a time when it had been little short of lunacy to believe that fire could be produced from friction, that an arrow could be as deadly as a spear, that animals could be domesticated more easily than hunting them wild, that plants would grow from seeds, that the world was round. People and tribes and nations had perished from wishful thinking. The ones that survived had learned to look facts in the eye and draw the unpopular conclusions.

If something had landed here, it had not been an accident. Surely, beings that could pilot a ship across the light-years of interstellar space could select a landing place with precision. Even in the unlikely event that only interplanetary distances had been involved, the same point would apply. Even man, with his primitive space technology, could land on a designated spot on the moon with some accuracy.

Question: Why land *here?*

Well, Royce thought, turn the thing around. Suppose that man had the capacity to explore an inhabited planet. Suppose that he was uncertain what kind of a reception he might receive. Would he plop himself down smack in the middle of a city? Or would he try to check things out first in a relatively empty area?

Of course, the chosen area should not be *completely* deserted. If you want to find out something about the natives you have to have a few to watch.

In a way, the Baboonery was ideal. It was particularly ideal if *they* were unsure of themselves, uncertain how well they could function on this alien world. There must be limits to what you can discover from a spaceship. Sooner or later, you must test your theories. You must open your door and check things out. You have to start somewhere.

All well and good. *Except* that he could not know their motives, any more than Montezuma could understand what Cortes was after or a chimpanzee could understand why he had been rocketed into space. *Except* that it did not explain the odd incidents with the baboons or the death of Kilatya or the fire.

When you don't know what is coming, you have to be ready for anything.

Royce screwed the bulb—only 100 watts, but it was the biggest he had—into the socket he had rigged and tried it out. Somewhat to his surprise, it worked perfectly.

It wasn't much—little more than a gesture, perhaps.

But he would be able to see a little farther into the darkness, and that was something.

Royce was finishing a late lunch when Mutisya called out to him.

"Mr. Royce! *Choroa!*"

"Oryx," Royce said, getting to his feet. "Meat, if we're lucky. Make sure Elijah switches on the lights if I'm not back by dark."

"You *be* back," Kathy said.

Royce grabbed his raincoat and the .375 and ran outside. The rain was still coming down but the visibility was good enough so that he could see to shoot if he could just get a target.

"*Wapi?*" he asked. "Where?"

Mutisya pointed down the road toward Matt Donaldson's camp. "Just now I saw him. A good one. Alone."

Royce hesitated only a moment. There wasn't anything much left of the road; the Land Rover could not make it through mud that thick. Too noisy anyhow, probably. He looked at Mutisya. The Kamba stood quietly, a dignified figure somehow despite the gnarled bare feet and baggy shorts and the battered olive-colored army-surplus overcoat he wore instead of a raincoat. "Can we get him, Mutisya?"

Mutisya smiled, showing his filed pointed teeth. "I will find him. You will shoot him."

"Okay, let's go."

Mutisya started off at an easy jog, his bare feet almost silent in the mud. Royce pulled his hat down more firmly on his head and followed him. The mud sucked at his boots and he sounded like an elephant. He veered off to the side of the road where the ground was higher and firmer and tried to pace himself. Mutisya was tireless, despite his age. The man's legs were as thin as sticks, but the long muscles in them were as tough as ropes.

It was eerie once they got into the bush—a dark, dripping world of long silences and glistening wet-black bark. The sky was close and gray, pressing down upon them. The rain-streaked air was heavy and still and Royce was sweating before he had covered one hundred yards. There was an expectant hush that hovered over the sodden earth like an electrical charge. Royce could almost see the vegetation coming to life—the bushes and the grass and the trees and the creepers, all of them drinking in the rain, waiting for the magic touch of the sun to explode into leaf and flower.

Tracking was simple enough as long as the oryx stayed in the road. The marks of his hooves in the mud were so clear that a child could have followed him.

Mutisya stopped suddenly and pointed to his left.

Royce nodded, panting. The oryx had turned off here, veering into the dripping bush to avoid Donaldson's camp. He could still make out the tracks but they were fainter now; the tangle of ground-hugging plants kept the animal's feet out of the mud. The spacing of the tracks showed that the oryx had increased his speed a little, but he was not running yet.

Mutisya left the road, moving fast, his body bent over almost double. He looked for all the world as though he were sniffing out the trail. Royce kept behind him, picking open spaces, keeping his head up. Mutisya could track better than he could; Royce's job was to look ahead to see if he could spot the animal.

Mutisya saw him first, though. Some sixth sense made him look up and he stopped at once, pointing.

Royce followed the pointing finger, saying nothing. It took him a moment and then the oryx seemed to leap into view. The animal was standing quietly by a baobab tree, his head raised, looking back. It was a long shot in the rain, better than two hundred yards.

Royce lifted the heavy rifle to his shoulder and slipped off the safety. He glued his eye to the scope. It took him a long agonizing minute to find the animal again in the scope, but then he had him. The two long, almost straight horns gave the oryx the look of a unicorn unless he was looking straight at you. He was a big animal, four hundred pounds or so, and there was power in that stout brownish-gray body. There were black and white markings on his face, and his black tufted tail was twitching slightly.

Royce took a bead just above the left shoulder and his finger tightened on the trigger.

The oryx moved. His didn't move fast or far, but he moved enough. He was screened by foliage. Royce knew about where he was, but he had no shot.

"Damn," he whispered. He lowered the rifle, wishing that he had a stand to steady his arm. The .375 was a heavy gun and a slight waver could make a big difference at that range. He had waited an instant too long. Next time…

He started ahead and to his right, trying to get an angle from which he could catch a glimpse of the oryx. He moved quietly, with Mutisya behind him now, taking advantage of every bit of cover he could find. He kept holding his breath and had to remind himself to breathe. He wanted that oryx. There was a lot of meat on him, enough meat to make a difference.

He thought he had lost him and then, quite suddenly, he spotted him again. The oryx was moving away and to his left. It wasn't a clear shot, but the animal was picking up speed. It was as good a shot as he was going to get.

Royce jerked the rifle up, peered through the scope, and squeezed the trigger. The loud crack of the big rifle seemed muffled in the rain but there was nothing subdued about the kick of the gun against his shoulder.

He lowered the rifle; he could not tell what was happening through the scope. The oryx, he thought, had jerked a little with the impact of the slug—but he couldn't be sure. In any event, the animal had not gone down. The oryx turned and broke into a run, headed straight for the Kikumbuliu. Royce snapped off another shot, hoping for a miracle. There was no miracle. The oryx kept going and was lost to sight in an instant.

They ran toward the spot where the oryx had been, not worrying about the noise now. It was hard going and Royce tore his raincoat in three places. He pulled up, finally, his chest heaving.

Mutisya found the torn-up patch in the mud first, and then the bright red smear of blood; the blood was fairly thick. They found another spot a short distance away. The rain splashed into the blood and trickled off as though it had fallen into a puddle of oil.

This was where the hunting got tough.

Mutisya took the lead again. He went slowly at first, watching for the smears of blood, but then he broke into a jog. The wounded animal was running in a straight line, headed for the river. He couldn't cross it, of course, but if he just didn't turn aside until he became weak and confused...

Royce ran in a kind of trance, one hand clutching his rifle and the other holding his raincoat tightly against his body so that it would not catch in the bush. The rain-pounded world was dreamlike in its emptiness; nothing seemed to move, and the only sound Royce heard was the rising roar of the river.

He saw the Kikumbuliu: a swollen brown giant of a river, choked with mud and brush and uprooted trees, a river that hissed and boomed and ripped at its banks. They started down the slope. The footing was tricky; the grade that led to the river had only a dead grass cover and the ground had turned into a slippery swamp.

Mutisya stopped and threw up his hand.

Royce snapped back to alertness. The oryx was in plain sight and less than a hundred yards away. He just stood there in the pelting rain, his back to the torrent of the river, his front legs wide apart for balance. His head was up, nodding slightly, as though the weight of his horns had become a burden too heavy to bear. He was looking at Royce, waiting.

Royce steadied himself, lifted the rifle, and fired once. The oryx crumpled in a heap.

The two men picked their way across the muddy earth and looked down at the animal. He was dead, his soft brown eyes already glazing.

Royce's first shot had hit him in the belly. His last shot had gone home in the chest.

"Well," Royce said. "Now the fun starts."

Mutisya grinned. "He is a big one. Very heavy."

Royce took off his hat and wiped the sweat from his eyes. The two of them could not possibly pack that animal back to the Baboonery. They would have to hack him up where he lay, and even then they would need more men. They were not far from the Baboonery—less than a mile, if one happened to be a bird.

He glanced up at the sky, letting the rain splash against his face. The clouds were black and heavy and it was beginning to get darker. There wasn't much time.

"Mutisya, I'll stay here and start cutting him up. Leave me that knife of yours and you get back to the Baboonery as fast as you can. If everything is okay there, come right back with four men and some pangas. Understand?"

"Okay, Mr. Royce."

Mutisya turned without a world of complaint and moved with his effortless stride back up the slope. He had vanished in less than a minute.

Royce fished out his pipe and got it going. He stood quietly for a moment. The rain continued to fall, cloaking the earth in sheets of silver. He was awed at the primordial loneliness that surrounded him. He thought: *I'll remember this time and this place. One day, if I'm lucky, it will all come back to me, fresh and new with the smell of rain. One day, when I need it, I'll take out this picture and see it again.*

He stared at the surging power of the dirty water in the Kikumbuliu. The once tiny stream was a great wide river, and the yellow-brown current was deep and strong. It carried broken black trees along like matchsticks, and its voice was a swirling snarl of fury. Nothing was going to cross that river for a long time to come. He could imagine what the Tsavo must look like now, and the Athi that separated him from Nairobi. And there were other rivers, too many rivers, too many little creeks and formerly dry canyons that were bursting with water....

He picked up Mutisya's knife and knelt by the oryx. This was a part of hunting that saddened him. There was death where there had been life, and the thrill was gone.

He went to work.

By the time that Mutisya returned with the men—who laughed and shouted when they saw the oryx—it was almost too dark to see. They hacked the animal crudely into sections with their pangas; they could carve it up properly when they got back to the Baboonery. Within twenty minutes, they had most of the edible meat piled into canvas carrying slings.

They started back through the darkness.

Royce could see the halo of the Baboonery lights ahead of him. He felt an icy chill that had nothing to do with the cooling of the night when he became aware of the presence of the *other* light as well. It was coming from the same place that he had first seen it, a seeming eternity ago. A soft, steady, pale glow, almost like moonlight.

They were still there.

Royce was very tired. He tried to concentrate on walking, on just putting one foot after the other in the mud. His brain was numbed. He was beyond mere worry.

He stared at those two lights shining through the darkness and the rain: two lights that were utterly different, separated by more than distance, and yet somehow linked.

We're all in this together, he thought.

Wearily, he put his head down.

He was going home. He held that thought in his head. He was going home, a hunter carrying his meat. He was at the end of an inconceivably long procession of men, stretching back through the ages, men returning from hunts long forgotten....

It was, somehow, a comforting thought.

There was a tie with the past, a continuity, no matter what the future might hold.

8

The long days passed, and the longer nights. The rain kept coming. It did not rain continuously—the sun even broke through the clouds a few times—but it rained enough so that the earth had no chance to dry out. The rivers roared and water dripped in a steady stream from the roof thatch. Clothing mildewed in the dresser drawers. The moist planks of the walls were streaked with mold. Outside, the world was a dismal gray, as though the rain had absorbed all colors and all life. The skies were gray, the bush was gray, even the mud was gray. The mud had been red once, the color of rust, but the red was gone along with the clouds of dust that had once hung in the sun-baked air.

Royce waited. There was very little else that he could do. Supplies were running a little low, but they were in no danger from that quarter yet. The meat from the oryx had helped. He still had plenty of fuel for the generator. The children were both healthy now, although they were cross and bored. The novelty of the rain had worn off, and Kathy had her hands full trying to entertain them.

There were nights when the strange pale glow was plainly visible, and there were other nights when the bush surrounding the Baboonery was black and still and lifeless.

Royce toyed with the idea of tracking that light down. He knew he could find the source if he put enough effort into it. He would have tried it if he had been alone; he was desperately curious about what must be out there in the bush, and he knew that there was a chance he might find out something that would be useful to him. But he could not risk it. As long as *they* did not attack him he was prepared to leave them alone. To go out there after them was asking for trouble. He could probably do nothing even if he found them, and if he got himself killed Kathy and the children would be in a hopeless position. That game wasn't worth the candle.

He waited, not knowing what to expect. Most of his fears were centered vaguely around the possibility of a direct attack under the cover of darkness. He was not quite ready for what actually happened.

It was daylight and a gentle rain was falling. Most of the men were in their quarters. Royce was standing at the kitchen window, looking out. A single baboon ran suddenly out of the bush and headed straight for the building that housed Royce's office and the operating rooms. For a long moment, Royce did not react. He noticed that the animal was wet and bedraggled and thin almost to the point of emaciation. The baboon darted into the building. By the time Royce had snatched up his rifle and lunged out the door, the baboon was outside again. The animal clutched a couple of pineapples to his chest and scurried away in a queer three-legged run. Royce snapped off one shot, missed, and the baboon disappeared back into the bush.

On the surface, that was all there was to it.

Royce, however, learned some important things from the seemingly trivial pineapple raid. It was highly unlikely that a normal baboon would behave as that animal had done. Baboons often helped themselves to a farmer's maize crop standing in the field, but they seldom ran through an occupied area and into a building after food. That was highly unusual, to say the least. If Royce had needed any additional evidence that some alien intelligence was controlling the baboons, he now had it.

More crucially, the incident taught him something that he should have realized before. If *they* had somehow taken over the baboons—not all of the baboons, of course, but some of them—the reason for the takeover was obvious. They could not function on this world without elaborate protective devices any more than a man could go for a stroll on Jupiter in his birthday suit. They had to work through a native animal, one that was already adapted to the environment of this planet. A baboon was a primate, like a man. A little simpler, a little easier...

They were practicing. The baboons were a means, not an end. A way station, a halfway house....

But if you take over a baboon and control him, that animal must still *live* as a baboon. He must eat, find shelter, ward off disease, protect himself from his enemies. Normally, he can do this readily enough. But if you short-circuit his brain, if you interpose an alien intelligence, what then? It is no help to a baboon to know philosophy or interstellar navigation. He has to know what insects to eat, which plants are nourishing, where the rock shelters are, how to avoid leopards.

The rains make things complicated, for baboons as well as men.

The baboon that had gone after the stored pineapples must have been desperate for food. He did not know even *what* to eat, much less where to find it. All he knew was that the captive baboons were fed maize and pineapple, and that traps were set with the same foods. The only certain source of those foods within miles was the Baboonery storeroom.

The next step was so glaringly obvious that Royce distrusted it on principle. Still, he could not afford to ignore it. He knew that a really hungry animal was a stupid animal. Even a deer will take long chances when his belly has been empty long enough.

Royce gave instructions that the outside door of the building that contained the storeroom was to be left slightly ajar. He locked the storeroom itself. He filled the syringe that was fastened to the pole with sernyl and put it in the lab, which was in the same building with the storeroom. From the inside, he unfastened the bottom of the lab window screen. The window was on the opposite side of the building from the bush where the baboons were.

He left the building by the door, went into the main building, and made himself a couple of sandwiches. Carrying the sandwiches and his rifle, he went outside again, this time using the front door. It was raining harder, and his boots squished into the mud. He walked a short distance through the muck that had once been the main road, left the road, and doubled back. He climbed through the window of the lab, refastened the screen, and sat down to wait. He kept his rifle ready on a lab table beside him, but he had the syringe pole in his hand. He didn't want another dead baboon. He wanted one of those creatures alive.

He sat there for hours, listening to the rain drumming on the roof. Absolutely nothing happened. He waited until almost dark and gave up. He could not risk it alone in the lab at night unless he turned the lights on. He left the building, locked the outside door, and posted a guard. The next morning, he tried his trick again.

Royce crouched behind the lab door, annoyed with himself because his hands were trembling. He heard Mutisya's shout and then a rapid scurrying sound in the hallway. He could not be certain, but from the amount of noise he judged that there was more than one animal in the corridor. He forced himself to wait, his heart thudding in his chest.

He heard a scratching sound as the animals tried the locked storeroom door. He knew that the creatures would have to move fast; if they could not open the storeroom door they would have to retreat quickly to have any hope of escaping. He waited until he heard them pass the lab door again.

Now.

He jerked open the door and sprinted into the hallway. There was a stench of baboons in the corridor. He saw them—two wet and skinny animals running for the open outside door. Royce did not hesitate. Just as the lead baboon ran through the door, Royce caught up with the other one. He jabbed the syringe into his rear end and jammed the plunger home. The baboon turned with a coughing snarl. Royce yanked out the bent needle and thrust the sturdy pole into the animal's chest, hurling him back. The baboon snapped at the pole with his long white teeth.

Royce dropped the pole, turned, and ran back into the lab. He slammed the door and locked it and snatched up his rifle. There was a thud as the animal's body struck the lab door. Royce did not fire. He stood there, rifle ready, catching his breath. He heard the baboon racing up and down the corridor. The animal was confused now, afraid to venture outside and trapped if he stayed in.

The sernyl began to take effect. Gradually, the baboon's movements slowed, became erratic. There was a long pause. Royce heard a sodden thump as the animal fell to the floor.

Royce waited a long minute, then opened the lab door. There was a smell of excrement in the hallway. The baboon was out cold, a huddled gray heap on the mud-spattered floor. He was breathing rapidly, the fangs bared in his long snout.

Royce felt a moment of pity for the creature. Whatever it had become, it had reached the end of a long and strange journey. In its own mind, it must have believed itself cornered by alien beings in an alien land. It had been wet and hungry and afraid.

"Well, pal," Royce said softly, "I didn't ask you to come here. Remember that."

He went outside into a driving rain. The other baboon had escaped back to the bush. Royce told Elijah to have the men carry a strong cage into the lab. When they got it into position, Royce and Mutisya lifted the unconscious animal into the cage. Royce put food and water in the cage, fastened the door, and put a padlock on it.

He instructed Mutisya to keep a sharp lookout and told Elijah that he would hold him responsible if anyone harmed the baboon. Then he locked the lab and locked the building and went inside to eat lunch.

There was nothing to do now except wait for the creature to recover.

As he ate his lunch, listening with half an ear to the chatter of his children, he was far from certain as to what his course of action should be.

He had his baboon, true enough. There remained the small problem of what the devil he was going to do with him.

Royce returned to the lab and hitched a chair up close to the cage—but not too close. He took out his pipe, filled it with Sweet Nut, and got it going. The rain pattered on the roof with a steady monotonous beat. A large black spider, like a burned pancake with legs, walked calmly across the floor and disappeared under a cabinet.

The baboon was awake. He sat in the far corner of the cage, as far as he could get from Royce, and stared at the man. The animal had eaten some of its food. He was an unlovely beast at best, and he smelled. Of all the primates, Royce thought, the baboon was the least attractive. A man felt an instant kinship with a chimpanzee, and gorillas could be charming despite their formidable size. Gibbons were endearing creatures, and orangs were fun in a lugubrious sort of way. Most of the monkeys were pleasant enough, if a trifle blunt in their manners. Lemurs looked like pets with their bushy tails, and tarsiers were clowns with their hopping legs and great saucer eyes. But it was hard to feel affection for a baboon. They were ugly and they could be dangerous, but it was more than that.

The baboon lived on the ground, like man. The two animals had been competitors, perhaps for a million years and more....

The animal in the cage was not a baboon, not any longer. Royce knew that, and the cold intelligence that looked out through the creature's eyes was all the proof that he needed. But he *looked* like a baboon. It took an effort of will to think of him as anything else.

Royce puffed on his pipe and felt singularly futile. He was almost close enough to reach out and touch the creature but there was no basis for contact. He did not even know whether or not *they* had a language, much less what it was. There was no convenient telepathy. He could not bring himself to utter, even in jest, the classic stock line: "Do you speak English?" Or Swahili, perhaps. Or Urdu. The idea was absurd.

He went to the storeroom, got a pineapple, and approached the cage. The animal snarled, watching him closely. Royce extended his hand, offering the pineapple. The creature defecated in fear. Royce put the pineapple in the cage and went back to his chair. The thing that looked like a baboon stared at him with something like horror and did not move.

Royce studied him as well as he could. The animal did not look healthy. His coat was dull, his eyes cloudy. He was too thin and there were vermin around his ears. Baboons were social animals; they lived in bands. A baboon alone, cut off from his society, would have a difficult time of it.

"You poor bastard," Royce said. "I'm not enjoying this."

He did not know whether or not he could keep the creature alive. Now that he had him, he was not sure that it was a good idea to keep him around at all. Would the others come after him? And *how* would they come—as baboons or as something else?

It seemed to Royce, as he sat there looking at the thing in the cage, that he had been wrong in thinking that *they* were simply controlling the baboons in some way. Surely, if that were the case, they could withdraw their control from an injured or captured animal. For that matter, they could release the baboons to forage naturally, then reimpose their control when it was needed.

It didn't work that way.

He knew that they had to catch a baboon and take it to their ship in order to use it. It took some time. And that meant...

They were not just manipulating the baboons. They were *in* the baboons. There must be some sort of transplant involved, perhaps an actual replacement of the brain....

He looked at the creature in the cage. He stared at the sick, alien eyes. He felt a sudden, irrational chill of dread. He was in the same room with one of *them,* face to face with...what?

"My God," he whispered. "Who are you? Why have you come here? What do you want?"

Royce thought: *He knows things I cannot know. He does not think as I think. He is trapped in a crazy body, locked in a cage, but he is smarter than I am. He might be able to do...anything.*

Slowly, almost mindlessly, his hand reached out for the rifle. Then he hesitated, stopped. He cared nothing for the scientific value of the creature now; his problem was survival. But shooting a baboon was one thing, and murdering an alien intelligence was something else.

He sat there, frozen into inaction, one hand touching the rifle.

A voice from outside: "Mr. Royce! Mr. Royce!"

He got to his feet, taking his rifle with him. He left the lab, locking the door behind him. He hurried through the corridor and out the door. He locked that door too.

The men were gathered in a knot by the baboon cages under the shed. Several of them were armed with bows and arrows. Royce ran through the rain and joined them.

"What is it, Mutisya?"

The African pointed at the bush. "Out there. Many baboons. Listen—you can hear them."

Royce held his breath. The patter of the rain and the muted roar of the distant river covered up all other sounds. He knew that his hearing was not as sharp as Mutisya's. He tried, straining his ears. He thought he heard a coughing and barking in the bush but he could not be sure.

He could see, though. He peered through the silver-gray sheets of rain at the dark and dripping bush. He saw shadows there, moving shadows.

"Our friend has company," he said. He stroked the barrel of his rifle, wiping off the raindrops with his fingers. Those shadows were within range. But if he shot them, what then? He had not forgotten the strange sharp tracks that he had seen. *They* could move with their natural forms encased in armor, he figured—unless the mud prevented them. For that matter, they could probably lift their ship unless they had had an accident of some kind. They could wipe him out from the air as easily as he could swat a fly....

One baboon-thing emerged from the bush. He advanced slowly across the clearing, moving gingerly, reluctantly. He stopped, started to go back to the safety of the bush, then came on again. Royce watched him with a grudging admiration. Either the animal was mad or...

Before Royce could act, a Kamba fitted an arrow to his bow and loosed the shaft. The feathered arrow whistled through the wet air. Considering the range, it was a fairly near miss. The poisoned shaft arced down within fifteen yards of the animal.

The baboon turned and ran for cover. The men laughed and slapped one another on the back.

Royce felt a quick surge of relief. He was not sure how to proceed, but he was suddenly certain that they were on the wrong track. A full-scale battle could have only one ultimate outcome, even if they managed to kill *all* of the baboon-things. There had to be a better way.

"That was a good shot," he said. "But I don't want to fight them unless they give us no other choice. Mutisya, I want you to stand guard here with your best bowmen. Don't let them move in close. Elijah, I want four men to help me carry the cage out of the lab."

Elijah looked at him his eyes hidden behind his rain-spotted glasses. "What is your plan?"

"I want to let him go."

Elijah shook his head. "Mr. Royce, that is wrong. Never fight a war with your finger. If you catch a Masai and release him he will not thank you. He will be back with his spear."

Royce hesitated. He had no right to give orders to these men when their own lives might be at stake. It was true that they could not understand the situation, but he could not be sure of his own tactics either.

"Those baboons are sick," he said. "They are not like other baboons. I think the sickness came down out of the sky. You know that we are trapped here by the rain—you are cut off from your people and I am cut off from mine. I am not trying to play the *bwana mkubwa* just because you happen to work for me. One of us must make the decisions. If you trust me, I will make them. If you do not, you can do what you think best. I am afraid that if we keep that sick baboon in the cage the others will fight to take him away. If we let him go, they may let us alone. I may be wrong, but if we let him go and they keep on coming anyway we are no worse off than we are now. Does that make sense to you, Elijah?"

The headman did not answer him directly. He walked off to one side and conferred with the other men. They talked a long time. Then Elijah came back with four men. He smiled. "Okay, Mr. Royce."

Royce said nothing more. He led them into the lab and they picked up the cage by the carrying rods. It was heavy and the creature in the cage snarled at them. Royce could smell his diseased odor. He could feel the stiffening of his hair on his scalp, feel an unreasoning terror. The thing was so close....

They walked slowly across the clearing with the other men fanning out on either side. Royce peered ahead into the bush but saw nothing. They set the cage down at the far edge of the clearing.

"Go on back and cover me," Royce said. "I'll let him out."

The men retreated to the shelter of the shed without argument.

Royce checked his rifle and slipped the safety off. He unlocked the padlock and unfastened the cage door. He prodded the door open a little with the rifle barrel and stood back.

The creature in the cage stared at him with sick, puzzled eyes. It made no move.

"Come on," Royce said. "I'm not going to hurt you."

The baboon-thing bared his fangs at the sound of his voice but still made no move.

Royce began to back away, his rifle ready. He backed a good forty yards across the clearing, his eyes fixed on the cage. Then he turned and ran through the mud to the shed. Standing with the other men, he saw the rain-blurred shadow of the baboon as it left the cage and disappeared into the bush.

"Go tell your friends," Royce muttered.

He locked up the storeroom building and wearily plodded through the muck toward the breezeway. He was wet and discouraged. There seemed to be no significant action that he could take. He had perhaps postponed a showdown but that was not good enough.

He could not wait indefinitely.

He had to *do* something.

When he had cleaned himself up and changed clothes, he went to locate Kathy. He found her in the kitchen supervising Wathome's cooking. Wathome preferred to do his cooking alone, but he had discovered that Kathy was less tractable than his own three wives. Royce sympathized with him, and he had a sneaking suspicion that Wathome pitied him for his inability to keep his woman in line.

Royce eased Kathy into the sitting room. He suggested to Barbara and Susan, who had their junk spread all over the dining room table, that they go and play in the bedroom. His suggestion met with a very cool reception, and he decided to let them stay where they were. The children were bored and fretful and the issue wasn't worth a fuss.

Outside, the rain had slowed to a gentle drizzle.

"I've got an idea," he said.

Kathy had dark shadows under her eyes. She looked older. Her hand trembled slightly as she lit one of her last cigarettes. "I think I'm about ready for it, whatever it is."

"I think there may be a way to get out of here."

"Don't build it up. Just tell me."

He took a deep breath. "Look, we've forgotten about something. We can't make Nairobi or Machakos. We can't make Hunters or Mac's because of the rivers. We can't even make Mitaboni. *But we don't have to.*"

"We can stay here, if that's what you mean. This isn't a good time for jokes, Royce. Really, your sense of timing..."

"We forgot about Bob Russell," Royce said quietly.

Kathy sat down on the hard leather couch. A flicker of hope showed in her eyes.

"Bob Russell's place is between here and Mitaboni. If I can get out to the main road, I'd only have nine miles to go—and that on tarmac of a sort. There's only one large draw on that stretch; I can probably get through the water. Russell has got a telephone. I could call the police in Nairobi and have them send a copter to pick us up."

Kathy drew on her cigarette. "You make it sound so simple. I'm a big girl now, Royce. You'd have to walk the whole way—that's nearly twenty miles. Russell probably got out long ago, and he probably thinks that we did, too. He wouldn't have known, or wouldn't remember, that Susan was too sick to travel. It would be a miracle if that phone was still operating. It would take you days, even if you made it. I don't want to be left alone here; I can't stand that."

Royce search for some words and didn't find them. He did the best he could. "You won't be alone. I trust Mutisya and the others—*have* to trust them. I think I can get the Land Rover through part of the way—not all the way to the main road, but maybe a few miles. I could make it to Russell's and back in thirty-six hours easily, even if I rested up when I got there. I'd only be gone one night. It's a chance, Kathy. *And we can't just sit here.* I'm afraid to risk it any longer."

"What about me? If I could go with you..."

"We can't leave the kids here alone. We can't take them with us; they'd never make it. My God, Kathy, do you think I *want* to leave you sitting here? I just don't know what else to do."

"You could send Mutisya, couldn't you?"

"I considered it. He's a good man. He could get through as well as I could, maybe better. But what if Russell isn't there? Mutisya can't use a telephone. Even if he could, would he get any action? I can go all the way up to the American representatives if I have to. I'm the one who has to go, if anyone does."

Kathy ground out her cigarette. She looked at him for a long time. "Tomorrow?"

"In the morning. Early."

"I'll pack some sandwiches for you," she said.

The rain began to fall harder and a cool wind blew through the windows from out of the darkening sky.

9

Royce left with the first light of dawn, partly to leave himself as much daylight as possible and partly with the hope that his departure would not be noticed. He had told Elijah and Mutisya of his plan the night before; he said nothing to them now. He did not awaken the children. He kissed Kathy lightly, almost casually. There were no words that he could say to her that would not sound hollow and forced.

The rain had slacked off during the late night hours. There was a fine mist in the cold morning air, but the road had drained fairly well. He had no idea how far he could get in the Land Rover, but even a few miles would help. It would save him time and it would save him strength; he would be needing both.

The Land Rover started sluggishly but the engine caught. He let it warm up for a minute or two; he didn't want to kill the engine in a crucial spot. He eyed the mud ahead of him without optimism. He took a deep breath and started out.

He kept it in two-wheel drive at first; he had no confidence in the mud gear. The vehicle fish-tailed through the muck and almost went into a spin. He hit a puddle that was virtually a miniature lake and began to lose traction. Despite his misgivings, he shoved in the mud gear. He had no choice. The low-ratio four-wheel drive would give him too much power and dig him in; the mud gear gave him less power but engaged all four wheels. The Land Rover kept going somehow and cleared the puddle.

Royce kept to the right, out of the ruts. His right wheels spun on wet grass and brush, but there was more traction there than in the slick, deep mud. He did not try to think. He just pushed the vehicle along, maintaining speed, trying not to stop. He could not maneuver; every turn of the wheel started a skid that was difficult to control. He hit rocks and roots and erosion cuts; he kept on going.

He passed the loading shed, bleak and deserted in the gray morning air, and jounced across the wet gleaming rails of the tracks. He negotiated the long sweeping curve, employing every ounce of driving skill that he had. The muddy trail was reasonably straight now. He picked up a little speed, praying that his momentum would carry him through the sticky spots.

The relatively open country was behind him; the bush closed in. He was forced almost into the ruts; there was no clearance on the side of the road. Wet branches slapped at his face. It seemed to grow darker. The great dripping baobab trees pressed in on both sides. The acacias were black as wet iron, the creepers were black and glistening snakes. He could hear the steady drip of the water above the whine of his engine.

He lost track of time. His knuckles were white on the wheel, sweat trickled from his armpits in icy streams. He hit a stump, spun off, skidded in a complete circle, kept going.

Every foot, every yard, every mile....

He saw it coming, but there was nothing that he could do.

The texture of the soils beneath him changed, with sands giving way to clays. He approached a long stretch that was gray-black in color and oozing water. The trail was very narrow; there was no way he could turn off.

He increased his speed as much as he dared and hit the muck with a splashing jolt. He didn't have a chance, and knew it. The Land Rover slithered wildly and slowly as the wheels sank in. He shifted to low gear and tried to bull his way through. All forward motion stopped and the wheels spun in the slime. He could smell the scorched rubber and see the steam rising from the mud.

He put the vehicle in neutral and wiped the sweat from his face. His hands were shaking.

Think, dammit.

He might get a few yards more by putting branches under the wheel, but he could never get clear to the firmer ground that was a good hundred yards ahead of him. For that, he would need a winch, a crew of men, and about six hours of work. It was time to hoof it. But he might need the Land Rover again on the way back; he had made five or six miles since leaving the Baboonery, and that was a far piece to walk. He didn't want to leave the vehicle stuck in the mud.

He climbed out into the drizzle and went to work. His boots made sucking sounds in the deep mud. He gathered dead saturated branches and inserted them behind the wheels. He lined the worst of the patch behind him with more wood and got back into the vibrating Land Rover.

He used the low-ratio four-wheel drive this time, putting it in reverse. He gave it short, sharp bursts of gas to get the Land Rover rocking. Then, before the wheels could dig in any more deeply, he floored the gas pedal and hung on. The vehicle came up like a stranded fish and lurched back over the shattered wood. He got it on more or less solid ground, found a small opening in the bush, and backed into it. The Land Rover was ready. One sharp turn of the wheel and it was headed back toward the Baboonery.

Royce switched off the ignition and pocketed the keys.

He wasted no time. He checked the wrapped sandwiches in his raincoat pocket, patted the box of heavy bullets. He stuck a short flashlight in his belt and slung a coil of light nylon rope over his shoulder. He picked up his rifle.

He started walking. It was slow going at first as he picked his way around the edges of the deep mud, but when he was able to return to the road he made better time. He stayed on the high center and the footing was slippery but firm.

The sky overhead was a thick, solid gray; there was no trace of sunlight. The bush on both sides of him was a dark wet tangle—twisted dripping trees, columns of motionless euphorbia, clumps of brush bent over by the weight of the water. Nothing moved. He saw no animals. There were no birds in the air or on the trees. It was utterly still except for the steady drip of the water and the splashing of his own feet.

It was really very simple. He lost some time detouring around thick mud and obstructions but he made better progress than he had expected. The country gradually opened up around him; the sensation of uncluttered space was refreshing after the dense bush. Even the air felt a little lighter.

He scrambled down a deeply eroded cut that was still awash with brown water, hauled himself up the other side, and felt tarmac under his boots with a sense of relief.

He had reached the Mombasa-Nairobi road.

It was only ten o'clock. He had been gone from the Baboonery slightly more than four hours.

The road would have been murder for a car—it was pocked with deep chuckholes and sheets of water in every dip—but it was not too tough for a man on foot. Royce was able to walk at almost his normal pace.

The road was completely deserted, of course. Nothing had passed this way for a long, long time. It was an eerie feeling, walking along that empty road under the leaden morning sky. It was as though Royce had somehow slipped back in time. The spasmodic bus service, the little cars with the men in turbans and the women in saris, the trucks loaded with produce, the government Land Rovers, the Africans pushing their herds of bone-thin cattle through the red dust that fringed the road—all of it had vanished. And before that: the missionary-explorers, walking this same route into the interior from the coast, sending out crazy reports of a snow-capped mountain not far from the Equator. And the old slaving expeditions, the Arabs and Swahilis plying their trade from Zanzibar to Lake Victoria. And before them Africans like the Kambas hauling ivory to the Indian Ocean in footsore caravans. And beyond all that an unknown land, a world never seen, animals so thick they covered the earth as the bison had covered the American plains, tribes and peoples whose very names had been lost, men and women who had lived and died long before the Kamba and the Masai had come....

All that, right here, where he walked in silence.

He was not the first to pass this way, in a hurry, his mind troubled with desperate problems. He would not be the last.

Royce did not push himself. He walked steadily but he conserved his strength. There was one deep draw between him and Russell's place. It was normally dry or nearly dry, but it would be a river of fast water now. He could never cross it in a weakened condition. And he had his rifle to worry about....

Take it as it comes. Take it as it comes.

There were times when the world seemed very small. There were times when it all came down to this: one man and a rifle and water to cross.

A century from now, it might not matter or be remembered. A century from now, even *they* might be forgotten—or man himself might have vanished from the earth.

But it mattered now. It mattered to him: what he was, and what he might become. He was just one man, but that was all that any man could claim.

He walked on, pacing himself. His shoulders began to ache. He shifted his heavy rifle from one hand to the other. The sky grew darker and fat drops of warm rain began to fall. He welcomed the rain, tepid though it was; he was hot and sticky and his clothes were damp.

Royce heard the water before he came to it. Not the roaring of a river in flood. No, it was a softer sound, a well-oiled sound, a hiss and bubble of swift water....

The road simply disappeared beneath the flow of yellow-brown water. There was no way to tell how deep it was. The current was strong and fast; there were sticks and tufts of grass and uprooted bushes rushing downstream. It had been worse: Royce could see the road damage that indicated that the water level had been far higher during the peak of the rains. There were good-sized trees strewn along the banks where they had been scattered by the force of the flow.

He estimated the width of the stream as about thirty yards. It was not an impossible distance, but Royce didn't kid himself. He knew fast water. A trout stream half that wide could knock a man down, and that was in clear water where you could see where you were going.

He stepped carefully into the water, testing it. He moved out a yard or two, sliding his feet in a fisherman's shuffle. The dirty water was up to the tops of his boots and the tug was strong. As he had suspected, the angle of dropoff was steep. It would be over his head in the middle of the river.

He backed out. There was no way he could cross here without swimming. He could not swim with a rifle, and he was not sure he could make it even without the rifle.

Royce forced himself to rest. He sat down on a rock by the side of the road. He unwrapped two cheese sandwiches and wolfed them down; they wouldn't be helped by being underwater. He fished out his pipe and got it going. The tobacco hissed when the rain hit it.

He got up after a few minutes, knocked out his pipe, and stuffed it in his pocket. He left the road and moved to his right, heading upstream. He had no idea of how far he might have to go, but he knew that the stream would have to broaden out somewhere. Drainages for flood waters seldom stayed in deep cuts; even rivers that always carried water had stretches that were wide and shallow.

It was tough going. There was no trail here, and there were places where he had to force his body through the brush. He stayed as close to the water as he could; the higher water of a few days ago had partially cleared a path for him. The mud was thick and great gobs of it stuck to his boots.

He lost nearly an hour before he found a possible crossing. He saw outcroppings of black gritty rock from an ancient lava flow and the channel of the stream widened perceptibly. The current was still very fast but it was broken into rapids and pools. There was white water mixed with brown. It had to be relatively shallow, but it was plenty deep enough to drown a man.

Royce moved another hundred yards or so upstream, giving himself plenty of room to move with the water. He found a stout tree near the bank and tied one end of the nylon rope to it. He tied the other end around his waist and carried the slack line in a coil in his left hand. He hefted the rifle in his right hand.

He started across. The bottom was good and firm. The dirty water boiled up around his legs, reached his waist. The current was strong; he could not move directly toward the opposite bank. He had to go at an angle downstream. He fought to yield as little ground as possible so that he would not run out of rope.

His right arm, holding the rifle clear of the water, began to pain him. Debris floating down the river almost knocked him from his feet. He had to move slowly, testing the bottom he could not see. For long, agonizing minutes he doubted that he could make it. He had actually reached down with his left hand to untie the rope around his waist when he hit the upward slope. The water dropped to his knees and he was able to move upstream, recovering some slack. He stumbled out of the river, put down his rifle, and tied the end of the rope to a tree. It would be easier now to cross again, if he had to.

Royce rested for a few minutes, but he was becoming concerned about time. He picked up his rifle and trudged back through the mud to the road. It was still raining but he hardly noticed.

It was almost three o'clock. It had been about nine hours since he had left the Baboonery.

Royce made steady progress along the deserted highway. He reached the Russell turnoff a little after four. The little road that led to Russell's place was not paved. Royce could tell at a glance that no vehicles had passed in or out for at least the past several days. Either Russell had cleared out early or he was still there.

Royce walked through the sticky mud with the open sisal fields on both sides of him. He was bone-weary. The driveway was a long one and it was ten minutes before he came in sight of the low stone-and-wood house with its long screened porch. He saw no signs of activity.

Royce stopped. He heard no dogs barking, and that was odd. Russell would not have taken his dogs with him; he would have left them with his African staff.

Think. This is no time to be stupid.

Royce left the road and entered the sisal field on his right. The footing was soft and the tough sisal blades were strong enough to impede his progress, but the sisal plants were tall enough to give him some cover. He worked around in a curve that would bring him in behind the house.

He got close enough to see the kitchen door. He stopped again, uncertain how to proceed. It was all very well to be careful, but it was dangerous to sneak up on the house. He was inviting one of Bob Russell's bullets in his chest. He decided to call out a greeting, but the sound never came.

He spotted them, sitting in an open shed near one of the outbuildings. Baboons. Two of them.

Royce ducked down in the sisal, his heart hammering. He slid his rifle into position.

They *might* just be baboons venturing in around an empty house. It was possible, but he didn't believe it. And if they were not just baboons...

The kitchen door opened.

Bob Russell came out.

The settler moved as though he were in a daze, or in the last stages of some crippling illness. His stocky body was canted at an odd angle. His long black hair, always brushed straight back, hung like a screen over his face.

Russell shuffled toward the baboons. He passed within five feet of them. They did not react, and neither did he. Russell entered the outbuilding, which was used for equipment storage. He stayed inside a few minutes and then emerged again. He walked slowly back past the baboons, entered the kitchen door, and vanished into the house.

One baboon got to its feet. It stood there in the shed, its limp tail drooping over the patches of bare skin on its rear end. The animal made a sound that was midway between a cough and a grunt. Its long snout, emerging nakedly from the thick ruff of its neck hair, parted in a cavernous yawn. Even at that distance, Royce could tell that the animal was a male by the size of its spikelike canine teeth.

Royce got down flat in the mud between the sisal plants. The implication of what he had seen stunned him. It was obvious that *they* had not confined their attentions to the Baboonery. The creatures had found Bob Russell's place. They had been successful here. They had done...something... to Russell.

Probably, Royce thought, they had gotten to Russell before the rains came. If they had taken a direct route through the bush, Russell's place was almost as close to them as the Baboonery. Had they taken Russell to the ship? Was it possible that they had simply worked on him *here?*

Royce bit his lip. *How* they had done it didn't matter. It was done. The problem was what to do about it.

He made himself as comfortable as he could. The rain had eased to a drizzle. With the clouds choking the sky, it would be dark in less than two hours. His chances would be better then.

He had to get into that house. There was a chance that the phone was still working. There was a chance that he might be able to help Russell; he could not just abandon the man.

Meanwhile, he could rest. He was reasonably safe where he was. He did not dare push himself to the point of exhaustion. Whatever else happened, he had to be able to get back to the Baboonery.

He cradled the wet rifle in his arms.

He lay there in the cool mud beneath the vast uncaring sky and waited.

10

Royce came to with a start. His body felt stiff and cold. The rain had stopped and there were a few early stars showing through breaks in the clouds. There was a pale light visible in Bob Russell's house. He judged that it came from the big sitting room. The kitchen was dark.

Royce did not bother with any fancy plan. If the baboon-things were watching the back of the house, they would be guarding the front as well. His best chance was to be *quick*. He checked his rifle as best he could.

He got to his feet and moved in a crouching run straight for the kitchen door. It seemed to him that his boots squishing through the mud were loud enough to be heard in Nairobi. He could not see clearly in the faint starlight, but there was no sound of alarm.

Royce grabbed the knob on the kitchen door, twisted it. The door opened. He slipped inside and closed the door quietly behind him. It took him long, slow seconds before he could see in the gloom. He crossed the kitchen and flattened himself by the side of the door that led into the house from the kitchen. On the other side of that door, he remembered, was the dining room. Beyond that was the main sitting room. Judging by the light he had seen, that was where Bob Russell was.

He stood absolutely still, trying to control his breathing. Now that he was inside, he was uncertain how to proceed. There might be some of the baboon creatures in the house. He did not know whether or not he could communicate with Russell.

He looked around him as his eyes adjusted to the darkness. There was no place in the kitchen where he could hide. There was a big iron stove and a box of wood next to it. There was a paraffin refrigerator; he could see the wick burning in the blue glass tube underneath. There was an empty wooden table with two chairs. A sink, with dishes neatly placed in a drying rack beside it. Shelves, lots of shelves. He squinted. There was the tea. There was the sugar.

Where were the Africans who worked for Russell? If they had been taken over too...

A sliver of yellow light showed suddenly under the dining-room door. Someone had switched on a light.

He heard Russell's voice. The words were muffled; he could not make them out. There was no reply. He heard a heavy sound as though Russell had stumbled. The light went off again.

Royce took a deep breath. He could not afford to lose any more time. He had to get close to Russell and he had to try that phone. He could accomplish nothing in the kitchen.

He crouched down, remembering the exact location of the rooms in the house.

He got his rifle into position.

Now.

He opened the dining-room door. It swung silently on its hinges. He went through, moving fast. He sensed the empty dining room around him and did not hesitate. He moved toward the light.

Royce stepped to the right through a hallway. He rounded the corner into the sitting room. He snapped the heavy rifle to his shoulder.

"Easy now, Bob," he said softly. "It's Royce. I mean you no harm. Just stay where you are."

Bob Russell was seated on the couch. There was a half-full bottle of Scotch on the long table in front of the couch. The old grandfather clock in the corner had stopped. The zebra-skin rugs on the red tile floor were dirty and twisted. The kudu head over the great fireplace was hanging crookedly.

Russell stared at him vacantly. His eyes were red beneath their bushy black brows. He needed a shave. His hard, capable hands were trembling.

Royce moved forward slowly. He lowered the rifle from his shoulder; it was too heavy and awkward to hold it that way for long. He kept it trained on Russell's torn white shirt.

"Bob! It's Royce Crawford. Can you understand me? What's happened to you?"

The settler made a strangled noise deep in his throat. He lurched to his feet, knocking the bottle off the table. There was no sign of recognition in his bloodshot eyes.

Royce took a step backward, his finger tensing on the trigger. "Hold it, Bob. I know you're not responsible..."

The being that looked like Bob Russell groaned. He shook his head. He advanced toward Royce, the fingers on his work-toughened hands opening and closing.

Royce felt a cold chill of horror but he could not bring himself to fire. He could not send a bullet tearing through the guts of whatever was left of a man who had been named Bob Russell. He knew that his failure to shoot was stupid but there was no time for second thoughts.

He reversed the rifle, holding it by the barrel. As Russell came closer, Royce swung the rifle butt. Russell ducked under it and the force of the swing turned Royce half around.

Before Royce could recover, Russell was on him. The hard hands dug into his shoulders, grinding against bone. Royce grunted in pain. He smelled a sick stench and there was black hair in his face. He felt a sharp burning at his throat.

My God, he thought. *He's trying to bite me!*

Royce dropped the rifle. He stopped thinking and let his reflexes take over. He twisted into position and brought his knee up, hard.

Russell shrieked an animal cry. His grip loosened. Royce pulled back a step and went for the face. He threw rights and lefts as fast as he could, more out of fear than anything else. He wanted to keep Russell away from him. Some of the punches landed but they did no damage. Royce's arms felt like cardboard—cardboard with puffs of cotton where fists should be.

Russell shook them off. He moved in, grunting. He threw a clumsy blow with his open hand that caught Royce on the side of the head. Royce went back against the wall as though he had been hit with a crowbar. He tried to brace himself. Russell came in low, using his head like a battering ram.

Royce felt the white fire of anger. He sensed his strength coming back to him, flowing into him like burning oil.

He had come too far to louse it up now.

"Okay, friend," he whispered. "Let's see how good a job they did on you."

Royce attacked, protecting himself with his arms. He was bigger than Russell and he used his reach. He backed Russell across the room, hurting him.

Lead with your left, stupid, he told himself.

He did. He threw no more wild roundhouse punches.

He jabbed with his left, keeping it in Russell's face. Russell was awkward; he could not counter. Russell's nose started to bleed. Royce used his right sparingly, going for the eyes.

Russell backed against the table. He groped for a wooden chair, lifted it over his head.

Royce went in under it. He drove a left to the belly, folding Russell like an accordion. The chair crashed to the floor. Royce swung a short right uppercut, straightening him up again.

Russell was helpless. He was a target, nothing more.

Royce took his time. He threw a left with all his strength behind it. Russell started down, his eyes glassy, his arms jerking spasmodically. Royce clipped him with a right as he fell.

Royce got on top of him. He took Russell's head in both hands, grabbing it by the long black hair. He raised the head to slam it against the hard tile floor.

He stopped before he completed the action. His anger drained away. Russell was completely helpless. That head he held in his hands harbored a brain. It might not be Russell's brain any longer, but still...

He lowered the head gently to the floor and staggered to his feet. He recovered his rifle and sank into a chair. He began to shake and his chest heaved. He felt sick at his stomach.

Where were the baboon-things? If they had not noticed all the racket in the house they must be deaf. Or else...

He looked at the beaten body on the floor.

"Jesus, Bob," he said in a low voice. "I didn't mean..."

The body stirred. The bloodshot eyes opened and looked right at him.

"Royce?"

It was the voice of Bob Russell.

Royce crossed over to him, his heart hammering. He knelt down and cradled Russell's head in his arm. "Bob, can you hear me?"

The sick smell of the man was overpowering. The eyes were filmed, distant. "Hear you," he said weakly.

"What's happened? What can I do?"

There was a silence that seemed long. Royce was afraid that Russell was...gone again. Then he heard the whispered words: "Kill me."

Royce, who had been on the verge of doing exactly that a few minutes earlier, groped for something to say. "'Tell me what happened."

"Hard...to talk. Can't most of time. Am caught...inside. Can't explain. *It* will be back. You...don't understand." The voice faded away.

"Bob, listen to me. I know about them. I know about the ship and the baboons. Did they take you to the ship? What are they after? What did they do to you?"

The eyes stared at him. The bloody face frowned in desperate concentration. "Came...before rains. Round metal, spider legs. Can't remember... things. Lights. Noise. Something...inside me. In my head. But all crazy, confused. Didn't work, Royce. They don't...know enough yet. Not even for baboons. They...it...so different...."

"*What do they want?*"

"Don't know. They're afraid. So different. Can't explain. Don't understand us, this world. My head...*it's coming back.* Don't let it. Kill me. Don't let it come back...."

Royce stood up, backed away. He had no guidelines by which he could act. He held his rifle ready and did nothing.

Russell's body twitched on the red tile floor. A groan of pain and despair was wrenched from the lips of the beaten face. The eyes opened wide. Strange eyes-seeing and not seeing, mirrors for an inner contest that had no name. The body got up on all fours, shuddered. The mouth whined. A foul, sick smell filled the room.

Royce watched in horror. The blows he had struck must have upset some delicate balance. If there were two...beings...in that body, he must have jolted one of them until it could not function. It was coming back, taking over, but it was hurt, crippled....

Bob Russell's body crawled slowly into a corner of the room. One arm reached up, groped blindly at the wall. The arm fell back. The body collapsed. It trembled for a moment and was still.

Royce walked hesitantly over to the thing that had been a man. He knew the signs; he had seen enough of death to recognize it when it came. He felt for the pulse to be sure. There was no sign of life. He forced himself to look at the face. He was hoping for some sign of peace, of calm, but he saw only agony.

Did I kill him...them? Was I responsible?

He sensed the room around him. The striped zebra-skin throw rugs, the kudu head, the cold massive fireplace. The pictures of Russell's wife and sons. The shelves of books. The African masks. The tall old grandfather clock, no longer ticking away the seconds of eternity.

It had been a good house. A happy and solid and productive house.

"I'm sorry," Royce said aloud. "I would have done better if I could."

He did not even consider trying to bury Bob Russell. There was no time for that, and perhaps Bob would have preferred to stay where he was. He picked the body up and put it on the couch.

Without hope, he walked into the hallway. The telephone was set into a niche about halfway to the bedroom. He did not turn on a light. He picked up the phone, lifted the receiver. The phone was dead.

Royce felt nothing at all; he was beyond disappointment. He went on into the bedroom, got a blanket, and covered Russell's body.

Numbly, he walked back to the kitchen. He opened the refrigerator, found some cheese that had not spoiled. He forced himself to eat it. He drank two glasses of water.

There was nothing more that he could do. He had failed, and more than failed. *They* had taken over Bob Russell, a human being. And he had left Kathy and the children at the Baboonery.

He could not get to Mitaboni. The river crossed the road about a mile from Russell's place and he could not cross it. He could only go back.

If he could make it....

If there was anything to go back to....

Wait a minute.

"The car," he whispered. "Bob had a car."

He went outside through the kitchen door, his rifle ready in his hands. He flattened himself against the wall of the house, letting his eyes adjust to the starlight. He saw no sign of the baboon-things. He believed that they were all so sick that they would not be dangerous, but he took no chances. He moved silently around the house. The night was very still.

He eased his way past the long line of the front porch and paused at the corner. He studied the outbuilding that Russell had used as a garage. The building was dark and silent.

Royce moved in a crouching run to the outbuilding, his boots sucking at the mud. There was no door. He slipped inside and almost collided with Russell's Land Rover. He worked the catch on the door and slid under the wheel. The door made a loud click when he closed it.

His fingers explored the ignition switch. The keys were not there. He remembered that Russell had once told him that he kept the keys in the vehicle, but he had not mentioned exactly where. He tried the panel that ran along the dashboard and found nothing. He checked the sunshades. Nothing but dust. There was very little space under a Land Rover seat, but he tried that, too. Nothing.

Royce forced himself not to panic. It was incredible that the baboon-things had not bothered him. Russell, of course, had been controlled from inside; he required no guards. But the baboons must have heard the racket in the house, and they must have seen him. The only possible explanation was that the baboons were not able to function properly. Royce knew that a wild baboon removed from its troop could not survive. It must be still worse for *these* baboons: robbed even of their natural behavior patterns, manipulated by an alien intelligence that had not yet learned to cope with a strange world....

Royce twisted in the seat. There were storage compartments lining both sides of the back. He tried the one immediately behind him. His searching fingers closed on two keys strung on a sturdy clasp chain.

A wave of relief almost made him giddy. If he could get the damned thing going...

He switched on the ignition and waited a long minute. He jabbed the floor starter with his slippery boot. The engine whined, sputtered, and died. No matter: the battery was okay. He tried it again and the engine caught. He gave it some gas. The roar of the engine blasted at his ears.

Royce set the knobbed lever in the four-wheel mud drive and backed the Land Rover out of the building. He turned on the lights; there was no point to driving in the dark with all the noise he was making. He turned the vehicle carefully and got it headed down the road. He picked up speed. The Land Rover slipped a little from side to side but it was not serious. He drove through the rows of dark sisal without incident.

He bumped out onto the paved main road and turned to the left. The road was in poor condition and the chuckholes and puddles of standing water forced him to take it easy. Nevertheless, it was a breeze compared to walking. There was no obstacle that could stop a Land Rover and he could almost relax as he drove.

He kept going until the beams of his headlights glinted on the river of rushing flood water that had washed out the road. He pulled over and stopped. The water level had dropped some, but the ditch of fast water was still a good twenty-five yards across. He turned off the ignition, cut the lights, and climbed out.

The easy part was over. He would have to walk again.

He gave himself no time to think. He plunged into the brush and picked his way to the bank of the swollen stream. He had more clearance now that the water had receded, and he was able to trudge through the mud at a fairly good clip. He did not need his flashlight. The scattered stars were clear and a warm yellow moon shone through rips in the clouds. There was no threat of rain.

Royce found his rope without difficulty and crossed the swift water. It was much easier this time. He sloshed back to the main road and headed for the Baboonery turnoff.

He walked as though in a trance, just concentrating on moving one heavy boot after the other. The stars turned above him and the moon faded to silver. He heard the calls of a few night birds from the wet black trees; once a leopard coughed from the bush on his left.

When Royce scrambled across the erosion ditch and started down the Baboonery road, it was almost four o'clock in the morning. His neck was sore and his shoulders were stiff. A muscle twitched maddeningly under his left eye. His legs were like iron posts. He kept going by setting himself a series of attainable goals: that baobab tree, that puddle, that rock.

He made it to his waiting Land Rover and stared at it almost without recognition. He climbed in and got underway. He drove clumsily at first with his numbed arms and legs. After he nearly got stuck in the mud, he forced himself to concentrate on what he was doing.

It was daylight when the vehicle jolted across the railroad tracks. A fat golden sun was floating up into a blue sky that harbored islands of dark-bottomed white clouds. The rain-sodden world seemed to be holding its breath.

When Royce pulled up beside the main building, he had been gone a little more than twenty-four hours.

He climbed out of the mud-spattered Land Rover. He did not even have time to look around.

The door opened and Kathy ran out.

As soon as he saw her, he knew that he was too late.

11

Royce took his wife in his arms. He could feel the tense trembling of her body. He held her tightly, trying to reassure her with a strength that almost failed him. The words they did not speak were the most important words of all. They said: *We're alive, you and I. We're not hurt. Whatever has happened, we're not licked yet.*

Kathy pushed him back finally. She held both of his hands in hers. She smiled a little, her tired eyes wet with tears. "You look terrible. I'm so glad to see you."

"I've seen you looking better yourself. You've been up all night, haven't you? What in the hell happened?"

She did not answer him directly. "Bob Russell? The telephone? Is help coming?"

"I'm afraid we're still alone in this, sugar. My big rescue mission was a bust." Quickly, as undramatically as he could, he told her what had happened. "But what went on *here?*"

Kathy took a deep breath, searching for coherent words. She shook her head. "You better... see it first."

She led him toward the shed that housed the generator. Even from a distance the damage was obvious. The flimsy structure had been ripped to shreds. The drainage ditches were intact, but their purpose no longer existed. The generator was wrecked. Royce took one look at what was now a pile of junk and knew that it was hopeless. He had repaired that cantankerous generator more times than he cared to remember, but his efforts had amounted to little more than inspired tinkering. He was not enough of a mechanic to rebuild a demolished generator from the ground up. In any case, he did not have the necessary equipment. The generator was finished and it would *stay* finished.

Tired as he was, the significance of the destroyed generator could not escape him. They had no lights except for a couple of camp lanterns. The freezers were out, which threatened their food supply. The pump would not function, but water at least was no immediate problem.

He thought: *They may have trouble with baboon behavior patterns, to say nothing of human behavior patterns. But they can damn well figure out a primitive electrical system. And they can set us up for a long, long night....*

"What else?" he said.

Kathy took him to the long-roofed baboon shelter. Six of the cages had been broken into. Six baboons were gone.

"I guess they needed some replacements," Royce said in what he hoped was a light tone. "The troops are getting a little thin."

377

"They waited until late. It must have been nearly midnight," Kathy said wearily. *(Midnight,* Royce thought. *Where was I at midnight? I must have been just about leaving Bob Russell's—could that have been just last night?)* "They knew what they were after—knew just where to go. They probably knew you were gone. They headed straight for the generator and the cages. The men heard them, saw them. They did what they could. They drove them off with bows and arrows. Mutisya was bitten in the leg. I cleaned it up, bandaged it. The men are afraid, Royce. They don't know what is going on. I can't even begin to explain. And I'm afraid. All those hours...no lights...not knowing if they were coming back.... The kids don't understand at all; they're so damned *cheerful....*"

Kathy's voice was rising, veering toward hysteria. Royce cut her off. "The things that came...just baboons?"

"They're *not* just baboons. You know..."

"I mean, just in baboon form? Nothing else? No machines, no armor, no men?"

"I—we—just saw baboons. Royce, what are we going to *do?* I can't face another night here in the dark. I'm only human, I'm scared, I've got Susan and Barbara to think about. I'll do anything you say, but we can't just *sit* here."

Only human. I'm only human, too. Is that enough? "Look, Kathy. I'm dead on my feet. I can't even think. I'm here and we'll be ready for them tonight. But I won't be of any use if I'm a walking zombie. Tell Wathome to rustle up some breakfast. I want to talk to Elijah and Mutisya. It isn't too likely that anything big will happen before it gets dark. I've got to get a few hours of sleep—you should too. Then we'll figure out what we can do."

Tears rose in Kathy's eyes again. She had hoped—believed—that help was on the way, that the nightmare would be over with his return. All through that terrible night she had kept herself going by holding fast to the thought that Royce would be back with the sun, that Royce would somehow take care of things. And now he was back, and it was all as it was before....

He held her, tried to comfort her. "Baby, we'll be okay. We can all get in the Land Rover if we have to. We can drive to a place where they can never find us." *(And where might that be, friend? At the bottom of a mudhole?)* "As our British friends say, you've got to keep your pecker up."

The phrase always tickled Kathy; she managed a feeble smile. "That's a hell of a thing to say to a woman."

"It refers, I think, to a bird's beak. Anyhow, you've got to trust me. I'm all there is."

She kissed him lightly. "I guess you'll have to do, then. Sorry to go all female on you. I'll get Wathome busy in the kitchen."

She left him and Royce almost staggered with the release from play-acting. He was so shot he could barely stand. His hopes, too, had gone down the drain. He saw no way out, no effective action he could take. Unless...

There was some truth, perhaps, in the old adage: *The best defense is a good offense.* He had been on the defensive from the beginning. If he could hit them where they lived...

Yeah, but *what* offense? Bows and arrows?

He rubbed his burning eyes. His head felt as though it were stuffed with cotton. It was dangerous to try to make plans now, he knew. He just wasn't tracking.

He walked on rubber legs to the men's quarters. Mutisya got up out of bed to let him in. Royce embraced the man without awkwardness. "I know what you did last night," he said. "I thank you for it. Someday, I hope I can thank you properly."

Mutisya retained his dignity. "A man does what he must do," he said quietly. There was a gentle rebuke in his tone. Royce should not have been surprised, he seemed to be saying, that the men had done their jobs properly.

Royce examined Mutisya's leg by loosening the bandage. The puncture wounds from the spiked baboon canines were deep but clean. There was no sign of infection. "We'll want to change that dressing before tonight," he said, pulling the bandage tight again. "Is it painful?"

Mutisya grinned, exposing his filed teeth. "Compared to a Masai spear, it is nothing. I am well."

"Give it as much rest as you can. I have a job for Elijah, but I want you to stay off that leg for awhile. Okay?"

"Okay, Mr. Royce."

Royce found Elijah and expressed his thanks to him. He told him to get a crew together and drag in some firewood. "Pile it in the places where the outside lights are." he said. "It will be better than nothing."

Elijah blinked behind his tinted glasses. "The wood is wet," he said with his customary optimism. "It will not burn."

"We have petrol—plenty of it now that we can't keep the generator going. The wood will burn."

Elijah looked dubious but Royce was too tired to argue. He plodded across the muddy ground with the welcome sun warm on his aching shoulders. He entered the breezeway, greeted Wathome who had a fire going in the cookstove, and slumped down at the wooden table in the sitting room.

"No place like home," he muttered.

He fought to stay awake until the food arrived, too weary even to attempt conversation with Kathy. He drank two cups of strong, black coffee, which had no effect on him whatsoever. He ate three fried eggs, six slices of fried Spam, and four pieces of charred toast. Surprisingly, it all tasted delicious.

He went into the familiar bedroom and felt better when he saw the kids still sound asleep. He moved to take a shower, remembered that there was no water, and simply piled into bed without any preamble. It felt great.

"Call me by three this afternoon," he muttered. "Don't forget, for God's sake."

Kathy smiled. "It's not likely to slip my mind," she said.

Royce buried his head in the pillows and closed his eyes.

Sleep was instantaneous.

When you get *really* tired, there are no thoughts at all.

"Royce!"

A detached part of him, floating way up near the surface, heard Kathy's voice. But it was far away, it could not reach the rest of him. If he could get down deep enough...

"Royce!"

He felt something digging into his shoulder. The whole bed seemed to be shaking. He swam up from somewhere, not without a flash of irritation. He opened his eyes.

"Look," he muttered. "What kind of a joint is this anyway? When I leave a call I don't mean..."

Kathy cut him off. "Royce, wake up, for God's sake!"

"I'm awake." He blinked. "What is it? What's..."

Kathy's fingers tightened on, his shoulder. "Barbara! She's gone. They've taken Barbara!"

Royce jerked up in the bed, his eyes wide and staring. He looked in confusion at the window, saw the curtains blowing gently and the sunlight beyond. "It's still light. What time is it? They wouldn't..."

"Oh, wake up, wake up! They came...the baboon-things...just now. I was in the kitchen with Susan. Barby wandered outside to play in the mud... I didn't see her at first... she was right outside the door...."

He felt a cold horror. "You *saw* them take her?"

"I saw them. They grabbed her and ran. I could hear her crying. Royce, we've got to get her back before...before..."

Royce leaped out of bed, threw on his clothes, yanked on his muddy boots. He grabbed his .375 and shoved Kathy ahead of him into the breezeway. "Show me. Quickly now. Exactly where did they go?"

Kathy pointed a trembling finger. Royce's eyes followed the line of sight, across the open compound, beyond the baboon cages, to the dark line of the bush still rain-wet under the bright afternoon sun. He saw movement there, shadows....

Royce was engulfed in an anger and a terror beyond anything he had ever known. He could face danger to himself with understanding if not with enthusiasm; he was a man, and he had years of experience behind him. But to seize a child, a little girl five years old, to carry her off into something she could not possibly comprehend....

It was *his* failure, of course. Barby could not defend herself. And he had been *sleeping.*

Even through his sick fury, the questions insinuated themselves. Questions and answers....

Why had they taken Barby? Obviously, because she *was* a child. They had learned something from Bob Russell, learned perhaps that they could not yet cope effectively with an adult. They had not been completely successful with the baboons. They might take Barby away with them, experiment with her, come back when they knew more....

Why hadn't they waited for darkness, after going to the trouble of knocking out the generator? Well, they were not fools, whatever else they were. They had seen him come back. They knew he would have to sleep, knew he could be ready for a night attack. They were at least as intelligent as he was. They had simply revised their plans.

And now...

His hatred drowned out everything else. He could *see* them out there in the bush, moving, watching....

He ran through the slow-drying mud beneath a deep-blue sky fragmented with drifting clouds still swollen with rain. He pulled up at the baboon cages, his heart hammering. He threw the heavy rifle to his shoulder, peered through the telescopic sight. He picked one of them up almost at once. His belly tightened as the cross-hairs centered on the olive-gray coat, the naked snout, the gleaming canines.

His finger curled on the trigger.

He did not fire.

Royce lowered the .375, his hands shaking. He swallowed hard to keep from vomiting.

Think, you fool. You've made enough mistakes. If you shoot every animal out there, what then? Will that get Barby back?

He looked more closely at those dark forms at the edge of the bush. What were they doing there? Why hadn't they gone with the others? Surely, they knew they were vulnerable if they did not run. What if they couldn't run? What if they were too sick, too weak to escape?

He had to get through to that ship, wherever it was. He had to get Barbara out of there. He couldn't storm it with a popgun and bows and arrows.

Whatever else he did, he had to get his girl *out.*

Royce spun around, shouting to Mutisya and Elijah. He sprinted to the lab storeroom, scooped up two bottles of sernyl. He filled the three pole-syringes he had. He hollered to Wathome to throw some maize and pineapple into the Land Rover and fill it with petrol.

With the rifle in one hand and the syringe in the other, he led the men on a dead run toward the creatures in the bush. He took no safety precautions. It was speed that counted now, nothing else.

The baboon-things saw him coming. There were four of them, all males. They coughed and snorted in fear. They tried to retreat into the tangle of the bush, but they could not run. They staggered and fell, saliva dripping from their snouts. Their eyes were cloudy and dull. The stink of sickness hovered over them like a preview of death.

The animals turned at bay. There was an alien intelligence in their primate skulls, but illness reduces all creatures to the same level. They functioned as sick and desperate beasts, nothing more.

They bared their fangs and waited.

Royce did not hesitate. He faked at the nearest one, drawing a weak lunge and a snapping of jaws. He leaped behind the animal and jabbed with his syringe. He hit him hard and rammed the plunger home.

The animal screamed, biting the air.

Royce backed away and refilled his syringe. Mutisya, despite his bad leg, already had another baboon cornered. Elijah, with the third syringe, was taking his own sweet time, protecting himself.

Royce stuck his second baboon, snatched the pole from Elijah, and went after the last animal. The baboon ignored his fake and attacked with a snarl of hate. Royce kicked him in the face with his boot, feeling a crunch of bone. He jabbed him in the belly with his needle, slammed the plunger with the heel of his hand, and leaped back.

He stood there, his chest heaving, sweat staining his shirt. The sernyl did its job. The baboons wobbled about on rubber legs, collapsed, twitched, and were still.

Royce eyed the thin bodies with a raging mixture of emotions: fear, anger, wonder, loathing, pity....

"Watch them," he said to Mutisya.

His thoughts on his child somewhere out there in the waiting bush, he ran back to get the Land Rover.

12

The warm afternoon sun stroked the rain-soaked land with golden fingers. The air was still and heavy. It was hot enough for wisps of smoky vapor to rise from the sodden acacias. The washed gray bulges of the baobabs stood impassively in the sunlight, indifferent to either rain or sun. Insects buzzed in the flattened grass and squadrons of birds feasted until they could hardly fly.

The back road to Mitaboni, thick with choking dust the last time Royce had driven it when he had checked his traps an eternity ago, was a trail of mud. There were no wheel tracks ahead of the Land Rover; no vehicle had come this way since the rains had started. The two rails that paralleled the road on the left had a thin patina of rust on them; no train had gotten through for a long, long time.

The slowing of the rains and the heat of the sun had helped to drain the road. It was not impossible now, at least on this side of the Tsavo. It was merely improbable.

The battered Land Rover was heavily loaded this time, which was both an advantage and a disadvantage. It did not skid and fishtail as it had done when Royce had driven it alone, but it dug into the soft spots more deeply and persistently. Royce had four men with him. Elijah and Wathome rode up front in the cab. He had taken Elijah so that he would not lose face with his men and Wathome because he was steady and reliable. Nzioki and Kisaluwa rode in the back with the unconscious baboons. They were both big strong men not unduly cursed with imagination. Whenever the Land Rover got stuck they vaulted over the side and pushed.

Royce had left Mutisya with Kathy and Susan. There was nothing else he could do, and in any case Mutisya was the best man for the job. He could not carry a load through the bush on his bad leg, but he could fight if he had to. Royce trusted him more than other man he knew in Kenya, white or black.

Royce tried not to think about Barbara. Whenever her image slipped into his mind his vision blurred and his thoughts went wild. He knew that he had to think clearly now, had to keep his emotions out of it. If he surrendered to hate, whatever small chance the child had was gone.

He fought the wheel, nursed the whining engine, picked his course his skill and care. He did not try to bull his way through the slop on the road. He stayed out of the ruts, took advantage of every patch of grass, every stretch of firm earth....

He forced himself to think about *them*.

He knew about where they were. The location of the eerie glow that he had seen was burned into his brain. It was this side of the roaring Tsavo River, thank God, off there to the right in the bush. He had gotten to within a mile of the source of that glow that long-ago night. He could have found it whenever he wished, even in the torrent of the rains. It would have been foolish before, perhaps suicidal. His chances were not good now. He knew that, but he had no other choice.

Would they know that he was not coming as an attacker bent on revenge? Would they even wait to see what his intentions were? If he ever got back to Kathy at all, would he still be Royce Crawford...or something else?

Well, he could always shoot himself if it came to that. And he could take a few of them with him, too....

Don't think that way. Choke it off.

What about them, those beings waiting for him in the warm mists of a world not their own? Could they understand him any better than he understood them? Could he see himself through their eyes? He had to try. If he miscalculated their response to his actions....

It came to him that he had never really seen them. A vapor trail in the sky, alien eyes staring from the skull of a baboon, a man who had once been Bob Russell, strange tracks in the African earth—these were their only visible signs. He could not imagine what they might look like. He supposed that it did not matter. They might be ugly or beautiful. They might produce no reaction at all. He might not even recognize them as living beings. It made no difference. It was what they *did* that counted. Octopus or dragon or blob of jelly—it was all the same.

He could not know what purpose had brought them to this world. He thought he knew why they had chosen this particular place; he could not believe that it had been an accident. This remote spot in the African bush must have seemed ideal from their point of view. They could operate with a minimum of interference and a maximum of safety. There were isolated human beings to observe, and there were simpler primates to experiment with—baboons that were enough like men so that men themselves used them for medical research. That was strategy, of course. It told him nothing about the nature of the game that was being played.

Royce knew one thing, at least. This was a dangerous world to them. They were running terrible risks. They were taking casualties. Whatever project they were engaged in, this was no picnic. They were vulnerable outside their ship. They were in a strange and hostile land. They must feel that they were surrounded by monsters, aliens bent on destroying them. They had killed, it was true, but perhaps they had only done so in what they regarded as self defense.

Suppose one day man landed on some distant planet. Why would *he* have come, what impulse would have driven him across the darkness and the light-years? Could he explain, and would he even try? If he set out to explore that fearful world, if he trapped some specimens, what would he do if he were attacked by monstrous beings he could not understand? Would he stay his hand, leave them in peace?

Royce knew with a hard cold certainty that the killing had to stop. No matter who had made the first false move, the chain of fear and destruction had to be broken. A man does not worry about a world or two worlds when the life of his child is at stake. It was Barby he was fighting for. But if she were to have any chance at all, there had to be a new kind of contact between him and them.

Somehow, he had to show them that man could be a better ally than an enemy. He had to prove that he was more than a mindless savage. He had to demonstrate that a man could be a friend worth having. If *they* could not risk compassion, then *he* must take that first tough step.

If his gesture did not move them—if they were so different from man that they could not be moved—then he had lost. But he could not get his child back by firing at a spaceship with rifle bullets. He could not induce an act of mercy by more killing.

Royce ground his teeth together. The muscles of his arms stood out like taut ropes as he gripped the wheel. He did not know whether he was man enough for the job ahead. There was another side of him, a side that shrieked for vengeance, that wanted to surrender to hate, that wanted to cut loose and take the easy way....

"Damn them," he whispered. "Damn them for coming here, damn them all."

He pushed the Land Rover as far as he could along the muddy trail, kept it going until the thunder of the flooded Tsavo was loud above the whine of the engine, and then jerked the wheel to the right. The vehicle jolted into the bush with a series of shuddering shocks. Royce engaged all four wheels but used his mud gear to maintain speed. He could not bull his way through thick brush and fallen trees, but it was surprising how much open country there was in uncleared land. There were lanes of wet brown grass and barren fields without a tree in them. The ground was more uneven than the road, but thick mud was less of a problem. He picked his course with care and he made good progress. He had trailed many an animal this way, and except for the jolts it was not particularly difficult.

Royce pushed the Land Rover on for nearly twenty minutes until the acacias and vines and thorny scrub brush thickened around him. Shadows darkened the land and the air grew still. A wall of damp vegetation confronted him, and he knew that he would have to make a long and time-consuming circle to get around it.

He stopped the Land Rover. There was a heavy silence in the air, broken only by the distant liquid roar of the Tsavo. Mosquitoes and flies swarmed through the open windows of the cab.

Royce leaped out, slapping at the bugs.

Now the fun starts, he thought.

It was a strange, slow procession that picked its hesitant way through the darkening wilderness. The men walked in single file, their footsteps cushioned by the soggy ground. Royce went first, a limp baboon slung over his left shoulder and a rifle in his right hand. Elijah followed him, staggering under the weight of a folded tarp and a canvas bag filled maize and pineapples. Royce wanted Elijah right behind him; he knew that Elijah had little stomach for this safari, and he needed to make certain that Elijah kept moving in the right direction. Nzioki and Kisaluwa came next, each carrying a baboon with something less than complete enthusiasm. Wathome brought up the rear with the last baboon and a sharp ax. Royce had confidence in Wathome, at least where cooking was not involved.

It was not, Royce thought, the most powerful possible assemblage to represent mankind in an encounter with an alien power. Perhaps, though, its very impotence constituted its best chance for success.

He forced his way forward, relying on his memory to take him in the right direction. There were no landmarks. He could feel the baboon stirring slightly on his shoulder. The dead weight dragged him down; it was like carrying a sixty-pound sack of lead. Insects bit his hands and face and he could do nothing to deter them. The clouds in the lowering sky grew thicker and blacker. If the rains came again...

He sensed what he could not see. He was getting closer to *them.* They were ahead of him. They must be very close now. He did not doubt that they were watching him somehow, waiting for him, sizing him up...

A brown flash bolted out of a clump of dead grass right in front of him. There was a snort of expelled air, a muted drumming of hooves pushing against the wet earth. Royce recognized the animal as a small bushbuck the instant he saw him, but his heart hammered so hard in his chest that he almost had to stop to catch his breath. He was keyed up so high that the slightest touch would have made him jump.

"Don't let it get dark yet," he whispered. "Don't let it rain." It might have been a prayer, though its target was uncertain. God, Mulungu, Allah, one of the local deities....

He fought his way on. Thorns ripped at his legs. The pounding sound of the flooded river came clearly through the screening trees but Royce thought he heard a new sound now. A higher sound, steady but taut, a vibrant hum of tingling power. It was like the hot buzz of electricity in a high-tension line back home on a still day....

He picked his way around a grotesquely swollen baobab tree, pushed through a curtain of clinging brush.

There it was, as he had always known it would be.

He stopped and stared.

It rested in the middle of a small clearing: white as new-fallen snow, smooth and featureless, terribly matter-of-fact and terribly *wrong* there in the confines of the African bush.

There was a cold white light coming from it, an aura that ignored the earthly shadows. The hum seemed louder and Royce almost thought he could see the thing move silently. It was *on*.

It was perfectly round, a great white globe. It looked like it could roll. It seemed to be resting on the ground but it made no impression at all, as though it were weightless. The blank smooth surface of the sphere looked more like plastic than metal. No, not plastic. Like a gigantic glowing white marble...

It was hard to grasp the size of the thing. The mind tried to find a slot to put it in, tried to check it against something known, and the mind failed. It was big, yes, but that was a pitiful word, an inadequate word. Mountains are big, oceans are big, men are big. It was not as big as the great rockets that men launched from this world—but it was far larger than the capsules that perched on top of those rockets. The thing was perhaps eighty feet across, perhaps more. The size of a house with rooms higher than any house, a vast shining bubble that moved through the dark seas between worlds and stars....

Royce thought: *Barby is in that thing. She has to be in there. She's in there with them, whatever they are.*

The men crowded in behind him, staring with more curiosity and fear than astonishment. They had seen so many astounding things in their lifetimes, things that had suddenly appeared in their world from outside—trains and planes and trucks that growled along the dusty roads. They were willing to accept anything now. They did not even ask questions, fearing to be thought ignorant. They simply waited for instructions.

Royce knew that he was close to death. He was certain that the beings in that ship could wipe him out as easily as he could step on a spider.

Act, he told himself. *They are waiting* to *see what we are going to do. Show them.*

He lowered the twitching baboon to the ground, gently. He took the ax from Wathome and told the men to remain as still as possible. He searched around in the brush, not venturing any closer to the sphere. He found some wood and hacked out six crude but sturdy poles. He fashioned a rough point on one end of each pole and chopped a notch in the other end. The sound of the ax blade biting into the damp wood worried him, but he knew that his fear was irrational. *They* would know that the men had arrived. It would serve no purpose to aim at concealment.

He gathered up the poles and returned to the waiting Africans. "Okay," he said. "Leave the baboons. Bring the tarp. Wathome, stay with the baboons. Holler if they come to enough to move away. Quickly, now."

He moved out into the clearing. He forced himself to walk toward the glowing white sphere. He went to within thirty yards of it. He could *feel* the thing as it towered over him. The humming tension that surrounded it was a palpable force that made his skin crawl.

Royce tried not to think, tried to shut off his imagination. He did not look at the snowy monstrous bubble that rested so lightly on the alien earth. He spread out the greasy tarp and arranged the poles at the four corners and the two canvas side loops. One by one, he drove the pointed supports into the yielding ground with the blunt end of the ax head.

The men hoisted the tarp up into position and tied it to the notched poles with the short ropes that were already fastened to the tarp. The heavy canvas sagged a little but the structure held. The tarp was only some four feet off the ground.

Royce went back and got the bag of food from Wathome. He walked around the shelter so that he was in plain view from the blandly featureless sphere. He took the maize cobs and the pineapples from the canvas container, holding them up so they could be seen. He placed the food under the tarp.

"Now," he said, trying to speak in a normal tone of voice. "Bring the baboons. Put them in there under the tarp. Be very careful with them. Don't just *dump* them, understand?"

They got the baboons. All of them were awake now but still confused from the drug. The men handled them gingerly. Royce had a bad moment when the animal he was carrying twisted in his arms and tried to bite him. He was determined to just let the creature bite if he had to, but the baboon-thing was too weak and fuzzy-minded to press home his attack. They placed the twitching animals under the tarp, their heads toward the food.

"Okay," Royce said. "Back to the edge of the clearing there. Don't run. Take it easy. Just walk."

The men withdrew, leaving the crude gray shelter with its strange occupants. The pole-supported tarp stood there in the field, a homely and somehow pitiful contrast to the massive glowing sphere that dominated the earth.

Royce turned to face the Africans. He felt himself trembling with relief. He did not dare to hope yet, but at least no new disaster had struck. He knew that he had been responsible for bringing these men here, and it was not really their fight. It was *his* child that was in that thing.

"*Asante sana,*" he said. "Thank you. I won't forget your help. There may be danger here; I don't know. There is no need for you to stay. Go on back and help Mutisya. Tell Mrs. Crawford that I am well and that everything is being done that can be done. Leave me the Land Rover. If you go now, you can reach the road before dark."

Elijah needed no urging. He adjusted his tinted glasses and struck off through the bush without a backward glance. Nzioki and Kisaluwa hesitated only a moment and followed the headman.

Wathome managed a tired smile. "I will stay if you wish," he said. "Miss Barbara was a friend to me."

Royce felt a stinging in his eyes. Mutisya, Wathome—they were good men. They had resources that he had not expected. He hated the barriers between them. Their differences were small indeed. Skin color, background, wealth—what did they matter in the perspective of that alien sphere from the depths of space? Men were men, that was all. "If you could help, my friend, I would ask you to stay." Royce tried to explain, tried to avoid the patronizing words of a *bwana* to a workman. "I am hoping that the ...the people who have taken Barbara will let her go. If they do, I will bring her home. There is nothing to do but wait. If they don't let her go, I don't know what will happen. You have a family of your own. I think it is my responsibility to stay here. I think it is yours to go back where it may be safer."

Wathome nodded. He seemed neither glad nor sorry. He turned and followed the others on the backtrail through the bush.

Royce was alone.

13

The African night fell swiftly. It was as though the sea of thick black clouds had fallen from the sky, shrouding the earth. The air was very damp and Royce shivered in the sudden chill. There were no stars; there was not even a faint luminescence where the moon should be.

A wall of darkness pressed in behind him, a living darkness that stirred with padded footfalls and called with the soft songs of night birds. It was a darkness that seemed to stretch away unbroken to the shores of the Indian Ocean where silver-crested waves washed over the clean white sands. Royce could feel that darkness, but it did not concern him.

He stood at the edge of the clearing, his eyes fixed on the great glowing sphere. He could see no change in it. In the cold radiance of its own steady light it was bland and uncaring, a huge egg of white marble that might have been deposited on the earth by some monstrous bird. There was no sign of activity, no alteration in the pitch of the taut humming that came from somewhere within its depths. It did nothing at all.

He could see the shelter clearly in the eerie glow. The baboon-things were still there; he could see their dark shadows beneath the tarp. The sernyl had long since worn off, of course. Royce figured that the creatures were so sick and weak that they could not move without great effort. In any case, they could probably not enter the ship unaided. Unless there was an atmosphere lock of some kind, they could not go into that alien interior without protection. Something would have to come out and get them....

Royce stood for what seemed an eternity, hardly daring to move. He had rested his rifle against a tree. He stood far enough out into the open to show that his hands were empty.

A light rain began to fall. It was just enough to be visible against the cold glow of the sphere. Royce fancied that he could hear it ticking against the surface of the tarp. The muted rush of the Tsavo seemed louder to him, but that was surely his imagination.

He trembled a little, colder inside than out. Unless he had made a terrible mistake, he was no more than seventy yards from his daughter. Not even the length of a football field. He could run to her in eight or nine seconds if he could just get inside that thing....

He could not shut off his mind forever. Barbara might already be dead. She might have been altered so that another mind was cradled inside her skull. *They* might be working on her even now, probing that small body that had known only a few short years, that had never known terror....

Royce cursed silently but viciously. He cursed *them* and he cursed himself. He had made too many mistakes. If he had acted differently, if he had made the right moves, she would not be in there now. He would not be standing here like a fool in the night and the rain, helpless and afraid.

Come on, come on. Do something. Do anything.

He could get his rifle. He could advance into that unearthly glow. He could threaten the baboon-things under that tarp. He could drag one out into the light and put a bullet through that implanted brain behind the animal eyes.

And then—what?

He did not move. He forced himself to stay where he was. He could not afford the luxury of action.

He looked at his watch. It was only ten o'clock.

He groaned aloud. There was nothing he could do, nothing.

He waited between the living darkness and the cold white light of the machine.

It was nearly midnight and the rain was pattering down in heavier drops when the frozen tableau suddenly changed. The change was minor at first, but it was startling in a scene that had been utterly without motion for so long.

Royce held his breath, staring. His knees were so weak that he almost fell.

In the exact center of the surface of the glowing sphere, there was an alteration in the intensity of the cold white light. A circular area about ten feet across shifted from marble white to a dull solid gray. It changed again, seeming to flow from one texture to another. It turned to a metallic glistening black that was sharply outlined against the featureless surrounding white.

It moved.

It bulged outward, a black swelling on the smooth white sphere. A circular black column descended from the bubble. The shaft came down without a sound, seeming to materialize out of the very air. It touched the earth.

The bottom of the column went from jet black to the dull gray that Royce had seen a moment before. For a long minute, nothing happened.

Then, abruptly, there was an opening. There was nothing that opened like a door or a hatch. What had been solid was simply transformed into a space that led inside. A cold greenish light spilled like smoke out into the rain.

Something emerged from the column into the clearing.

Royce stood his ground, afraid to move and afraid not to move. The thing that had come out of the ship looked like a strange fat shining worm with legs. It seemed too large to have come out of the shaft. Its swollen, flexible body shimmered with white light. The light was intense; it hurt Royce's eyes. There were six legs: strong jointed black metallic appendages that blurred where they articulated with the serpentine body. The thing looked cumbersome and poorly designed, but it worked with fluid ease. The legs left sharp round depressions in the damp earth but they did not stick. The shining white body moved above the legs almost independently. Perhaps, Royce thought, the legs were not supports at all but served some other function....

The thing was obviously not alive. It was a machine of some sort, a shell, a container that held life forms that Royce could not even imagine.

He *knew* that the thing was not empty.

The glaring white caterpillar flowed with an improbable grace through the rain. It gave off a crackling buzzing sound, different from the hum of the looming sphere. It crossed the space to the crude tarp shelter and stopped.

The fat worm's head seemed to grow longer. It dipped down and probed under the tarp like the questing trunk of an elephant. The shimmering white light illuminated the waiting baboon creatures as though a flare had been stuck in the soft earth.

There was a slow leakage of smoky cloudiness, a blurring of light and form. The four baboons remained motionless. The smudge of smoke-blue vapor surrounded the animals, obscuring them. The baboon-things were *absorbed.*

The cloudiness disappeared. The head of the shining caterpillar shrank to its former size and lifted in the wet air. The swollen sinuous body turned with precision and flowed back to the sphere, buzzing loudly. It seemed to coil into the cold green light that spilled from the bottom of the black shaft. The green light...stopped. The foot of the column went back to a dull solid gray.

The shelter was empty. There was nothing under the tarp.

The only sounds were the taut humming of the sphere, the distant roar of the Tsavo, and the gentle splashing of the falling rain. It seemed much darker despite the white glow of the sphere.

Royce stood in an agony of fear and indecision. He had played his only card. He had made the only move that was open to him. He had gambled on the psychology of the beings in that ship, hoping against hope that they were not as totally alien as they seemed.

If he had thrown away Barby's last chance...

If that glistening black column were withdrawn...

He swallowed hard. "Come on, come on, come on," he whispered.

It seemed to him that hours passed with that great white sphere resting impassively in the clearing. His watch told him that it had been only ten minutes.

The gray area at the bottom of the shaft...disappeared. Smoky green light eddied out into the rain. The shaft was open again.

Royce's hands were wet with sweat. He could feel cold icy drops dripping from beneath his arms. His heart thudded against his chest with a force that made him sway. He crossed his slippery fingers.

The shining worm-thing came out again, buzzing and clicking. It looked smaller now. It wound its way above its six-legged frame back to the shelter. The swollen head stretched down beneath the sagging tarp. The light almost blinded Royce but he kept his eyes riveted on it. The blurring vapor swirled like blue smoke. He could not see what was happening.

The head withdrew. The strangely graceful caterpillar made no attempt to approach Royce. It turned in a blaze of white light and went back to the sphere. The opening filled in behind it, shutting off the smoky green light. The dull gray color of the bottom of the column shifted to a jet black. The black shaft lifted without a sound into the air, seeming to flow upward into the dark bubble in the center of the glowing sphere. The swelling on the smooth globe collapsed and was gone. The circular area where the bubble had been went from metallic black to dull gray to marble white.

The sphere was as it had been: bland, featureless, an uncaring egg resting on the alien earth.

Royce moved. He could not wait any longer. He walked slowly out into the clearing. He felt the cool raindrops on his face, the ache in his stiff legs, the yielding softness of the wet turf. He kept his eyes fixed on the small, lonely shelter. He thought he could see something under the water-heavy tarp, something still and motionless....

There was no visible reaction from the white sphere.

He ducked under the edge of the tarp, crawled into the shelter on his hands and knees. The animal smell of the baboons was very strong. There was another smell, too: an acrid oily smell that suffused the close air.

The shelter was not empty. There was a form, a bundle, curled up on the flattened grass.

Royce touched it, feeling dry cloth and warm flesh underneath. He turned it over, gently. He stared at a pale drawn face, close-cropped hair, a small still body dressed in wrinkled blue jeans and a smudged yellow T-shirt.

"Barby," he whispered. "Barby, honey."

The child stirred at his touch, shivered. She opened her eyes. They seemed blank at first, disoriented. Royce felt a chill of terror when he saw those eyes. But the eyes cleared. There was recognition.

She reached out for him.

"Daddy?" she said weakly. "Daddy?"

Royce scooped her up, pressed her to him. "Everything is okay," he whispered. "Hang on now."

He lunged out from under the shelter, his child in his arms.

He ran.

Royce never knew how he got through the dark and dripping bush. He did it mindlessly, never stopping, never hesitating. He made no false moves. He did not give a thought to snakes or wild animals, despite the fact that he had left his rifle back at the edge of the clearing. He simply clutched his child tightly to him and *ran*.

The Land Rover was waiting. He put Barby in the seat next to him, her eyes wide with excitement now. He kicked the engine into life and churned the vehicle through the trail he had made, following the tracks of his wheels. The path was clear in the bright headlight beams. It was still raining, but the rain had not been hard enough to make new mud a problem.

He skidded out onto the road, spun to the left, and gave it some gas. The tires took hold. The Land Rover whipped and jolted between dark lanes of dripping vegetation. Barby held on tightly to the gray metal shelf that stretched under the instrument panel. Her small body bounced alarmingly on the lightly padded seat but Royce was not about to slow down now. He shouted encouragement and maintained all the speed he dared.

He saw the welcome lights of the Baboonery at last. The men had lit the fires and kept them going somehow. There were paraffin lamps gleaming through the windows.

Royce hit the horn in sheer exuberance. The Land Rover skidded to a stop. There was a sudden silence as he cut the engine. He jerked open the door and almost fell in his haste to get out.

"It's okay!" he yelled into the shadows. "I've got her! Everything is okay!"

Figures, running figures. Laughter, that wonderful long-absent sound. Clutching hands. Faces: Mutisya, Mbali, Wathome, Kathy, Susan....

Kathy almost smothered Barbara as she lifted the child from the Land Rover. Tears were streaming down her haggard face. Susan jumped up and down, half with glee at her sister's return and half in annoyance at being left out of things.

"We don't have any electricity," Susan said, yanking on Barbara's arm. "We don't have any water."

"A baboon almost ate me," Barby said solemnly, topping Susan's best effort.

Royce started to follow his family through the breezeway door and then stopped when he felt a touch on his shoulder. He turned.

"Mr. Royce," Wathome said, pointing. "Look!"

He could not miss it; it filled the sky. Back there where he had been, back there in the dark bush between the Mitaboni road and the lost and lonely Tsavo, an intense white light pulsed upward through the blackness and the rain. It grew brighter still as he watched, a miniature sun that transformed night into day.

He could hear it now: a taut throbbing hum that stirred like a keening alien wind out of that distant clearing and whined through the swollen baobabs and the dripping branches of the acacia trees.

He called out to Kathy and she came to stand by his side. He wanted to say something, but no words came. There were no words. They were witnesses to an event that had no parallel on the earth, an ending or a beginning....

He took her hand, knowing that it was a childish gesture. He felt small and powerless and he reached out for comfort, for warmth, for reassurance.

The white light seemed to explode. There was a dull and muffled report, not unlike the detonation of a few sticks of dynamite deep underground. A wave of warm air touched his face and was gone. The explosion of white light... vanished.

There was a whistling roar and an arc of silver mounted into the sky on a column of thunder. The sound was gone in an instant. A silver glow lingered briefly beneath the torn clouds and then it, too, was gone.

There was only the great night and the feeble fires that man had made.

Royce felt a curious mixture of weariness and exultation, joy and a kind of sadness. The tension that had filled him for so long drained away. He felt an unutterable relief, a sense of triumph, a strange awareness of loss.

"They're gone," he said softly. "Whoever they were, whatever they wanted, they're gone."

And the dark world around him, no longer threatening, seemed to stir and rustle and murmur in the gentle rain that fell from a known and familiar sky: *gone, gone, gone.*

14

The rains were over. There would be no more rain in Kenya for many months. The golden African sun blazed in a vast and cloudless blue sky. The swollen brown rivers retreated from the ravaged floodplains and flowed clean and fresh between shattered banks. Standing water was absorbed into the earth, finally, and the trails of mud dried and cracked with long fissure lines.

The land was reborn in a miraculous and astonishing burst of life. Green was everywhere: a crisp new green that soothed the eye and refreshed the mind. The bush, once a barren world of dry gray-brown branches and dead grass and blowing red dust, was a riot of living things. It was a new earth, a different earth. Rain in an arid land had done its age-old work, touching seeds long dormant, patiently waiting grass, questing roots, budding leaves...

The vegetation was taller than a man and so thick that Royce could not see through it. Even the baobabs were lush and green. The cactus-like euphorbia seemed to grow before his eyes. The convolvulus had sprouted into clumps that were eight and nine feet high, and the plants were covered with white blossoms that looked like morning glories. Bees droned in the warm, still air.

The toy whistles of the busy trains were heard again and the rust stains were ground from the gleaming tracks by heavy wheels of steel. Crews of sweating men worked on the roads. Bridges were rebuilt across deceptively gentle streams. In time, even the red dust came back again to settle on wax-green leaves and the tough pitted hides of rhino and elephant.

The main road was open, to Nairobi and beyond.

It was all as it had once been, and yet for Royce it could never be the same.

The generator was repaired with monumental labor and minimal cost and the Baboonery lights came on again in the black velvet of the African night. The staccato sounds of drumming came once more from dances near the station. Piles of supplies were unloaded from the Nairobi train. Matt Donaldson came back to supervise the repairs to his battered safari camp.

Royce tried to pick up the threads of his life. It was a curious life certainly—he saw it now as though through alien eyes—but nonetheless he had a job to do. He was not a man to quit without warning; he would do what he had to do until he could be replaced. He owed that, at least, to the Africans who worked for him; if the Baboonery operation collapsed, they might all be fired. He did not regard his decision as being in any way heroic. The threat was over, after all. There was no point in scurrying for safety on a retroactive basis.

He set his traps, caged his animals. He resumed the shipments of baboons to the United States. He told himself that what he was doing was good and valuable. He tried to remember the benefits that would come from medical research. It was not easy.

Royce was not fond of baboons. Certainly, he did not idealize them. But the parallels were too close; they made him feel guilty and uncomfortable. *They*, too, had taken baboons, experimented with them, used them for purposes that had seemed worthwhile to *them*. *They* had done it for the same reason that Royce was doing it: the baboons were a lot like human beings. There was a kinship there. Perhaps there was also a responsibility....

And he looked closely at every baboon he trapped. He looked for signs of weakness, of sickness, of an alien intelligence staring out through desperate primate eyes. Not all of the transformed baboons could have made it back to the ship. He doubted that any of them had survived, but how could he be sure? Were any of them still out there in the bush, bewildered and alone, stranded voyagers in a world not their own?

No, he could not ever again see a baboon without wondering, without remembering....

He wrote to Ben Wallace in Houston, asking that a replacement be sent. He gave reasons, but not the real ones. He told about the fire and the floods and said that his family wanted to leave, which was true enough. He detailed the fine work that had been done by the men and recommended raises for all of them. In particular, he singled out Mutisya and Wathome. He suggested that Mutisya be given enough training so that one day he could manage the Baboonery himself. He made no attempt to tell Wallace the true story of what had happened. Houston was far, far away in another world, and Ben Wallace was only a man.

Royce returned several times to the place where the great white sphere had been. It would have been fitting, he thought, if no grass had grown in that lonely clearing. It should have been marked somehow; it should have carried the imprint of the strange visitation it had known. But the grass grew there as everywhere, and the flowers nodded in the sun, and the warm wind rustled through the leaves.

They had come and they had gone, and they had left no sign upon the land.

Royce had taken no photographs. He had been fighting for survival, and picture-taking had never crossed his mind. In any case, he knew, photographs would prove nothing. Pictures could always be faked.

The bodies of the baboon-things he had stored in the freezer had decomposed in the weeks before the power from the generator had been restored; they were only stinking chunks of decaying meat. He had buried the bodies without attempting an autopsy.

Bob Russell's corpse had been found in his house, still on the couch where Royce had placed it. Royce read the obituary in the *East African Standard* that came in on the train. The death was ascribed to natural causes. Russell's death had created no special stir. He had not been the only man to perish in the isolation and confusion of the floods.

Royce had not the slightest desire to live out his life as a freak, and he was not anxious to get involved with the Kenya Police. No action of his could help Bob Russell now. He knew that Russell would not have held him responsible for his death. He would probably have agreed that there were some things better left unsaid.

Royce knew, too, what would happen if he tried to tell his story, the story of what had really happened during those strange days and nights at the Baboonery. He would be thought mad at best, and at worst dismissed as the sorriest kind of publicity-seeker. The situation was a profoundly curious one. Mankind had reached the point where people could discuss such things in the abstract and believe in the possibility—even the probability—of non-earthly life. At the same time, if you met a man or heard of a man who claimed that an alien spaceship had landed in his backyard—that was a different proposition. People were not ready for *that*. Royce himself would have dismissed such a story as absurd only a few months ago.

No good could come from blurting out such a yarn. Royce felt that he owed his family something better than that. And he did not try to kid himself. He was what he was; a man can be marked by a strong experience and even changed somewhat, but he does not suddenly become a totally different human being. Royce had his own values, whether they were right or wrong, and they did not include a desire to be a celebrity, a martyr, or a nut to be paraded on television. He wanted a chance to live his own life as best he could, a life that was satisfying and meaningful to him. It was not an outrageous ambition, despite being somewhat unfashionable. Royce believed that perhaps he had earned the right to be himself.

It might be that one day *they* would come again in another place and under other circumstances. If that happened, he was prepared to tell what he knew. It might serve a useful purpose then. It might possibly help to know that *they* were not totally alien, however inexplicable their actions seemed to be. It might help to know that there was a gulf that could be bridged....

Royce did not know and could not guess where the great white sphere had come from, or where it had gone. He did not pretend to understand why the ship had come or what its inhabitants had sought. This small corner of the African earth had been a port of call, a mysterious island touched in the course of an alien Odyssey. Somewhere, perhaps, on a world lost in the deeps of space, there was a Homer who would sing of that voyage, sing of Earth and the beings who lived there.

Royce dared to hope that *they* had learned something good about man. He dared to hope that the songs—if songs there were—might say that men were something more than savages, that they had a capacity for understanding, that there was something in them that could be respected. Yes, and that there was a toughness in man, that they were not to be despised as potential friends in the maelstrom of the universe.

It was only a hope, but it was something.

It could have been worse, for both of them.

Meanwhile, Royce had his own life before him.

It wasn't much, one man's life.

But it always came down to that in the end.

One man. One life.

15

A day came when work was done, a time when Royce could take off on his own without guilt and without worry. It was not his last day at the Baboonery but the end was in sight. It was a time of hiatus, a time of waiting, a time for winding up one phase of his life. The new man had not yet arrived but Kathy had started her packing. The kids were playing with furious energy, excited at the prospect of flying away to a distant land called home.

It was a day that had to be.

Royce knew that he would see Buck again this day. He knew that he would have his chance. Call it the sure instinct of the hunter or give it a fancier name, it did not matter. Buck would be waiting.

He took the .375 and the cameras and the glasses. He took one man with him—Mutisya.

They set out together in the battered Land Rover, an unspoken bond between them

It was a perfect afternoon for hunting: a time of golden sunlight and soft shadows and cool green leaves. Royce. drove slowly, savoring it all, wanting to remember. The Land Rover whined and growled along the weed-grown trail. Through the thick bush where the tsetse flies waited, past the clearing where Matt Donaldson's camp was neat and clean again in anticipation of a fresh covey of hunters from Nairobi. Across the sparkling silver of the Kikumbuliu, once more a gentle stream, and finally out into that great green plain that swept away to the Tsavo. Under that immense African sky, a sky empty now of menace but still a vast sky that went on forever....

Royce saw game that quickened the heart, game that was plentiful with the new grass and water, game that lived as it had lived for uncounted thousands of years. Gray-brown kudu, long-horned oryx, striped zebras that ran in a field of yellow flowers, ungainly ostriches trotting along with the single-minded determination of long-distance runners, dignified old elephants secure in their conviction of immortality. It required a conscious effort of the imagination to realize that the United States, too, had once presented such a picture. The animals had been different, of course, but the scene had been much the same: buffalo and antelope, bears and bobcats, deer and coyotes in an unspoiled land. It took even more of an effort to realize that the days of the old Africa were numbered, that this Pleistocene panorama before his eyes would be gone within fifty years or so.

Royce knew that he was seeing something that would never come again. It was a terrible loss, no matter how inevitable it might be. It left a hole in the world. He wanted to fight it but he recognized that the odds were hopeless. He, too, was an anachronism. He was out of step—or other people were.

He took some pictures. They were not for himself; the only pictures he wanted he carried in his head. The photographs were for the magazine articles he would be writing. A man had to eat.

He did not use his rifle. There was only one animal he wanted now.

He could smell the big river, a cool fresh wetness carried on the rising wind.

He stopped the Land Rover on the rim of the Tsavo valley. He climbed outside, the breeze from the river stirring against his skin. The Tsavo seemed still and quiet in the distance, a river of glass winding across the earth. The flood scars were still plainly visible but there was no fury now. The green meadow sloped peacefully away to the river, alive with new grass and flowers and the rustlings of the wind.

He lifted his binoculars, but it was Mutisya who spotted them first.

"*Kuro,*" he said, pointing to his left. "Waterbuck." Royce nodded. Buck would be there, waiting.

He took the .375 from the cab of the Land Rover. The rifle was cold and heavy in his hands.

The two men moved down into the valley on foot, quartering across the gentle slope. There wasn't much cover-the tall, swaying grass, a few clumps of commiphora—but the wind was right. If they were careful, they should be able to get very close.

Royce was certain that he had him. He had been on too many hunts not to know.

They worked their way down until they were within two hundred yards of the unsuspecting animals. Royce stopped, half hidden in the grass. He stood very still, watching.

There were four of them, all males, standing quietly in the grass near the river. Royce caught their scent clearly—a strong smell, rather like turpentine, but with a heavy animal muskiness. There were four of them, but he saw only one.

Old Buck stood a little apart from the others. He was not a herd animal.

He was a stately creature; he carried himself with aloof dignity, his head up, his splendid horns like a lyre above his alert, rounded ears. He was a majestic animal, a great stag of legend come to claim his world. His sleek coat glowed redly in the westering sun. The white lines that striped his eyes gave him a painted, ceremonial look. The deep curve of his chest told of power that had never known defeat, while the white on his rump hinted at an odd and unexpected playfulness.

Buck must have weighed a quarter of a ton but he stood as delicately balanced as a gazelle.

Royce knelt down and raised his rifle. He got Buck's big chest in the cross hairs of his scope. It was easy, very easy.

He felt nothing, nothing at all.

His finger tightened on the trigger.

Royce made no decision with his conscious mind. The choice came from deep within him. His rifle moved. Not much, just a little. But enough. There was only a small brown rock in his scope.

He fired.

The flat sound of the shot cracked and echoed in the valley of the Tsavo. A puff of dust and splinters exploded from the rock. The four waterbuck were catapulted into sudden motion. They bolted for the river, Buck in the lead.

They ran without hesitation into the water. The animals were strong, graceful swimmers. They made it across with effortless ease. Royce watched them climb out, dripping, on the far bank.

It was still an easy shot. He held his fire.

The last sight he had of Buck was his white rump—a neat circle like a painted target—vanishing into the high grass.

Mutisya was utterly disgusted.

"Missed him," Royce said, grinning broadly.

Mutisya was not fooled. He felt cheated. "Someone else will kill him, Mr. Royce."

"Not today, anyhow. Maybe he's got a few years left."

Mutisya shook his head. He had no sentimentality about animals. Meat was meat.

Royce felt good about what he had done. There were times when a man had a choice. He had no compulsion to explain his actions even if he could find the words. He thought that he understood a little about himself now; perhaps in time he would understand more. It was not a new thing with him but it was a conviction that had been strengthened by what had happened to him-and by what had not happened. Surely, if man could find a point of contact and identity with beings from another world then there must be a kind of continuity between the creatures that shared the earth. There would be other days when choices could be made. His gesture had been a small one; he was only one imperfect human being. Still, there were articles he could write, pictures he could take, actions that were within his grasp. Perhaps there was a place on this earth where something could be saved....

The two men walked slowly back up the slope to the Land Rover. Mutisya said nothing more, but the burden of his disapproval was heavy.

Royce did not doubt that Mutisya would be leading the new man down to the Tsavo for a crack at Buck before long.

Well, maybe the new man would be a lousy shot.

Maybe not.

They climbed into the Land Rover and started back toward the Baboonery. Long before they reached the Kikumbuliu Mutisya spotted some kudu on the grassy plain. He looked a question at Royce.

Royce stopped the Land Rover. He handed the rifle to Mutisya. Mutisya's seamed face creased in an eager smile. He was out of the vehicle in an instant, maneuvering for a clear shot.

Royce watched him and responded to the ancient thrill of the hunt. There was a streak of common clay in him; he could not think of himself as a vegetarian. Man had been a hunter for hundreds of thousands of years before he had sown his first crop. The plants of the field have shallow roots; there are other roots that go deeper.

It was an old drama that was set in its ways and it was soon over: the stalk, the crisp shot, the fall, and death where there had been life.

He helped Mutisya drag the heavy warm body to the road and heave it into the back of the Land Rover. The two men climbed back into the cab and started off again. Mutisya was pleased and happy.

The dead kudu flopped and rolled bonelessly in the back of the vehicle. The soft liquid eyes were dull and glazed, like blobs of old jelly. The dry horns scraped and clicked against metal. There was a lot of thick blood. The big flies covered the animal, feasting.

The great dark shadows were gathering again in the bush. The wind stirred across the lonely land with the first chill of the approaching night.

The dead kudu was very close behind him but Royce tried to force it from his mind. This had been one of the good days. There were other things to remember.

He looked up when he could, out through the dirty windshield, up at that tremendous arch of blue African sky. It was a more mysterious sky to him now, a sky filled with danger and promise, but still a sky that touched the world of man. It was a sky as boundless as it had been when the earth was born.

Life was just beginning, even now.

If he could have a little luck—if he could remember well enough and long enough—he could carry the memory of that free African sky with him wherever he had to go.

It was a long way home.

Royce hoped that he would not lose it, somewhere along the way.

The New England
Science Fiction Association (NESFA)
and NESFA Press

Recent books from NESFA Press:

The New England Science Fiction Association:

NESFA is an all-volunteer, non-profit organization of science fiction and fantasy fans. Besides publishing, our activities include running Boskone (New England's oldest SF convention) in February each year, producing a semi-monthly newsletter, holding discussion groups relating to the field, and hosting a variety of social events. If you are interested in learning more about us, we'd like to hear from you. Write to our address above!

Acknowledgments

NESFA Press Books depends on volunteers. These are the people who helped make this book happen:

Proof reading was provided by a stalwart band: Pam Fremon, Deb Geisler, David Grubbs, Tony Lewis, Mark Olson, amd Sharon Sbarsky.

Rick Katze and Lis Carey helped with scanning.

Mark Olson kept the computers (and the editor) up and running.

George Zebrowski nagged me (in the very nicest way!) to finish it.

Thanks to all.

—Priscilla Olson
November 2007